OPERATION SEAL

CAYCE POPONEA

D1519510

WHITE HOUND
PUBLICATIONS

This is a work of fiction. Names, characters, businesses, places, events and incidents are either the products of the author's imagination or used in a fictitious manner. Any resemblance to actual persons, living or dead, or actual events is purely coincidental.

© 2017 by Cayce Poponea @Write Hand Publications

Cover design by Jada D'lee

Editing by Elizabeth Simonton

So many people contributed to the elements of this story. From the SEALs I spoke with to the wonderful lady who gave me the name of my hero.

As always, I wish to thank my husband, Patrick. Hours of hearing me say, "just one more paragraph." Letting me be as creating as I needed to be.

To my editor, who without your red pen this would be a travesty. Thank you Elizabeth, now on to the next.

Jada, my graphic designer, creater of all things pretty on my covers. You never fail me and I appreciate all the patients you show me as I make up my mind.

Julie McCleary who responded when the call went out for the name of my unsung hero. Letting me borrow a name close to your heart. It is my hope Ive done you proud.

HM Brandon Sparks, your stories of living in the desert, finding the roadside bombs and the amazing things you had to endure. For planting the seed of a mad man and how he could be so deceptive.

To all the men and women of our Armed Forces and the loved ones you left behind.

But most of all, to you, the person who is taking time to read my words, escaping life if only for a moment.

I dedicate this to all of you.

PROLOGUE

"No regrets."

Diesel's words echo in my head, digging up memories I've worked hard to bury. A promise made in the heat of battle gave me a mission I've failed to complete. Sunlight glistens off the polished wood of Ramsey's coffin, bright concentrations of energy broken by the six Trident shields hammered into the solid surface. A handful of mourners gather around, making a promise to a dead man to help those who could not help themselves; by finding the truth beneath the lies.

How would they feel if they knew the lie I told? The amount of regret I carry every day from a promise I will never be able to keep?

Would Diesel have the same look of respect on his face if I told him of a hot day in Afghanistan, months before I became a SEAL, when I made a move to run from my inability to face my demons? Could I look him in the eye and swear an oath, forgiving the one regret I can never rid myself of?

Chapter One

LOGAN

September eleventh, a day not many Americans will ever forget, while thousands of pimple-faced young men rushed to the recruiting office to join the war on terror, I boarded a plane to Afghanistan, ready to do some real medicine, the kind I was trained for. Just as those starry-eyed young men imagined themselves running down the battle lines, kicking Al-Qaida in the face and grabbing the victory flag, I imagined my hands like Harry Potter's wand, healing wounded victims with a single, skilled touch. The reality for both of us would make any horror movie ever watched seem like a Saturday morning cartoon in comparison. I never imagined the unending supply of heat, sand, and broken bodies; both the enemy and ours. Or how the sounds of helicopter blades, filled my chest with dread, instead of adrenalin as it did back in the States.

Death had already filled his quota for the day as far as I was concerned, when the helicopters landed once more, bringing more bodies of men who came here with a dream, only to find a nightmare waiting instead. As I stood under the blazing heat of the desert, the sun seeming to get closer to the Earth every time I left the protection of the shade, I once again questioned why I thought I could save anyone with death swirling around like the never-ending dirt and sand.

My team of nurses and corpsman rush from behind me, ready to do their part as we stitch the holes created by a faceless enemy, the action to be repeated over and over. IV bags hung from strips of metal, designed to secure machine guns to the inside of the cabin, the medics using anything at their disposal to carry out their duty. The floor of the aircraft was stained in blood, no time to rinse away the evidence of the previous battle.

Hands reach in, pulling out the board where a set of boots is connected to the body of my next patient, and author of my regretful lie. The noise of the blades was too much to ask many questions about the patient, their story could be found written in magic marker across their forehead and chest. As the last of the board comes toward me, I notice the uniform of the marine is drenched in his own blood, black against the tan material. I know before I look at his face, this man has minutes before death does another victory dance.

The lights of my exam table give me no better news. The marine, whose name tag is unreadable from dried blood mixed with the elements he was pulled from, is tugging at my arm, demanding I lower my ear to his mouth. My team tries to assure him, giving him an ounce of hope he will walk away from this, with a scar and a story to share. But my eyes betray me, telling him the fear in his own is warranted.

"Sir?" his voice cracks, a trickle of blood rushes from the corner of his mouth and down his cheek, blending with the sweat and filth collected there. Reaching into his pocket, searching for something deep within its hidden compartments, his eyes close in relief the second his fingers land on their intended target. With his left hand wrapped tightly around my right, he places his treasure against the skin of my palm.

"Tell her I always loved her."

I want to tell him he will have the opportunity to give this back to whomever *her* is. Instead, my mouth betrayed me, letting loose a promise I will never keep, to a man I don't know.

"I promise."

Hours later, I watched the sun dip behind the horizon, the chill of the night air wrapping me in it's freezing clenches, teasing me with reprieve before the sun of a new day bakes me to a crisp. Glancing down at my bloodstained boots, I scoff at all the time I once spent agonizing over keeping them dirt and lint free. After the events of the last six months, I no longer give a fuck, when all my attempts to keep the blood inside the bodies of the men instead of caked on the leather of my boots, were all in vein.

Two marines walk past me, mutter their required greeting, and then approach a team of SEALs who had reported early this morning. Their presence indicates a serious mission, one they would never be able to talk about around a campfire, wrapped around the girl they loved. They lived a secret life, one where they approached an enemy while their eyes were closed, took what they needed and disappeared into the thickness of the night. Any injuries suffered, were attended to by a member of the team who stood beside you, not a helicopter ride away.

The epiphany hit me so hard, I bent over laughing, garnering me strange looks from the SEALs and two men who stood with them. As if slapped by the hand of fate herself, the Commander of the base walked past me, returning from the mess tent.

"Captain, do you have a free moment?" The sounds of more helicopters in the distance snagged both of our attention, warning us of more wounded fast approaching.

"Honestly, yes. Your name crossed my desk earlier and I meant to have a word with you, but—" Tipping his head to the team approaching the helicopter.

"My office," he shouted, leaning as close as he could so I could hear, squinting his eyes as the sand kicks up from the rising helicopter.

"Earlier today we had a number of injuries—" Not waiting a second to dive into how my name crossed his desk. This seasoned officer knew how quickly things could change around here.

"One of the men you worked on was the nephew of the Secretary of Defense, William Burge. He was at his sister's house when she got the call from her son, detailing the quick actions a Lieutenant Forbes used to remove the bullet in his thigh."

Keeping my resolve, I remembered the kid in question cried as if his leg had been shot off, instead of the graze I found when I cut his pants open. There was more damage done from his thrashing than what I could give the bullet credit for. Two stitches and some silver nitrate to cauterize the bleeding, and he was off having chow with his buddies.

"Mr. Secretary extends his gratitude and his offer to return you to Bethesda for the remainder of your time." Had this offer been made yesterday, I would have taken it and run. Back to air-conditioning and running water, to food made fresh and not out of a sealed pouch, a bathroom connected to plumbing and not a hole in the ground.

"Respectfully, Sir, I'd like to counter his offer." Captain leaned back in his chair, its legs creaking in protest of his movement, disbelieving eyes squinted back at me.

"He can keep Bethesda, if he will open the door for me to attend SEAL training."

Leaning forward on his desk, the salt and pepper color of his hair reminding me of his age and wisdom. "Lieutenant, do you have any idea what you're asking? Do you know the amount of men, twice your size and a few years younger, who don't make it much past the front gates?"

These young men he spoke of didn't have the same open eyes I did, no longer shocked by the cruelty of men and how hard we worked to destroy one another.

Three months later, I found myself standing in a line of forty men, the average age twenty-three and rank no longer a factor, unless you were an instructor. Two-thirty in the morning with the frigid chill of the ocean surrounding me, I readied myself for the next drill. I hadn't slept more than four hours in the nearly two days since I'd arrived, which for me and the conditions I left in Afghanistan, wasn't unheard of. But for the man on my left, Aiden Sawyer, this was where his comfort zone ended and his fear began.

Aiden woke up one morning, bored with his desk job in Rota, Spain. His career counselor gave him a multitude of suggestions on to how to advance in his current position, none of which were new to him. As he got to his feet, about to leave, he noticed the photograph of an older gentleman on the desk. When he inquired as to whom the man was, the young sailor shared the story of her father's time in the Special Forces, along with his untimely death when she was three. He figured since he joined the military for all the wrong reasons, he may as well continue the tradition and completed the paperwork for SEAL training.

He and I bonded quickly, both of us barely a step ahead of the demons licking our heels. Aiden, with his heart torn apart by a girl with a pretty smile and a forked tongue, diving head first into one of the most dangerous jobs on the planet. With one incredible fear hanging over his head: his aversion to being under water.

At first, I laughed when he swore under his breath as they pulled us from the piece of cardboard they called beds, running us down the beach and into the putrid smell of low tide approaching, face down in the wet sand with our arms above our heads. One by one they made us stand, keeping our arms overhead. I side glanced at my new friend, his face full of determination as the instructor orders him to charge into the surf and retrieve the small boat waiting out there in the darkness.

I don't have time to think about the pain starting in my shoulders as I'm shoved in the same direction, my feet moving as fast as I can in the restricting sand. Lightning off in the distance lights up the sky enough so I can see Aiden struggling, and the outline of the boat we are tasked with finding. It's pitch black out here, and I have to wait for the next flash of lightening to get a better visual. I keep swimming, my adrenalin negating the chill of the water as Mother Nature cuts me a break and lights up the sky as if it's high noon instead of the middle of the night.

Aiden has almost made it to the edge of the boat, but I can tell he is struggling. Digging deep into the last of my reserves, I make it to his side as we both reach for the cording along the perimeter of the boat. His breathing is labored, and he could either be exhausted or about to go into shock. It's just the two of us out here; no one to report back if this is panic setting in. I won't let him fail or be the first in our group to ring the bell.

"Sawyer, you okay?"

His eyes are fixed on the side of the boat, fingers wrapped in a death grip around the cording. His bottom lip is trembling from the cold, and I need to get him to pull himself out of this.

"Hey!" I shout at him, praying we are far enough out the instructors won't be able to hear me.

"Don't you let the bitch win, you hear me?" As we stood in line to eat yesterday, I told him of my family and the reason I was here— minus the big favor a man with a powerful pen made good on—the need to do some good in this world and not feel defeated all the time. He razzed me about doing my time at Bethesda, switching to plastic surgery and looking at beautiful, naked women all day.

I fired back at him, wanting to know why he gave up a tour in Spain to be surrounded by a bunch of sweaty men and horrible food. His eyes lowered to his tray as he told me of his high school sweetheart who used him for the notoriety he gave her as an All-American running back for his State. He went to work, saved a little money and bought her an engagement ring. While hanging out with one of his buddies one night, they came across a web page advertising naked girls who wanted to chat with lonely men. His girlfriend was the model they used to separate men from their hard-earned money. When he confronted her, she justified her actions by comparing the web to a dirty bar full of men. He wasn't amused and returned the engagement ring he had purchased earlier in the day. Wanting to get far away from her, and the pitiful looks in his hometown, he joined the military. When the ex-girlfriend heard he was going to Basic Underwater Demolition/SEAL (BUD/S) training, she spread it around town he wouldn't last a week.

While the women in my life didn't complicate things like his, I labeled all my demons female and we entered into a pact, vowing to remind each other to never let the bitch win. A wave of water crashes around us at the same time Aidan's fight or flight instinct kicks in, sending me a nod of his head as he pulls himself into the boat. By the time the sun came up, four men had tagged out, ringing the bell three times before walking out the front gate. Two more would ring out before the sun set behind the buildings and I collapsed onto the cardboard mattress I'd been assigned.

During combat training five weeks later, I landed wrong on the side of my ankle, screaming like a bitch with the pain. The guy who had flipped me, a kid from New York City named Vinnie, had remained undefeated all week with his quick reflexes despite his mammoth size. I wanted to give up, go back to the desert and never complain about the conditions again. But Aiden got down on his hands and knees, his face right next to mine and repeated the words I had said to him. It worked and I was able to get to my feet, using my good leg and flipped Vinnie over, winning the match. Sadly, Vinnie rang the bell three weeks later, returning to his old unit where he was medically discharged a year later.

Ten days before graduation, an event in name only for so many, I assumed the intensity of our training would decrease and become more administrative. I was proven wrong when the lights came on in the middle of the night and all hell broke loose, as we were shoved down the hall and into the mess hall.

Several square boxes, which looked as if they fell off the back of a *Guns N' Roses* concert stage, sat in puddles of water. Where I had enjoyed dinner from a pouch, razzing Aiden about the real reason his girl chose porn over him, now rested a piece of plywood with straps and jagged-edges covering most of the visible wood.

Before I could digest anymore of my surroundings, an arm reached out pulling me off to the side and into one of the roadie boxes. Ordering me to get on my knees and lie down in the bottom, slamming the top closed as I complied. Where the majority of SEAL training is physical, it is also a test of your mental capacities. The worst possible situation for one person can be a walk in the park for another. Stuffed in a dark box was an invitation for me to fall back asleep and the breaking point for one of the other remaining men.

Two days and a hot shower later, Aiden and I shared what we had witnessed. He watched as the latest man to ring out, who had bragged of how he lived in the water during his off time, surrendered when it was rained down on him while strapped to the board. Aiden thanked me for the advice I had given him, explaining how the mind is a powerful thing, and to try repeating to himself this wasn't real.

On the final night of training, Aiden received word his father had been taken to the hospital by ambulance. He was allowed a one-minute phone call, as well as the opportunity to ring the bell and return when the next class started. His father refused to hear anything about him leaving California and made him swear to finish what he started.

Nine days later, I stood beside my friend as he said his last good-byes to his father. We hadn't hesitated as we jumped in a rental car the second graduation was over, driving through the night to be by his father's side as he lost his battle to cancer, something he had hidden from him for years.

Later in the evening, I dragged him off to a local bar, one he and his friends had frequented. We would be leaving in the morning, boarding a plane for Honduras and our first official mission. As we enter the bar a number of heads turn in our direction, including the girl he once loved. She was working behind the bar, and as I took in the sight of her, I prayed time had not been her friend. Her short, straw-like hair stuck out in every direction, with skin looking more like chewed up leather than skin, highlighted by bright pink lips. The second she recognizes him, she is around the edge of the bar and headed in his direction. Spending the past six months with Aiden, I can tell when he is disgusted by something, and right now that some-thing is wearing cut-offs and a halter-top, the lack of self-control hanging over the edge of her pants like an apron. Using his ninja skills, he stepped around her and slid into the seat of a booth.

A part of me wanted to feel sorry for her, but I knew the history between them, and the amount of time since they last saw one another hadn't softened his hatred for her. If anything, it had reas-sured him he had made the right choice in leaving her behind.

Photos on the wall confirmed the stories he told me of his time as a youth. His old football jersey was framed beside the newspaper article announcing a hometown boy who had been selected to become one of the elite. The owner came over shortly after we settled in. His former coach who helped him every step of the way in getting the All-American title, as his family was too poor to afford the fees which went along with any sports team.

Vernon Holt, or Coach as he preferred, purchased this bar the year after Aiden left for the military. Coach freely offered a plethora of embarrassing stories featuring Aiden as the ringleader, including one involving his youngest daughter, Jordan.

At first, I assumed this would involve a backseat and being caught in a compromising position. The truth was a rescue from a burning car, a frightened eleven-year-old and a drunken mother who perished. The mood at the table turned somber until Coach mentioned Jordan was growing into a fine young lady, working for his sister over at the diner on the weekends.

The next morning, Aiden pulled into the parking lot of the diner, which was buzzing with activity. Coach had spread the word around we were pulling out this morning. The townsfolk stood and applauded as we took a seat at the counter. A dark haired, fresh-faced girl came shyly over to pour each of us coffee. Aiden introduced the young lady as Jordan, although I could have sworn something flashed between them as they shared a look.

If I had to guess, I would put her in her late teens or early twenties, based on the way she carried herself and how her gray, nearly violet, eyes stood out against the sun kissed tones in her skin. With her hair in matching braids on each side of her head, she was the poster child for what I would coin a 'country girl'. Once our meal was ready, Jordan placed the plates before us, and then disappeared into the back. We didn't see her again before we left.

I will never forget the first mission we did as trained SEALs, suiting up on the deck of an Aircraft carrier, sitting in a room with the President of the United States on a monitor, calling us by name and wishing us luck. Dropping out of a C-160 and parachuting to the tropical terrain below, feeling the incredible force of adrenalin as the ground rushed toward me.

None of the scenarios we practiced ever prepared me to have mosquitos attacking my neck, my need to remain still preventing me from killing them before they sunk their teeth into my skin, leaving behind the relentless itching I endured for days later. Balancing my feelings for the man I had to kill as we breached the security of the compound, against my years of training to save lives. I learned to trade the victory of rescuing the captive as justification for taking a life. Celebrating each completed mission with a cheap beer and an attempt to forget the envelope I kept in my shirt pocket, and the promise I made to find the owner.

Chapter Two

HARPER

The hum of the ceiling fan gently wakes me, its poor motor exceed the life expectancy the manufacturers had given it years ago. Dusty blades rotate in the center of my bedroom, offering more white noise than actual cooling, but the effort is appreciated.

Traces of light and the sweet smell of rain filters through the sway of the curtain from the open window. I can feel the chill in the air, a subtle reminder of the change in seasons, as autumn arrives clearing a path for winter and all she has planned. I'll attempt to remember, to slow down and enjoy the pictures Mother Nature painted for us in the leaves on the trees, and the flavors of the season.

Deep green eyes greet me from the bedside table, a toothy grin full of mischief and dreams. His picture does him no justice, as his warmth has the ability to erase even the deepest chill old man winter can brew up. The love in those eyes, so all-consuming and reserved for me, reveal a softer side of him kept private from the prying eyes of those around us.

Alexander Gray, my brother's best friend and resident pain in my behind growing up, managed to stitch himself into the fabric of my life, making his hold permanent and everlasting.

Snuggling into my pillow, I recall with fondness how he and my brother would run off behind the house to play Army men, while I surrounded myself with stuffed animals and a tea set. I would sing songs and entertain myself until the boys became tired and hot, stealing my lemonade and cookies, leaving me a crying mess only to do it all over again the next day.

As we grew older, the games and interactions changed, the relationship morphing into something new. Books became my solitude, my nose proverbially buried between the pages, lost to worlds where knights slayed dragons before they could kidnap the princess. My brother and Alex discovered organized sports, specifically football.

As they grew and their skill level increased, the eyes and attention of girls their age zoned in on the ever-growing muscle and definition of certain charms. With the newfound status and attention, their view on me changed as well. My brother, Ross, began picking on me, showing off for his new friends and never ending line of female admirers.

Sadly, I became victim to several schemes in an attempt to get closer to him. After a while, I placed a wall between us, limiting the people around me to those I knew before the popularity began. Alex was the guy everyone wanted to be friends with, the one who helped with every good cause, volunteered for countless organizations, and lended a helping hand to everyone he knew.

The summer of my freshman year became a game changer for me, while Ross and Alex went off to football camp, my body developed overnight, giving me curves and, more importantly, boobs. Rumors would have started accusing me of stuffing my bra, except the city built a swimming pool and it was the place to be the first day of summer vacation. I showed up with my friends, wearing a bikini, which left no room for the rumors to grow. By the end of the first week, I had a tan and my first boyfriend, Mark.

The relationship lasted two weeks, long enough for my brother and Alex to get wind of it and scare the piss out of him. Poor Mark was one of many that particular summer the pair of them intimidated from two states away, calling the guy on the phone and handing out threats as if they were compliments.

Any attempt at getting help from my father resulted in increased frustration as he agreed the young men pursuing me were not right for me if they scurried away with their tails between their legs after the slightest amount of pressure.

"Harper, you need a man who is strong on the inside as well as the outside. Able to hold his own and stand up for what he believes in."

At the time, it was wasted words on the broken heart of a young girl, one who would grow to appreciate the wisdom in his love.

Right before Christmas that year, a new boy by the name of Brady moved to the district. He was tall and handsome; with a smile perfect enough to melt the hardest heart. Every girl I knew wanted to be wrapped around his arm, labeled as his girl and have all the benefits associated with the title. Just before the holiday break, I received a note in my locker, letting me know Brady had an eye for me. I remained calm, as much as a young girl could when a boy she liked returned her feelings.

Brady approached me later in the day, asking if I was available to go out with him that weekend, I accepted and rose to cloud nine, convinced Heaven could not possibly be any better than this. Friday morning I walked with a smile on my face, dreaming of how the day would be filled with glances from Brady. However, as I rounded the last corner to get to my locker, Alex hovered over a cowering Brady his index finger planted in the center of his chest. I didn't have to hear the words or see his face to know the date would never happen.

For nearly a month after, I refused to speak to Alex or my brother, my father kept his distance as he and my mother had begun to have problems in their marriage. When Valentine's Day came around, Ross tried to bribe me with flowers and candy; I tossed them both back at him and slammed the door closed.

As quickly as my body turned from bomb to bombshell, I stepped back into myself. I quit wearing makeup and pretty clothes, avoided social events and concentrated on my studies.

One afternoon, as I was sitting in the library, I overheard some students discussing the prom and how the administration had opened it up this year, allowing freshmen and juniors to attend. Slamming my book closed, the frustration of the past few months creating a new sadness in my chest. Had I been speaking to my brother or Alex, I would have accused them of ruining everything. In my haste to get out of the school, away from the colorful posters and announcements of the ticket sales for the event I would never attend, I ran into Oliver Pittman, math club president and king of the pocket protector wearing clan. He fumbled around, shoving his glasses back up the bridge of his nose, his inhaler to his lips as he recovered from the wrecking ball of my life. He scooted off at a hurried pace, glancing over his shoulder twice as he put as much distance between us as possible. As he ran through the final exit door, he moved quickly enough to the side giving me an unobstructed view of Alex singing to the head cheerleader, Laura Fiddler, his subtle way of asking her to the prom.

I wanted to hit him, make him feel the level of pain I did, have him look into my eyes and see what loneliness looked like. Instead, I turned on my heels and cut through the science lab, using the exit at the side of the building to avoid watching Laura as she cheered her acceptance of his proposal. I was almost to the sidewalk when I heard my name called, the voice changing octaves as if struggling to make it through puberty. Glancing over my shoulder, I caught sight of Oliver walking quickly in my direction, his fingers pushing back his side-combed hair as the breeze whipped it around his face. His breathing was labored, his index finger pushing at the middle of his glasses, sliding them back into place.

"Harper, please forgive my rudeness. I've meant to make an appointment with you, but my schedule has not permitted me to do so."

Oliver had the IQ of a genius and the social graces of a slug, still, I couldn't erase the smile he created on my face.

"Would you consider going to prom with me?"

His voice cracked as he managed to get the last word out, swallowing hard to clear his throat and tame the hormones, which wreaked havoc on most boys his age. Oliver was a senior by GPA, testing out of most of the curriculum and leaving his teachers scratching their heads as to what to teach him. Several colleges had made offers, but he wanted to spend one year having *the* high school experience, which apparently included attending prom.

"If you're willing, we could do a compatibility experiment by attending the basketball tournament in the gymnasium tomorrow afternoon."

Our high school won the district championship, giving us home court advantage in the state playoffs. Alex and my brother had both made the team and would be there. Given the silence they had received from me, they wouldn't know it if I attended or not.

"I'd love to come with you, Oliver."

Like most nights at our house, dinner was less family time and more of how creative we could all be in avoiding one another. Dad and I tended to gravitate to the bar, while our mother and Ross sat at the table in the next room. Tonight Alex came over, which sent me upstairs to my room and my mother in the den with a liquid dinner, instead of the meatloaf she made for everyone else. A little after midnight, I crept back downstairs to put my plate in the dishwasher and see if mom had made anything for dessert, but Alex was crashed on the couch, an empty pie plate on his chest. Breaking my mother's rule of cleaning up after yourself, I tossed my plate into the sink and ran back up the steps. I hated Alex and his ability to destroy everything for me, my love life, and the relationship with my family, and now the last bite of my mother's homemade pie.

The next morning, both plates were clean in the dish drainer and both boys already out the door, on their way to the championship game. Mom came out of the den, her hair a mess and the look of sleep on her face, all clear signs she had slept in the chair I last saw her in last night. Her eyes looked empty and sad, reflecting the feelings I had hidden behind baggy clothing and clean skin.

"You're such a smart girl, Harper."

She praised around a cup of coffee. Her encouragement was meant to make me smile, but she had no idea the torment I felt, being smart didn't get you anything but good grades.

The gym was alive with the sounds of cheering, whistle blowing and the squeaking of shoes against the polished wood of the court. Oliver and I arranged to meet at the edge of student seating. Scanning the sea of students, I found him three rows from the top, his focus attuned to the game. Keeping to the edge of the court, I made my way to where he sat, his eyes following the action, the white collar of his shirt peeking out of the top of his red school sweatshirt, the eyes of our mascot, a wolf staring back at me. I never bothered to purchase any team spirit items, as I coined them, not caring enough about the team to waste my money.

Taking the first step on the bleachers, metallic red and black pom-poms flashed in my peripheral vision. Chancing a look, I found Laura and her copy-cat friends, dressed from head to toe in red and black, Alex's number painted on the right side of her face. Laura had a repu-tation for sexual conquests, which matched the number on her cheek. She had a preference for men at the top. According to my brother and his talk with my father I accidentally overheard one night, Laura had given him all the signs she wanted him, but he was inter-ested in another girl, one who didn't make the roster in the popularity game. Our father told him if he worried his buddies class ring would fall out of her, it was best to leave her for the next guy.

Oliver's eyes finally landed on me, a smile of recognition as he stood from his seat and motioned me toward him. Acting as the gentleman I assumed he would be, he allowed me to sit on the inside of the bleachers. We spent the last minutes of the game with Oliver asking me questions about my likes and dislikes; his questions appearing rehearsed. I imagined he wasn't as versed at speaking with girls as he was at mathematical equations.

When our team won, he jumped to his feet, and I briefly consid-ered how he was a contradiction in terms; a mathematical scholar who was also a sports fan, the two not being mutually exclusive when it came to the norm. As the players left the court, he offered to grab me a drink and popcorn, but I declined, he hurried off to grab something for himself, assuring me he wouldn't be gone long.

Several minutes later, the next game began but there was no sign of Oliver. I needed to use to restroom, so I asked the guy sitting beside me to save our seats. As I exited the gym, I saw the line to the ladies room was so long it came out the door and down the hall. I knew the location of a much smaller bathroom, one the janitorial staff used to store brooms and mops. As I hurried down the hall, I noticed my father talking with Ross and Alex, towels wrapped around sweaty necks and proud smiles on faces. I hurried down the hall and around the corner to avoid them seeing me.

Walking through the janitor's office, I stilled as the lights were off except for the closet on the back wall. I listened to see if someone else knew about this bathroom and had beaten me to the punch. When I heard nothing, I walked hurriedly across the carpet and opened the door, letting out a bone-crushing scream as I caught sight of what, or rather who, was inside. Leaning against the large tub sink, his sweatpants down around his ankles, stood Coach Loft, his hand buried in Oliver's hair while he plunged his dick inside his mouth. Oliver was completely naked, his glasses on top of his neatly folded clothing, the hand not tugging at Coach's balls, wrapped around his own dick, masturbating as he gave the much older man a blow job.

I heard my father's voice first, as the pair separated and attempted to look a lot more innocent than they were. It was the large arm, that wrapped around me, pulling me against a wet chest, which I recall with more clarity than what my father said to the pair of them. Alex picked me off my feet, running down the hall and into a vacant room, asking me repeatedly if I was okay?

The police were called, Coach Loft was arrested, and my mother came to the school to take me home. Alex and my brother went back out on the court and won the championship.

Monday morning came and with it the rumors flying around. Coach had been placed on administrative leave pending the outcome of his trial, and Oliver and his family had packed up and left in the still of the night. An assembly had been called to congratulate the basketball team and give the students as many facts about what was going on as they could. Laura and her friends sat in seats two rows ahead of me, close enough where what she chose to share got the attention of enough people to spread through the ranks.

"*Apparently holding hands with Harper Kincaid will turn even the most desperate man gay.*"

Oliver had taken my hand in his as we sat together on the bleachers, a couple of students below us noticed, but I assumed they didn't care. As the laughter broke out in the seats around me, the walls Oliver had began to knock down fortified themselves as I leapt out of my seat and headed for the nearest exit. As I pushed the release bar for the door, I could hear my brother call my name followed by someone yelling, *"stupid bitch,"* but I kept running until I made it to the safety of my bedroom.

The next day, my parents allowed me to stay home from school, and I plotted how to convince them to let me go live with my grandparents. But as afternoon rolled around, my father knocked at my door, asking to come in and talk with me. He reminded me none of this was my fault and no one can make a person feel anything they don't allow them to. It was time I took back any power I had given to the kids who laughed along with Laura Fiddler.

"Harper, people like her tend to get what they deserve. You just have to be willing to wait long enough for it to happen."

As I came downstairs later in the evening, the doorbell rang. I opened the door to find every member of the basketball team standing on our front lawn with Alex in the center of the group, a guitar on his knee and several bunches of flowers around him.

"Harper Kincaid, will you go to the prom with Alex?"

They sang in unison as Alex continued to strum out a tune about the color of a girl's eyes.

After I stormed out, Alex caught wind of what Laura had said, my brother had to abandon his pursuit of me to keep Alex from beating the crap out of one of the guys sitting close to Laura, who she had been messing with all along. Alex took back his invitation to prom and announced to the entire student body how Laura had a third nipple. Not like a tiny mole, but almost a third boob, and it was as flat as the other two she used padding to enhance.

I'm not sure what made me agree to go to prom with Alex, something deep inside telling me this was the path my life was destined to follow. Just as chasing him around the yard as a little girl, getting angry when he teased me, and forgiving him when he apologized for being the reason behind my tears. Years later, the cycle was continuing, and yet changing direction.

Alex arrived at our house in a fresh tuxedo and corsage in hand, it was the first night in years my parents remained in the same room and held hands as they wished us a good night from the front steps. I had assumed it would feel strange sitting so close to Alex, like one of those sad stories of how the girl had to go to a dance with her cousin, but it wasn't. Alex held my hand and pulled me close as the photographer took our picture.

He introduced me to his friends as his date, not his friend, and kept me close as the conversations continued. When the music changed and the soulful voice of the current chart topper spoke of being in love and belonging together, Alex pulled me close and swayed as the colorful lights danced off both of our faces. His lips absent of a smile and the seriousness in his eyes ran deep.

"Harper, I'm about to change everything." With confused eyes, and a quickened heartbeat, I scanned his face. *"I want to kiss you. I need to make you understand how I feel about you, leave you with a firm understanding of what I've been fighting. All those boys I chased away? I did it, not because of my need to protect you, but my need to posses you."*

He gave me an opportunity to object, to walk away and remain as we had before, but when he found none in my eyes, his lips descended to mine. Alex, being nearly a foot taller than me, lifted my feet from the ground as his lips parted and the tip of his tongue introduced itself. I'd been kissed before, but never like this, and never by someone who knew how.

"Every time you kissed me, you set my world on fire." Running my finger down the glass of the frame, I'm still able to recall every detail of the moment the photo was taken, a moment in time I have frozen forever. Alex had been right; everything did change with his kiss.

The next morning, he came over and spoke with my father, gave him his word to treat me with respect. Then he and Ross took off for the backyard where they played as young boys, returning a few hours later with an understanding forged between them.

I became Alex Gray's girlfriend, and for the remainder of the school year the envy of half the female student body. Ross finally asked the girl he had eyes on, Holly Edwards, out for a movie. They dated for four months before her family had to move to Germany.

When graduation time came around, I expected Alex to break things off as he had a full scholarship to the University of Michigan, but he didn't. For two years, we sent letters back and forth, called every chance we got, he was home every school break and made a special trip to escort me to prom.

When my senior year ended, he was sitting beside my parents as I walked across the stage. We celebrated all weekend, as I had been accepted to the same university. Alex found an affordable apartment and we would be living together for the first time in our lives. It took some getting used to, but Alex didn't pressure me when it came to sleeping together and as August of that year turned into September, I couldn't imagine my life could get any more perfect.

I woke up on a Tuesday morning, my only class free day with the intention of creating a romantic atmosphere for Alex and I to have sex for the first time. He had been patient long enough and so with a mission in mind, I set about making plans. I'd barely gotten out of the shower when Alex and my brother came rushing in the apartment, he turned on the tiny television in the corner and we all watched as a single airplane smashed into the World Trade Center. Chills ran down my spine, as we remained silent while the news anchor spoke of the horrific events, while the smoke and debris filled the streets of New York. My legs gave out and I leaned my body against Alex, who was shaking so bad it made me gasp. He held me closer as we sat on the floor of our apartment and watched the world change around us.

The next morning Alex woke me before the sun came up, telling me to pack a bag as we were going back to Virginia. Ross joined us as we loaded Alex's truck for what I assumed would be a short trip home. But when he and Ross disappeared on Saturday morning, not returning until after midnight, I knew something big was about to happen.

My father woke my mother and Alex's parents came from three houses over as Ross and Alex announced they had joined the marines.

No one was surprised as this was who Alex was, the guy who did the right thing and helped every stranger in need.

We drove back to Michigan, packed up the apartment, and I withdrew from school, transferring to a community college close to my parents' home. Alex didn't like the thought of me staying in Michigan, and honestly neither did I.

Three weeks later, at a dinner to say goodbye to Alex and Ross, with all of our friends and family setting around the table, Alex dropped to one knee and asked me to marry him.

"Baby, you plan the wedding of your dreams, and the first chance at leave I get, I'll be standing at the end of the aisle to make you my wife."

As the time for the pair to go away to boot camp grew closer, I planned for our last night together to be spent in a hotel where we could be alone one more time. Alex carried me over the threshold, calling it practice for when he came home.

We loved each other soft and slow, he even apologized for hurting me as he broke through my barrier. He asked me to shave his head, knowing all of his beautiful hair would be swept up in a pile and tossed with the rest of the new recruits. I picked up a curl, wrapped it in a tissue and stuck it in my purse. Picking up the silk nightgown I'd let him peel off me, I snapped the satin ribbon he spoke so fondly of. Cutting a lock of my hair, I braided the ribbon into the long strands. He took the ribbon and wove it into the band of his watch, and then pulled me close as we once again lost ourselves in each other.

The next morning, before the sun had an opportunity to come up, we stood in a huddle as Ross and Alex joined the ranks of the men who would serve our country. We were given thirty seconds to say our final goodbyes, so Alex wrapped himself around me and swore to take care of me.

"I'm coming back to you, the first chance I get, I will be right back here, in this exact spot." He teased me, and then kissed me soundly, *"I love you, Harper."*

His mother called our names and as we turned to face her, she snapped a photograph, framing it so I could have it close to me. I placed it beside my bed, its permanent home until he returned to me.

November found me writing every day to Alex. When his mother contacted me about sending a box to him for Christmas, I argued they might get to come home for the holiday, but a letter crumpled in her hand told me different. Alex had sent word to his mother he had been selected to deploy to Afghanistan, lacking the courage to tell me himself. Three days later, I received word Ross would also leave for the Middle East, so Bonnie, Alex's mother and I went to work putting boxes together.

The New Year came and with it a phone call from Ross, he would be assigned to a new base, Camp Leatherneck. It had been six weeks since I had heard anything from Alex, his last letter told me how hot it was in the desert and how much he missed me, but nothing about a change in station.

Valentine's Day came and with it a letter, Alex had promised me so many things, some promises he kept and some of them he didn't. Taking care of me and making sure I had what I needed he excelled at, but today wasn't a day to think of the promises he forgot. Celebrating the joy around me, looking forward to the new and exciting life I was about to live, beginning with the bridal shower I was going to be late for if I didn't get a move on. Looking at the diamond on my left hand, I kissed the photograph and crawled out of bed.

Chapter Three

LOGAN

Korengal Valley hadn't changed much since my first visit all those years ago. We were still battling a man who had more aspirations than brain cells, carrying on a tradition passed down to him from an ancestor who made a fortune from the poppy fields. The players may have changed, but the rules had not and winning was still the goal of the game.

The unease in my gut started the minute Viper told us what our next mission involved. Getting the medical convoy across the valley wasn't necessarily difficult so as much as it was deadly. Aarash Kumar was one of the players who had changed since I had last visited, he and his younger brother now controlled the crops being harvested. It was big money filling pockets from here to the middle of the US. Not a single member of this team hadn't been personally introduced to Aarash and his brazen ways of doing things. For him, and his men, there are no rules. Which is why they have sent us on this mission, the rules of engagement aren't found in any of our rulebooks.

As we sat against the hillside, the fresh-faced boys who would become men, hardened and irreversibly changed by what they see here, measure the six of us up. By the look in their eyes, they are trying to see if the rumors are true, if what they have read in books and seen on television is facts or Hollywood's way of selling more tickets. I'll leave them to wonder as the reality, the true story, would scare them more than the people who live in the shadows behind them. I listen as Havoc shares a little of what he knows, a decent enough warning to keep them safe, and yet not enough to give them nightmares.

I hear the rumble of the trucks a few beats before the rest of my team, a skill I always possessed, yet never admitted to. Ghost has been waiting on a letter from his girlfriend, or slut-bag as the rest of us call her when he isn't around. When Aiden made Chief, we celebrated by going to a hole-in-the-wall bar just off base where we met Ryan Biggs the night before he reported to our team. He had been in a heated conversation with her on the phone as we walked into the bar. Chief made the comment how he didn't miss the arguments of having a girl-friend, he and Jordan had exchanged a few letters but they were strictly in the friend zone. Years later, Ghost is still chasing after her like a dog searching for its tail. She has been caught more times than I can count in the bed of one producer or another, always with an excuse, managing to keep him trapped in her web of lies. I look forward to the day when a girl comes along and changes his world.

"Doc, this one has your name on it."

Ghost hands me the white envelope, the postmark dated from late last year. Checking the return address, I'm confused as to who the hell Harper Kincaid was and why the fuck she was writing to me. Searching my brain, mentally checking off the list of girls I'd been with in the last few years. I'd always been careful with where I stuck my dick and even more so, with who I shared my real name with. There had been a number of attractive ladies to walk through my life, a set of best friends in Malaysia who wanted to have a vacation of firsts, a threesome included. I left them sated, wearing smiles on sleeping faces, but none of them had been named Harper. Just as those doe eyed men had dreams about becoming one of us, women around the world fantasized about bedding a SEAL. Being protected by the muscles under my uniform or provided for by the tiny paycheck the government deposited in my account twice a month. While I came up blank for any Harper, a light bulb flashed in my head at her last name.

"Hey, anyone know if Kincaid has a sister or a wife?"

"Both. Why do you ask?"

I met Ross Kincaid almost a year after I completed SEAL training. He had been captured by a pack of Guerilla rebels who had tortured and killed the rest of his team. By the time we reached him, death was trying to take him out the back door. I worked on him for hours after we drug him out of the jungle, tossing everything I had at him to keep him alive. We shipped him off to Germany to finish recovering, six weeks later he was back in his boots, joining me on another mission. Kincaid, and a friend of his, joined the military as a knee-jerk reaction to the Twin Tower attacks. Not long after, the pair was given different duty sections and Kincaid landed in a spotlight, which sent him back to the States for SEAL training. He helped us out when Havoc was shot in the chest and if what I suspected the military was about to do was true, he would replace him on a more permanent basis. On Havoc's last exam, I found an area of scar tissue in the pleural space between his lungs and heart. To the average Joe it was no big deal, to the killing machines we were trained to be, it was a career ender. I never bullshitted Alex when I told him, looked him square in the eye as I explained what I found. In typical Havoc fashion, he laughed it off and made a comment about his momma being the death of him instead of Aarash Kumar and his illegal weapons.

"Because I got a letter from one of them."

Chief sat down beside me, snatching the letter out of my hand, "You lucky, motherfucker. Harper Kincaid is the sister *and* one of the sweetest ladies to walk the planet." Tossing the envelope back to me, he adjusts himself against the hillside.

"She works with the USO and Navy League to make sure single soldiers aren't forgotten during the holidays."

Ripping open the letter, the elegant script on the envelope matched the writing inside. Long hand was becoming a lost art, tossed away with the invention of the typewriter and made ancient with modern computers.

Dear LT Forbes,

Please allow me to begin this letter by thanking you for your service. As the sister of an active duty, I know how difficult it can be going for long periods of time without word from the home front. Good news! We are still here. Sorry, my lame attempt at humor.

My name is Harper Kincaid and I currently reside in Chesapeake, Virginia where I own a small shop. As I mentioned before, I have a brother who is active duty, a SEAL to be more specific, excuse me for title dropping, I don't do it to carry airs. I noticed when your name came across my desk, you had the same specialty code as my brother, who ironically is responsible for the idea behind the packages you will receive. When he first joined the military, I came across a flier for the USO needing volunteers for assembling Christmas packages for the single soldiers. I jumped at the opportunity to help. Hours later and hundreds of boxes stacked neatly in a warehouse, I asked the director when the next shipment would go out? My heart sank as she told me this was a once a year event. I looked over all of the boxes representing the faceless men and women who would be forgotten before the New Year came. Inspiration hit me as I collected all of the names we had assembled packages for, pinned them to a wall and, with a tried and true scientific method, I closed my eyes and tossed a wadded up tape ball at the sea of names on the wall. Every month for a year I package up specific items requested by the soldier I adopted, exchanging sometimes daily emails from each one over the course of the year. I do feel the need to give you a little tongue-in-cheek history on these packages, each soldier I have adopted has fallen in love with one of my friends. Now, I didn't really count my brother as being one of my special package recipients. My friends had called them a number of things over the years; love-grams, cupid packages, boxes of muscle. Sorry, getting ahead of myself there.

My first adoption was Asheton Dawson, a First-Class Petty Officer stationed in Djibouti, Africa. He and I exchanged information and I mailed a care package every month as promised. I included my phone number and address. He was so grateful he swore to me he was going to thank me in person as soon as he was back in the States. He was originally from Texas, but his parents told him if he joined the Navy he was dead to them, so he had no one. It was the same year my friend, Amanda, came to me asking if I knew anyone who was looking for a good hairdresser. I had been thinking of renting out the small space I had beside my shop, so I asked her if the person she had in mind, would like to rent the space from me. She said she would talk with her sister and get back with me.

Several weeks later, I was hanging up a new dress in my front window when Ross, my brother, came through the door. I dropped the dress and ran to him. We clung to each other for ten minutes before he put me down. Ross was about to leave when Amanda walked in the door. It was love at first sight for them and they married thirteen days later before he shipped back out.

Amanda's sister, Stacy, took me up on my offer and opened up a salon next door. A few weeks later, Amanda got in a heated argument with her boss and quit her job. She went to work for Stacy as a makeup artist. November of the same year, Asheton made good on his word and came into my shop. Stacy happened to be getting some coffee when he walked in. They made it nine days before he carted her off to the Justice of the Peace and got married.

The next year, I got a call from another friend of mine, Sarah, who had split with her long-time boyfriend. Sarah wanted a new start so I offered her a job as a seamstress in my shop. When she showed up, Stacy and Amanda took one look at her and dragged her off to the salon. When they were finished, Sarah cried when she looked in the mirror and told them she felt just like Cinderella. The very next day, we had a sign made for the salon; Cinderella's.

The same year, I selected Chief Mitch Riley in Okinawa, Japan. Mitch, as he preferred to be called instead of Chief, had more time on his hands and chose to call instead of write. More often than not, Sarah answered the phone. I had barely gotten two boxes sent to him when Sarah asked to take over. By the time the third box was due to go out, Mitch asked if she would consider visiting him in Japan. Sarah jumped at the chance and when she returned, she was sporting a diamond ring. Mitch was up for a promotion and if he didn't get it, he was going to retire from the Navy and move to Virginia. Everything changed six weeks later, when a tearful Sarah told him over the phone she was pregnant. He handed in his retirement letter the next day and five months later, he arrived in town, they married, and he opened an electronics store down the street.

I could go on and on, tell you of all the packages, which united a couple together, but I won't. What I will tell you is you can relax, as I am out of friends. You can let out the breath you may have been holding as this year the only thing you can count on is a package in the mail and a listening ear if you need it. I

assure you this is not a joke, or some crazy Officer and a Gentleman fantasy.
Consider it my way of serving those who serve.

Your friend,

Harper Kincaid

I read Harper's letter three times, unable to decide if she was telling the truth or was a professional bull-shitter. Since she wasn't asking me for anything, I would see where she took this. I would however, need to talk with Blaze the next time I saw him, let him know I was corresponding with his sister. For now, I needed to get my shit together and get ready for this mission.

When we finally finished getting the medical team across the valley floor, after a brief encounter with Aarash, which opened a door for Chief and one of the nurses to get cozy. The smile she put on his face and holding him back long enough to make him run for our ride back home was a little too obvious if you ask me. Chief could be, and had been, a huge flirt; not going any further than what the lady was ready for. He gushed about the cute nurse, Rachel, but I don't exactly get a good vibe from her. As long as all he does is talk, I'll keep my opinion to myself, my friendship with him is more important than being right.

* * *

Arriving back at home base, I found a box waiting for me. Harper Kincaid practiced her own brand of magic as she defied the laws of physics with how much you can shove in a small box. I spent a good twenty minutes pulling out shaving cream, shampoo, body wash, cough drops, icy hot, several different magazines, a thumb drive, batteries, nuts, and even Cheez-Whiz.

TO: AlexGrl17

FROM: Logan.Forbes.LT@ OPS

CC:

SUBJECT: *Hello*

Dear Harper,

First and foremost, I cannot begin to thank you enough for your devotion to our service members. You are correct in thinking that many Americans think of us during the Christmas holidays, but sometimes forget us the rest of the year.

You did give me a much-needed chuckle with your claims of not being psychotic. I will have to have further contact with you before I can give you my full diagnosis. I would never, however, question one sibling as to the sanity of the other.

As you know, my name is Logan and I am, as you suspect, a SEAL. My reasoning behind joining the military would make you feel the need to sit down, so go ahead and take a seat.

After finishing my undergrad, I had been accepted to medical school. I've dreamed of being a doctor since I was a little boy. My family owns controlling interest in a fortune five hundred company and my parents were heavy into different philanthropy projects. They entrusted my uncle to run the daily operations of the company, which he failed to do, choosing instead to funnel large amounts of money into an offshore account. When a routine audit found the company's holdings hovering above bankruptcy, all of our assets were frozen— including my tuition. Funny thing about medical school, they expect payment in order to allow you to learn how to become a doctor. I was staring at failure directly in his condescending eye. A friend of mine had a relative who had served in the military as a physician, paying with his time the money they spent on his education. Having a family with money and power, you can imagine my father knew a few Senators and Congressmen. A couple of calls and a signature on my part and my tuition was taken care of. A year later, the missing money had been found and returned to my family. I could have asked my father to make my contract with the military go away, but it wouldn't have been the right thing to do. My last day as an intern was September eleventh. I woke up in a luxury apartment near Bethesda and went to bed in the back of a C130 headed for Kuwait. A few months later, I was given the opportunity to go to SEAL training, it's been an adventure with moments I wouldn't trade for the world and others I wouldn't wish on my worst enemy.

I apologize for not writing sooner, as you may know my job keeps me busy and never knowing where I will be next. I am so happy your package found me.

At the end of this letter, you will find not only my new address, but also my personal email so we won't have to worry about being censored.

I do have a confession to make; I know your brother, Ross. I served with him a few years ago and I consider him a true friend. I have always told my family not to send me anything as the military sees fit to give me my basic supplies. I will say, though, that you get a gold star from me when you sent me Cheez-whiz. I mean, who doesn't love the stuff?

So please, tell me more about Harper Kincaid. What is your favorite candy? Or better yet, how about this, the next package you send to me, make it as if you were sending it to yourself. Pack it full of your favorite items, sans the tampons and lady razors of course.

I will share with you this about me; I was born in New York and lived there until I went away for medical school. I have no brothers or sisters, but I did date Lisa James in high school—yes, the Victoria's Secret supermodel. It was a long time ago, but we still keep in touch.

Waiting patiently to hear from you,

Logan

Chapter Four

HARPER

Today was one of those days where I knew good and well I should have pulled the covers over my head and kept the shop closed. As much as I loved helping the wives of our military, they could be whiny bitches sometimes.

Take one Ophelia Mosley, current wife of the base Commander and self-appointed queen-bee. I met her during one of the USO events, just after she and her husband arrived, she was all toothy grins and firm handshakes, and I was baffled by her bullshit facade. We were introduced and she became quite animated with excitement when I invited her to come by and take a look around my shop. She came in on a Monday, took a detailed tour, and then returned on Tuesday with a back seat full of clothes. Our first transactions went fine, and her clothes sold in a matter of weeks. She returned a few months later with another back seat full, but this time the clothes looked to have been pulled from her grandmother's basement. I reminded her of the possibility these clothes may not sell, but I would try my best. She signed the agreement I had all of my clients sign, clarifying my responsibility to show the clothes for one hundred and twenty days—thirty days past the state requirement. After the allotted time, the seller would have the option of picking up the clothes, paying my twenty percent commission, or forfeiting the clothing to a charity I ran for women attempting to return to the work-force.

"Harper, retro is in. I paid top dollar for those clothes and they're still perfect!"

I was at the end of my rope with Ophelia. I knew damn well she didn't spend a dime on them, stole them out of the donation bin at the local thrift store maybe. She huffed and slammed her purse down on my glass counter, her bright red curls bouncing from the force.

"Fine, Harper, I'll take my clothes and find someone else to sell them."

"Ophelia, you're too late," shaking my head as I turned the form she signed around to face her. Pointing at the date on the page.

"I've already sent all of those clothes to Horizons, as stated in the contract you signed." Tapping my index finger on the white paper, lifting my eyes from the date to the angry face of Ophelia.

"You had no right."

Flipping the page over, "If the owner fails to appear within five business days after notification—"

"Exactly!" she screamed. "You never notified me. Now give me my clothing or pay me what we agreed on."

Slamming her hand on the glass of my desk, confusing her ability to tell the wives of her husband's men what to do, with the independent and clearly in charge person who stood before her.

I turn my attention to my computer, opening the file with her name on it, "Ah, here we go. You were notified, by email, five days prior to the expiration of the contract, and again on the day your grace period began."

"I never got any email, this isn't my fault." Clicking on the command to print, I waited in vain for my computer to make up its mind to send the read receipt to my printer. The tapping of her nails on the glass of my display case was scratching at my last nerve. I reach over and twist the monitor so she can see what I have on the screen.

"Sorry, Ophelia, *Microsoft* has no reason to lie to me. You opened the emails and read them both. For whatever reason, you chose not to come in." I left the accusation hanging in the air, pursing my lips as I elevated my eyebrows in a quick motion, crossing my arms over my chest.

"My email was hacked, someone else read them."

"Tell it to your bank or credit card company, as it is no concern of mine. You signed a contract and I held up my end." I didn't give her time to think about it or even answer me.

"Well, I never!" she exclaimed as she turned and stormed out the door, causing Sarah, my assistant to jump out of her way.

"You know, you should have tossed her out last year when you saw her with Mayor Craven." Sarah stood back against the edge of the display window, my silver laptop clutched tightly to her chest, eyes wide in aggravation with Ophelia's behavior.

Ignoring her taunting, "Please, tell me that is my laptop in your hands?" I look down at the computer screen as the sound of the printer coming to life pulls at my attention. It's the story of my life, everything a day late and a dollar short.

"It is, but I'm holding it ransom until you tell me everything that happened at your shower last weekend." Holding the silver contraption I've dubbed the Silver Devil, as it has given me nothing but trouble since I purchased it less than a year ago, in her right hand, twisting back and forth at her wrist as her face turns from perturbed to inquisitive.

Sarah and her husband, Mitch, had planned a vacation for this past week almost a year and a half ago, way before my bridal shower was scheduled.

"Fine," wadding up the paper I no longer required, I toss it into the recycle bin. "My mother showed up, wearing a dress you could see her crotch through, sans panties but at least a complete wax. My future mother-in-law failed to show, or call, and has avoided speaking to me since then. Oh, and I broke the heel of my shoe when I had to carry my own gifts out of the restaurant." Sarah's eyes flicked between mine, her level of amusement fueling my need to animate the story.

"Wait," Sarah placed the computer on the glass of the counter, folding her left arm over the cover, and then aiming her index finger in my direction.

"His momma didn't show? After all the fuss she raised to have a vegetarian menu available." Nodding my head as I allowed my shoulders to shrug, this had been one of the many hurdles I've had to overcome since the wedding date was chosen and rescheduled once already.

"Has he spoken to her? Made sure she isn't lying in a ditch somewhere."

Taking in a deep breath through my nose, not ready to share with Sarah the entire conversation.

"Yes, apparently there was some issue with her transportation or something." Shaking my head and holding my hand out for my laptop. "He spoke with her right after I got back from the shower," *minus any gifts from his side of the family*. I kept the last part to myself, no need stirring up trouble when it didn't really matter to me to begin with. What I did care about was talking with my brother, Ross, hearing his voice and assuring myself he was doing okay. I hadn't gotten an email from him in a while, as he was transferring to a new SEAL team.

"She better not decide to drop in on your bachelorette party as an apology. I have plans to get your liquored up and stick some hot naked men in your face." Resisting my attempt to take the computer from her. "Not so fast, Harper." She pulls the laptop off the counter, twisting her body to the side. "I have good news and bad news, which do you prefer first?"

Letting out an exasperated breath, my threshold of allowable negative things reaching a critical level.

"Bad first, so you have an opportunity to rebound my pitiful mood."

"Okay, your motherboard is fried."

"But—" waving my hand in a circle attempting to speed up the recoil.

"But you're still under warranty, and Mitch is putting the last of your files on the new computer. He will have it here before we leave for *Thunder Nation*."

Sarah has wanted an excuse to visit one of Chesapeake's more controversial clubs. Opened by one of the original Chippendales dancers, *Thunder Nation* was an all-male strip club. Certain organizations had tried and failed to shut down the club, but with all the military influence, the city council allowed it to open.

"Are you sure we can't go to *Aries*?"

"No, we can't go to *Aries*." She tossed back at me, changing her voice to emphasize the condescending tone of her words. "We are going to surround you with hunky, muscled men who want to grind their dicks in your face and take your money."

Aries was another new club in the area, opened by the same people; it boasted modern lines and a state of the art sound system. Mitch had won the bid to install all the equipment so Sarah had gotten to attend opening night along with some high-profile celebrities. According to her the hype was overrated as it lacked a decent clientele.

"You can have that man of yours take you dancing at *Aries*."

"Right, you know he doesn't go to clubs." Scrunching up my nose, I try to hide the aggravation I felt with our lack of social interactions. A flaw I had to add to the enduring qualities list when it came to him.

"Maybe I'll get dressed up and go by myself." My back straight as I faced her, challenging her to call my bluff.

"Keep telling yourself that. We both know you'll park your behind in front of the television just like the two of you do every other night." The bell over the door signaled a new customer. Glancing over, a smile spreads over my face as Lance Ranoka, the delivery guy, walked in with a smile on his face and a white cup in his left hand.

"Hey, Harper." He called as he allowed two ladies behind him to walk through the open door. "I thought you could use a cup of coffee this morning."

Lance was a sweet man, who worked for one of the local delivery services. When I first opened this shop, he came by and introduced himself, offering the use of his truck transporting the donated clothing over to the small shop behind the local church. He came in one day and noticed the cup I had from the gas station several blocks over and offered to bring me a cup of coffee whenever he made a delivery over there.

"You're a lifesaver." Taking the cup from his hands, he tips his hat down, and then pushes his dolly into the shop. Lance blends into any room he is in, not drawing attention to himself or creating a scene. Most of the time he leaves and I never hear the bell sound.

Sarah was attending to the ladies who walked in. She has never been a fan of Lance's, no real justification behind why, but she avoids him when he comes in. I turn away from Sarah and the new customers to ask Lance a question, but like most days, he pulls his impression of a ninja and silently leaves. I'm about to click out of my email when I notice Ross has sent me something. Swinging my eyes over to Sarah, confident she has the sale in the bag, I click on the letter and begin to read.

TO: AlexGrl17
FROM: Ross. Kincaid ENS @OPS
CC:
SUBJECT: Hey Sis!!
Harper,

Hey, Sis! Finally made it to Afghanistan and am now waiting for the team I'm joining to get back from Korengal Valley. You remember when I was there before, right after I joined the military? Anyway, they are finishing up a mission and I expect to meet up with my new LT in the next day or so. I'm excited for this one, as I've worked with the team before. Anyway, I heard from dad. He mentioned you had your bridal shower recently and something about mom showing up. I understand why you're inviting her to your wedding, but I don't want you to get your hopes up she will be anything like Amanda's mom when we got married. She isn't exactly mother of the year material. In any event, I have my ticket purchased and I will be there to help you celebrate this new chapter in your life, the two of you deserve all the happiness in the world. My Skype and Face time are working if you want to talk.

Love you, Sis,
Ross

My brother may not understand why I wanted both of my parents there, as the divorce was messy and dragged out for many years. My father came home sick from work one morning, and found my mother in bed with his best friend. They tried counseling, but during one of the sessions my mother made a pass at the counselor and my father filed for divorce. During the court proceedings, she admitted she wasn't sure if Ross or I were my father's children, and the judge ordered paternity testing. My father held me tight as the judge read the report and whispered he didn't care what a piece of paper said, I would always be his baby girl. Luckily for everyone, the report confirmed both Ross and I were indeed his children.

She took off with the best friend, but it didn't last long. She came back in the middle of the night crying when he tossed her out of the house, but my father handed her money and pointed in the direction of the nearest hotel.

Their divorce affected Ross more than it did me. He was, and I suspect still is, angry with her for what she did to my father. Ross is an old soul with beliefs, which run deep; giving his heart away to one girl and keeping her until the day he died.

"Harper, these ladies wanted to meet you." Sarah approached from across the room, two dresses draped over her arm and a smile depicted across her face. "Miss Mona here, heard you are the lady in charge of Horizons." Shifting my attention from the screen of the computer, I take in the face of Mona Jackson. Mona was one of those ladies who boasted about all the charity work she did, using her generosity as nothing more than an excuse to look down her nose at others. Her checkbook could afford her the price of admission to most of the charity events in the city. One good smile from her and my little shop could afford to come out of the church basement.

Extending her hand out, blood-red lips framed a set of commercial grade teeth, so sharp she could bite through a steel cage. Pitch black hair, pulled back in a severe bun, she was grace and pearls on the outside, with venom and knives on the inside. Still, I would gladly dance with this devil if it meant helping out the women who came to the center.

"Pleasure to meet you, I'm Mona Jackson." Handshake like a wet noodle, and anyone with computer access and twenty minutes to kill would know her southern accent is as fake as the reason she is standing before me. Mona, or Monique as her birth certificate reads, is from a piss-ant town in West Texas. Her first husband hit it big on an oil rig, and she managed to suck as much money as she could from him before she landed herself a much wealthier man. Peter Jackson, owner of several sports teams here in the state.

"Your name has come across the circle of friends I keep close to me. Everyone tells me all the wonderful things you are doing at your little center."

I smiled and nodded my head in the right places, while wiggling my toes so as not to get bored listening to the tale of all the starving children she fed on a trip to Thailand. Twenty minutes of my life I will never get back later, and I had an appointment with her to tour the facilities at Horizons.

"This is a good thing. Right, Harper?" Sarah kept her focus forward as we both watched Mona and her friend get in the back of a town car.

"Absolutely, but so is a root canal when a tooth is damaged beyond repair."

Silence filled the space between us for a moment, then as the town car disappeared from view, we both collapsed in laughter.

"On the bright side, you did get a response from your Lieutenant."

Tapping her chipped nail against my computer screen, as she reaches for the mouse. Sarah has no boundaries when it comes to the letters I get from the people who have benefited from one of my care packages. She reminded me this was the first year these boxes would not bring a couple together, and how she felt kind of sad that the magic was gone.

"Oh, look. You were right, he is a SEAL."

I tried my best to ignore her, concentrating on getting to know the new friend I hoped to make. A smile tickled at my lips as I read how he knew Ross and wondered if there was a chance they would be on the same team. My eyes flew over his email several times before his request finally registered. No one had ever asked what I would want in a care package, and honestly, I'm not sure what I would ask for.

"He seems nice, apologizing for not responding quicker." I'd noticed this first off, reminding me of how much I missed Ross and his gentleness. "Reminds me of someone." She nudges my hip as the sound of the bell over the door announced the arrival of another customer.

* * *

One of the first lessons I learned as a business owner is the value of good marketing. Didn't matter what kind of product you had, if there were no buyers, you were destined to fail. The man who owned *Thunder Nation* was the poster child for how to market to the masses, as the line to get in wrapped around the side and down the back of the building. Giant spotlights swayed back and forth and a photographer stood on a red carpet as anxious ladies melted themselves against shirtless hard-bodies. Tan, sculpted muscles, the result of hours in the gym, and bright white smiles designed as a distraction, capturing the attention of the unsuspecting victim, much like the carnies at the fair. Using the desires naturally found within us, cashing in on the impulses of the heart.

Sarah jumped from the limo, hands over her head and a hot pink boa around her neck, whooping and hollering before her feet ever touched the ground. She showed up at my house nearly two hours ago, a bottle of champagne in each hand ready to, as she said, pre-game. From her zealousness and exuberance one would assume she was the bride instead of me.

"Come on, Harper, we've got VIP seating tonight."

Sarah had surpassed her alcohol threshold, as this was the fourth time she announced our seating assignments since we left my house. Her cheeks are stained red and eyes glassy as she stumbled her way to the front doors. One of the attendants, dressed in classic Chippendale attire, caught her as she missed the last step and nearly fell to her knees; which considering where we are would have been appropriate.

She pointed to me, letting everyone in line know I was getting married in a few weeks and this was her last attempt at introducing me to the rest of the male population before I sealed my doom.

The shirtless man, who introduced himself as Garrett, wrapped a protective arm around her and helped us find our seats. Handing each of us a wristband, he shamelessly flirted as he placed a flashing engagement ring on my finger. Between its flashing light and the glow-in-the dark penis necklace I had around my neck, I could land a 747. Which was good considering the size and length of the stage.

Four tables sat on either side, three across the end, which is where Sarah had managed to put us. Against the back wall was a line of silk fabric, the pink and blue lights on the floor creating a haze effect from the silk. Rope lighting outlined the edge of the stage and several steps down to the main floor.

Next to our table was an older group of ladies, they were having as much fun as Sarah was, laughing and tossing back shots as if they were water. The lady in the middle of the table had a necklace to match mine, she also sported a tiara with the word bride flashing across the top.

When the house lights dimmed and a silhouette stood at the center of the stage, a sultry voice boomed overhead and the ladies around me went wild with excitement.

"Ladies, are you ready to have every fantasy you can imagine come across this stage?"

The screams are so loud there are no devices able to register the volume. I had to cover my ears as the noise caused them to begin ringing. Rolled up dollar bills came soaring through the air, landing on the polished floor of the runway.

"Well, all right then."

The lights went dark and the music began, a deep base with a sound I recognized right away. The back of the stage lit up, creating another silhouette. This time, I could make out the broad shoulders of the man, and a hat setting atop his head. Green lights bathed him in the deep color, creating shadows across his chest and arms.

When the light switched with the beat of the music, a bright spotlight, much like the ones outside, danced over his body to reveal the camouflaged face of a solider. Amanda grabbed my hand as the man tossed his hat into the crowd, then reaching up to rip the muscle shirt in half down his chest. I could feel his eyes on me, gyrating his hips as he dipped lower on the stage to create the illusion of having sex. Just as he was about to reach down into his pants, the room went dark and the music stopped.

Some of the crowd assumed this was part of the show, but when I noticed the wait staff running around in confusion, my eyes began scanning the room. Grabbing my cellphone, I flipped on the flashlight, as did a few other sober women around me. Sarah was still whooping at the table next to ours with the older ladies.

A chill runs up my spine as the seconds ticked by and we remained blind in the darkness. The sound of boots against the floor came from my left and I reached over and grabbed Sarah pulling her into my lap.

A booming voice, the same who had started the show, called our attention from the center of the stage. A hard face, bathed in LED lighting from the massive flashlight in his hand stood at the end of the stage, tossing on a friendly smile. Due to the angle, he flashlight made him look like the Joker without makeup.

"Ladies, there is no need to panic! I've just been informed a transformer has blown on the corner of our property. The power company has been called, and are enroute, but cannot give me a time as to when the lights will be back on."

Several audible jeers rang out around me, followed by the bride at the next table reminding the man on stage how lights got in the way when handsome men were naked.

He ducked his head and, if the lighting had been better, I'd bet his face would be tinged pink.

"While this beautiful lady makes a valid point, as the owner of this establishment, it is my duty to give you what you've paid for."

Cheers roared once again, not quite as deafening as before, but enough to coax out a cringe and pucker my eyebrow.

"Each of you will receive a voucher good for one year from today, where you may return and enjoy the show. For tonight, and as an apology from me and my staff, the first round and cover charge is on me at *Aries*."

A wave of relief floods me as the prospect of going back home and into my pajamas is within reach. Sarah will never go for a night at *Aries* and opt to grab more bottles of wine or champagne before heading for my house. But she let out a holler, topped off with a swirl of her hips against my lap and glanced over her shoulder as she shouted, "Looks like you get your wish, babe!"

* * *

Where Thunder had been dark inside, giving me the illusion of being in a man's bedroom, *Aries* was much brighter, filled with hard lines and sharp contrasts. Sarah told me the downstairs had been decorated in white, and she questioned why until Mitch helped put the lighting system up. Now, with the base bumping so hard I can feel it in my chest, the room is teal-blue with silver lights bouncing off the bodies on the glass dance floor.

Sarah grabs my hand, dragging me, and my four-inch heels, down the steps and along the edge of the thick dance floor. Out of the corner of my eye, I notice the guy whose time on the stage was interrupted, his hat on backwards and his hands on the bride from the other table. I imagined he assumed the older woman was a safer alternative than the wild woman dragging me to places unknown. I suspected she may have a few miles on her tires, but she could give him a ride for his money.

Focusing my attention back to Sarah, she lets go of my hand long enough to hug a tall blonde standing by a sectional couch.

"Harper, this is Mercedes, she's married to the owner."

Sarah leans over in my direction shouting into my ear, as the bright smile of the gorgeous woman grows bigger.

"I met her when Mitch was installing—" she waves her hands, motioning to the lights and speakers over our head. We exchange pleasantries and a waitress shows up to take our order. The drinks are weak, and I'm both grateful and a little perturbed, as I know the drinks in here are going to be expensive.

Thirty minutes later, when Sarah slides back into her seat after saying hello to another woman she recognized, the waitress hands us each a refill and a bill for nearly one-hundred dollars. Sarah reaches into her wallet to get her credit card when I stop her with my hand. I'm about to tell her I've got this, when Amanda coughs in her drink and whisper- shouts, "Oh my, God!"

Everyone stops what they are doing and focuses on her shocked face; I use the distraction to slip my credit card into the hand of our waitress.

"They aren't even trying to be discrete."

Sarah smacks my hand, no longer interested in what is going on behind me. "Harper, this is your party and we had planned to pay for our drinks." Circling her finger around the small space indicating the group of women surrounding me.

"Sarah," Stacy placed her hand on her thigh, her eyes wide with panic. "I think we should go."

I caught the shift of her eyes as they darted behind me. Curiosity taking over, I slowly look over my shoulder.

At a seating area, which mirrored ours, two women sat on either side of a man who had his head tossed back, their faces hidden from my view, but not what they were doing to the man's cock.

With his knees spread wide and his arms stretched along the back of the sofa, the girls take turns between pleasuring him and sampling the lips of one another. Dipping my focus down, I followed the girl on the left take him all the way to the back of her throat, pausing at the reason for Stacy's sudden suggestion to leave.

Several lines of what any fool would recognize as cocaine, is setting on the glass of the table at his feet. The man, whose face had been toward the ceiling before, is now in clear view as he reaches down to pull the girl off his junk.

Brown eyes lock with mine, a set I would know anywhere, even in a crowded room. The same set which greeted me with coffee and small trinkets. The same set, which waited patiently as I turned him down for over a year to have dinner with him. And the same set who put the diamond on my finger when he asked to marry me almost two years ago.

My body moves of its own volition, crossing the distance between us, the beat of the music changing as I took the first step, his gaze remaining fixed and his expression emotionless. His hands go to the backs of the two women who in turn face one another and begin kissing. His eyes never leave mine as an evil smile crawls onto his face, shattering any kindness I once found there.

"I thought you were going to the strip joint."

"Funny, I thought you never left your house after dark."

His head tilted as he raised the eyebrow over his left eye, the corner of his mouth lifting in a condescending smirk. The man sitting here looked and sounded like the Lance I knew, but his actions, surrounding himself in women and drugs, was a man I had never, and would never, consider meeting.

Lance proclaimed to have an aversion for going out after dark, spouting off statistics on the amount of crimes, which increased once the sun disappears behind the horizon. At the time, I added the peculiarity to the pile he had for me, which included my disinterest in affection.

"As long as you're here, why not take your place where you belong?"

Removing his hands from the backs of the two women, their attention remaining on each other, he motions to the floor between his parted knees. Lance had come into my life when I was drowning in my own tears, lost in the darkness my grief had created. He was funny and polite, helping me forget about the sadness, which surrounded me.

"What about this?" Pointing to the cocaine, a razor blade resting on its side the bottom edge muted from the powder. "Is this part of where I belong?"

Leaning forward, ignoring the girls hovering over his lap, and picking up the razor blade, he slides the edge under the line closest to him, gathering a significant amount along the sharp edge. With his eyes locked with mine, he brings the metal to his nose, but changes his mind and hands it to the waiting girl on his right.

"In service of me, yes. The chemical benefit will make you more tolerable."

Lance had given me the impression he was a kind man, willing to be my friend when I couldn't offer anything more. Chastising people who were cruel to others, claiming to believe in a spiritual equalizer to right all wrongs.

Listening to him now, the man who held me as I cried the last time my brother went back to the Middle East, brought me chicken soup when I complained of an upset stomach, and every night, sent me a text wishing me sweet dreams, was a product of my imagination, conjured up to deal with the challenges in life. Lance Ranoka, the man who sat before me, was cruel and sinister, and a stranger to me.

"It was all a lie, wasn't it? The compassion, the understanding? Hell, even your lack luster proposal."

"You saw what I wanted you to see, felt what I needed you to feel. But don't think you are blameless in all of this. You accepted the relationship I offered, you welcomed the lack of emotions I took from you. All so you could keep the memory of a dead man in your dreams."

"I can't believe I was so blind, trusted you were a good man."

"Which is one of the reasons I chose you; your blind faith in humanity. Ignoring every warning sign you ever passed, you never questioned anything about me. Not my job, or the way I lived, hell you never asked to meet my parents, which turned out to be good for me." He shrugged, a knowing smirk on his face. "Had you questioned one thing about me, you would have known the woman I said was my mother, was nothing more than an actor I hired."

Leaning over, I place my open hands parallel to one another, my face even with his. "Don't you darken my front doorstep ever again. I never want to hear my name cross your lips in the future. Don't think about me, don't ask about me, as a matter of fact, you need to forget we ever knew each other." Lifting my hand as if to slap him, I lean toward the table containing his snowy entertainment.

"As for your ability to tolerate me, here's a little help."

Turning my hand to the side, using the plane edge, sweeping the top of the glass, sending the powder into his face and eyes. Not waiting to see if he has a rebuttal, I turn and grab my purse from the chair behind me, walking with a new purpose to the front entrance, and away from a life I never wanted.

Chapter Five

LOGAN

"LT, I understand your position and believe me, I'm sympathetic to your request."

"But?"

When Viper announced, he was done with the military, he spoke the words, which had been running around in my head. I have time remaining on my contract and I will serve it with pride, but I've spent too much time in the desert and been away from my family far too long.

"Your skills are needed here, helping these men who are pouring in with more injuries than we can keep up with some days."

I had heard rumbling from some of the corpsman how staff numbers were down, a product of advancements and change of duty stations. This base needed two surgeons, and for the next little while, it appears I will be one of them.

"Perhaps if things settle down, or if I can get someone from NPC to send me some additional bodies."

Navy personnel command had a reputation for doing things in their own time and ignoring most phone calls unless you held a high enough office. I could tell by the look on his face and the way his eyes shifted, he had no intention of helping me. Captain Vale had an agenda, which didn't include my personal tragedy.

"Thank you for your time, Sir."

Arguing with the man would get me a letter of reprimand. If I'm honest, I don't give a fuck about the potential loss in pay, or achieving any additional rank. What I do care about, what would affect me, is the look in my team's eyes when the news reaches the rest of the base. Honor and integrity are important to a SEAL, especially among one another.

All those years ago, when I left this place in order to find a way to beat Death at his own game, convincing myself if I could be closer to the action, I would be in a better position to save more lives. Years of fighting against men I didn't know, rescuing civilians and doing anything else I was commanded to do, has taught me it didn't matter if I was standing beside a man as he was shot. If the bullet was meant to kill him, nothing I did would stop it.

As I walked across the yard, the heat of the day already climbing into triple digits, a gust of wind stirs up the dirt and sand. I can hear trucks enter the front gates bringing with them supplies and, hopefully, a few new men. I'm not the only one who has noticed the new arrivals as Ramsey stands just outside the Mess hall, a bottle of water tipped back. The fear he showed during the last mission needs to be contained and harvested to motivate him to stay alive. He needs conditioning, and I need to release the tension forming in my shoulders.

"Ramsey, get over here!"

I catch him off guard, which is evident in the way he spills half his water down the front of his uniform.

"You ain't worked hard enough today, let's go." His wet clothes forgotten, he tosses the bottle into the bin and jogs in my direction.

"LT, you need me to do something?"

"Yeah, keep up."

Not elaborating any further, I take off in the direction of the front gate. One lap around the camp is close to a mile and we are going to keep circling until this tension is gone. Carrying a gun and knowing how to shoot is half the game out here, I could stick him with Reaper for a few days and he would be well on his way to becoming an expert marksman.

Out here, you have to be conditioned, able to use the elements to your advantage. I can give him a taste of the training I have under my belt, giving him the skills he needs to survive his time in this hell.

Ramsey is sucking in serious air as we finish five miles. My breathing is labored, but not a tenth of what he is doing. "Meet me here every day at zero-five, and if I'm not here, you start running without me." Ramsey has his hands on his knees, unable to speak, but his head is bobbing in agreement.

"You want to be a SEAL?"

I listened to the guys talking as we patrolled earlier, heard him speak of being better than his brother who found it easier to steal from people than to work hard. Ramsey spoke of his father dying in prison, and his mother pushing herself into an early grave from the choices she made in life.

"I can help you get yourself ready, condition your mind and body to survive Hell week, and the time you have left here." Ramsey pulled his body to his full height, face flushed and covered in sweat.

"It will get worse before it gets better, so if you're not sure, better say something now."

Fatigue rolled off him in waves, but his eyes showed the determination of a warrior.

"I'll be here."

***

"I will kill him." As I was about to open the door of my room, I caught the rush of words behind me.

"I don't give a fuck what my sister did, I will kill the motherfuck-er." Crossing the hall, I ignored the protocol to knock before opening the door. Someone threatening to kill another individual gave me the needed permission, and urgency for that matter.

Pushing the door open, I startle the dark-haired man who sat with his side to me, his profile one I recognize. Ross Kincaid pounded his fists into the wood of his desk, the face of a beautiful woman filling the screen. Kincaid turned his attention to me, our gazes colliding as his fury seemed to pitch.

"Who are we killing? 'Cause you know I'm always up for a good fight."

Not waiting for an invitation, I cross the room and sit on the edge of his bunk. My eyes swing to the woman on the screen, flashing her a smile of assurance. Her blue eyes are full of sadness, clouded with a burden she didn't own. Kincaid stands from his desk, his anger forgotten for the moment.

"Doc, how the fuck are you?" Capturing me in a side hug, knocking the air out of me with his firm hand slapping against my back.

"I'm good, it's been too long." I pull back, glancing to the screen and tipping my chin. "Looks like the company you keep has gotten better."

"Fuck you." He jokingly points at me, and then sits back into his chair. "This is my wife, Amanda. Babe, this rude bastard is Logan Forbes, the doctor I told you about last time I was home."

Leaning over his shoulder, donning the friendliest smile in my arsenal. "Mrs. Kincaid, it's a pleasure to meet you. You may call me Logan."

A pleasant smile meets watery eyes, sitting up a little straighter in what looks like a chair in a barbershop.

"I'm Amanda, and I apologize for my husband's outburst, we were discussing some unpleasant news about his sister."

Kincaid huffs as he leans back in his chair, turning the screen to the side and offering me a seat.

"Doc, I assume they have told you why I'm here?"

Nodding my head, "Yeah. Havoc is getting Med-Boarded because of his lungs." The CO had asked to have a word with me after the rest of my team left his office. Command had sent the official word of his impending discharge, and while these things took months to finalize, our missions went on.

"Yes, and it fucking sucks. I feel as if I'm betraying him by being here."

"Don't." I warned. Kincaid was an unofficial member of my team and my responsibility as his teammate was to tell him the truth.

"Havoc is looking forward to going home to Florida, getting back to his family's business and his mother's relentless search for his future wife."

"Well," he looked to his wife's smiling face. "At least someone's happy."

Crossing my arms over my chest, the metal of my dog tags clink together from the movement. "I'm going to have to ask you to elaborate." I out ranked him but it didn't matter, being a member of this team was like a brotherhood of unspoken valor.

Kincaid shifted his eyes to mine, the peaks of anger brewing in the hazel orbs. He sits silent for a few minutes, contemplation reflecting in his features. "How much time you got?" Tapping his fingers against the edge of the desk.

Crossing my boots at the ankle, "As much time as it takes for you to tell me who we're going to kill."

"Okay, but I warn you, this isn't a pretty story."

"The good ones never are." I admitted.

"I have a younger sister." He started and my heart sank. I'd nearly forgotten about the connection between the woman who had given me something to smile about and the man who sat before me.

"Harper, right?"

An instant look of suspicion covers his face, competing head to head against the protection he felt for his sibling.

"Calm down, Blaze. She chose my name this year." Suspicion turned to elation as he let out a victorious laugh, which rocked the room.

"Then you may end up just as pissed off as I am, considering."

My attention captured, I motioned for him to continue. The frayed edges of anger beginning to simmer in my chest. From my brief encounter with Harper, I found her to be someone I would like to get to know. Anyone who went to as much effort as she did to help complete strangers was someone worth knowing.

"When Harper and I were younger there was this kid, Alex, who lived not far from us. He and I fell into an easy friendship and spent countless hours being boys. As we got older, Alex found more reasons to be close to Harper. I was oblivious to his attraction for her until one night I found him standing outside her bedroom door listening to her sleep. I threatened to kick his ass if he ever touched a hair on her head. Alex was a popular guy who had sampled his fair share of the female population of our high school. While he respected my wishes, he also made it impossible for anyone else to date her. There was this asshole that tried to hurt my sister and Alex stepped in and took care of things. When I saw for myself how much he cared for her, I gave him my blessing to ask her out. They dated for a while and when it came time for us to head off to college, Harper, and myself, assumed he would break things off with her. When I confronted him, he said he loved her enough to become someone so one day he could put a ring on her finger and be a part of our family. Everything was great until the Twin Towers came crashing down and he and I chose to go beat the shit out of the bastards responsible. He made good on his promise and bought her a ring, asking her to marry him. We headed off to boot camp and in the blink of an eye, found ourselves in the middle of the desert, only in different countries. He was placed on the front line and I was at the right place at the right time to save the ass of a dignitary. We were able to keep in contact until just after the New Year when his company was ordered to go out and find a missing group of soldiers. According to the report I read, Alex found the group being held prisoner and led his team into the camp, lighting up the enemy with enough C4 and bullets to kill everyone twice. As they were pulling the injured guys out of the building, a rogue sniper shot Alex in the chest. He lived long enough to make it to a field hospital, where he died from the severity of his injuries. My father was with Harper when they came to the house to tell her the news. It was Valentine's Day and she assumed the knock at the door was a delivery for her."

Kincaid's voice cracked as he spoke of his friend's death, and my heart went out to Harper for the love she lost on what was designed to be such a special day.

"Alex had all his benefits in Harper's name, including a life insurance policy which she used to open the shop she has now. She dove into the business from the moment she was handed the keys. The town hailed Alex a hero, building a park with a statue of him in the center, named a street after him and every year there is a memorial to honor him. Our old high school has a scholarship in his name, one Harper laid out the initial money for. On the anniversary of his death, she started a charity where unemployed women could come in and get a suit or dress so they could go to interviews. She teamed up with my wife and sister-in-law, who run a beauty salon next door, to get these ladies a cut or color to help boost their confidence. One afternoon, a new delivery guy came into her store, he joked around with her and developed a friendship with her, taking his time progressing the relationship further. Whether out of pressure from our family or loneliness, she caved and let him take her out. According to our father, the guy Lance, has shifty eyes and something about him rubs dad the wrong way. Two years ago, he got down on one knee and asked for her hand, she surprised us all when she said yes."

Not certain if I agree with Kincaid, two years is enough time to heal from a death, and moving on can sometimes be the best medicine.

"Babe, you tell him the rest, you've been with her for it."

Turning to the monitor, Amanda had composed herself, looking more like a proud wife than the distraught woman she was a few minutes ago.

"Lance gave Harper what she needed at the time: a relationship with no expectations. There was no chemistry between them, no sweet kisses or pet names. He let Harper hide in her shell and continue to grieve Alex's death. He also fooled her into thinking he was something he wasn't."

Kincaid's knuckles cracked as he listened to Amanda, the tension in the air thickening with each word spoken.

"He never ventured out after dark, reasoning the statistics for crime increasing when the sun went down. They were together for years, but she never spent the night. As far as I know they never slept together. According to her, his religion forbade it. He would come by the shop almost every morning, with a smile on his face and, after this past weekend, a lie on his lips."

My curiosity piqued, "What happened this weekend?"

I had visions of a massive girl fight with hair pulling and one of them ending up naked and arrested when an old girlfriend showed up to express her disapproval of the couple.

"Her bridal party took her to a strip club, but the power went out and we had to move the party to a club Harper wanted to visit. Long story short, the lying bastard was there with two girls sucking his fucking dick as he fed them cocaine. She left when, instead of trying to lie his way out of it, he told her to get on her knees and join them."

This time it was my knuckles cracking as I pictured the mother-fucker hurting the selfless girl who had befriended me. Just as Kincaid had shouted earlier, I was going to kill him.

"She got up the next morning, contacted all the venders, cancelling everything and apologizing to me for the money we had to spend on airfare for Ross to come home."

Glancing over to Kincaid, his eyes looking lovingly at Amanda.

"And now you know everything."

I remained in Kincaid's room for a few more minutes, gaining information on this Lance Ranoka. After he ended the Facetime session with Amanda, we spoke of the mission coming up that, if the CO had his say, would be my last with this team. Bidding my friend, a good night, I checked the time and couldn't help the smile as I calculated the difference between here and Chesapeake. Signing onto my computer, I felt good as I clicked the mouse several times and sat back, anticipating the smile I hoped would grace her face.

Chapter Six

HARPER

Securing the last strip of tape on the latest box for LT Forbes, made as he requested sans tampons, using anything I could to ignore what day it was.

Amanda and Stacy had been hovering over me, trying desperately to get me to express my feelings about the breakup. Did they really want to hear how I came home and danced in my living room? Or how I took all of three seconds to pull the ring off and remove every trace of the bastard from my life? No, they wanted to hear of the ice cream diving, and marathon movie watching which never happened. The lake of tears I cried for a tainted love, which was a twisted tale of bullshit.

Lance Ranoka didn't break anything in me, he made me remember the truth I had always known, men will do and say anything to get what they want. All of the good guys were either married, dead, or gay. Granted this jaded view I had was manufactured in response to their hovering, something I said to get them off my back and away from my front door. Good men still existed, my brother and father are living proof, but none of them, none of the good ones anyway, seemed to fit into my life.

"I have something you really want!"

Sarah called as she came through the door. The morning after the club, I had to call Mitch when the wireless system in my shop failed to connect. He came over and broke the news of my router's death. I added it to the growing pile of corpses that lined the space around me.

Taking my dead router and the loaned computer with him, he promised he would have everything working by the time my shop opened this morning.

"Actually, it's me that has it, she's just my sexy assistant."

Looking up from the box, Mitch crosses the space with a smile on his face and a large box under his arm.

"Give me a kiss, a screwdriver, and twenty minutes and I'll have everything working." He winked as he leaned his cheek down to my level, eliciting a smile from me as I added in a tight squeeze around his neck.

"What would I do without you, Mitch?"

"You'd have to find another way to watch *Pornhub*, that's what."

Hands down my favorite thing about Sarah and Mitch was their ability to see the true me. They both allowed me to deal with the Lance situation, as I felt best.

"Then thank God I won't have to find out."

Mitch disappeared into the back where my electronics were housed.

"Sarah, I'm headed to the Post Office to mail this." Raising the box from the counter, my purse resting on the top. "I'm going to stop at the cemetery on my way back."

Not waiting to hear her question if I wanted company, I practically ran out the front door and jumped into my car. Even with the early morning hour, the line at the Post Office was several people deep. Melvin, the same man who had taken care of me for years, stood ready to assist as my turn finally came.

"Different address this time. Your friend get new orders?" Melvin was the biggest gossip in town, next to the Mayor's wife. I wouldn't be surprised if he had an x-ray machine back there to look inside the box.

"He did," I admitted, withholding how this was the same base Ross had been assigned to according to Amanda.

"Guess I won't see you at the ceremony this year, with you getting married and all."

"Sorry to disappoint, but the wedding was canceled. Found Lance doing something he shouldn't have and we are done. So, yes, you will see me at the ceremony." I'd never been one to show rudeness on purpose, but with recent events, perhaps he could make up a better story to pass around.

"I'll get this out first thing," he replied with a smirk. "Never did care for Lance, something about him didn't add up." Instead of breaking into the meaning behind his cryptic words, he tossed my box in the bin and wished me a good day.

* * *

The bitter cold wind of this February morning stung my cheeks as it pelted my skin. Snow flurries danced on the air as I stood looking at Alex's grave. A fine layer of snow covered the dead grass, and made the black leather of my boots stand out in contrast to the pure white.

"Ross told me when we buried you here, you would be looking down on me and keeping me safe. He's never lied to me, so you must already know what happened the other night." Stepping closer, running my fingers along the letters of his name, tracing the crevices each one created.

"I should have known he was full of shit when he said I could keep your photograph beside my bed, the one we took before you left." I waited for the emotion to choke me, filling my throat and halting my ability to free my thoughts.

"I think you would like the soldier I adopted this year, he's a SEAL, like Ross." Stopping short, feeling lost as for the first time as to what to say. "I'm sorry, you already know that too, don't you?"

The sound of a train off in the distance pulls my attention to the horizon; the creaking of an old oak tree as the wind tossed its dormant branches back and forth interrupts the stillness.

"I didn't love him, Alex. I'm not sure I have the ability to love anyone after you." A strong gust of wind hits me hard enough to push me back a little, nearly knocking me off balance. The cold surrounding me pushes its way past the layers of clothes and into the depths of my bones.

"All these years and I still can't let you go, can't move past what could have been and let myself live." Sniffing as the cold air causes my nose to run.

"Maybe one of these days you'll send me someone to take over where you left off. Someone strong enough to live with the ghost in my heart."

* * *

The memorial ceremony for Alex was much the same as it was last year. New faces filled the seats of those we lost this year; a number of military uniforms came to honor the man they knew back in Kuwait. I'd heard the stories so many times I could tell them myself, of how he saved a dozen men before sacrificing himself. For years, I resented Alex for the heroic action he took, giving up his life—our life—for the men who sit in this room with me. But as I look at the face of the young person who was awarded the scholarship, I knew Alex would have been proud. It was enough to keep me going for another year.

I pondered this year's winner, a young man with the same spirit as my Alex. A smile brought to my lips as he spoke of honoring his memory by doing many of the same tasks he was noted as doing: volunteering with the younger children, helping with various charities, and being accepted to the University of Michigan. Rationalizing with myself this was Alex's way of reminding me life went on without him.

Sarah returned my smile as the bell rang above the door, announcing my return. The smile lasted long enough for my eyes to see Lance exiting the door of his car, sunglass sliding into place—something he never wore in the past. Thankfully he stayed away from the memorial service, keeping her from causing a scene by calling the police. Pretending as if I hadn't seen him, I cross the threshold and shrug off my coat, the warmth of my store welcoming me with open arms.

"Don't think for one second I won't call the cops. You say the word and I will hit the green button on my cell." Sarah's cell is in her hand, the face illuminated and I could see the three numbers on the screen.

"He knows not to come in here." My confidence was too much as the bell rang and the man I hated most in this world walked in. Sarah raised a single brow, waiting for me to say the word. Storing my coat and purse, I turned to see him standing beside the window display of a wedding dress, the one I purchased to marry his sorry ass, surrounded by red and pink hearts, tiny reminders of what today represented.

"Harper, I deserve to be heard. What you saw the other night wasn't what you think."

Sarah looks for confirmation, but I place my hand on her arm. "Let's get a few things straight from the beginning, here in the light of day and absent of musicians singing about sex, and how many ways they can do it. Minus the two human lips enjoying the tiny as fuck dick you're carrying between those thighs. I do *not* owe you anything; my time, my attention or my affection. The minute you chose to let the first girl take your dick in her hand was also the minute you lost any right to have a say in anything I do. You're lucky I was able to get the majority of my money back for this sham of a wedding you fooled me into; otherwise I would have taken your sorry ass to court. Now, for the last and final time, you are not welcome in my shop, or in the shop next door. Leave before I let Sarah call the police and have you arrested for trespassing."

Lance lowered his gaze, laughed thickly and then pointed his sunglasses toward me.

"When you've come to your senses and can have an adult conversation, one not filled with juvenile threats, you know where to find me."

He left just as he came, with a new swagger and attitude to match. How long would it have taken for me to see this side of him? The man he truly was when no one was looking.

"One thing always bugged me about that piece of shit." Sarah watched him get into his car, both of our eyes fixed on his retreating form.

"Just one?" I teased, bumping her hip with mine.

"How does a man who makes a stitch over ten dollars an hour, shares a studio apartment with two other guys, and owns two pair of jeans, afford a car like that?"

Sarah waited until he drove off down the street before she told me the internet was fixed and my new computer was ready for me to take a test drive. She had some alterations to complete and excused herself to the back of the shop. Excitement filled me as I lifted the lid of my laptop, the larger screen came to life and a picture of my three nephews greeted me.

Signing into my email, I waded through tons and tons of junk until I came to one from Ross. I didn't have to guess what he would say, most likely telling me he was sorry for what happened. I'd call him tonight, let him know I was fine and not to worry. I needed to send Logan an email, giving him a heads up a new package was on it way.

TO: Logan .Forbes.LT@ OPS
FROM: AlexGrl17
CC:
SUBJECT: Heads up!!
Dear Logan,

I am so glad you got your package and are enjoying its contents. I can tell you over the years, I have had some strange requests for follow-up packages, but I do believe yours is the strangest. You want me to send what I would want in there...hmm. All right, but you should really be careful what you ask for. However, I have to ask you not to tell Ross or make fun of me for what the box may contain. I mailed yours this morning and you should have it in a few weeks.

Lisa James, huh? I knew a guy once who said she had legs all the way to her ass. At the time, I didn't understand what he meant as this is traditionally where your legs end. However, the first time I saw her on a runway, I understood what he meant. She is a seriously beautiful woman and has an amazing set of legs. I read something in People magazine where she hasn't been linked to anyone in Hollywood, so it would seem you still have a chance.

You wanted to know something about me that no one else knows. Well, here goes. I found my fiancé cheating on me, with two women. Everyone, including

Ross I suspect, is waiting for me to curl into the fetal position and cry. How can you mourn something you didn't want in the first place? How can you pretend there is an emotion where nothing, and I mean absolutely nothing, exists. Lance gave me what I needed at the time, allowing me to hang on to something I wasn't ready to let go of. In the light of a new day, I feel exactly the same as when I woke up the day it happened, only twenty grand richer! Yes, I managed to cancel everything at the eleventh hour before I lost the right to a refund. There, now you know a secret of mine, something I haven't even taken the time to write in my journal.

Anyway, I'm glad I have the opportunity to get to know you and I am positive we are going to be amazing friends.

Your friend,

Harper

The ringing of the bell over the door jarred me from the smile I allowed myself to enjoy as I hit send on Logan's email. I smelled them before I saw them; white roses. The bouquet was so big it hid the person carrying them. The poor delivery person barely made it to the counter where I stood gawking. With a moan of exertion, the vase slid across the counter in front of me.

"I have a delivery for Miss Harper Kincaid." Standing like an idiot, recalling a time where I hoped Alex had remembered my love for roses. Instead, the men who stood on the other side of the door held the news which had shattered my world rather than of the joy I anticipated. The clearing of a throat, brought my attention to the man in a ball cap, with Holly Farm's embroidered across the face. His outstretched hand with offered pen and clipboard, waiting patently with a smile on his face. Signing my name, I handed back the clipboard, reaching into my pocket for a tip.

"No need, Miss Kincaid, everything was taken care of by the sender." Tipping the bill of his cap at me, "I have two more for you, be right back."

Amanda appeared out of thin air, as I never heard the door to her shop open, "Harper, who are they from?"

"Is there a card?" Sarah must have heard the door and came to see if I needed any help as she was now standing on the opposite side of the counter searching the stems for the missing card. Her perusal proved successful as she handed me what looked to be a business card. "Oh, my God! These are from Holly Farms." Sarah had lived a tough life, having several jobs at one point in her life just to keep her family afloat. She shared how one summer she worked for a nursery, helping customers pick out flowers for summer planting. She didn't mind it so much, growing flowers being her second love next to sewing.

The delivery guy returned with two more vases of flowers, each as enormous as the first. A sliver of anger reared its head as the thought of Lance sending these came to mind. I had to take a minute and remind myself he had never sent me flowers in all the years we were together, no reason for him to start now.

Nestled in the sea of white petals was an elegant card on thick stationary, not the standard business card size you expect when receiving flowers such as these. A gold sticker, embossed with the image of a tree in the center of a circle, secured the flap of the envelope closed. Carefully, I lifted the edge of the flap, my curiosity nagging at the back of my mind, who would do this for me?

Stacy had her nose buried in one of the open blossoms, taking in the scent, which filled the space around me. Looking closely at the edge of the petals, I could see what looked to be tiny raindrops and I assumed with the snowfall outside.

Harper,

Every beautiful woman deserves to have flowers surrounding her. I take great pleasure in being the man who gets to make it happen for you. Valentine's Day is a celebration of love, a day set aside so millions of men can remind the women in their lives how special they are. You have given a stranger the gift of friendship, something not many people are willing to do.

The first vase, and if you're reading this you've already noticed the crystals adorning the petals, are to remind you of the glimmers of hope and joy you have given all the other couples who've crossed your path. Uniting two souls, who may have been searching their whole lives for one another, needing a guiding hand to help them find their way. Enjoy the fragrance these flowers bless you with, sharing the only gift they have to give.

Yours,

Logan

Tucking the card back into the envelope, my heart races as I looked to the next vase. Amanda, enjoying the pearls springing from between the blooms, hands me the sealed envelope, a teary smile on her face.

Harper,

Pearls of wisdom, or at least that is what my aunt calls them. A tradition she started when she purchased Holly Farms from its original owner. In her younger days, she spent time traveling as a photojournalist, capturing the faces and exotic treasures all over the world.

Here is my pearl of wisdom which applies to you: kindness isn't always convenient, but it has the potential to change everything. You showed kindness to so many and it is my wish you receive some back.

Yours,

Logan

The third vase sat off to the side, and while the flowers were beautiful, they lacked any fancy additives to make them stand out. Stacy admired the blossoms, her chin propped up on her hands, eyes lost in a moment of admiration.

Harper,

The last vase was the hardest for my aunt to arrange. When I requested the final arrangement to be as plain as possible, she sent me an email chastising me for sending a girl something so lackluster. When I told her the story of why I was doing this, she reluctantly agreed.

The last vase represents the future, one with a blank slate and endless possibilities. The world is ever changing and with change comes uncertainty. You have come into my world like a breath of fresh air, giving me a reminder of the good things in life. For the rest of the year, and as our relationship grows, we get to choose where our friendship goes. And who knows, maybe I will find myself

standing in your shop one day, thanking you for leading me to the special
someone I was destined to meet.

    Yours,

    Logan

No one had sent me flowers since Alex. Avoiding relationships tends to limit the customary gift from a man of interest. Lance preferred to bring me coffee, or a sandwich from around the corner.

As I flipped the open sign to closed, twisting the lock on the door, I turned and leaned my body against the metal and glass. My heart felt full as I took in the gifts Logan had taken time to send. Mitch came by just before lunch, their two children in tow, with gifts in their hands. Sarah kissed her girls' cheeks, giving Mitch a look lending suspicion another baby could be in the making.

Ross and Ashton made their wives teary as balloons and flowers were delivered shortly after lunch. Love hung heavy in the air, marrying with the sweet aroma of my roses and Sarah's chocolate. The spirit of the holiday wrapped me in a warm feeling, giving me a new outlook on the world around me. And for the first time in several years, I didn't hate Valentine's Day.

Chapter Seven

LOGAN

TO: Logan. Forbes.LT@ OPS

    FROM: AlexGrl17

    CC:

    SUBJECT: Thank you

    Logan,

For the first time in a long time, I am speechless. I feel thank you somehow just isn't enough. You should know you have impeccable timing as your flowers came at a time when my world was really sucking. Valentine's Day historically has not been my favorite day, you helped to make the day, and what it previously stood for, a little more tolerable. Your advice on kindness is the truth, and the way I've chosen to live my life. Giving back as much as I possibly can. Thank you for taking just a few minutes out of your already hectic day and making mine so much better. You didn't have to, but I am so glad you did.

    Stay safe,

    Harper

I found myself reading her letters all too often, practically memorizing them and using them to bring a smile to my face. My Aunt Lila had been all too willing to help me with the delivery, she was also a big mouth when she called my mother and told her what I had done.

Meredith Forbes waited all of thirty minutes before sending me an inquisitive email in regards to who Harper was. I gave the excuse of needing to go on patrol, something I should know not to even think about as the second the lie left my fingertips, the call came out. We were needed to go handle a situation where others may have failed.

With barely enough time to grab all of my gear, I hadn't been able to send Harper an email. The omission plagued me as we sat under a flea-infested brush for two days waiting for movement. Aarash Konar was on the move; the wires had come alive with chatter. I sat beside Ghost as he wrote frantically in his book, using the codebook buried in his head to tell us where the strike would happen. Ghost let me listen as Aarash chastised someone for acting like an idiot. His name, Ecnal, was one we heard a few months ago, but he held no threat to us. By the way Aarash was yelling at him, whatever he did warranted penance.

Ghost was able to translate there was a scheduled attack on a village not far from our location. Composed of mostly women and children, he wanted to make an example out of them for their lack of cooperation during his harvest. When his trucks finally moved out, they were greeted with a few rocket launchers resulting in the destruction of the convoy. We returned to base haggard and tired, and ready to sleep for a week. In our abrupt departure, there hadn't been time to check Kincaid into the team, he remained back at base with instructions to keep Ramsey motivated and to show him why we gave Kincaid the name Blaze.

"Doc, you coming?"

Havoc pounding on my door pulled me from my flashing cursor. "Yeah, I'll be there in a second."

Blaze wanted to have all of the team in his room for a little get together. He mentioned something about an old friend of his he found wondering the base, a Chief he knew from back home. As the interim appointed leader of this group, I felt obligated to go over there. My need to know more about Harper and what she was like had nothing to do with anything.

TO: AlexGrl17
FROM: Logan. Forbes.LT@ OPS
CC:
SUBJECT: You are my favorite girl on the planet!!
Harper,

My sincere apologies for the lapse in time since you last heard from me, I'm counting on your being a seasoned military sister to know these things sometimes cannot be avoided, or explained. Your last email brought a smile to my face and has kept it there for the past few weeks. Knowing I was able to bring a glimmer of hope into your dreary winter made the desert heat and sand fleas not so terrible.

Your latest box greeted me when I walked in, covered in sand and the amount of dirt I won't dare describe to a lady such as yourself. I dove into the white box as if a kid at Christmas, laughing until my face and abdominal muscles hurt from the tension. You shared a great deal about yourself in what you sent me. For example, the chocolate you sent; not your standard drug counter variety, but from a genuine chocolatier, albeit a famous one. It tells me you have a taste for the finer things, yet keeping your expensive taste in a reasonable price bracket. I, too, enjoy that particular brand. Sadly, it did not survive the heat of travel.

Next, your choice in lotion, a brand I'm all too familiar with. Lisa and I have kept in touch over the years, and the last time I saw her, we had dinner following a photo shoot highlighting the fragrance you sent me.

The most surprising of the items you sent were the collection of romance novels by CJ Reece. Soft-core porn is what you enjoy? Harper Kincaid, you naughty girl! Not to worry, I'll read them later, treating it as if I'm peaking at the opposing team's playbook.

Still smiling,

Logan

When Viper got ready to leave, he pulled me aside and handed me the jar of moonshine he had. Giving me strict instructions to welcome the guy who joined our team the way boys in the South did it. Tucking the half-full jar into my pants pocket, I shutdown my computer and headed across the hall.

I knocked softly on the metal door, avoiding calling attention from the last door at the end of the hall which housed a new Lieutenant I was warned about. The door opened slowly as Blaze stuck his head around the edge. "Thank God, it's you and not Oxford."

Closing the door behind me, I had to blink my eyes several times as I took in the room. Last time I was here, the sparse furnishings I was accustomed to surrounded us as I spoke with his wife. Now, two flat screen televisions hung on the wall and a leather couch, similar to the one in the officer's lounge, sat against the left side of the room. Numerous gaming systems filled the bookshelves lined up under the television screens.

"Do I even want to know?" Fanning my hand around the room, Ghost and a man I never met glanced at me briefly as they continued the racing game playing on mute.

"I didn't steal it, if that's what you're wondering. I have a buddy back home who can get me any electronics I want at cost plus shipping."

"Wasn't accusing you of anything," molding my tired body into the leather cushion of the couch. "But I did bring us a little something to celebrate with."

Pulling the jar from my pocket, the man in the corner pauses the game as his eyes register what is in the jar.

"Tell me that ain't bug juice." Rising to his full height, the anchors on his collar tell me he is a Chief and I wonder if this is the friend Blaze mentioned earlier.

"I'm sorry, I didn't catch your name." Standing to match him, my blouse draped over the chair in my room, my t-shirt giving nothing away in significance of rank. With my hand extended, "Logan Forbes, but my guys call me Doc."

His grip is firm, and it tells me he isn't intimidated by who I am. "Ashton Dawson, but everyone calls me Master Chief."

Tipping my head to the side, his name stirring up a familiarity. "Have we met before? Your name sticks out for some reason."

Blaze picks up the jar, removes the lid and takes a sniff, shaking his head and squinting his eyes.

"Nope, Ashton, pure moonshine." His tone says it all, conveying the thrill of getting his hands on some true alcohol. Tipping the jar back, Blaze coughs a few times as the liquid lights him up.

"Ashton was the first guy to get Harper's packages." He clarifies, his voice gravelly from the moonshine, pointing at his friend.

"This is the guy who she picked this year." Taking another gulp as Ghost moves in and takes the jar from his hands.

"Really? Congratulations man." Holding out his hand to take the jar from Ghost, "Harper is a goddamn angel. Helped me find my Stacy, who gave me my two kids." Ashton moves the jar to his mouth, tipping it back and swallowing several mouths full.

"She blessed us both." Blaze stood with hands on hip, his eyes hovering over the picture of his wife.

"Gave me a reason to try harder and make the system work for me." Dragging his gaze to Chief who nodded his head in agreement.

"Can't say as I was upset to hear about her and what's his name." Chief mirrored Blaze's stance, his focus on the jar still in Ghost hand.

Feigning ignorance, "What guy? The one she was engaged to?" Holding my hand out for a sample of the rapidly disappearing drink.

"Forbes, you can drop the act, we all know about the flowers you sent her. My wife saw the email she wrote to you when she was ringing up a customer for Harper. But yes, I'm glad she called it off with him. Although Harper won't say anything to me, Amanda says he's come by the shop a few times, trying to get her to change her mind. Sarah had to call the police this last time as he refused to leave until she agreed to dinner with him."

"She take out a restraining order?" Ghost inquired as he handed the jar to me.

"Ain't worth the paper it's written on if the man is determined." I hadn't noticed Reaper come into the room; he shot me a quick nod and then held up two jars matching the one in my hand.

"My new neighbors in South Carolina introduced themselves." Reaper had purchased an old farm outside of Charleston, his need for solitude after the life we have lived these past several years, had him searching for a place away from everything and every one.

Someone attempts to open the door, smacking the edge into

Reaper's back. "Hey, motherfuckers, let me in." Aiden's voice rang through the crack in the door. He had received a letter from Rachael and wanted to try and call her. He planned to take leave soon and wanted to get-away with her, but she wasn't being cooperative. By the sound of his voice, maybe he was able to change her mind.

"Sorry, Chief." Reaper apologized, moving to the side and offering one of the jars in his hand.

"Oh, yes. Apology accepted."

"Aiden Sawyer." Master Chief called from my left, moving around Ghost to shake Aiden's hand. "I thought I heard your name being passed around, how have you been?"

"I'm good, brother. When did you arrive in Shangri-La hell?"

"Two weeks ago, the call went out for a critical fill and I can't say no to the money. I'm retiring in a few months and this will be my last tour." The two Chiefs stared at one another, nodding their heads, as they appeared to understand the struggle of the other. Aiden hands the jar to Ashton and then turns to me.

"Doc, you remember me telling you about the guy I almost landed in jail with during boot camp?"

"Oh, Lord. Tell me you aren't still sharing that story with everyone?" Ashton snickered as he brought the jar to his lips.

"He hasn't told us, but by the color of your ears, I damn sure want to hear it now." Sure enough, the tips of Ashton's ears were a deep red.

"Forget it. The story involved a beautiful woman who turned out to be underage, and hiding in a dumpster for three hours in the sweltering heat." Aiden waved his hand in the air, dismissing the story and the embarrassment.

"What I do want to hear, is the two of you comparing notes on the lottery you both won." Perplexed with his meaning, I narrowed my eyes and tipped my chin.

"Harper Kincaid, this fucking grizzly's baby sister."

Flashing my attention back to Blaze, I give him a hard look and let out a belly laugh. Aiden was spot on with his description of Blaze. He was well over six-foot tall, with tan skin and dark hair and eyes.

"Hey!"

"Sorry, Blaze. I haven't given you a hard enough look before, but he's right. You do look like you could use a good waxing." Pretending to pull at a hair poking our of the collar of his shirt.

"Yeah, well, this Lance guy better hope I don't find him when I'm home on leave next week." Blaze stiffened as he uttered the name. I couldn't control the growing agitation I felt myself as a result.

"Tell me again, besides the whole cheating part, what made you uneasy about him?" Taking a seat on the couch, my elbows on my thighs. Blaze takes a seat in his chair, mimicking my position.

"He's—odd."

"Define odd?"

"He delivers for one of those carrier services; you know the box trucks you can buy at auction?"

"Yeah." Nodding my head, lacing my fingers together. Reaper and the rest of the guys circled around us, the video game remaining on pause.

"He drives an Audi RS8."

"Okay, so? Ever heard of a lease?"

"He paid cash."

"So?"

"I don't know many guys who work for ten bucks an hour who can afford to lay down one-hundred-thousand dollars on a car."

"He could have saved, won money in a lottery scratch off, a relative died and left him money." With the amount of resentment in Blaze's attitude, I would keep the bottom line of my finances to myself. And no way was I telling him what kind of car waited for me in my parent's garage.

"I'm not trying to challenge you, but having money doesn't make someone a bad person."

"He has an arrest record."

"Okay, he rebelled as a youth."

"For possession with intent to distribute."

"And he just became a piece of shit. Let me know if you need bail money or legal representation when you find him."

I have zero tolerance for the poisoning of our streets back home. If this Lance guy was harassing Harper, I knew of a few guys who could step in and give him a warning.

"Harper doesn't know this, but my friend Mitch sent me an email the other day with the information.

"Mitch Riley?" Aiden interrupted, as the sound of knuckles hitting the door thumped once again.

Blaze held up his clinched fist signaling us to stop and motioned for Ashton to grab a rope tucked behind the monitor of his computer. Stepping lightly, he crossed the room and opened the door a crack.

"Oh hey, man." Opening the door fully, allowing Havoc to step into the room.

"Sorry, y'all. But the weasel dick LT down the hall is as nosey and by the book as they come."

"You mean Lieutenant Oxford? Way I hear it, he hasn't seen the outside of an office since he got his silver bars." Aiden huffed, humorlessly as he scooted over to let Havoc sit down.

"Caught him watching me as I went down the hall after my shower. I dared him to say something about this beard."

Looking around the room at my team, Aiden and Reaper are the only two who hadn't picked up a razor after this latest mission.

"Y'all gonna keep those things? You forget about the fleas out there?" I snickered, as the need to get rid of those nasty things haunted me for the past week, the beard came off before anything else did.

"Hey, I'm Alex Nakos, these guys call me Havoc." Leaning his body in Blaze's direction, hand outstretched in invitation.

"Ross Kincaid, or Blaze as Doc saw fit to call me. And I'm sorry to be the one who's taking your spot on this team."

"Don't apologize, this is a good thing, and I'm not upset in the least. I've had my adventure and made some kick ass friends. Now, it's time to go home and get a real job." He eased back in his seat, "But you have to tell me how you got the name Blaze."

Just as Blaze takes a breath to start the story, one which will make him look as crazy as Diesel and his ability to make water flammable, an alert sounds from his computer, one most of us are familiar with as it announces the face of a loved one.

"Hang on, let me see who this is."

Turning his chair to the computer, tapping the spacebar as the photo of him and three little faces surrounding his.

"Hey, Sis." Blaze boasts as the screen changes from a black box to an animated photo with Harper's name under it.

"Ross? Are you there? I can't see you." Her voice is angelic and captures my attention, freezing me in my seat. I watch with anticipation as the screen once again goes black and then slowly progresses to brown, and finally reveals the face of one of the most beautiful girls I have ever seen.

Brown hair similar to her brothers, with lighter shades blended throughout. Pale skin, that of a woman who takes great pride in the health of herself, protecting the delicate organ from the sun's harmful rays. Eyes blue like the shallow pools of a tropical beach sparkling with hints of amber and green around the edges. Her face is full, signs of a body with curves and character. Lips, which hold a smile, one of joy at seeing her brother, covering the white teeth, which from the little I can see, are straight and nearly perfect.

"There you are." She giggles and I cannot hide the smile she evokes from me. "This isn't a bad time is it? Amanda just left the store to get the kids, so I hoped to catch up with you."

"You're fine, Harper. I was having a little get together with my new team."

"Oh, I'm so sorry, I didn't know. Give me a call when you're free, there's nothing wrong. Be careful and I'll see you next week. Love you."

She was gone before Blaze could say anything, my soul crying out for her to stay, to say my name so I could watch those lips of her move and tempt me further.

"And that was my crazy sister Harper." Blaze laughed as he closed the program, "Always afraid she's bothering me."

My eyes remained on the now black screen, her laugh running around in my head, making a place for itself in my memory. Until now,

I never understood those poets who prattled on about instant love, believing soul mates were something found in fairytales and the books my aunt wrote.

"Logan?" My name combined with a set of fingers snapping in front of my face temporarily stopped the progression of my inner thoughts. Harper Kincaid had changed me. The tough as nails, seasoned physician who walked into this room was a new man, one with a deep raging desire to get closer to her.

"Awe hell! I know that look." Aiden punched my shoulder, gaining an angry oath from me, robbing me of the last frame of her face I had been holding on to. "Looks like Miss Harper made an impression on Doc."

"Can you blame me? The woman is fucking gorgeous." My mouth failing to rationalize with my head and heart, giving no consideration to the men around me, including her brother, whose smile had faltered and bewilderment filled the corners of his eyes.

"She's been hurt, not by this Lance guy, not really. But by my best friend who didn't come home to her like he promised."

Feeling braver than I should, new purpose bubbling in my chest giving me immeasurable amount of courage.

"Good thing I'm a doctor then. Healing people who are hurt is my specialty."

Cocky words hung in the air between us, I hadn't meant them to be, and by the flame in Blaze's eyes he didn't care.

"How many kids you got, Ross?"

Choosing to use his Christian name as to clear any confusion as to who was having this conversation. Two men who cared for the same woman, not members of the military governed by rules and regulations.

"Three boys." Turning back to his computer, he clicks the mouse several times and opens a blue folder. The game disappears from the large screen television; the smiling faces of three small boys light up the room.

"My oldest, Adam, is four and can't wait to start school next year." The picture on the screen looks to have been taken during Halloween, as he stands proudly in a Superman costume, a bright orange pumpkin behind him.

"Jason is our three-year-old, who looks the most like his mother out of all the three." He's right, the bright smile on the toddler's face matches the one I was graced with three weeks ago. The photo shows him hugging a chocolate colored puppy, the dogs tongue flat against his cheek.

"Hudson is the baby, born the last time I was home." The photo had been taken at a park, the baby cradled in the arms of the girl who stole my breath earlier. The two older boys hugging her on each side, her smile wide, reaching her eyes.

"Take a hard look at those faces. Every one of them holds a reason for me to stay here until my time is up. You were chosen by some random selection she uses to keep Alex's memory alive. Yes, she has this weird way of pairing up people with these boxes, but if the look on your face tells me what I think it is, I don't care what cosmic intervention is going on; hurt my sister and you will deal with me."

I'm unable to put myself in Blaze's position as I've never had any siblings, but it wasn't too hard to transition his love for his sister and how protective he was of her as I was of my mother.

"Listen, Blaze, we're brothers in this, and I won't hand you any lies in order to look like someone bigger or better than anyone else in this room. I came in here tonight, not to ogle your sister or test your defenses, but when I saw her face, heard her laugh—"

Words evade me as the memory of her clogs my throat, filling me once again with warmth and purpose.

Ashton pushed the jar toward me, the hush of the room resembling the quiet we demanded during a mission.

"I remember when I talked to her at Christmas, she joked how you would be the first one who would get a box without a bonus. Granted, she was engaged at the time, but she still felt as if she was cheating you somehow, hoping she picked the one guy who already had someone back home waiting for him. When I was first introduced to Harper, I was jaded against most women, having been lied to and cheated on. But one look in Stacy's eyes and all the wrong ever done to me vanished."

Before I could take a drink, Blaze reached over and pilfered the jar from me, "Every box has a story, and every damn one of them has a happy ending." Tipping the glass to his mouth, his eyes locked with mine as he takes several swigs.

"What will your story be, Logan? Can you erase the bad taste of a love gone sour? Or will your happy ending vanish like the dew in the morning?"

I knew my answer before the alcohol stopped burning his throat, but as I was about to answer, tell him how I planned to make her smile so much her face hurt, he leveled me with information I hadn't considered.

"Before you answer, you should know, my wife and Ashton's have been trying to set her up with the eligible men around town."

A flash of anger builds in my belly and I'm ready to jump to my feet and pound on my chest like a goddamn idiot. I had resources, lots of them, and I was more than willing to use every fucking one of them to keep those faceless bastards away from Harper. "And what would it take to make these men go away?"

"A phone call from me, letting them know you're interested. Knowing our wives, something monetary or the equivalent."

Reaching over, I take the nearly empty jar from Havoc's hands and lean into the space, which separated Blaze and me.

"Tell your wife to name her price. Operation SEAL has just been ordered," clinking my glass against his. But before the toast can be consumed, a loud knocking at the door fills the quiet of the room.

"Captain Kincaid? It's Lieutenant Oxford, I need to have a word with you."

Blaze jumps to his feet, "Awe hell."

Grabbing the rope behind him and tugging twice, a screen comes down covering the large televisions and bookcase. Reaper tucks the jars behind him on the couch and Ghost pushes the gaming chairs under the bed.

"Okay, let the rat bastard in."

Chapter Eight

HARPER

TO: AlexGrl17

FROM: Logan. Forbes.LT@ OPS

CC:

SUBJECT: Just thinking

Harper,

Ever get up at the crack of dawn just to listen as the Earth comes to life? How the shadows of the night retreat into the fallen areas of our surroundings? Watch as the animals venture out to explore, trusting the light of a new day to give them security? Maybe it's just me, and the way I try and appreciate the world around me, celebrating each sunrise as a new gift from Mother Nature.

This morning, as the sun crawled over the mountains, I didn't look for the lizards who watch me from their boulder perches, or listen as the men around me talk of their plans as they stand in line for chow. Today, I tried to imagine how you begin each day. Do you rise early and greet each day with a renewed anticipation? Or are you one of those who love to burrow under the covers, hitting the snooze button until the last possible second? Are you a coffee drinker or do you follow the English and enjoy a spot of tea?

Saint Patrick's Day is just around the corner, a time where everyone becomes Irish as a justification to celebrate and partake in the various celebrations. When I was in college, I had the opportunity to visit Savannah, Georgia during spring break, which coincided with their celebration. My friends and I drank beer as the water in the river downtown turned green to match the festivities. I don't recall much after that, as the drinking continued, erasing any memories I may have made.

What about you, Harper? Any plans to celebrate with the Leprechauns, drinking green beer until your cheeks turn a rosy pink? Or do you perhaps have a date with some lucky fellow? One I will willingly threaten bodily harm to forcing you to stay home and pine for me.

My celebration of the event will be limited to rounds on the patients, and eating dried out corn beef at the mess tent, thinking about the blue-eyed girl I managed to catch a glimpse of as she rushed to tell her brother she loved him. As you have gathered, or perhaps I'm not as coy as I give myself credit for, I was in the room when you contacted your brother. Harper Kincaid, you are, by far, the most beautiful woman I have ever seen, and I cannot wait to get to know you better.

Yours,

Logan

I read his email over and over. If I didn't know better, I would have sworn Logan was flirting. Closing the email and chastising myself for the crazy thought. Logan Forbes was most definitely not flirting, he had no reason to. There is a wide gully between gratitude and flirtation, the two having no reason to meet—ever.

A cold front had moved in overnight, sending the early morning commuters scurrying down the sidewalk, their scarves trailing behind them. Wrapping my hands around my second cup of coffee, I attempted to fend off the empathy chill from people watching.

Sarah called a little while ago, letting me know she would be late this morning as she had to go into Mitch's shop and help him with something. Things traditionally didn't get rolling around here for another hour, so I busied myself moving some racks of clothes around.

The bell above the door jingled and I assumed it was Sarah, but as I waited for her usual greeting, the voice of the local radio announcer prattled on about the chance of snow later.

"Hello?" A female voice called out, not one I recognized, so I placed the gown back on the rack and turned around.

"Good morning, welcome to Second Chances, can I—" My words dying in my throat as the face of the woman came into view.

"Good morning, my dear beauty!" Her sultry voice matched the image I had for her. I would recognize her anywhere as her face graced the back cover of at least a dozen books I owned upstairs.

"Oh my, God! You're CJ Reece."

"Yes, and I am hoping you are Harper Kincaid as I have something special for you."

I couldn't move. Here stood the woman who had, for years, taken me away to a place where men treasured women and loved them with amazing passion. Where love conquered all and always won in the end.

Finally finding my voice, unwilling to let the chance to talk with her slip out of my hands. "Yes, I'm Harper."

Crossing the distance between us, and raising her hand to cradle my cheek. "His description did you no justice." Her smile electric, as her other hand caressed the other side. "It's a good thing I'm the writer in the family, huh?"

Calling over her shoulder, "George, put the boxes over there." I watched slack jawed as the man placed the large box on the counter. CJ walked over ripping the tape from the top and took out what looked to be a manuscript. "Now, my dear, Harper, let me show you what I've brought you," pointing to the sofa placed just outside of the dressing area.

"Come, sit, I have so much to share." I wanted to pinch myself to make sure this was real. I cautiously followed and sat down next to her.

"Please forgive me for coming unannounced, but when my nephew called me and told me how the two of you met, I had to see this for myself."

Something about this didn't feel right. Why would a New York Times bestselling author come to my shop, on an ordinary Tuesday, to talk with me? I hadn't won any contest, nor had I entered any for that matter.

"Harper, you look like a deer caught in headlights." Patting my pant cover thigh, "Let me back up a little and tell you how I came to see you today." Returning her hands to the manuscript on her lap, *The Hands of Fate* written in bold block letters across the page, a novel by CJ Reese.

"My pen name is CJ Reese, but my legal name is Valerie Forbes. I am Logan's aunt. He and I have always been close, and he encouraged me to submit my books to a publisher. When he went off to the Middle East, I made him promise to always remember who he was, and be kind to everyone. He called me in the middle of the night when he decided he wanted to become a SEAL. I cannot tell you how much sleep I lost for those six months." Waving her hands wildly, leaning into to me to emphasize her point.

"He's worked so hard at being a good doctor, and I've worried he would spend the rest of his life off doing one mission or another, giving up his chance at a family. When he called me yesterday and told me all about you and the wonderful things you were doing, not only for him, but also for your community; I knew he was on the right path. This, my dear beautiful girl, is my next novel."

My hands were trembling as I slowly opened the page. I could hardly believe this was happening to me of all people. I blinked my eyes several times as I read and re-read the words that sat on the page.

"Go on, Sweetheart, read the dedication."

Logan and Harper,

Fate has a habit of taking the ordinary and making it extraordinary. Finding lost souls and reuniting them with their perfect match. There is no ocean, amount of time, or stretch of road which can keep two hearts destined to be together apart. Eventually, they will find each other and create their own version of happy ever after.

"Valerie, please forgive me, but I honestly have no idea why you're here or how Logan ties into all of this."

Handing her the manuscript back, her green eyes bright with mischief. "We really don't know each other—at all. We've exchanged a few emails and I've mailed him a couple of care packages."

Her expression changes, eyes full of joy and her smile now dazzling. "I'm here because you, my dear, are about to have your socks knocked off." I'm about to open my mouth in protest when she raises her hand to stop me.

"Let me tell you about a call I received from a room full of military men." Fanning herself as she rocks back and forth in her seat. "If I was twenty years younger, there was a couple of them I would have taken for a test drive. Anyway, I had the pleasure of speaking with your brother, who is a huge flirt by the way." Her admission makes me laugh, as I agreed with her.

"You have caught my nephew's attention with your generosity and both internal and external beauty. He, and his team, have banded together in an effort to see if he can win your affection."

My gut was screaming that something vital was missing. "And he knows you're here, to tell me all of this?"

"Well, not exactly."

"I see." And there it was, the joke, which always came when real feelings rose to the surface. Rising to my feet, I'm prepared to seal up the box and escort her out the door.

"Harper, wait, he knows I'm here. He did call me and ask me to deliver the books in the box over there. When I saw the sparkle in his eyes and heard how the guys around him spoke so highly of you, I had to come and make sure you were for real, and not some opportunist. I'm happy to say you are exactly as he said you were, a genuine person."

Valerie left me an autographed collection of her books, and her contact information. I promised I would keep her posted on the progression of my relationship with Logan. As she waved her final goodbye, I reasoned with myself how she had to be a romantic at heart, creating a world where fantasies were born. I lived in the real world, one where men didn't fall for women they never met.

Removing the manuscript before a customer could see it, I turned and caught my reflection in the full-length mirror. I had a closet full of gray and black, a few reds thrown in as sweaters and blouses. Genetics gave me large breasts and larger hips; rolls of skin came from lack of visits to the gym. As I locked eyes with my reflection, it became clear to me it was Amanda who Logan saw talking to Ross, not me. "No one would ever consider this beautiful." My eyes drift to the window where my wedding dress still hung on the dress form, "Even someone who was pretending."

* * *

"Sorry I'm late." Sarah rushed through the front door, the chill of the wind following her in. "Mitch had an order come in from out of state and he wanted me to look it over for him." Setting her purse down on the counter and shimmying out of her coat.

"What's this?" Sarah stops, pointing to the box I hadn't managed to move to the back. Lifting the flap on the box, I grab the first book I come to and pull it out. I had been reading CJ Reese's novels since I had found one left behind at a Laundromat. It was *Love's Never Ending Journey*, a story about two star-crossed lovers who lived in the Wild West. I read the entire book in less than five hours.

"Lieutenant Forbes is related to Ms. Reese and sent her over here with this box of her books for me."

"Shut the front door." Her eyes widen as she takes the book from my hand.

"He told her how much I enjoyed her writing and she wanted to do something nice." No way in hell was I going to tell her about the mix up in me and Amanda.

"You must have made quite an impression if he went to all of this trouble to get her to come over here." Sarah thumbed through the pages, ones I knew she had read time and time again. Placing the book on the counter, she reached over and took the manuscript.

"Holy shit, Harper! This one isn't due out until this summer." Reaching over, I try to take it out of her hand, not wanting her to read the nonsense in the dedication. She gives me a stern look as she steps away from reach, taking the book with her. I want to hide as she reads the words, her smile growing as she gets to the dedication and my name big and bold next to his.

"Harper! Do you know what this means?"

"Of course," attempting to reach the book one more time, the need to hide this small piece of a lie somewhere safe is overwhelming. "It means I accomplished what I set out to do. Pay it forward."

"How can you say that? CJ Reese is the most read author in romance."

"Exactly, she writes fiction. Happily ever after with each issue, fabricated in studios with high tech equipment and photoshop."

"Says someone who's never been in love."

"That's not true. I was engaged to be married."

"Doesn't mean you were in love."

"That's crazy! Why would I marry someone I'm not in love with?" Her eyebrows disappearing into her hairline, eyes challenging me to return a rebuttal.

"Lance and I were together for years—" I attempt to rationalize, but Sarah knows me well, and heads me off with my own brand of logic.

"Time doesn't make you in love, dear, it makes you comfortable." I couldn't argue with her. She was absolutely correct. Time meant nothing in matters of the heart. Historically, men and women met on a Thursday and married on a Sunday.

"Sarah, I've never met him, or even spoken to him, not outside of email."

"You think just because you haven't been face to face with him this can't be possible?" Tapping her index finger over the scripted lettering. "What, are you worried he is five feet tall with warts all over his hands?"

"No, looks wouldn't matter to me, but I still haven't been face to face with him." Reaching one last time, snagging the edge of the paper and pulling it into my arms.

Sarah folds her now empty arms, crossing them in front of her and leaning over the counter. "Then explain to me how people who are blind fall in love?"

Not certain where she was going with this, "Well, they get to know each other's character and spend time getting to know one another."

"Which in a sense is what the two of you are doing via email, right?"

"It's not like that." Shaking my head wildly, the need to change the subject nearly choking me as I placed the manuscript back into the box and pulled it from the counter.

"Tell me something, Harper? When you ended your engagement, what left you the most broken? Was it the way he kissed you goodbye in the morning? Or the fact you wouldn't be getting laid every night?"

"We never—"

"Wait, you and Lance never fucked?"

Bracing myself against the counter, I hadn't meant to say anything, keeping my lack of a healthy sexual relationship to myself. With a deep sigh, "No, the relationship hadn't evolved toward anything quite so deep."

"Then I'm going to go out on a limb here and say you've never been pushed up against the wall, gasping for breath, while your panties are ripped from your body, as a man, one who knows you better than you know yourself, takes you to places even a well written book like these can't reach"

I had read about the kind of passion she spoke of, gasping into my hand as I imagined the characters coming together in such a way. My one and only encounter with Alex had been tender and sweet, like the love he had for me, and how much we treasured one another. He had taken his time, made sure I was ready for him, never taking more than I was willing to give.

"You're right, I've never experienced the type of unbridled passion you describe. But you know what? Even if I had, it still wouldn't make the words in the dedication true."

Sarah silently nodded her head, something brewing in the depths of her hazel eyes. "You're absolutely right, it doesn't make any of this true. But I know you and I can tell by the way you were trying to hide it from me there's more you're not sharing. Something he's saying in those emails you've been exchanging."

Sarah may know my body language, but I knew she would never pry into my personal email if I weren't reading it myself.

"You're free to have a look, but prepare yourself for disappointment. They're filled with a lot of gratitude and what he would like to have in the next box."

She surprises me, turning to look over at the computer screen. "Maybe later, I have something else I need to talk with you about. I need to ask you a favor."

"Ask away."

"Well, you know it's no secret this is by far one of the busiest shops in our area. Mitch was wondering if he could install some electronics over here for advertising purposes?"

"Why?"

"Well, he's trying to increase the number of television sets he's selling and his surround sound equipment, so he figured if he was to install a few items in this store, and then place his business contact information on them that word would get out."

"Tell him to install whatever, just clean up after himself."

* * *

TO: Logan. Forbes.LT@ OPS
    FROM: AlexGrl17
    CC:
    SUBJECT: I had a visitor
    Logan,
    You are a sweet and thoughtful man. I thoroughly enjoyed meeting and visiting with your aunt. Having been a fan for several years, I loved listening to how her creative mind works and getting a glimpse of the wonderful stories she plans to create. I cannot thank you enough.

You know, I didn't send you the box as an attempt to create an atmosphere of obligation. I do this as a way of giving back.

As to your comment of me being the most beautiful girl you have ever seen, I assure you the girl you saw talking with my brother was his wife, Amanda. You and every man who sees her is captivated by pretty much everything about her. Don't worry, I won't say anything to my brother, your crush is safe with me.

Saint Patrick's Day will be just another day for me, tucked away early in my bed, reading one of these books your aunt signed for me. In regards to your question of my rising in the morning, I will admit to enjoying watching the sun come up, savoring the quiet before the world wakes up. Taking my time as I sip my coffee.

I do look forward to Easter. Spring has always been a time of renewal. I will help my friends celebrate with their children, hunting eggs in the park and feasting on a meal together.

Sorry to hear about the dried out corn beef. How about I send you some jelly-beans from the candy shop across the street? Name your favorite flavor and they will be in your next box.

Your Friend,

Harper

Chapter Nine

LOGAN

"I need to talk to you."

Kincaid stepped in pace with me as I started my run. Ramsey had watch this morning, so he would be running with Reaper and Ghost later in the day.

"Okay, what's up?"

"You're collecting attention, and not the kind you should be if you're serious about being with my sister." His features are hard, his face giving the impression he was concentrating on his run and not controlling the burn filling his belly.

"From who?"

"The newly advanced Lieutenant Goodman." Her name coming off his tongue like a bitter pill, the valley above his brow dipping to painful looking levels.

"Rumor has it, she wants to celebrate by spending some quality time in your bunk."

Three marines are a few paces ahead of us; I choose to wait until we pass them before hounding him for information. I know the nurse he's talking about. When the Captain made it clear I would be spending my downtime with my team as a physician in medical, he took me around and introduced me to the staff. Goodman had volunteered to escort me around, offering to make my first few days a little smoother. I shut her down as I told her I spent a fair amount of time at this particular field hospital and I could figure out for myself what I needed.

"Logan, I know some guys feel the rules from back home don't apply here, but they aren't sniffing around after my sister."

"Sniffing? Is that what you think I'm doing? Looking for little tail when I get back home?"

"No," he shoved me, taking off to the left through the dry brush toward Freedom Rock. "I haven't been in this position in a while; fielding rumors which could hurt my little sister. Who, according to Mitch, via his wife Sarah, has surmised your recent attempt at impressing her as the result of some lavish way of saying thank you."

Sometime after midnight, as I crawled into my bed, I heard the ping of my email. My need to hear from her again drove the exhaustion from my body. What I read did not surprise me, but gave me direction and confirmed what I had suspected. In my experience, women who try and deny the beauty everyone around them sees, has been taught this, told by some jealous male or female they don't measure up. If I ever found the person who told this lie to Harper, I would rip out their tongue for lying to her.

"I know, she emailed me last night. She also thinks I'm mistaking meeting your wife for her." I nearly collided with him as he abruptly stops before hurling over a bank of rocks.

"Are you serious? Do I need to call her and set her straight?"

"No, don't call her, I have something else in mind. Did you confirm with Mitch about the equipment set up?"

Nodding his head, he checks his watch, "Yeah, everything is ready to go. Sarah made it sound like he was asking to do some product placement in her store. And Mitch is in love with you and the way you made his bottom-line not so bleak this month."

Tossing me the first smile I had seen on him since we started over his shoulder as he picked up his leg and hurled over the rocks.

"The girls loved their flowers, and all plans for setting Harper up on a blind date is history. Mitch will come in while the girls are getting ready for Easter service and disable the internet on their side of the shop."

I put a lot of thought in what I had planned for Easter, letting her know what I really wanted and who I wanted it with.

"And in other, less stimulating news, according to Goodman you spend too much time out here with some kid when you could be playing with her."

Tugging him back, "That *kid* is doing everything I tell him to do to become eligible for SEAL selection. He's also following every word of the rest the team to learn from seasoned soldiers."

Worry crosses his face and his hands find his hips as he turns his attention, looking at the ground below. "The whole team or just a few of us?"

Kincaid is a big guy, with finely-tuned skills which could kill a man before he blinked, but on the inside, hidden behind the ingredients for a lethal cocktail, is the soft heart of a man who cares. "He could use some more help controlling his breathing."

Satisfied with my suggestion, his head tilts up and we're back to running. Letting the silence settle comfortably between us, I waited until we were around the main gate before resuming our conversation. Goodman is standing beside a number of nurses, listening to Lieutenant Oxford complain about a certain member having too many privileges. I know the bastard is talking about me and my team. The CO has the same opinion and has made it his mission to find tasks for the guys to do while we wait for an assignment. Just as I didn't dignify the CO with a response, I ignore the greeting Goodman sends my way, not allowing her to think there will ever be anything between us.

"What? No words for your fan club?"

Quickening my pace, a silent reminder I'm his leader until I leave this team.

"You mentioned how some people make excuses for how to act when they are away from home, justifying their need for companionship with the lack of correct partner. Now, I won't proclaim to be a saint, having had my fair share of women to help me spend some downtime and get rid of the dust of the road. It was all done consensually and as a single man. Goodman is the type of girl who possesses no boundaries, following those justifications as guide maps to get what she wants. I won't congratulate her on her advancement, as she did nothing except her job in order to receive it. I won't pretend to be her friend, as this would inspire her to become bolder than she already is. I have a chance with Harper, granted it's slim, and she is fighting me with everything she has, but I'm no stranger to challenges as the finish is always worth the effort."

* * *

"Girl, as if this heat isn't enough without men like him walking around."

I tried not to listen to Goodman's conversation as I pulled my scrub top over my head, hopefully she was talking about someone else.

"I wouldn't mind taking a bite of Chief Sawyer's ass, as long as we are discussing hot men."

Aiden would get a big kick out of that one, he's always been a big flirt and a real hit with the female population. Who knows, after the disaster of his last conversation with Rachel, he might take her up on her invitation.

"What we need to discuss is the snub you got from Lieutenant Forbes this morning."

"It wasn't a snub, it was—"

Not interested enough in what she had to say, I grab my equipment and head out. I haven't seen this side of medicine since I took my first assignment as a SEAL. Keeping my men alive long enough to get further treatment had been my primary goal and I've loved it. My first stop involved a check on a set of sutures placed by Lieutenant Oxford. The area around the site looked red and inflamed, as I got closer and felt around, I caught a putrid smell coming from the wound. When I pressed along the edges, the poor guy winces in pain.

"Sorry," I empathize, my anger bubbling as I continue to press along the suture line.

"I may need to remove the stitches and clean out the infection." Malodorous smells are never good in any situation, but here in the ward, they are inexcusable, as everything is clean and sterilized. There's no reason for a wound like this to become infected and go unnoticed.

"I told Doc last night it was hurting me, but he said it was because it was healing." Checking his chart, I notice a dose of pain medication was given at twenty-ten, the notation indicated clean and dry with absence of redness and odor. The signature belongs to Lieutenant Goodman.

"HM2," looking to the corpsman who was taking vitals on the patient in the next bed. "When you're finished with him, I need your help with this incision."

Twenty minutes and a hanging bag of antibiotics later, the wound had been drained and a culture ordered. I didn't need to wait for the results to know this guy had a nasty case of MRSA.

"Go ahead and isolate him until we can positively rule out the infection." The corpsman nods his head and turns to carry out my order.

I checked the last patient, a kid who failed to check his boots before sliding his foot into them, a scorpion stinging him twice on his big toe. The area around the sting had turned white and cool to the touch.

"Never knew that level of pain could exist until the damn thing stung me."

The kid had been here less than three months, admitting to joining the military due to lack of funds for college. Examining the rest of his leg, I deem him ready to join his unit and get back to work.

"You're lucky it didn't do more damage, I've seen bigger men than you die from the venom of a baby one."

Signing his paperwork and warning him to check his boots in the future, I hand off his chart to the waiting corpsmen.

My shift had gone by remarkably fast, considering the amount of non-urgent patients. Coffee sounded good and I was about to let one of the nurses know I was stepping out when Lieutenant Goodman brushed up against me.

"Hey, Lieutenant. Want some company with your coffee?" Batting her eyelashes as if they were some crazy seduction charm geared to work on me.

"You know, you shouldn't wear false eyelashes out here in the desert, too much sand and dirt."

Assuming she had an ounce of humility, my exposure to women who wore accessories to improve their looks gave me the knowledge they didn't want anyone knowing something wasn't natural on them.

"Then I'm glad I have you around a help me." Lowering her voice, taking the slightest of steps closer to me. Clearly Goodman not only lacked boundaries, but she was fresh out of common sense.

"LT, you know I'm not an optometrist and wouldn't want to step on any toes. Besides, you're the one who wanted to show me around, surely you know where the eye wash station is."

Leaving her wanting is something I plan to keep doing, as I stepped into the bright light of the day and come face-to-face with Aiden and Ashton.

"Hey, Doc, you ready for chow?" Aiden wears a smirk on his face, his eyes fixed on something behind me.

"I was headed that way, come on gentleman, I'm buying." Not waiting for a quick-witted comeback, I walk as fast as I can away from medical and into the mess tent.

Snagging a cup of coffee and a clean table, I wait for them to get their food. My appetite leaving me the second I started working on the kid's incision. Keeping my attention on the table, I take away the need to address anyone who passes by.

"Do I have shit to tell you."

Aiden slides into the bench beside me, his tray full of food temporarily forgotten as he leans in toward me.

"That stunt you pulled this morning, has most of the nursing staff in an uproar."

"Whatever." Frustration filling my body, wishing like hell this bitch would find another swinging dick to focus on.

"You have Goodman trying to rationalize why you ignored her. Apparently the crazy bitch doesn't handle rejection well."

"Well, the crazy bitch, and one of her friends, wants to take *your* ass for a ride."

Sliding my attention in Aiden's direction, gambling on what kind of reaction I can get out of him.

"Fuck that! The way I hear it, her pussy has a set of golden arches over it." Ashton nearly chokes on his drink, coughing and turning red. "You okay over there?" Aiden hands him a stack of napkins, turning back to me when Ashton nods his head and quits coughing.

"Got an email from Jordan today."

"Oh, yeah. How's she doing in school?"

"Graduated," he looks at me perplexed. "Nearly a year ago." Shaking his head as he digs into his food.

"Sorry, man. Time slips away when you're not paying attention."

"Nah, it's all right. You met her once a long time ago, I don't expect you to keep up with her. She wanted me to know she's started dating this guy, some new kid who moved into town."

I've known Aiden for a long time, watched him do some crazy shit, but something is brewing behind those eyes of his. A new emotion I can't place a label on yet.

"You gonna check the fella out?"

Without hesitation, "Fuck yeah, I am."

TO: AlexGrl17
FROM: Logan. Forbes.LT@ OPS
CC:
SUBJECT: You are wrong.
Harper,

The longer I live, the more things amaze me. Recently I've come in contact with a few people, each one unique in their own way. The first, a man, I've know for years. Been to Hell and back, twice, and we are still friends. Today, he showed me a side of him I haven't seen. A possessive side, one I had never considered lived inside him. The second, a harpy, which is the harshest word I am going to use as I am speaking with a lady. This harpy has, in my opinion, shamed herself with her actions. *Giving those around her an impression of who she is, which, again in my opinion, is deplorable. Sadly, she has the power to change it, but it is my doubt she will ever choose to do so. The third is a beautiful woman, one who gives so much of herself, she finds it difficult to accept a gift from anyone. Including an honest opinion from a man who has been blessed with knowing her. Harper Kincaid, you may not have sent the care package to me in hopes of getting anything in return, but you are so wrong if you think you don't deserve it.*

Definitely yours,

Logan

Chapter Ten

HARPER

There are certainties in life: growing old, death, and paying taxes. In my world there are additional ones, including the comic relief I have as I watch Amanda and Stacy run like mad women to make it to their shop on time, balancing cups of coffee and oversize bags while teetering on sky-high heels.

This morning, however, as I open the back door of my shop, the aroma of fresh coffee and sugar hits me. Our shops share a back loading area and if their door is open, like today, you can see all the way to the front desk.

Amanda and Stacy are fawning over two massive potted plants, the lettering on the side the familiar trademark for Holly Farms.

"Logan is too much, sending these—"

I don't need to hear how kind Logan is. Despite the email I received last night, there is another certainty in my world; Logan Forbes most definitely did not see my face on the screen.

As the morning begins and the streets come to life, I watch Mrs. Mona Jackson stroll along the sidewalk, tailored suit with the skirt ending at her knee. Clipboard in hand, with the Mayor on one side and the City Planner on the other.

I had hoped she would have kept her appointment to tour Horizons, but I heard through a third source, she chose to write a check to the garden club instead, spending thousands on window boxes and plants to fill them. A part of me prayed for a deep frost, temperatures plunging deep enough to ruin her plans of decorating downtown for Easter.

"What time is Mr. Woods coming?"

Sarah had her hands full of clothing as I came in this morning, sorting out the items we needed sent to Horizons.

"Lunch time."

Keeping my focus on Mrs. Jackson who laughed at something the Mayor said into her ear. One would think if a couple cheating on their spouses wanted to keep it a secret, they wouldn't allow such obvious closeness.

"Okay, I'll cover until you get back, and then I'll drop this batch of clothes off at the church."

"You don't have to. When you leave for lunch, lock the door and I'll see you on Sunday."

"Are you sure? You gave me Friday off already."

"Of course, you deserve an afternoon to yourself."

Giving her a gentle smile, she moves the clothes to the counter. With a smile reflective of mine, she hugs me tight as she sways us back and forth.

"You're good people, Harper."

She's wrong. If I was as good as she says I am, I wouldn't have assumed the money I had from Alex's insurance would run the charity until the end of time. The church had slowly increased the rent over the years, and I foolishly assumed this was a perfect situation.

Three months ago, the church sent me a letter advising they had purchased a new building and would be moving, with the additional overhead of a mortgage, they needed to raise the rent, again. This time to nearly three times what I had paid in the past, an amount I had no hopes of meeting. My lunch with Mr. Woods would center on helping the clothes to find a new home.

Amanda had fluttered in and out as the morning progressed, sharing her grand plans for the new flowerbeds Ross promised to dig for her while he was home next week. I avoided her, not intentionally, but my heart was too full of sadness to embrace her joy. As the clock struck noon, I turned the sign to closed and wished the girls a good afternoon.

The mood was somber as I met with Mr. Woods. He extended the church's regrets in not being able to continue the charity, but gave me forty-five days to have all of the clothing out of their back room. He offered to hire a crew of men and a truck to take the items to the local thrift store, but I declined. I started Horizons with a hope and a prayer, needing to help women who were in a position not of their own doing. I would collect every article of clothing and see it through to the end.

After the meeting, I was lost as to what to do next. Preparations were going on in the local park, the gazebo in the center already coming to life with an area to meet the Easter bunny.

As I rounded the edge of the park, I stopped at the site of the memorial statue dedicated to Alex. I allowed my eyes to drift up, squinting as the midday sun glistened off the bronze statue. Alex always seemed larger than life, and the people of Chesapeake immortalized him as such.

The number seventeen stamped on his chest, his arm pulled back as he threw the winning touchdown, clinching the state title and the hearts of this community. The memorial had been built over the old bus station, ironically the last place I saw him alive.

Emotions gripped me and I hurried back to my shop. There would be no one there to see me cry, allowing the bitterness of the day to claim me. When I was younger, I would seek out my father when I needed a shoulder to cry on. But as an adult, I had scolded myself, demanding I grow up and handle things on my own.

Today, however, the need for rational thought called to me. As I closed and locked the door behind me, I dropped my purse to the floor and ran to my waiting laptop.

A few clicks later and the sound of Skype ringing had my heart pounding. Glancing at my watch, the anxiety coursing through my veins confused me too much and I gave up on try to configure the time difference. Relief washed over me as the bright smile and loving eyes of my brother came on the screen.

"Hey, Harper. I didn't expect to hear from you until next week." His voice full of laughter, matching the thrill written on his face.

"Hey," my voice cracked from the emotions and I watched his smile fall and the crease in his brow form.

"I know you're coming home next week, but I needed to—" I swallowed the tears clogging my throat, threatening to burst from my chest.

"Talk with you and I didn't want to pull you away from Amanda and the kids just so I can cry on your shoulder." Closing my eyes, my chin finding refuge on my chest as I allowed the sobs free.

"Harper?"

My breath caught in my throat as the husky voice called my name. Embarrassment filled my chest, kicking out the sadness and forcing my head to rise. Wiping the tears from my face with the edge of my sleeve, I tried hard to recover.

"Yes, I'm sorry. I didn't think you would be busy."

Turning my head to the side, as the last of my unshed tears blurred my vision. I hate to cry, as I'm not one of those people who are blessed to be a pretty crier with glassy eyes and a watery smile. I am a full on red faced, body jerking, and a distorted smile crier.

"Please don't hide from me." My reaction is involuntary as the voice pulls every ounce of embarrassment out of my body, filling it with a strange calm and need to hear it again.

"Never hide from me. I want to know what's going on in your beautiful head."

The face belonging to the voice was of course not my brother's, but a man who snatched my breath away. Dark brown hair, that appeared to be wet from a shower, and eyes a pale blue, which sparkled mysteriously. His features formed hard edges and shouted sex appeal. I can't pull my eyes from the definition of his arms, the muscles flexing as he leans into the screen, his white tank allowing me a glimpse of the tattoo on his left peck.

"Harper did someone get hurt?" I found myself unable to open my mouth and answer, too lost in admiring the man staring back at me.

"Harper?" My brother's voice pulls me from the inked skin beside him. My mouth still refusing to connect to my brain, as all my motor skills are trying to engage. Shaking my head, the best I can offer, as my senses begin to return to me, and the shock of my behavior surfaces.

"Did somebody do something to you? Did Lance show his face?"

This beautiful man knows who Lance is, which leads me to believe this could be Logan, or someone Ross has confided in.

"No, everything is fine. Lance has kept his distance since the police came by and I made a complaint."

"Are you sure, beautiful? I can have a friend of mine to your house in a matter of hours."

"I'm sorry, I didn't catch your name, Sir." Leaning back in his chair, those massive arms of his dropping to his side and I can see his dog tags dangling between his pecks.

"My apologies, Harper, seeing your beautiful face again made me forget the advantage I have over you."

My heartbeat quickens, and I try with all my might not to dwell on his use of the term beautiful.

"I'm Logan."

The way he says his name, the tone of his voice dipping to levels that make my body quiver. Logan is a dangerous man, one who has the potential to melt a few hearts, and awake the naughty girl in a few more.

"Oh, Lieutenant Forbes."

Trying my best to recover and steer the conversation into neutral territory, no reason for him to hear about my personal tragedy.

"Uh-uh, I'm Logan to you. Only these guys over here have to call me Lieutenant. You're special, Harper, and someday you and I will come to an agreement on another name you will have for me." His commanding tone was a little unsettling, but immensely erotic.

"Now, how about you tell us why you were crying, so I can get busy finding a way to kick somebody's ass."

Swallowing thickly, I shift my eyes to Ross who has his arms crossed and one eyebrow cocked.

"I'm sorry, Harper. I don't mean to make you uncomfortable."

"You didn't, it's the situation I find myself in today. I met with an adviser friend of mine," swallowing my pride, I told them the story of my morning. The anxiety, which riddled me earlier, slips from my body, allowing me to feel lighter and less pessimistic.

"So, now I have a little over a month to get about a thousand pieces of clothing out of a church basement and into a few thrift stores." Logan had listened intently, his eyes squinting when I mentioned Mona Jackson's decision.

"Let me ask you," Logan moved closer to the screen, his muscles flexing as he rested his forearms against the desk. "If you could find a new benefactor, would you be willing to help men as well as the women?"

"Of course, the idea originated from an article I read one day. I had the resources at the time and tagged on to someone else's idea. Like I said, I have the option to keep the charity open, but I can't see paying three times the rent I charge the girls next door. Not to mention the insurance and small amount of overhead."

"So you're talking about a building and operating expenses."

"There isn't really any overhead."

"Who hands out the clothing, keeps track of stock?"

"Well, I have the volunteers at the church."

"You *had* them, sweetheart. Now you need to think bigger, hire at least three staff members to keep the doors open. Give someone, or a few someone's, a permanent day job."

"I can't even dream about something so wonderful."

"No guarantees, love, but I do know a few people who may be interested. I'll give them a call here in a little while and see what they have to say. For now, I'm going to make sure you have a way of contacting me. I want you to feel free to call me anytime you want, and I mean it."

"That's very generous of you."

"I'm not being generous, Harper. I'm trying to make you understand I'm being honest in my attempt to get to know you better. I want you see what we could have together, if you would allow yourself to believe in the possibility of an us."

* * *

Easter Sunday came with the sun shining and the weatherman predicting seventy-degree temperatures. Sarah had a customer come in a few days ago with a lavender and yellow dress, I couldn't say no to. I had assembled my nephew's baskets the other night after I got off the phone with Logan. Finding myself in need of a distraction, I invited Mitch over to set up the new television and additional internet speed. Using the excuse of him being here as a reason to stay away from my email. Logan both thrilled and scared me shitless. I had lied when I said he didn't make me uncomfortable. He made me question things, dissecting moments in my life I had accepted and tucked away as a learning experience.

Yesterday, as I spent time rearranging a few displays, Mr. Simpson from across the street brought me a crystal candy dish filled with my favorite candy, along with a beautiful lily. The note attached was an email sent to Mr. Simpson, folded and sealed with a gold sticker.

Harper,

My aunt sends her apologies as she found herself in short supply of this seasonal flower. In a recent discussion with Ross, he led me to believe you had a fondness for this chocolate confection. Easter back home in New York is celebrated with mass at midnight, followed by brunch at Tavern on the Green. Next year, I hope to start a tradition of our own.

Waiting patiently and ready to be yours,

Logan

I watched mesmerized as the rays of sunlight danced through the prisms of the crystal. I sat on the couch watching until well after the sun had fallen behind the buildings and the shadows stretched, covering the room in darkness. My upbringing dictated I contact him and offer a thank you for his generous gift. But something deep inside kept me from sending the email, or using the number and Skype user name he gave me. I would try later, after lunch was served and the kids had crashed from their sugar highs.

Ross and Ashton were scheduled to call after we got back from church so they could wish the kids a happy Easter. It was planned for me to be included in the call, as the other night had been a moment of weakness. I considered skipping the phone call, but I hadn't spoken to Ashton in almost a month.

"Harper!" The panicked voice of Amanda cried out from her side of the shop. I hurried over to the back door, worried something bad had happened to one of the boys.

"Oh my, God, please tell me you have internet over here?"

My heart settled back in my chest, and I wanted to fuss at her for scaring me. "I should, Mitch was here and worked on it the other day." I hoped she wouldn't question why I hadn't used it.

"Maybe he's the reason mine isn't working." Amanda pushes past me, Hudson babbling on her hip, Jason and Adam running behind her.

I barely turn around when Stacy comes jogging by her tight skirt keeping her stride short and bouncy.

"Thirty seconds, Manda."

Her voice is tense as she heads toward the television. I'm confused as Amanda picks up the oversized remote, pointing it at the television, but I assume she is turning it on to keep the kids occupied as we wait for Ross to call. Jason is whispering in his mother's ear and shooting me an excited look.

"Happy Easter, Mrs. Kincaid." My eyes shoot to the television as the sultry voice echoes through the speakers overhead. Logan's face and torso fills the screen of the massive television. His smile seems bigger and he is dressed in his uniform, his hair, which was as a dark brown is lighter now, a slight wave to his thick locks. His skin is sun-kissed golden, making his eyes seem so much brighter.

"It's been awhile since we visited. Did you enjoy the flowers my aunt sent over?"

Jason is pointing to Logan, his eyes wide and his legs jumping up and down.

"Yes, Logan, we did thank you. I plan to put my husband to work planting them next week."

"I wish I could be there to help," sliding his eyes toward me. "And get a chance to take my girl out and show her off." Jason tugs his mother's skirt, pulling her attention back to him.

"You look beautiful in lavender, makes those eyes of yours call to me." Finishing his compliment with a wink. He is such a mystery, confidence exuding from every pore, yet I feel as if I know him and can anticipate his next move.

"Logan, Jason is about to bust if he doesn't get to do his job."

His eyes leave mine and settle on my nephew, who has a blue bag in his hand and his patience wearing thin. Adam, his older brother, has his hand on the handle of the bag, his smile broken with his two front teeth missing.

"Go ahead boys, give your Aunt Harper her present."

Two happy faced boys cross the room, the blue bag dangling from their outstretched hands. The bell above my door jingles, but I refuse to take my attention away from my nephews.

"This is for you." They say in unison, and I laugh at how adorable they are. "Uncle Logan said you get two presents because you're so pretty."

Taking the bag, I pull them close and kiss each of their cheeks. "If you look under the counter, you can check and see if the Easter bunny came by last night." The two take off, rounding the counter, squealing as they find the baskets tucked under the cabinet. I'd ignored the uncle reference, words and titles don't solidify anything.

"Come on, beautiful, open your present."

Shifting my attention to the blue bag, the white tissue crinkling under my fingers.

"This is unnecessary, Mr. Simpson brought me the candy yesterday. I should have sent you an email thanking you, but—"

"But I took you out of your comfort zone." My hand stills as my eyes flash to his and his cavalier tone.

"I showed you an example of a strong Alpha male, and not the lap dog you had up until recently."

Leaning back in his chair and crossing those massive arms across his chest, the evidence of all his many hours in the gym rippling in the corded muscles flexing with his movement. My breath catches, and I pray he doesn't hear me.

"Harper, you need a strong man. One who can challenge you, pulling you out of this shroud of doubt you've dressed yourself in. Someone who will treat you like a lady, and not a girl from around the corner."

Lacking the courage to retort his words, I lower my eyes and continue examining the signature blue bag. Inside, wrapped in white tissue paper was a small wooden box. Setting the paper and bag on the coffee table, I take the lid of the box between my thumb and index finger, tugging until the latch releases and allows me to see the single charm resting on the pillow of cotton.

"Ross mentioned you suggested he start a charm bracelet for Amanda, something he can add to on special occasions and holidays. He said you spend a great deal of time admiring them in the store, but haven't pulled the trigger and started one." The silver package, designed to look like same ones I used to mail all of those soldiers over the years.

"I have nearly a year before my obligation with the military is over. During this time, I will send you a charm to place on your bracelet. Giving you tiny reminders of who I am and what we can be."

"Lieutenant!"

"Name's Logan, beautiful, we've had this discussion."

The look on his face fueled the fire in my chest, motivated me to remind him I had not agreed to anything he has proposed.

"*Lieutenant* Forbes, you had this discussion, I listened. I never agreed to anything."

Carefully placing the charm back into the box, I would send it back with Ross when he came next week. I neither needed, nor wanted, a man to buy me trinkets.

"And there's the fire I wanted to see. I knew it was in there, trapped behind all the bullshit you've swallowed over the years."

I want to scream at him, tell him he is wrong and knows nothing about me, no real idea of who I am. But I can't, because he is right.

"I'm sorry to interrupt." A delicate voice sounds from behind me and I turn abruptly to find a petite woman and tall man standing just inside the door.

"I'm Meredith Forbes, and this is my husband Weston. I would ask if I found you at a bad time, but I have a feeling I've arrived in the nick of it."

Not waiting for an invitation, Meredith crosses the room, winding her way around the racks of clothing, and takes a seat next to me. I glanced around to find Amanda, Stacy, and the kids have disappeared.

"Harper, it's a pleasure to meet you," a tiny hand shot out to mine. "As I said, my name is Meredith and I am here at the insistence of my son." Tipping her head in the direction of the screen, a look of annoyance crosses her slender face. "Who is more and more like his father every day."

A throat clearing behind her belongs to the tall man who Logan favors, with the same hair and eyes, a little worn from age and wisdom. Placing a single hand on her shoulder, he leans over and places a kiss to her head.

"Oh, my love, you forget how much you love the strong side of me." I feel wrong to have heard him, like a voyeur peeking into an open window.

"He's right, I do love his strength." She admits with a smile, the love between them filling the space around me and I crave the warmth it brings.

"Logan," Meredith turns to the screen, reaching her hand to her shoulder where Weston hand rests, intertwining their fingers together. "Would you like to do the honors, or shall I?"

"Go ahead, this is technically your project. I'll finish what I have to say when you're done."

His eyes don't leave mine as he speaks to his mother, his stare intense as well as captivating, leaving me helpless to look away.

"Very well."

Meredith adjusts her position and pulls a file from the oversized purse I failed to notice on her shoulder. The bag is expensive, the same as her shoes and the watch on Weston's wrist.

"I'm going to assume by your lack of incoherency, you have no idea who we are outside of being Logan's parents?"

"No, Ma'am."

"Good," she smiles. "This will go so much better then."

Placing the file on the glass table, she reaches back into her purse and pulls out a set of reading glasses.

"Logan has brought to our attention your involvement in various charities, including the packages you send to single soldiers. I've been in contact with Earnest Woods, your adviser for the foundation."

Her glasses rest on the end of her nose, the gold frames contrasting against her skin, making the blue in her eyes come to life.

"I've seen pictures of your facility and am impressed by what you have been able to do with so little. According to my son, you are open to taking the next step by making Horizons available for anyone in need?"

"I'm open to discussion, yes." My words have bite, although I don't mean them to. Logan has somehow conjured up something in me, some hidden warrior I didn't know existed.

Her smile gets a little wider. "Very good, Harper, you do have a fire in you." As she opens the folder, I can't help but glance down and see photos of a building with a for sale sign in front. "You're going to need that fire in order to survive this business. Mona Jackson has already shown you how ruthless people can be." I'm surprised by her words, assuming this community has been forgotten by the rest of the world. I'm not certain I want to know her affiliation with Mona Jackson.

"Harper, for generations my family has been in the business of helping those who cannot help themselves. Weston is a physician who has traveled the world over, rendering aid where it is needed. My focus is on literacy and the education of those who want it. With what you have started, and I hope you will allow us to help, we can make it into something many more people can benefit from."

Lifting the photo from the stack of papers, she pushes what appears to be a contract in front of me. "Reese International would like to purchase, and maintain, the building Mr. Woods spoke highly of, as the new location of Horizons. Furthermore, we would like to award you a grant for all operating costs, including employee wages, taxes and insurance. At the end of five years, Reese International will evaluate the continuing need and any improvements the board deems necessary."

Using the tip of her high-quality pen, she ticks off the requirements her foundation will insist upon. It's nothing drastic, no selling of souls or pacts with the devil. From the brief period of time I've spent with her, I get the impression she doesn't hear the word no very often.

As she speaks of paint colors, placement of computers, holiday pay and Christmas parties. Much like her son, she assumes I'm onboard.

"You make it all sound so simple. Just a snap of your fingers and my little shop gets to stay open."

"More like three snaps," she teases, but I find no humor in this conversation. "Yes, we've done this long enough to have ironed out all the wrinkles."

"Yes, well, Meredith, you will have to excuse me and my narrow way of thinking. While all of this sounds perfect, it's my experience great romances have a honeymoon phase, where hearts and flowers camouflage the imperfections. It's when the blinders come off and the sourness of life opens our eyes, we see each other for who we really are."

She studies my face and I wait for her to protest my unwillingness to fall at her feet and thank her for being the mighty savior who rescues me from certain doom.

"You chose well, Logan." Her eyes are calculating and I can't put a label on the feeling I get as I hear his laughter at her comment.

"You're a smart woman, Harper. I'm glad to see you stand your ground, willing to let your ship sink rather than be overthrown by pirates. The offer is good for thirty days, you have my contact information here."

Rising to her full height, smoothing down the material of her skirt, Weston is there to take her hand, a knowing smile touching his lips. Reaching over, she extends her hand, "Harper, it was a pleasure to meet you. I hope to hear from you soon. I do wish to leave you with one piece of free advice."

Rising to meet her, our height is relatively similar, but the heels on her shoes gives her an advantage. "The Forbes men have a fierce fight in them and Logan has been given more spirit than any of his ancestors. Every time he's set his sights on something: class valedictorian, getting into medical school, joining the SEALs, he had done everything in his power to achieve it. Do yourself a favor," glancing at Weston.

"Don't give him reason to make you his next challenge. Let him show you how right you are for each other." Turning to the screen, placing the wide strap of her purse on her shoulder.

"Logan, you were missed at brunch this morning. Hopefully next year we can have you both at our Easter celebration."

"No guarantees, Mom. I still have time on my contract."

"You know—"

"Yes, Mother, I know I could get out of it. If I did, then I couldn't look myself in the mirror or expect Harper to view me the same."

Meredith and Weston look around my shop, complimenting on the beautiful wedding gown in the front window. I keep to myself who the gown belonged to. With a final wave, they both duck into the back of a limo and drive off down the street.

"Harper, we've been called up for a mission, one you know I can't talk about." Nodding my head, I keep my back to him, watching the people on the street as they gossiped about who was in the back of the car that just pulled away.

"I'd like to ask you a question, but I want you to think about it and give me your answer when I get back."

Turning my body in his direction, I walk with purpose back to stand in front of the television. The silence remained and I questioned if the signal had been lost.

"Go on."

"When you broke up with Lance, what was the one thing you regretted? Think about it. When I get back you can tell me, and yourself, the truth."

Chapter Eleven

LOGAN

TO: AlexGrl17
 FROM: Logan. Forbes.LT@ OPS
 CC:
 SUBJECT: tomorrow
 Harper,
 Tomorrow you are going to wake up and try to convince yourself the last few days never happened. How you hit your head or dreamed the whole conversation we had earlier. Trust me when I say my mother was right in how persistent I am.
 Logan

I hadn't meant to send an email, feeling it was better to leave her alone with her thoughts. As I packed my gear, Kincaid came in, telling me it was to my advantage to give her something she can view over and over. Since I couldn't get on a plane and tell her myself, this would have to suffice.

I hated last minute missions to check out intel, stepping close to the enemy to listen in on his conversations. This one, in particular, would be the hardest, as it was to be our last as a group.

When we met for briefing, the message had come in halfway through the CO's speech on rules of engagement. Reaper and Chief would be going home in a few weeks, Havoc received orders to begin his discharge process. I would be advanced to Senior Medical Officer, in charge of overseeing every aspect of the medical department.

Recent monitoring of radio chatter hinted at a possible meeting between Aarash and a known member of organized crime, Pavel Kumarin. According to conversations, the pair is in talks to move a lot of product from here to Russia, where Kumarin will disperse it to various sources. The agreement isn't anything out of the ordinary, but it does involve a Mafia Family, one who has been skirting the line of boundaries even criminals consider taboo. The location of the meeting was sketchy at best, but our team had enough of a history with Aarash, we knew where the bastard would be.

Sitting in the back of the Blackhawk, I scanned the faces of my team. Memories of celebrations and a few arguments flooded my head. The time Reaper found a little girl buried under the rubble of a blast. How she clung to him for hours, refusing to let anyone else touch her.

Havoc and the moments after he was shot, when I didn't know if I would be able to save him. Aiden, when he helped me deliver a baby for the family we discovered as we took refuge from a storm. How his eyes teared up as he handed the baby to the father, and then went outside and took out the men who had been tracking the family.

Red lights at the edge of the open door turned to green indicating it was time for us to jump. The area where we suspect Aarash to be was surrounded by hills filled with loyal villagers. We would use the cover of darkness to drop in and put an end to this meeting. Reaper would go in first, his keen eye and accuracy with his gun would benefit us the most on the ground.

Havoc and Chief would go together, increasing boots on the ground without attracting unwanted attention. Ghost and I would go last, his priority would be keeping his ear on the radio, checking for any changes or reports of our sighting.

I'd always enjoyed the feeling of free-fall, the wind rush past you as you descend into the pitch-black darkness. My mother would faint if she ever saw me do this. The first time I went home to visit after training, I stumbled into a situation where a construction worker lost his footing and was dangling by a safety line. The company had called the fire department, but with the traffic in the city, his chances didn't look good. I had climbed up the rig, used my belt to pull him up and had him on the ground when the ambulance pulled up. My poor mother watched from the restaurant window, her hand covering her mouth. My father made her sit and have a stiff drink.

Climbing the edge of the ridge line, a few flickering lights from the burning fires reveal the location of Aarash's hiding spot. Using the cover of an overhanging rock, we tucked in so Ghost could have a listen.

Havoc and Reaper scan the area with night vision. "I've got movement at three o'clock." My eyes automatically find the coordinates he called, watching as five bodies get out of a truck.

"Aarash is moving up in the world, got himself a Hummer." Chief joked, his knowledge of what was going on, even in the dark, astounds me.

"Wonder if this was a gift from Kumarin, or if he has been swinging on the pole?" I'd laugh at his attempt at humor later, when we were back at base.

"Doc, we've got chatter about Ecnal again." Ghost called into my ear, the edge to his voice unsettling. He had scanned every channel he knew since the first time he heard the name, but nothing had surfaced except how much he had pissed off Aarash by failing to do something. Maybe the bastard knew his days were numbered and went into hiding.

"Anything relevant?"

"Depends. He's the one who sent Aarash the Hummer."

"Chief?"

"I'm on it." Aiden would be able to search any shipping records, narrowing down who this Ecnal is and what business he has with Aarash.

Two more trucks pull in stopping short behind the hummer.

"Doc?" Reaper calls, his rifle pointed at the men standing around the Hummer.

"I see them, let's see what they have to say." Ghost pulls a cord from his gear bag, the end looks like a tiny suction cup. Pointing at the men by the truck, he pressed several buttons but can't get the conversation to come in.

"Motherfucker got smarter," Ghost complains through clenched teeth. "He found a way to block me." By the tone of his voice, it's more than the inability to give us what we need, it's the result of a long-standing game between Aarash and us. For all the ways we have to stop him, he figures out how to get around us. Sometimes I wondered how he managed to get the information he did, who he found desperate enough to sell out their own country?

"All right boys, let's go kick some Hummer tires."

We have at least three hours before the sun will take away our cover and we are going to need the time to get in and out of this place. Villagers around here profit greatly from Aarash and will kill us without a second thought.

Skirting the edge of the ridge, Reaper and Havoc silence a few guards who were focused more on the game they played than the men they needed to protect. Our plan was to come in from the top and ease our way into the cave Aarash had carved out for himself. We knew where it was, but what rested inside remained a mystery.

Keeping Aarash and his guests on the left, and the rocks on the right, it didn't take as long as I thought to get around to the other side. Chief had one of his many gadgets out, searching for anything he could use to help get us inside. Just as Ghost was pulling out his listening device, Chief held up his fist, silently telling us to stop.

Getting low to the ground, "Every cave needs ventilation." Holding up one of his meters, the green numbers going wild. He takes two steps over, pulling away some dead brush revealing what looks to be a metal cylinder.

"Bingo," he celebrates, taking his own sense of pride from narrowing the playing field between Aarash and us. The hole is big enough for a grown man to crawl through, a way for Aarash to escape if things ever went wrong. Knowing the rat-bastard, he told the people who dug it he would use it as Chief said, for ventilation.

Chief is the first one down, his reward for finding our way in. This tiny win is enough to wet his appetite and make him search for more. As I lower myself into the hole, my nerves grip me as I fall a few feet into a room, landing on solid rock. I do a mental check of my extremities before standing to my full height. Havoc is searching for a door, while Ghost tries to check the radio. Reaper finds the exit, motioning for the rest of us to follow.

Just outside, the escape hatch is at the top of an intricate system of steps, each going off into various rooms. The astounding part, and one I didn't consider, is the interior looks more like the inside of a warehouse instead of a mountain. Industrial looking sconces are attached to the wall every few feet. With the amount of light they are giving, there must be a massive generator around here somewhere.

"No wonder I couldn't hear him," Ghost taps the metal of the walls. "Reinforced titanium-alloy." It's the combination of the two metals which cut our ability to listen. The capability to get past one or the other is easy, but combined creates a new problem, one Ghost will figure out if I know the man at all.

"You have strange accommodations, Comrade." A chuckling voice drifts from below, the Russian accent bounces off the walls and confirms what intel rumored to be true. We each hold our position as Havoc edges over to investigate.

"Strange it may be, Kumarin, but safe and well protected as well. No American has ever taken a breath behind these walls and lived to tell about it."

"So, it is true then, what they say about your capabilities?"

"My abilities to trick the American military is one of many talents I possess. But this isn't why you are here my friend."

"You are correct. Shall we see to an arrangement?"

"Are we waiting for Andrey?'

"My son won't be joining us."

"Forgive me, I misunderstood."

"No, my son is a weak man who would rather meet old enemies than build new relationships. He does not have a strong business mind like yourself."

"Shall we get started then."

Their conversation lingered, fading into the shadows as they moved into another room. With the all clear, Chief has another gauge in his hand, hovering it under one of the sconces. Turning over his shoulder, he motioned for us to go down the steps for two measures. Keeping our shoulders to the wall, we followed the stone steps as they descended deeper and deeper into the fortress. As we step on the second landing, Chief raised his closed hand for us to stop. Leaning his ear against the metal door, he listens for a second, and then pushes the door open.

Deep inside this mountain, walls giving him more protection than the vaults in Fort Knox, the room behind the door looks to have been stolen from NASA. Multiple television screens cover three of the walls, the height of each seemed to touch the clouds. Several rows of long tables hold computers and monitors, each alive with color and a multitude of activity.

Ghost's face lights up as he rushed over to one of the monitors, staring wide-eyed at the information scrolling across the screen. On the wall behind us are more televisions with the news broadcasts: American, British and a few Arabic.

"This motherfucker has his hands in everything." Chief had found a port to plug into, his fingers flying across the keys as his eyes followed the screen. "Banks, insurance companies. No wonder Kumarin wants to dance with him."

As I walk around the room, Reaper maintains his post at the door, his gun ready to silence anyone who comes through.

"Doc, how the hell does your family own a fucking private jet?" Turning back to Ghost, his face looking back at me over his shoulder. Crossing the space between, I look to the screen where I find what looks to be my sealed file with the government. Most of my credit accounts and expired driver's license are there for everyone to see.

"Look, he has a file on all of us: school records, where we grew up. Hey, Reaper, your taxes on your house are due. You might want to send in a check before Aarash adds your shit to his vast property holdings."

"Fuck!" Havoc comes around the corner of the table, his tone abrupt as if he had remembered he left the coffee pot on. "That's how he knew about Viper and how his brother hurt his knee playing pro-ball."

Last year, on one of the last times we went out with Viper as the leader, we had been given the task of escorting a medical team across a valley. Aarash and his men were there, we exchanged a little gunfire and Aarash said some things he shouldn't have known about Viper.

"He knows about all of us, our families included."

Without hesitation, Harper's face is in the forefront of my mind. "Copy what you can, let's set this bitch on fire."

Giving Havoc an excuse to play with fire was the equivalent of offering a small child a second bowl of ice cream. Chief and Ghost wasted no time downloading files as Reaper and I helped Havoc wire this bitch to burn. In theory, the amount of force we were creating would cause the walls to become brittle and cave in on themselves; anything flammable would turn to dust within seconds.

The tricky part is being far enough away to avoid getting hurt, yet close enough so the detonators would work. Chief came up with using a few of the burner phones I found while keeping an ear on Aarash, something we'd all seen in the movies but never used. Using every ounce of firepower in our arsenal, we prepared for this shit to register on earthquake monitors around the world, as we found our way back outside the fortress.

Climbing down the side of the hill, I realize we spent more time in there than I'm comfortable with, as the sun has already announced its arrival. With our choices limited, I looked around until an idea hits me. Hoping Aarash had more confidence in his assumption of our ignorance to his location, than in his rational side of thinking.

"Come on, I've got a plan."

Charging down the side of the hill, guns fire, taking out the handful of men who stood guard, jumping over the last man who would soon succumb to the multitude of bullets I filled his chest with. Opening the door of the Hummer and climbing in, and sure as shit, Aarash had indeed left the keys in the ignition. As Ghost jumped in through the back shouting, "Go, go, go!" I pushed in the clutch and shifted into gear, tearing out of the compound like I was trying out for NASCAR.

"Whoever this Ecnal is, he didn't skimp on the accessories." Chief rejoiced as he pressed the button for the popup navigation. The sounds of a ringing phone came through the speakers, followed by the first of many rumbles in the Earth. Pushing the accelerator to the floor, not certain of the distance we needed to avoid the fallout, the wheel begins to jerk as the ground shakes and a large yellow cloud shows up in my rear-view mirror.

Cheers echoed through the cab of the Hummer, high-fives and happy faces as the realization we had successfully ended whatever plan Aarash and Kumarin were brewing. More than that, we had killed the man responsible for more evil than Satan himself.

"You know, I wish Viper and Diesel had been here to see this." Reaper spoke from the passenger side. "As a team, we've tracked that son-of-a-bitch for years, he always found some dark corner to hide in." Shaking his head as he looks over the miles of endless desert, "Rest in hell, motherfucker."

Hours later, as we pull into the gates of the base. Wide eyes take in our group of SEALs inside a non-military vehicle. Ramsey comes around the corner, his t-shirt wet with sweat from his run, stopped short, much as the others around him. Captain and Lieutenant Oxford stepped out of Administration, as I jerk the wheel to the left. A cloud of dust swirls around the car as we jumped from the Hummer. Men with eyes of wonder came closer, if only by some deep-rooted instinct we as men have in admiration of a well-made machine.

Walking as if I owned the world, and with what we had just accomplished I felt as if I did, I toss the keys to the Hummer in the air toward the CO. His eyes are wide as he catches them against his chest. My eyes focused on the door leading to my bed and a shower, but a Cheshire grin makes a home on my lips. "There, now you can't say I never bring you anything home."

Chapter Twelve

HARPER

"Reese International, this is Leslie. How can I help you?"

"Hello, this is Harper Kincaid. May I please speak with Meredith Forbes?"

"Just one moment, Ms. Kincaid, she has been expecting your call."

Leslie sounded far too chipper for the early morning hour. Maybe she was, as I am, in the early morning riser category.

"Please hold."

It had taken me four days of near constant war with myself, battling between what I wanted to do, and what was best for everyone involved. Countless numbers of people turned to me, needing my help in taking another step in their recovery or independence.

I stood for hours inside my office, staring at the bulletin board covered in thank you cards and photos, graduation announcements and business cards, reminding myself why turning Reese International down was such a bad idea. Questioning the validity of the offer and the timing of Logan's confession. Would anything change if I said no to one and not the other?

Early this morning, I sat inside my shop sipping a fresh cup of coffee, enjoying the quiet before the sun took its place in the sky and watched the birds as they fluttered around the sidewalk, searching for tiny morsels of food. The first rays of the morning allowed enough light for me to see the window boxes Mrs. Jackson chose over doing some real good for the community. Her ambition to make the streets beautiful had backfired, as an arctic blast hit the area, sending temperatures into the teens and the plants into an early grave.

"Harper?"

"Yes, is this Meredith?"

"I was about to give up on you. What took you so long?"

Baffled by her question, she had given me thirty days and not half of those had passed. "I'm sorry?"

"I expected a call from you before Weston and I were on our plane back to New York. You took your time, I like that."

"Yes, well, this was a big decision. One I had to look at from all sides before making this call. I'd like to accept your offer and give this proposition you have a chance."

"Excellent, I'll send my attorney over with the paperwork. Tell me, Harper, are you opposed to a few high-end dresses in your shop? According to my calendar, the annual Navy Ball is coming up."

Spinning on my heels, three racks of evening gowns stood in the middle of the room. The annual pilgrimage of wives and girlfriends had begun last week, bargain shoppers not wanting to spend an entire paycheck on a dress. Sarah had begun to drop hints about hiring a second seamstress to handle the workload.

"What do you mean high-end?"

"Well, I have a closet full of dresses I've worn the past six months to various events. They will likely remain on the hangers until my stylist takes them wherever it is she takes them. I also have a few friends who would willingly do the same."

I had no doubt Mrs. Forbes belonged to an impressive circle, one with a few names holding celebrity status attached.

"Of course, the ladies would love it."

"Excellent! I'll have a friend of the family come with my attorney later today. I'll be in town next week so we can do a walk-through of the new building with the contractor."

"I'll be ready, and thank you, Meredith, for saving this program." I tried not to let the emotion in my voice slip through. She didn't need to know how much I had cried over the possibility of closing it. How I apologized to Alex's picture for not being smart enough to keep it open with the money he left me.

"It means so much to so many."

* * *

As I was about to close the shop for the day, a black limo pulled up front. The back door swung open and a tall man unfolded himself from the back, his designer suit, slicked-back hair and large briefcase screamed *lawyer*.

He turned, over his shoulder to look at the street around him. His eyes covered by a pair of sunglasses, hindering my ability to read his face. But as the long, sexy leg of the second occupant slid out of the darkness of the limo, he turned back, offering his hand, helping the legs become a quite attractive woman dressed in red.

Miss Legs took a look around, pointing at various shops along the street. A gust of wind of the waning day causing her perfect blonde curls to whip across her face. The bitterness of the weather makes her rub her gloved hands up and down her slender shoulders. It's amusing how she stomps her feet on the pavement as a protest against the cold temperatures.

The pair head for my door and in an instant I know who they are. Adjusting my skirt, the wool material perfect for the temperatures, but not so much for flattery. Considering who the gorgeous woman headed my way is, I'm left feeling inferior.

Even in her thick coat, the blonde is skinny and reasonably so, her job dictating it. I knew the moment she pushed off the last of the wayward hair who she was, having seen her practically naked body on more advertisements and store windows than I could count. Lisa James is at the top of the food chain when it comes to supermodels. She is every straight man's fantasy and I'm sure a few gay ones too, she is the face of *Victoria's Secret*.

"Oh my, God." Lisa gushes, her arms circling me as she rushes through the open door. "You're prettier than Meredith said you were." For as tiny as she is, Lisa has some power behind her, rocking us side to side in dramatic motions.

"Isn't she something, Houston?"

"Yes, Lisa, she's everything I would expect from a friend of Logan's." His words aren't harsh, but they aren't comforting either, his attention focused on the briefcase he slid on the counter behind me.

"Logan told me all about your pen-pal friendship, and I think it's wonderful how you remember our men over there." The grinding of brakes brings the odd conversation to an abrupt end as all of us look to the box truck parked in the middle of the street. Two men jump from the cab, dressed in uniforms, with the company logo on their hats.

"Right on time," Lisa comments as she rushes to the door, our conversation forgotten, calling after the men to grab their attention. While her efforts are appreciated, they are unnecessary as she need only step onto the street to get their eyes on her.

"You must excuse Miss James. While she's beautiful, she has the attention span of a grain of rice."

I snicker and turn to the man beside me, "Excuse me?"

"Josh Houston, personal attorney for Meredith Forbes." He stretches out his hand, a Rolex peeking from beneath his jacket sleeve, a platinum band on his left ring finger, and the edge of a tattoo on the side of his pinky.

"As I said, Lisa is many things, including beautiful, but she has no boundaries and lacks any filters in what she says. Take nothing she eludes to as the whole story, and assume nothing with her." His handshake is firm, something I find important in business. He's also blunt, a character trait I find lacking these days.

"Nice to meet you, and thanks for the advice. But do you really think you should talk about the woman you work for that way?"

Josh slides his eyes in my direction as he stacks several pages in piles on my counter. "First, you're welcome. Second, I work for Meredith, not Lisa. And if you were to ask Meredith, she would say the same thing. Now, I know what you're thinking." Shifting his body so his arm rests on the stack of papers closest to him, his hazel eyes serious as he captures my attention.

"Neither one of us missed how she labeled your relationship with Logan. That's what I mean when I say she has no filter; she spews out the first thing on top of her head. Meredith likes you and she has spoken with her son," adjusting his eyes back to his task, he pulls an expensive pen from his inside jacket pocket, tossing it carelessly onto the table.

"Who, by my understanding, has begun his pursuit of you." Tapping his fingers on the edge of the discarded pen, "Do yourself a favor," pointing in my general direction. "Give in now and save yourself the trouble. The Forbes' always get what they want."

Any further explanation is interrupted by the commanding voice of Lisa as she pushes open the doors, the two delivery men behind her, each push a dolly packed with wardrobe boxes.

"Harper, there's another truck coming on Friday. My friends heard about what I was doing and they all want to help." As I readied to thank her, the ringing of her cell pulls her smiling face and clear blue eyes to the offending object in her hand. Quicker than a blink, she answers the phone and turns her attention away.

"See what I mean?" Josh nods toward the back of Lisa, who is repeatedly asking the caller if they are kidding her. "Attention span of a grain of rice." Shaking his head, he motions for me to come join him.

"Meredith wants to be called when we are signing the contracts." Reaching into the belly of his briefcase, he pulls out a fancy looking laptop. Pushing several buttons, the screen brightens and Meredith's beautiful face appears.

"Harper, do not believe a word Josh says about me." Meredith tries hard to hold back her humor, but the glint in her eyes says it all. "He has a bad habit of telling the truth."

Josh doesn't even try to hide the smile, his eyes focused on his writing. "I haven't told her the story of how you stole me from Lloyd and Bernstein."

Maybe he wasn't name-dropping, but I was impressed with the name he bounced on the table. Lloyd and Bernstein was a major law firm with offices in New York, Los Angeles, and Miami. Last year they represented a big Hollywood divorce case, which turned ugly and into a murder for hire trial.

"Feel free to listen to how we saved him from a life of long nights and endless weekends. Rewarding him with a house where his children get to enjoy being tucked in my him every night, and hasn't missed a moment of their lives since we stole him."

Josh pulls a set of papers forward, placing them in front of me and setting his pen on the top. "Like I said, Harper, they always get what they want." With cautioned eyes glancing at me, a knowing look on his face. "And since my youngest is teething, I'd like to get this over and back to my little girl."

Meredith places a pair of glasses on her nose, "She likes the frozen bananas, they helped her to get to sleep this afternoon when I saw her." I feel as if I'm listening in on a conversation I shouldn't, too personal and among family, so I distance myself and pretend to pull a piece of lint from my skirt.

"Harper, I spoke with Logan a few minutes ago. He was excited about a mission he returned from. Something he said we would hear about on the television in the next few days."

"Oh, that's good news, then." Trying too hard not to give her any clue on my decision about Logan. "I mean he made it back safe, with his team and all." Kicking myself for stumbling over my tongue, giving her justification for the smile on her face.

"Yes, it is great news, although he was disappointed to return with no word from you waiting for him. I assured him you were considering all the options, weighing your heart against your mind." Tapping the end of her pen against her desk, there are no emotions tied to her words.

"Josh?"

"Yes, Meredith. Harper, If you will open your packet, we'll get started."

* * *

One hour, twenty-seven minutes and a threat to never speak with Lisa again if she didn't leave my things alone later, I waved a final goodbye to the pair. Josh shared photos of his two little girls, Courtney, who is two, and Zoi, age ten months, who is testing his last nerve with her teething. He married Erin, his college sweetheart who almost got away. She heard a rumor about him and decided he wasn't worth the effort. He spent most of his senior year convincing her he was the man for her. They married the summer after he graduated law school and had been trying to have a baby and buy a house, but his long hours at the firm and student loans, were making it impossible to achieve either one. Meredith Forbes saw his rebuttal in a case she was testifying in and decided she wanted him to come work for her. When the three incredible offers she tempted him with failed, she pulled out the big guns and spoke with Erin.

I understood how he felt, as I held a check with too many zeros attached to the end, a lot of money earmarked to help even more people than I had ever dreamed of. Lisa left over two hundred dresses, beautiful pieces of clothing made by names which have made women gasp for years and years. The generosity of this family had no measure, rhyme or reason. They were simply good people, who wanted to give back to those who needed it.

Smiling to myself, I turned off the lights and secured the check in the safe. I'd deposit it in the morning, not comfortable with that kind of money hanging around, even if it was a check.

As I walk around the edge of my counter, I see the big screen television sitting silently on the far wall. Recalling how excited Mitch was to install it and give me way too much information on what all I could do on it. Sitting on the sofa, one of the best purchases I ever made for this shop: too many husbands and boyfriends have fallen asleep on these cushions as they waited for their girls to try on clothing.

The console to turn things on looked more like a mini computer than a remote control. Pressing the green button, which read power first, as it seemed the obvious choice. I wanted to have a Skype conversation, so I pressed the button with that icon. A list of contacts came on the screen, a plus sign at the bottom. Logan had given me all of his contact numbers including his connect name. Typing in his information, I am nervous and make a mistake. Pressing the red circle on the bottom, I get frustrated when the mistake doesn't disappear. Searching in frustration until a blue button with an X in the center appears, and the mistake disappears with a single touch. Pressing the big green button with the camera icon in the center, I hear the tone telling me the call is trying to connect.

The screen on the wall goes from blue to black as the tone continues, my hands are wet with perspiration from the nervousness in my chest. The tone continues three more times and I'm about to end the call and leave him an email instead when the signal changes and the call connects. The screen goes from black to a grainy picture to that of a beautiful woman, who looks completely sexed up.

"Hello?" Her voice is as beautiful as she is, inky black hair framing a set of ice blue eyes. Her makeup is smeared and her hair is in a messy bun on the top of her head. "Are you there?"

"Oh, yes. I'm sorry, I must have the wrong number."

"Who are you looking for?" Wiping the mascara from under her eyes, short manicured fingernails absent of any polish. But it isn't her nails or how nice they are that catch my attention, but the t-shirt she pulls from the back of the chair she sits in, showing me the edge of her naked chest in the process, a perfect nipple flashing in the center of my screen.

"Leu-Logan Forbes."

"Then you have the right number, but *really* bad timing." She mutters as she slips the shirt over her head, the Navy logo now covering her naked chest.

"He's in the shower, cleaning up." Her bottom lip slides over as her top teeth capture the edge of her lip, keeping it in place. She doesn't need to clarify what he is cleaning; her wearing his shirt says it all.

"You want me to take a message?"

I don't know who this girl is, and frankly, I don't care. This is a sign I was about to make the wrong choice, placing my trust in someone who doesn't deserve it.

"No, thank you. I ran into a friend of his and wanted to say hello, I can do that anytime."

"So you and Forbes are friends from back in the States?" Her interest is transparent, and I can see right through it. I've listened to enough conversations between bitchy women who are clawing their way into someone else's bed to know when feigned concern is involved.

"Friends, no. We have a mutual business interest." Not allowing this conversation to go any deeper. "I'm sorry I interrupted, hopefully you can finish what you started. Have a good evening."

Ending the call before she can open her mouth to rebut or add to the web she is weaving, I lean against the back of the couch and shake my head. Josh was right, the Forbes do get what they want, and by what I just witnessed, it clearly isn't me.

Pulling the bracelet from around my wrist and tossing it to the table, the charms left leaning against the remote. I'd found a quiet moment a few days after Ross left the box with me. A single rose, the note included read, *this one won't wilt and die*. Too bad the sender collected women, a life like keepsake to use at his disposal. I've never fancied myself as a possession, I'm not about to start now.

Chapter Thirteen

LOGAN

Being in the military has taught me a myriad of things: how to shoot an assault rifle, slit a man's throat in a single swipe, and how to masturbate in silence. I've used the latter of the three more times in the last few weeks than in my entire career. Tonight is no different. After the CO found his tongue, spewing some bullshit about our latest mission being a career changing win, I excused myself and ducked into the privacy of the showers.

Harper's face fills my mind, the roundness of her cheeks, her haunting eyes and lips, which beg to be kissed. Wrapping my hand around my cock, I close my eyes and imagine for a moment it is her delicate hands instead of my massive ones sliding up and down my shaft. Using the oil of my soap to make the journey easier and allowing myself to believe it is her mouth. My fantasy Harper knows how to bring me to the edge, where to place her tongue and when to tug at my balls, humming around the head as she begins her circuit all over again.

Hot water doesn't last long around here, and as the last of it takes the evidence of my activities down the drain, I reach over and cut off the water. Running my hands over my tired face, I can taste the sweetness the endorphins bring, calming me and making me crave any sleep

I can steal. Havoc, Reaper, and Ghost are leaving later tonight, back to the States and a normal life. I'm jealous as fuck, wishing like hell I could have a seat beside them on the transport back, but my sense of honor won't allow me to make a call, putting an end to this existence I have here in the desert.

Wrapping a towel around my waist, I open the door before any of the other guys waiting for the showers start pounding, demanding their turn at the sad imitation of a shower. Rounding the corner I notice my door is open, something I know I closed before I left. Edging the door open slowly, the groaning of old metal lets anyone inside know I'm here.

Everything looks just as I left it, clothes I wore for the past week on the foot of the bed, and my desk chair still turned slightly outward, fresh clothes draped over the back. Sliding my eyes over, I notice the screensaver for my laptop is still on, something that should have faded to black some time ago. Pulling my pants from the chair and sliding them up my legs, I notice my t-shirt is nowhere to be found.

Kneeling down, I check under the bed and desk, but find nothing. Unease fills my chest, as I know I pulled the shirt from my trunk, my last clean shirt to be specific. Jumping back to my feet, I flip open the trunk at the end of my bunk, finding the empty bottom looking back at me. With hands on my bare hips, I scan the room around me. Someone has been in here, taken my shirt and possibly looked at my computer.

Tapping the spacebar, the screen comes to life and I know for sure someone has been looking around as I'd purposely left Skype and my personal email open so I wouldn't miss anything from Harper. Both programs are now closed. How they got past the password is beyond me, but I sure as shit am going to find out. Pulling on the cleanest shirt I can find, I make sure the screen goes black before locking my door.

* * *

Blinding sunlight hits me as I push open the exterior door, my eyes squint in reaction as I slide my sunglasses down. The team wanted one last opportunity to say goodbye without the whole camp walking around us, able to allow the truth to flow and keep the emotions a secret.

I notice Reaper first, the larger than life fucker is hard to miss, sitting with his back against the rocks, his hands dangling between his knees. Ghost paces to his left, cellphone to his ear and pain written all over his face. I don't have to question what the issue is as it is always the same, Lindsay Jennings. I sure hope this high-profile girlfriend of his is worth the misery she puts him through.

As I step off the last step, my attention focused on joining my brothers, when the sound of hard and fast boots come up on my right.

"Doc," Ramsey calls my name, labored, yet hopeful. He has kept his word and worked like hell to get into shape.

"Hey, man." Not stopping my forward progression as he easily catches up to me. I have to hand it to him, in the last few months he has managed to bulk up at least twenty pounds and cut nearly six minutes off his run time. Reaper spent extra time getting his mind right, showing him how to separate himself from the reality the instructors will create and the real one he needs to remain in.

"Chief sent me to give you a message." Ramsey's sweat covered face grows closer, his rhythm somewhat impressive and much improved, able to speak clearly despite his work out.

"He got a call from Rachel, and will join y'all as soon as he is finished."

I wasn't particularly happy with the way this meeting was turning out, first Harper and the lack of response I was getting from her, and now this shit with Lindsay and Rachel.

"Thanks, Ramsey. How's it going, man?"

His smile is immediate and electric, and I can feel the positive energy beaming out from every pore.

"Couldn't be better, I sent in my packet while you guys were out."

"Congratulations."

"Thanks, Doc." Ramsey nods his head and then checks his watch, "Good talking with you, but I have work to do."

"Take it, easy man," I say to his back as he digs in and continues his run, tossing a blind wave as he picks up his pace and disappears around the corner of the building. If I was smart, I'd dig in and run with him, burn off this edge I feel from not knowing what Harper is thinking.

Just as I'm about to reach my team, Chief runs up beside me, smacking me on the back of the head and then jumping on a boulder to avoid my retaliation. By the smile on his face, I question my earlier assumption of his phone call not going well, perhaps he has finally convinced her to take some leave and spend some time together.

"Motherfucker! You better sleep with one eye open tonight." Chief fakes fear, wiggling his fingers as he backs away from me.

"We should all sleep with one eye open." Reaper's voice has an edge of seriousness, enough that everyone picks up on it and all eyes fall on him. His eyes say it all, deep hollows of concern, speckled with suspicion.

"Wanna share what you know, big guy?"

Reaper drops his head and allows his hands to relax enough his fingers touch the ground, picking up a hand full of pebbles and tossing them out into the rock ledge.

"LT Goodman is on the prowl. I saw her coming out of Oxford's room, naked as the day she was born. She dipped into your room, Doc, and then back out wearing one of your t-shirts before I could get down there."

"Where is the bitch now?"

"Surgery, according to Oxford." Reaper leans back on his arms, a satisfied look on his face. "Although he wasn't too happy I was asking about her."

"Looks like she has eyes for more than our pretty boy, Doc." Chief wraps an arm around my shoulder, playfully slapping my face, and then grabbing my chin and shaking it.

Shrugging him off and slapping his hand away. "Knock it off, my ass ain't pretty." Adjusting my shoulders, trying to save the last ounce of masculinity I need to prove.

"I'm fucking ruggedly handsome." A round of laughter sounds all around me, Chief bends in half, leaning into my side.

"Keep it up Giggles McGiggleson, glad to see your phone call went so well you can pick on the rest of us."

Chief wipes his face, trying to gain his composure. "For your information, my phone call went shit side up. Rachael would rather hang out with her friend Vivian, than spend time alone with me."

Chief collapses down on the ledge beside Reaper, his eyes, and the clenching muscles in his jaw, telling the story of his frustration. None of us care for Vivian as she and her bitchy attitude nearly got us killed when we helped her team cross the Korengal Valley.

"Sorry to hear it, man."

"Eh, no big deal." Shrugging his shoulders, knowing Aiden like I do, he always has a plan in the mix. "Told her we were never solid, no damage done. Got an email from Coach, though. He wants to sell the bar to me."

"The one where your ex-works behind the bar?"

"Not anymore. She's landed a new man, one who wants her to stay home and cook for him or some shit."

"This something you want to do? I mean running a bar when you've lived the life you have for so long is a big change."

"Pfft, if I don't like it, I'll hire someone to run it for me, or sell it to someone else." Aiden was easy like that, never letting the little things in life complicate it.

"Speaking of bars," Ghost pulls a bottle of clear liquid from his boot, twisting off the cap and holding it out in front of him.

"I'd like to make a toast. A man who sat behind a computer brought this team together, his job to fill empty positions with fresh bodies. We came together by happenstance, but we've stayed together because we became more than a group of guys, we became brothers. Later today, each of us will take different paths. Chief will buy a bar and marry the first woman who talks dirty to him."

Chief kicks Ghost in the shin, as our laughter swirls together, the ease at which we welcome the jabs is part of our unity.

"Havoc will sit his broken ass on a Florida beach while his mother parades young girls all around him. Each barely a cunt hair away from being his first cousin."

Havoc raises both middle fingers, but his smile and laughter show his true nature.

"Reaper will go off into hiding, becoming one of those scary stories the young shits tell about the burly man who lives in the woods. Stealing goats and sheep to have a little something warm to slip his tiny dick into every night."

Reaper looks over, his face tilted slightly as he lets a handful of rock fall to the dirt.

"You're half right. I'll pass on the goats and sheep after what you said the last time you tried them."

Eyes flash wide as Reaper's comeback hits its target; the pink of Ghost's cheeks has us laughing that much harder.

"Doc will continue his bedpan duty until he is a hundred years old. Yelling at poor corpsman on how they don't do anything right, until they get sick of him and try to give him to one of the farmers around here, who won't be fooled by his good looks and require a deposit before they take him away."

"What about you, Ghost? What will happen to you?"

Ghosts looks at his feet and then back to each of us, the eyes of a torn man full of uncertainty and fear. He takes a deep breath before pushing his chest out and shoulders back.

"You're looking at Ryan Biggs, Special Agent to the President."

Reaper is the first to hop to his feet and congratulate Ghost, pulling him from the ground to offer him a backslapping hug.

"You got the job, that's great man." Ghost nods his head but remains silent and I know this has everything to do with Lindsay. I hate what she has done to him, taking a man like Ghost and twisted his emotions, playing with his heart while she got off with every news producer she ever met.

"Ghost will save the day when a routine check of Air Force One lands him in the middle of a bunch of secretaries trying to take it for a spin around DC."

* * *

I watched as the dust whirled in the air, the deserts last goodbye to my brothers. We spent the better part of the afternoon along the ridge, retelling stories of close calls and sticky situations. Ghost shared his appreciation for my dig at his new job, and how once again Lindsay was making his life difficult. He had phoned her when he got the news, assuming she would want him to move in with her and finally be together. She crushed him once again with some bullshit about the rules of her co-op agreement and cohabitation.

Making my way back to my bunk, the smell of tonight's dinner drifts through the air. I'm half tempted to grab something, but the possibility of Harper emailing me is too overwhelming to ignore.

Lowering my tired body into my desk chair and rubbing my eyes with calloused hands, I pray to whatever God was available to make an email spontaneously appear. Entering my password, sliding myself further into the plastic of my chair, my left leg bounces a mile a minute, running a race against my heart.

My breath catches as an envelope on my screen now has a single digit on it, and I jump to click on the link. My body sinks, along with my heart, as I see the email is from Ross and not Harper. Tossing my anxiety to the wind, I hover the mouse over the link as I read the subject line.

TO: Logan. Forbes.LT@ OPS

FROM: Kincaid, Ross @ Hotmail

CC:

SUBJECT: You have serious issues

Attachment: Crazybitch1

Logan,

Something you will learn about me is I hate when people take advantage of situations, using the opportunity for their agenda. Now, before I tell you anything about what I just found out, you have to understand how technologically challenged my sister is. Maybe you should consider investing in one of those voice-operated controls, as this may be the only way she will be able to operate your entertainment system.

Anyway, earlier I came to my wife's shop with her when she forgot she had to meet with her accountant. I decided to skip over to my sister's shop and take advantage of the television you bought for her. Just as I'm about to sign on to the internet to kill some Zombies, I see she has been using Skype to call you. Being the nice guy I am, I notice she has managed to record the session. Now, Logan, I wasn't trying to be nosy, but I clicked on the recording and fuck!

Goodman answered your Skype naked! Now, I know you weren't with her, as the crazy bitch didn't try to lie and say you were there. I'll let you watch the clip, but man, you have to show this to the CO. I've called Harper and told her to get her ass down here as I'm going to bat for you. Watch your six and I'll have Harper give you a call as soon as I straighten this shit out.

Ross.

Clicking on the attachment, I waited as the clip loaded. Anger simmers in my blood as my fingers join in with my leg, tapping hard enough my mouse rattles against the desk. Harper's face fills the screen as I stop all the bouncing and push myself up in the chair, leaning as close as I can to get a good look at her.

Harper's features are filled with courage, as she doesn't let Goodman, or her fucking tit, get to her. I want to punch the screen as I hear the crack in Harper's voice as she calls herself my friend from back home. Then cheer slightly as she cuts Goodman off, not letting her have the last word.

Pulling a thumb drive from my bag, I copy the clip and sign out of my computer. I should send Ross an email thanking him, but I don't want to spare the time getting to CO's office before he goes to bed for the night.

Jiggling my doorknob, making sure it's locked, I turn to head down the hall when the skanky bitch pokes her head out of Oxford's room.

"You!" I shout at her, dismissing any idea she may have of ducking back into his room.

"I'm going to hang your fucking ass! Take your career and piss the fuck all over it!"

Her eyes go wide as I storm toward her, not giving a fuck if I call

136

attention to us or not. Oxford sticks his half naked ass in the doorway beside her, "What is going on out here?" Pulling his blouse over his shoulders, fake concern written all over his face.

"I've got you on film, on my computer, naked as fuck, making my girlfriend think we are fucking. You broke into my room." Raising the thumb drive to her eye level.

"Stole my fucking shirt and now I catch you coming out of this fucks bed." Oxford opens his mouth to protest, shoving Goodman behind him and I notice she still has the shirt in question on. Several people have come out of their rooms, snickering behind strategically placed hands and whispering to one another. Ignoring anything Oxford is trying to say, I let the anger in my voice get my point across.

"Don't try and hide that shirt, cause all these motherfuckers have seen you in it! I'm going to the CO and show him exactly the whore you are. And trust me, when I'm done with you, there won't be a soul who will hire you!"

Slamming my body into the door release, I walk with purpose to administration, determined to grab the ear of the CO and make him listen to the bullshit Goodman has been up to.

The administration hall is silent, not surprising with the hour of the day, the evening meal is well under way. The desk where his assistant sits is empty, but his door is open and I can hear him laughing. Gripping the thumb drive in my fist, I round the desk and poise my hand to knock on his door. Protocol dictates I wait for him to conclude his call, but my anger overrides my better judgment. Rapping my knuckles against the wood of the door, ripping into the silence in the room and capturing the attention of the CO. His eyes flash to mine, motioning with two fingers for me to come in his office and have a seat.

Captain Jim Sloan, as his desk plate reads, was more of a placeholder for his position than someone who knew what they were doing. According to the reports I have on him, he accepted this deployment to gain a skill set and make him a shoo-in for a spot in the White House as an adviser. He's spent more time on his knees, sucking the dick of any man who could help him climb the ladder and get to where he wanted to be, than learning the fucking job.

Ending his call, he turns to me, "Your ears must have been burning, Lieutenant." Tenting his arms on the single file on his desk, the chair squealing in protest from the movement his chuckling creates.

Captain Sloan couldn't be a day over forty, but the fat rings along his midsection begged to differ. I'd question how he passed his physical exams, but I didn't really give two shits about him.

"That call was from personnel, regarding the remaining months on your enlistment." Excitement danced in his eyes, giving me all I need to know about where my future is headed. Captain Sloan has never hidden his desire for me stay here and work for him, my hard-core work ethic makes his numbers look better, ensuring his selection for adviser.

Knocking at the door behind me steals his attention, reviving the anger seething in my veins. There is no need to turn and see who stands in the doorway, I can smell his fear from here. I would never label Oxford an intelligent man, and attempting to shove his balls in my business, confirms my assessment of him.

"Can I help you with something, Oxford?"

"Yes, Captain. I believe I can shed some light on the accusations Doc is harboring against—" Standing to my full height, Oxford makes the mistake of capturing my full attention, something a countless number of men have taken their last breath after doing. His words falter as I turn my body in his direction, crossing my arms over my chest, showing force by not saying a single word. From his hard swallow and widening of his eyes, my message is heard loud and clear.

"What accusations?"

Oxford jerks his head in Captain's direction, "Um—"

I almost feel bad for him, but the memory of hearing Harper refer to me as a friend slaps me back into the highway of determination, fueling my inner fire for action.

"I don't have accusations." Tossing the thumb drive on his desk, the plastic and metal toppling end over end, skidding to a stop against Captain's elbow.

"Indisputable proof is what I have." Drifting my eyes from the face of the Captain to Oxford's impression of a flopping fish searching for a pool of water. Pulling the chair I just vacated to the side, "Have a seat Oxford. You need to see what your girlfriend was doing while she waited for your Viagra to kick in."

Captain pushes the thumb drive into the USB port on the side of his laptop, his brow puckers as his eyes flash back and forth over the screen. His right hand comes to rest under his chin, seconds later, his eyes flash wide and I assume it's a result of Goodman's tit filling the screen. My heart aches as I hear Harper's voice, the braveness and disbelief wrapping itself around her words. This girl owns me, and I'll be goddamned if I allow some bitch in heat to ruin this before it becomes something wonderful.

Captain's eyes jump from the screen to Oxford's face. "Have you seen this, Lieutenant?" Unmoving, he waits for the quivering man to respond, a fragment of fire growing in his eyes. This isn't something he needs going on around his base, investigations are never good, no matter who you are.

"No, Sir." Oxford sits up straighter, his lame ass attempt to shake off the fear he has pouring off of him. "I've considered the source and know the allegations to be unfounded." I give him credit for at least attempting to defend his fuck buddy, justifying her attempt at slithering her way into my bed.

"Then perhaps you should." Captain turns the screen to face the two of us. Harper's downcast face frozen on the screen, as she reaches over to end the session. I want to reach through the screen, tip her face back up and kiss the hurt off her lips.

"No thank you, Captain."

"It wasn't a suggestion," the room is deathly silent from the cold and hard words Captain tossed at Oxford, rocking my stance slightly as I never really thought he had a decent set of balls on him.

Oxford, nods his head, his shoulders slumping as Captain plays the clip for him. I can smell the despair seeping out of his soul, his actions with Goodman have all but guaranteed the pair of them an automatic discharge.

As the clip ends, and Harper is once again frozen on the screen, Oxford clears his throat, lowering his head in defeat.

"I never thought I could capture the attention of a beautiful girl like Goodman."

I'm skeptical of the emotion in his voice, the defeated look in his posture. I've met far too many evil men who have cried crocodile tears and then tried to shove a knife in your heart. "I take full responsibility for this."

Captain leans back in his chair, his silence is unnerving and I question if he has the same suspicions as I do as to the validity of Oxford's statement.

"I can appreciate your willingness to take the blame for this. Don't think for a moment I'm not going to begin an investigation into the relationship between you and Goodman. Furthermore, I will have her in the chair you presently occupy as soon as I've finished my conversation with Doc. She can explain why she felt the need to visit the male barracks in the first place, not to mention naked."

Oxford recognized defeat when he saw it, asking the Captain if he could be excused if there was nothing further. Closing the door behind him as his fate and dignity was about to take a hit.

"Take a seat, Doc."

The man who sat behind the desk now was not the same as when I originally came in. This man, is the seasoned and hard faced leader who had been on the giving end of more life-altering punishment than he cared for.

"Goodman is no stranger to questionable activity. Her last command didn't have the courage to ignore the fact she was a woman and charge her for her misdeeds. She came here thinking she was bulletproof. Thanks to you, and this beautiful girl of yours, her time in the military has come to an end."

I would enjoy sharing this tidbit of information with Harper, seeing how big I can make her smile or watch as she attempts to hide her enthusiasm.

"I do have something else I need to talk to you about." Removing his elbows from his desk, opening the lone folder on the middle of his desk.

"I had an interesting call from your detailer. He and I agree, based on your current position and our need for a skilled physician, you are most needed here. You will remain here until your current time is up."

Walking back to my room, Captain's words echoing inside my head like lines from a horror movie. Frustration replaces the anger I felt an hour ago, disgusted with my inability to toss my sense of honor out the window and get the fuck out of here. I needed to call Ross and find out if Harper knew the truth or if she was still blinded by Goodman's bullshit. But my head wasn't in it, I wasn't ready to listen if the latter was true.

With the final rays of sunlight wishing the world a pleasant good-night, I turned away from the barracks and headed to the track, determined to clear my head of all of this fuckery.

Chapter Fourteen

HARPER

"Who sent this to you?" Unable to remove my eyes from my brother's cell screen, the events playing out take my breath away, leaving me with an unyielding intrigue to find out what the problem is.

"The guy who sleeps across the hall from me." Ross had called me down from my apartment upstairs, teasing me for my inability to work a simple remote. He and I watched as the conversation I had with the naked girl transpired on the big screen again. Ross didn't bother hiding his feelings about this girl, Goodman, from me.

"We've been waiting for something like this to go down. Hoping to catch her in the act so she can't lie her way out of it."

"Why was she in Logan's room? I mean, perhaps he was taking advantage of having a girl with him."

Ross drops the phone to his lap, wrapping his left hand around my neck, forcing my face to align with his.

"She was in his room because she is a sneaky bitch." Dark eyes, bordered by serious features convey much more than any words, leaving not a sliver of space for any doubt in the truth.

"My buddy came back from chow and saw her sneak down the hall, from Oxford's room to Logan's. He managed to pull out his phone and catch her as she stripped naked before entering Logan's room." Softness filled the once angry eyes of my brother.

"Listen, Goodman is an opportunist, looking under every grain of sand for her next victim." Squeezing my free hand tightly, an assuring smile growing from the corners of his lips.

"Believe me, Logan isn't the kind of guy to get mixed up with a predator like Goodman."

Something in me wanted to believe in what he said, trust he knew Logan well enough to make a judgment call and for it to ring true.

"Tell me, Harper, why were you calling Logan?"

Letting my body relax back into the cushions of the couch, I release a puff of air, which tosses a strand of my hair into the center of my face.

"Partly because I wanted to tell him about signing with his mother. And—" Feeling foolish for my skittishness in telling my brother the truth, not having any real basis for the butterflies bouncing around in my stomach.

"And?" He prodded me, playfully shoving his shoulder into mine. His warm smile, always something I found comforting and on occasion annoying, has taken over his face.

"And I decided to give this a try. To let my guard down and see what a real relationship feels like."

His eyes search mine, blue orbs on a mission to peer into my soul, see for himself the truth that lies there. Ross has always looked out for me, taking his role as protector past the limits. In this moment, I've never been more grateful for his love.

"You know," shifting his eyes to the entertainment center, and then back to me, picking up the remote from the coffee table.

"If I was Logan, and I had a day like he did, one where I had to go sit in my boss's office, sharing the bullshit story he has been handed. I would be sitting behind my computer, needing to hear from the girl who was hurt the most from all of this."

Ross motions to the television, as he presses the power on and the screen changes from black to blue, pressing far fewer buttons than I did earlier. Although, my ignorance of how to properly use the program proved to be a blessing and not a curse.

"Are you sure it isn't too late? I hate to wake him." I'm too overwhelmed with everything I've learned in the past few hours to do the conversions of the time difference. Not to mention I am slightly intrigued with the way his body moved as he tore down the hall and verbally throttled the half naked woman. I knew his arms were covered in muscle from the brief time I spoke with him, but to see how he towered over the men around him, commanded attention and didn't let anyone interrupt what he had to say did something to me. Men who carried themselves with authority have always been a turn on for me. Having not been close to one in a long time, seeing Logan has woken the need in me.

Ross chuckles to himself as we wait for the call to connect, "Guy rule number two, it's never too late for a call from a beautiful girl." Relaxing back into the couch beside me, taking my hands in his, squeezing gently several times, a warm smile across his lips.

"What's guy rule number one?"

"If your girl is crying, no matter whose fault it is, you need to fix it." The deep, husky voice stealing my attention back to the screen, too enamored with the handsome face to question why I didn't hear the signature tones of the program.

Two sets of eyes, thousands of miles apart, take advantage of technology, allowing the invisible cords of a blossoming relationship weave their way to one another, connecting in a silent but solid bond.

"Logan."

"Harper."

Words so soft they could have been carried on the backs of Angel wings, sighs of relief their traveling partner. Locked eyes never waver as twin smiles come to life.

"I'm sorry you were exposed to the lunacy of a deranged woman."

Logan runs his hand against the back of his neck, the edges of a tattoo look out from his t-shirt, ribbons of dark ink, their pattern swirling so severe it's impossible to tell what it is.

"I swear you will never have to deal with her again." His words are the truth, stamped and sealed by the code he lives by, the same set of rules I've known from my brother my whole life.

"I saw you in the hall." I blurt out, needing him to know I never believed the lies of a desperate woman, a fantasy cast in deception, her goal to distance our affections lost to the truth.

"It scared me a little," I admit, unable to forget the passion he displayed or how it started a fire in my core, one no amount of water would ever extinguish.

"Collins showed me the clip, told me he sent it to you, Kincaid." My heart jumps a little, so lost in this bubble we have created I forgot my brother was sitting beside me. "Captain is including it in the charges he is bringing against Goodman and Oxford."

"Charges?" I question, confused as to what illegal misdoing this couple stood accused of. "How can she be charged for telling a lie?"

Logan licked his lips, something everyone does subconsciously, yet when he did it, my breath hitched and my pulse reacted, my heart hammering against my chest. His mouth composed of two equally soft and supple pillows, separated by genetics and so unbelievably sexy.

"She broke into my room, touched my computer and stole an article of clothing from me. All fairly minor in the scope of things, a verbal reprimand at best."

Leaning his upper body on his crossed forearms, the muscles in his arms expanding behind his already tight t-shirt. Ripples of testosterone causes a shaking of my core and my mouth to go dry, my eyes devour the cut of his chin, follow the sharp line so rigid he could cut glass.

"But she was sleeping with someone in her direct chain of command, a violation of the UCMJ, conduct unbecoming an officer. Her actions warrant immediate discharge from the military."

Ross props his feet on the coffee table, placing one ankle over the other.

"Oxford is finally getting what's coming to him. That cheese-dick motherfucker walks around like he is the poster child for the Naval Academy." Tucking his hands behind his head, a new glint in his eye.

"The bastard had the nerve to come knocking on CO's door while I was in there."

"Seriously? What a pussy."

"Yeah, he tried to pull some martyr bullshit." Logan's brow bent creating a deep crevice between his eyes, waving his hand around in a circle.

"But I don't give a shit about Oxford and his lack of courage, I care about what you said earlier, how something you saw me do scared you, Harper."

"Maybe scared isn't the right word," I confess hurriedly, not comfortable with how my earlier statement affects him. "More like—"

"Hold on, babe." Logan interrupts, sending me a wink to make my heart race. "Ross, you and I can talk about all of this when you get back here. How about you give Harper and I some privacy?"

Ross extracts his feet from the table, smacking me upside the head as he brings his arms down.

"Oh sorry, Sis." He laughs, rubbing the side of my head as he sends my hair flying.

"I know when I'm not wanted." Grasping my head between his massive hands and placing a kiss to the middle of my forehead. "I'll talk with you later, after the two of you iron out your wrinkles."

I wait and watch as Ross leaves my shop, waving one last time as he goes out the side door to his wife's store. Turning back to the handsome man on my screen, his focus seems to have never left my face. Grabbing one of the throw pillows, cradling it against my chest.

"I missed those beautiful eyes of yours. I had a few moments where I didn't think I would see them again."

"I wouldn't have done that to you. I made you a promise and I would have kept sending you packages every month."

Logan leans forward, tenting his hands together and tilting his head to the side, "I know you would have, but it wouldn't have been the same. I don't —" The dip between his brows is back, his face contorted in what I fear is anger.

"Logan, what is it? What's wrong?'

He shakes his head several times, a war within himself evident in his actions. I wish I could reach out and touch him, erasing the tension pulsing in his twitching jaw. Finally, he raises his face, "I heard you tell Goodman I was a friend from back home."

"Yeah," I answered cautiously, not understanding why this was upsetting him. I'm trying to push down the anxiety I feel reaching through my chest and wrapping around my throat.

"I didn't like it," he snaps, not in a hateful or spiteful way, his eyes filling with sadness as he cringes from the sound of his own words.

"I'm scaring you again, and it's not my intention. Harper you have to understand when someone comes after the people I care about, I will do everything I have to in order to protect them. Goodman made the mistake of putting doubt in your mind, I saw it in your eyes when you ended the call. Oxford had every intention of trying to discredit you to my CO, and I couldn't let that happen."

Hugging the pillow closer to me, a warm feeling filling my body, chasing away the anxiety and returning the smile to my face.

"Thank you, Logan, for caring enough about me to defend me like you did. You should know, although I did assume you and Goodman had slept together, I didn't believe you were in a relationship with her."

"Harper, there was never anything between Goodman and I. Not a kind word or hello in the morning. I've avoided her since the first time I laid eyes on her. You, on the other hand, are all I think about. No matter what I'm doing, you're in my mind, invading my every thought."

Logan's voice dips to this incredibly sexy, gruff tone, setting my soul on fire and my thoughts to mush.

"You do the same to me."

"You're not wearing my bracelet."

Looking down, my fingers automatically wrap around the naked flesh of my wrist. I hadn't wanted to take it off but knew it needed to go back to him. With new light shed on the truth, I needed to correct the wrong and put a smile back on his face.

"I have it."

Moving the pillow over and grabbing the box I tucked the bracelet into. "I took it off," shrugging my shoulders.

"Well, you can imagine why I did." Sliding the cold metal over my hand, resting in the center of my wrist, the tiny package sparkling from the light of the lamp.

"I can't say as I blame you."

His eyes are fixated on my wrist, a new smile spreading across his lips, the very set I want to touch and get lost in.

"Although, seeing you wear it now does some pretty powerful things deep inside."

I can't help the smile, which takes over my entire face, filling me with a level of happiness I haven't experienced in a long time.

"What would you think about keeping it on? Letting the rest of the world know you belong to me."

The way he says, belonging to him does something to me, his possessiveness is sexy, which surprises me and yet makes me feel incredible.

"I think, considering how much time you have left in the military and the miles which separate us, wearing this, and calling you mine, is one of the best decisions I've made in a long time."

The beam of his smile matches mine, and I can't help but giggle like a schoolgirl, covering my mouth with my hands, pushing myself into the back of the couch.

"Harper, I know you're no stranger to this life I live. The months we have before us, unable to be a normal couple, going out to dinner and movies. But I promise, if you can be patient, I'll make up for every single mile that separates us."

I'm mesmerized by the scruffy beard on his face, how it makes him look intimidating. For a brief second, I wonder what it will feel like against my thigh?

"I'm going to hold you to it."

Squinting my eyes and pulling my knees to my chest, "As long as we're discussing keeping things on."

I pause to collect my hormones, the need to rub my thighs together to relieve the pressure building in my core.

"What's the chance you can keep this ruggedly handsome thing you've got going on?" Tapping my finger against my chin.

Logan takes in a deep breath, moving his large fingers against the scruff of his face and my mind wanders to what those fingers could do if I allowed him to explore me.

"With my new orders, this is the last you'll see the beard on me for a while, but I promise to grow it out for you the second my time with Uncle Sam is paid."

"I can live with that, and who knows, by the time you're back in the States I might prefer you clean shaven."

He has less than a year left on his contract, and until this moment I've never thought about where he will live. I assume since his family is from New York, it would make sense he would return there. I won't think about it now, I'm too happy to let the thought of this being a temporary thing ruin it.

"Whatever you decide will be fine with me, babe. I'll follow your lead."

Chapter Fifteen

LOGAN

"LT, the guy in triage one is asking for something for pain."

Glancing up from the lab work of the young man I would be taking to surgery soon, my HM2 replaces his stethoscope around his neck.

"The one I discharged twenty minutes ago?" Using everything he has to keep the smile off his face, pausing for a moment before confirming.

"Yes, his wrist is hurting now."

Tossing the lab report into the bin to be filed, not having the energy to deal with people who cried wolf to get out of doing their job.

"Tell him to quit jacking off so much and get the fuck back to work."

As I suspected, not everyone was receptive to how I did things, as many complaints had come across my desk. Most from disgruntled corpsman who didn't appreciate being called out on their shit. I had been schooled in the thought if you were going to do something wrong, you better be available to have your ass chewed.

One young man, in particular, felt his time was more precious than the rest of us, and became upset when I didn't agree. Today's complaint was a nonexistent rash on his arm, and in his mind, it rendered him unable to stock the rooms and take the vitals of our patients. The kid with abnormal labs had a hot appendix and it needed to come out, something that is truly deserving of my time.

Crossing the yard, heading toward the mess tent, I felt the hairs on the back of my neck stand up, that eerie feeling you get when someone is watching you. I drop to one knee under the pretense of tying my boot laces as I scan the surrounding terrain.

My first pass catches nothing out of the usual, but as I study the ridge line, I find the reflection of a signal mirror. Looking over my shoulder, I see a response from the ditch beside the road that leads into the compound.

Something's about to happen, I can feel it in every fiber of my being as my heartbeat quickens and beads of sweat collect along the back of my neck. From the corner of my eye, I notice the Captain walking around the Hummer we stole from Aarash. He is proud of the vehicle, and has been trying to figure out a way to take it back home with him.

Returning my attention back to the ridge line where I saw the signal, buried behind dead bushes and barely hanging on trees, I find nothing. Just as I'm about to check the signal from the ditch, a man steps out from the cover of the rocks, his white clothing rippling in the breeze, as he takes a rocket launcher from around his back and aims it in the direction of the Captain.

I don't have the luxury of my gun, or half the equipment I would have carried with me during a mission. The only thing I can do is get everyone's attention and get them as close to the ground as possible.

"Get down! Get the fuck down!"

I scream and several frozen eyes turn toward me as I take off running toward the Captain and the Hummer.

"Goddamn it, get the fuck down!"

I try again, as Ramsey comes around the corner, gun still around his back as he walks his patrol. He notices my fix on the ridge line, and just like Reaper showed him, he drops to one knee and lines up his sights.

I press on full force, attempting to get to the Captain before the motherfucker with the rocket launcher can. His eyes find me, terror and confusion blocking his ability to do anything except stare open mouthed at my approaching form.

"You need to hit the fucking dirt!"

I roar at him, just as I launch myself into the air, my arm catching his chest as the hissing sound of the released rocket whizzes past me, hitting the armored vehicle and sending it into a ball of flame. I can feel the heat from the flames, the intensity of it something I will never forget.

The Captain is still under my chest, dirt smeared all over his face and the sleeve of his uniform torn. I look up as Ramsey pulls the trigger, his confidence from the last time I saw him in this type of situation is off the charts. He will make an incredible SEAL, one I would fight beside any day.

Jumping to my feet, men with fire extinguishers are already spraying down the now worthless Hummer, its charred remains still smoldering, black smoke from the burning carcass clouding the sky.

"You okay, Doc?" Ramsey runs over, his gun secured on his back, a look of pride mixed with smatterings of being scared shitless marring around the edges.

"Yeah, I'm good, but this one—"

Extending my hand down to the Captain, his hand is shaking so severely I'm going to have to check him for shock.

"Sir, let's get you over to medical and checked out."

Standing on wobbly legs, his hair disheveled and covered in dirt, he nods his head in agreement and allows Ramsey and I to escort him to the hospital.

"Forbes, you saved my life." Captain had a few scrapes and most likely would have a multitude of bruises, but he was alive. I put a butterfly dressing over a small gash he had above his eye, head wounds being notorious for bleeding like a sieve. He would be good as new once his nerves calmed down and we got a little sugar in his bloodstream.

"I won't forget it. As soon as I can get back to my office, I'm calling your detailer and getting you back to the States."

I wasn't going to hold my breath. Not even a month ago, the man making this vow to me claimed we were too short staffed to let me go back home.

"I appreciate it, Sir."

* * *

"Good morning, beautiful."

Harper and I have adopted a schedule, she calls me every morning as she is having her first cup of coffee, and I am getting ready to fall asleep. Tonight, I managed to get done with work early, as this afternoon was the sentencing for Goodman.

With all the evidence stacked against her, she remained motionless as the board handed down a unanimous decision to end her career. She was no longer allowed to enter the hospital and was confined to her quarters until time for her to leave. Her nursing license was revoked and she would face military jail time for theft.

"Um, what?"

Her eyes were focused on my bare chest, something I had wanted to do since we began dating. I'd caught her several times appreciating the way I looked, and wanted to show her what was waiting for her when I got back home.

"My eyes are up here, sweetheart."

Tapping my temple, I was enjoying this far too much. Harper's eyes go wide as she averts her eyes from my chest, focusing her attention to the bright pink cup in her hand.

"I'm sorry, I didn't —"

"Harper, stop." She looks at me with pink cheeks and the tips of her ears growing deeper red by the second, "I was teasing you, love. This is your chest, covering the heart, which belongs to you as well. Someday, and I hope it's soon, you will lay your beautiful head on it so I can hold you as long as I want to."

"I think about that too, when you're here in the States."

"Yeah, what kind of thoughts do you have?" She looks at me with those big blue expressive eyes, thick lashes framing the pools of warmth I fall into every time I look at her.

"Honestly?" She hesitates, looking down at her mug and then back at me. "I question how this will work with you living in New York and me in Virginia."

We'd never discussed it, stupid of me not to tell her what I planned to do when this was over. Right after my team left, Reaper called us from Viper's house introducing the team to the new love in his life, Rayne. He shocked the shit out of all of us as he had shaved the beard and had a girl living with him, something he vowed never to do.

After listening to how each of them found the rules of civilian life too constricting, we decided to form a team, a pack of mercenaries for hire. Viper and the girl who wrote to him by mistake, Kennedy, became the group's first clients. I had no plans to practice medicine, my heart no longer feeling the need it once had to heal the sick. Now, I wanted to protect those who couldn't protect themselves, not giving a fuck what the overcrowded court systems thought.

"It will work perfectly fine since I'm not returning to New York. I need to stay in the south where my heart has lived since you stole it."

I wasn't ready to tell her the rest. Since her brother had returned, he wasted no time airing his displeasure at being here. He, like me, was full to the brim with being away from the ones he loved.

He shared with me how he wanted to open a kick-ass gym, one with physical therapy and private trainers. He had a business plan and a fair amount of money saved to get the gym off the ground. I tossed out the idea of going into business with him, teaching self-defense when I wasn't off working with the team, and he accepted.

Ross found some new storefronts going up on a popular street, not far from where Harper's new building was. I called our family attorney and had him get the process going.

"You're moving here?"

Harper's voice shoots up a few octaves as the surprise of my announcement registers on her face. Those sweet lips of hers upturned into a delighted smile, one I've labeled my favorite.

"That's my plan, know any places I could stay?"

Tossing her my best smile, throwing in a little sexy edge to up the game. Harper was the type of girl who appreciated honesty and being up front. I appreciated how she returned my honesty with a brand of her own.

"Well, there are these new condos going up not far from here, I saw the announcement in the paper. There's also a couch directly above where I'm sitting I could let you have for free."

"I was thinking a little closer to where you lay your head at night."

"You know, it just so happens I have a vacant space on the right side of my bed."

"Right side you say?" Playing along with her, enjoying the fuck out of the way she flirts with me.

"Did you know the right side is my personal favorite?" Her hand comes up to cradle her face, and my bracelet dangles from her delicate wrist. Seeing her wearing something I gave her makes me want out of this place that much more.

"Shall I put a hold on it? Save it until you get home?"

"Put a reserved sign on it, babe. Being beside you is where I belong."

* * *

Morning had come before the sun took its place in the sky. I wanted to check on the Captain and make sure he was doing all right, but as I opened my door to begin my day, Ramsey is hurrying across the yard, his heavy steps telling me he is on a mission.

"Hey, Doc."

"Hey, Ramsey, you ready for a run?"

"No, Sir. I was sent by the CO to have you come to his office right away."

"Is he okay?"

"Oh, he ain't hurt. He's been on the phone since a little past midnight."

"Thanks, Ramsey. I'll head over there now."

With the earliness of the hour, the amount of people around was low, making my trip across the yard pleasantly quick. The offices outside the CO's were dark and quiet, giving me the ability to hear him talking to someone at the back of the building. As I approached the open door, he was sitting in his chair, talking to his computer screen, his normally pressed uniform exchanged for a college t-shirt and sweatpants.

"I love you too, I'll call you later." He smiled at whoever he was talking to, my approach to his door catching his attention as he ended the call. The smile created by his call didn't diminish as he motioned me forward and offered me a seat.

"Forbes, sorry to get you out of bed, but I have news that I didn't want to sit on."

"Did I or did I not tell you to go to your bunk and get some rest?" Ignoring the offered chair, choosing instead to lean over his desk, my arms locked and supporting me.

"You did, and I attempted it, but I made you a promise and I am a man of my word."

"Clearly, by the way you ignored my instruction, your word includes the things you are interested in. As far as waking me up, I was coming to see you after I got some caffeine in my system."

CO laughed, easing himself back into his chair, his night of not sleeping was catching up to him as dark circles were beginning to form under his eyes.

"Forbes, have a seat, would you? The quicker I share the news with you, the quicker I can get to bed."

"Fine," I agreed, dropping into the seat directly behind me. "Let's hear it."

Shaking his head, a genuine smile on his face, "You're something, you know that, Doc?"

"So I've been told."

"As I said before, I've been on the phone with your detailer, pulling more strings than a bass guitarist at a rock show. I managed to get you transferred to Twenty-Nine Palms. You report in two months."

Twenty-Nine Palms was clear across the country from Harper. What the fuck was I going to do for the remainder of my time in the middle of nowhere?

As midday allowed me to take a lunch break, I declined an invitation to eat with Kincaid and stormed to my room. I had sworn to myself I would keep my word to Uncle Sam and remain in the military, but being close to Harper was more important than saving face with my family.

"Fuck it." Picking my cell off my desk, I scroll through my list of contacts until I locate the number I need. A quick look at my watch, not taking time to calculate the time difference, I pressed send on the green button.

"Congressman Green's office. How may I direct your call?"

"Yes ma'am, I need to speak with Congressman Green, please."

"May I ask who is calling, sir?"

"Tell him it's Logan Forbes, Meredith and Weston's son."

"P-please hold."

Goddamn, I hated name-dropping, but from the stutter his receptionist showed, my parent's name still held enough clout to get me through to him.

"Logan Forbes, to what do I owe the honor of this call?"

Congressman Green and my father had attended college together, pledging the same fraternity and ran in the same circles. A few years ago, his wife was diagnosed with a brain tumor, my father stepped in and helped save her life. He told my dad if we ever needed anything from his office not to hesitate to give him a call.

"Congressman Green, I hate to bother you, but I need a huge favor."

"It's David to you. After what your family has done for me, you name it and it yours."

"Thank you, David. I need you to get me assigned to Norfolk, Virginia."

Chapter Sixteen

HARPER

The dreaded day had finally arrived, the last twenty-four hours I would have to enjoy my brother's company before he had to return to Afghanistan. I had assumed he would want to spend the day wrapped in the love of his wife and children. However, I had been wrong, as he insisted I join them for a family dinner and casual drinks after the kids went to bed. I didn't hesitate to accept, having grown used to having my brother around, watching him play with the neighborhood kids, and dancing with Amanda as she tried to sweep hair off the floor.

I enjoyed how his smile covered his face as the baby pointed to him and screamed dada. Witnessing my brother's interaction with his three boys these past few weeks had me questioning if Logan wanted children. It was far too early in the relationship to discuss such things. However, not wanting kids was a deal breaker for me.

"Stupid bastard doesn't know when to quit."

Sarah's harsh tone snatches me from my thoughts. She had offered to help me make a side dish and dessert, as she didn't feel like going home before heading to her doctor's appointment this afternoon. She and Mitch have been actively trying for a baby, and with her period a no show this month, she made an appointment.

"Clearly having Ross threaten him within an inch of his life did nothing."

I didn't need to look out my kitchen window to know who she was talking about. Lance had shown back up in the neighborhood over a week ago. At first, he stood by his car, parked across the street, sunglasses on as he watched my shop. When his gawking got him no results, he started sending me flowers, scheduling the deliveries to coincide with his perusal. Lance had chosen the wrong week to mess with me, Sarah's period may have been MIA, but mine was present and accounted for. Using every evil hormone I had, I ripped the blossoms off the stems and tossed them into the window boxes to join the rest of the dying flowers. He had shaken his head but sent another bunch the next day, the backup flowers meeting the same demise. Too bad for Lance, as Ross saw my destruction of the petals and connected the dots, tearing off across the street and leaving a centimeter between their faces, barely.

My brother is a mountain of a man at nearly six foot five and well over two hundred pounds, his broad shoulders are able to hold all three kids at once. And while Lance is tall, he can't match the sheer size of Ross.

"How do you know what Ross said to him?"

Letting the knife in my hand fall to the cutting board, the metal thud echoing off the walls. Sarah glances over her shoulder briefly, a condescending spike in her brow. Her eyes flash to the knife and then back to the street below, the water from the faucet splashing over her hands as they continue to clean the vegetables.

"You didn't have to hear what he said to know it wasn't hello and how are you doing."

Shutting off the water and shaking the globes of vegetation to free them of any remaining water, she turns around.

"He threatened him, plain and simple. Your brother is a SEAL and doesn't live by the same rules the rest of us do. In his world, when an enemy presents itself, he takes it out. No man with a gun and badge needed."

Sarah was right. There was no doubt in my mind Ross pulled out every swear word in his arsenal as he told Lance to get lost. He never cared for Lance, and the disdain he had for him had come from the opinion our father formulated. Nothing changed once Ross and Lance met face to face, neither man impressed the other.

"Anyway, your salad shit is rinsed and ready," tossing the hand towel she used to dry her hands on the counter beside me.

"I have to get out of here and see if that man of mine managed to knock me up." Grabbing her purse strap she had laid over the back of one of my chairs, dropping it on her shoulder as she pulled her keys from her jeans pocket.

"Do you think the test the doctor gives you will dispute the ten you took this week?"

"No," Sarah turns to face me, her fingers wrapped around the door handle, twisting it open and stepping onto the threshold. "It won't change. But the insurance company has a nasty habit of needing to hear news from the doctor, not my excited husband."

Returning an understanding smile, "Sorry, I forgot about the necessary evil that is insurance." Picking my knife back up, raising the handle to resume my chopping.

"No worries, Harper. You'll see how big a pain in the ass this is when you and Logan start having babies."

Sarah's words hung with me as I finished making my part of dinner and long into the drive over to Ross and Amanda's. Where I knew it was normal to daydream of what any future children would look like in a new relationship, I felt strange hearing Sarah mention it, as I never shared much of our private conversations.

"Aunt Harper, Daddy helped me catch a frog today." Adam says proudly, a fork of mashed potatoes raised to his face. "But Momma said he had to stay with his family." His face and his voice fall as he recalls the story, while Amanda covertly rolls her eyes and hides the smile she has for her son.

Ross puts down his fork, reaching over to grasp Jason's face. "Hey, you remember the promise I made you, right?"

Adam nods his head, his brothers joining in the celebration and my heartbeat quickens as I wait for them to share the news.

"Aunt Harper." Adam jumps from his chair, nearly tripping over his shoes to get to me.

"Guess what?"

Quicker than I can blink, I have Adam and Jason vibrating with excitement, the baby squealing from his seat in the highchair, frustrated he can't join his brothers surrounding me. The excitement filling the air is contagious as Ross leans back in his chair, sporting an amused smile across his lips.

"Daddy said when he gets to come home forever, he's getting us a puppy."

My eyes instantly water at the thought of Ross coming home for good. He and I had lunch last week, and he made it clear he was finished with the military, there were too many events in his life he was missing out on. When we finished eating, he took me to a new store front in the beginning stages of construction. He had contacted the owners and was in negotiations to open a gym and physical therapy center.

"A puppy!" Joining in their excitement. "No way." The baby slaps his open hand on the table of his high chair, demanding a slice of the excitement be given to him and adding in his shrieks of babble he assumed we all understood. Two dark haired, cherub-faced boys look back at me in sheer bliss, pearly white teeth adding the crowning finish on those smiles.

"He said we could have any dog we want."

Amanda opens her mouth, in what I assume is instruction for the boys to finish their dinner, when a sharp alarm comes out of the television speakers. With this being the last meal as a family, some rules had been bent, including the no television on during dinner.

"We interrupt this program for this special report."

Ross tears his eyes from his children's joy as the middle-aged man on the screen starts to apologize for the interruption, pointing the remote at the television and increasing the volume.

"Last week's breaking story of an unexplained earthquake which rocked an area just outside the US occupied Korengal Valley, is now confirmed to have been a massive explosion by Military Special Forces in the continuing war on terror.

Officials released a report moments ago, confirming this was indeed a mountain fortress where Aarash Konar had been evading military capture. Positive DNA identification of at least one well-known individual has been recovered. Pavel Kumarin, leader of the Russian organized crime Family, who has been under investigation for the murder of his first wife and the family of his close associate, Viktor Petrov"

Behind the anchor, in a square box appears the picture of a man surrounded by lots of suit wearing men, his hair is dark with a dusting of white at his temples. When he turned his face toward the camera, I could feel a chill run down my spine. I had seen this man before, a story a few months back where he had been taken in for questioning on the death of his latest wife.

"Sources close to the Kumarin family confirm Pavel's son, Andrey, has traveled to Afghanistan to retrieve any remains. Andrey ignored reporters who questioned him why his father was in a mountain fortress with a known terrorist."

The photo switched again to an incredibly handsome man. Dark hair, with features that would make a nun moan, and a swagger in his walk which would rival any super model. My breath hitched as I took him in, gaining the attention of both Ross and Amanda.

"Don't waste your admiration on him, Sis. He may be something to look at, but he would slit your throat in the blink of an eye."

Ross rose from his seat, pulling out his cell phone and pressing several buttons. Turning my attention back to the screen, having learned long ago there were conversations I could never be part of.

"The remains of Aarash Konar proved to be a little harder to identify, however with his brother Aaron attending school in the US, a close match was identified using a blood sample. According to US officials, Aarash Konar was killed by a team of SEALs acting on intelligence collected recently. We will continue to follow these stories and update you with any updates."

Amanda had cleared the table during the time my nose was buried in the news report, a bowl of ice cream now in front of the boys whose attention was focused on the creamy goodness. With Ross out of the room, Amanda turns the television off allowing the welcomed silence to fill the room. As gently as possible, she began to clean the baby's face, his bright eyes drooping from the sleep wanting to set in.

A familiar line of worry appeared on her face, reaching past her beautiful features and into my chest. This time tomorrow, Ross would be back in the thick of things, back where this Aarash and Andrey made all the rules, killing whomever got in their way, not caring who was left behind.

The sound of Ross's boisterous laugh echoes down the hall, ironing out the worry lines and replacing them with a painted on smile.

"Just for that, I won't hand the phone to my sister like I was going to."

Ross rounds the corner, his phone pressed to his ear and an evil smile on his face. Amanda plants her hands on her hips giving Ross a not so subtle warning.

"Hang on fu—" Amanda tosses the rag she was using to clean the baby into his face. Her warning turning into pissed off. "Er—hang on a minute, I mean." Lowering the phone and sending Amanda an air kiss.

"Okay, Doc. You're on speaker phone, but be careful, my boys are in the room."

Booming laughter comes from the phone, a magical tune which sings to me and brings my smile to life.

"You mean your beautiful wife is in the room about to kill you because of your mouth."

The beating of my heart increases and my mouth begins to water. Having conversations with Logan using Skype has been the highlight of my day, giving me a new goal to focus on.

"Careful, Doc. I can take you off as quick as I put you on."

"And I can tell your wife about the file on your computer she told you not to get."

You can tell Ross wants to say something incredibly witty and completely X-rated by the way his face is turning red and his features are contorting into an angry look. Shaking his head and lowering his gaze to the hardwood of the floor, "And I will share something equally as damaging with my sister."

Amanda mutters something under her breath, and I step in to help her collect empty ice-cream bowls and wrangle rapidly tiring children.

"There isn't much you could tell her about me she doesn't already know." Logan tosses back, a bite of humor woven in his tone. He always appears so confident, so sewn together it is intimidating.

"Oh, I'm sure I could come up with something. Although it happened before you started dating her."

"And she would give me a pass because of it. Exes are in the past for a reason."

"Speaking of exes," Ross snaps, turning a dining chair around and straddling it. "I had to have words with a certain ex of Harper's who insists on sticking around."

"Lance?"

"Yep. Caught him watching her office from across the street the other day, he had the balls to send her some cheap ass flowers."

"Tell me these words started with F and ended with a kick to his family jewels."

Amanda had taken the boys out of the room, instinctively knowing where this conversation was headed. "You guys can use adult words, the boys are upstairs in the bathtub." Ross stood up suddenly, running around the corner to the banister, yelling up to Amanda he would be there in a second.

"No, we can't, babe, my favorite lady is still in the room."

"I have a few customers who would beg to differ with you." Mona and her endless list of followers coming to mind. I'd seen the scowl on her face, no matter how hard she tried to hide it when I let it slip Reece International had granted me so much money.

"Isn't it late there?" Doing my best to keep the conversation flowing, praying he didn't detour back to the subject of Lance. I planned to give my brother a piece of my mind the second this call was over.

"It is, but Ross managed to catch me as I was ending an urgent call to the States. I'll tell you more when I have things firmed up."

Ross takes his chair again, folding his arms over the back of the seat. "What did I miss?"

"Nothing. I was just about to ask Harper why she didn't tell me Lance was bugging her." I never cared for being talked about when I was in the room, something Alex and Ross frequently did when we were younger.

"Need I remind you, I'm still in the room. And the reason I didn't call you and say something, is because there wasn't anything you could do about it. Furthermore, I didn't say anything to Ross, he managed to catch him doing it and got in his face."

Ross raised his eyebrows, but said nothing, shaking his head in silent disagreement. The sly smile on his lips hiding a secret I wasn't sure I wanted to know.

"Harper Kincaid don't you underestimate how far my arm can reach. If Lance steps a toe over the line you've drawn, I better get a phone call, and I don't care what time of day it is."

Frustration bubbled inside, I was a big girl and could take care of myself. I hadn't asked Ross to step in this time, but my mind betrayed me, as I allowed my emotions to take over my thoughts.

"Well he was sitting across the street this afternoon." Ross's head snapped up, the vein in his neck swelling.

"He say anything to you?"

A new edge sharpening Logan's tone, causing goosebumps to form on my arm as a trickle of fear crawls up my spine. I had backed myself into a corner, unable to look at Ross while telling the both of them a lie. Ross knew of one flower delivery, and the times he found Lance in the street. I hadn't told him, or anyone for that matter, of the numerous occasions I found him sitting in his car in the middle of the night.

"No, he never says anything, just stands beside his car and watches me."

It was the truth, Lance hadn't approached me in a while, remaining near his car as he watched my shop. I had mentioned his actions to one of my regulars who is a police officer, but she let me know standing in the street isn't a crime, and there was nothing the law could do unless he did something to hurt me or destroy property.

"Okay, Harper. I don't want you to worry about him. I've got a few friends who can drive home my warning."

I didn't want to know what he meant by that. Logan was a man of considerable means, and I wasn't certain how many influential pockets he had his hands in.

"Doc, I called to razz you about the mission you did without me. Lucky bastard taking that prick out."

"Who Aarash?"

"Yeah, the news broke the story a few minutes ago. Andrey Kumarin is on his way to picking up his daddy's ashes."

Ross scoffed, his hands clenching into fists and then relaxing. There was a history there, not one I wanted to know anything about. How they could speak so nonchalantly about a known criminal, I would never understand.

"If I hadn't heard Pavel saying his son wasn't there because he was weak, I would have assumed Andrey planned his father's death."

"Either way, there's about to be a shortage in heroin production for a while."

"Not long enough if you ask me."

"Small battles, Doc, small battles."

I didn't understand what they meant, fearing the worst when they mentioned heroine and a known Mafia member in the same conversation. Preferring to live in my little bubble, I stood from my chair and chose my exit.

"Gentlemen, it's been a long day, and I have a meeting with the contractor in the morning. Ross, you have a flight to catch and Logan, I'm sure you would like to get some sleep while you can."

Wrapping my arms around Ross's neck, giving him a tight hug and a kiss on the cheek.

"Harper."

"Yes?"

"I'll never be too tired to talk with you."

"I know, but this is the last night I have with Ross for however long, and I need some time with him before he goes."

Motioning the ceiling, letting Ross know I would be upstairs while he finishes his call with Logan.

"I understand, babe. Let me talk to Ross for just a second, and you can have him until he has to get on the plane."

"Thank you, Logan."

"For what?"

"Understanding how important my family is to me."

"No thanks are ever needed. I'll talk to you later tomorrow."

"Good night, Logan."

"Night, beautiful."

As I climbed the steps, I focused on the splashing sounds of the bath going on a few feet above me, and giggling voices of my nephews as they played a game involving a pair of super heroes, instead of the conversation between two of the most influential men in my life. As I crested the top of the stairs, I couldn't fight the smile which captured my face, hoping someday the men downstairs would be in the same room, and the children in the tub would be mine.

Chapter Seventeen

LOGAN

"Lieutenant Oxford, you stand accused of fraternization with a lower ranking member of your chain of command. How do you plead?"

Oxford stood with his head held high, eyes focused forward and a blank look on his face. After Goodman had been sentenced, she wasted no time giving details about their relationship, sighting days and times where they had sex during their shared shifts, and on more than one occasion, included another staff member in their activities.

"Guilty, sir."

I wanted to scoff at him as I knew he stood there, smug instead of sincere. His guilty admission the only path he could choose as the other nurse who had been involved, gave birth to a little girl a month ago, DNA confirmed ninety-nine point nine percent likelihood Oxford was the father of the baby. Bastard didn't need to open his mouth to admit his guilt.

"Are there any character witnesses here on your behalf?"

Keeping my eyes on Oxford as no one in their right mind would stand up for the dirty bastard. There had been an overwhelming sigh of relief when word got out Oxford had been busted.

Our CO didn't believe in closed-door hearings, a bonus which was taken advantage of by the standing room only crowd. When enough time had passed, giving anyone in attendance an opportunity to speak, the CO handed down his ruling, ending the career of Lieutenant Oxford.

"Is this going to affect your leaving here?"

Kincaid leaned over in my direction. He hadn't wasted a second since getting off the plane, handing in his separation request, turning down a decent size reenlistment bonus in the process.

"No," mimicking his sideways lean, using my fingers to muffle my answer. Gossip was worth more than gold bars around here, partial truths spreading like wildfires, searching for a listening ear and a wagging tongue. "I dare any motherfucker to stand up to Senator Green."

The same day Kincaid came back, the CO came stomping into the hospital, slamming my new orders on the empty exam table. His face was a red as a beet, the veins in his neck so distended a blind man could see them.

For twenty minutes he threatened to call Washington and have my ass in front of a review board for blackmailing a Senator into helping me. I stood to my full height, six inches further than he stood, and let him know anytime he wanted to contact my friends in Washington, I had a long list for him to chose from.

"Have you told Harper the news?"

Shifting in my seat as the CO slammed his gavel against the wood of his desk, dismissing the proceedings. I wanted nothing more than to call her and tell her the good news. In eight weeks I would be allowed to serve my remaining five months as a physician in one of the branch clinics in Norfolk, Virginia. A mere thirty-minute drive from Harper's shop and the new gym I was partnering with Kincaid on. I nearly called her when I got the confirmation I was going to Virginia, but I wanted to surprise her, and I was using Josh to help me with my plan.

"No, and neither will you."

"You have no worries here, but I want to go on record stating I advised you to tell her and not do whatever those gears in your fucking head are telling you to."

Twisting his index finger in a circular motion next to his temple, wearing a Cheshire grin on his freshly shaved face.

"Whatever," I brush him off, the anxiety of it all mounting inside my head. "I have a plan, one I know will work out in the end. I have my attorney, Josh, working on some things for me, and he's sending the paperwork for the incorporation, it should be here tomorrow." Kincaid and I came to an agreement in the partnership of our gym. He had a friend of his who was a personal trainer, looking for a new gym to bring his clients to. Kincaid was scheduled to leave the military three weeks after I left for Virginia, and he would run the operation until my time had been paid back.

"Well," Kincaid paused as he rose from his chair, pushing his palms against the tops of his knees. "I speak from experience when I tell you Harper will be pissed when she sees you and is unprepared. But go ahead, do whatever you're thinking." Ducking his head down slightly, the curl of a smile forming on the edges of his lips.

"Better make sure to have a backup plan of where you will sleep that night, and save me a spot, as Amanda will be just as pissed since I haven't told her our plans either."

I had to check in on a patient, but didn't want to get anything on my uniform, having made that mistake once already. Years ago, I'd attended a change of command before beginning a shift, as I was leaving the parking lot, a group gathered around one of the active duty who was in attendance. He had been pre-gaming a bit excessively, tripping in his drunken haze and cracking his head open on the side of his car. By the time I got to him, blood was everywhere and the concussion he suffered caused him to vomit all over me.

As I closed my door behind me, I automatically looked at my computer screen out of habit to see if I had any new mail. My breath hitched when I noticed I had not one, but two pieces of mail waiting for me. Ignoring my need to change and get to the hospital, I slid into my chair, clicking the envelope on my screen.

TO: Logan.Forbes.LT @ OPS
FROM: Sawyer, A @ Gmail

CC:

SUBJECT: Answer to your question

Logan,

So I found the guy you asked me about, Lance Ranoka. I followed him around Chesapeake today, as he went from delivery to delivery until about one this afternoon when he pulled into one of the ugliest apartment buildings I have ever seen. This thing would scare the shit out of any street thug and make him run home to his momma. After what I assumed was his lunch break, he jumps back into the delivery truck and heads to a storage unit where he trades the delivery truck for the sweetest looking Audi I've ever seen. He proceeded to drive around, and I assumed he spotted me tailing him, but I stayed on him as he pulled up across the street from your girl's shop.

He sat in his car for at least thirty minutes before a delivery truck pulled up, and the guy took in an armful of flowers. This Lance kid planted his ass on the hood of his car and watched Harper refuse the flowers and ignore the bastard. After I was sure Harper was busy with a customer, I went over and relayed your message to him.

Logan, I don't know what it is, but this guy is weird, like there is a screw loose or something, because as I'm telling him to stay away from her, he pulls out a fucking joint and starts smoking the thing in the middle of the street. I called Austin Morgan and had him run this guy's information through his sources. He called me back and said Lance has a record, paid cash for the Audi and has a number of storage rentals in his name.

I don't know, Logan. This all seems too odd for me, and I can't shake the feeling we haven't scratched the surface when it comes to Lance Ranoka.

Aiden

Ten seconds after I got off the phone with Kincaid, I called Aiden, waking him out of a sound sleep. I apologized, but by the feminine laughter in the background, he wasn't too pissed at me. Rachel, the nurse from the medical convoy we assisted with, had called him a few minutes after he landed in the States, having reconsidered spending a weekend alone with him. He picked her up from the airport and they hadn't seen the light of day since he pulled into one of the hotels close by. With Aiden confirming the unease I felt from the news of Lance still stalking Harper, I knew I needed to act fast. Do everything I could to protect her.

TO: Logan.Forbes.LT@ OPS
FROM: Sawyer, A @ Gmail
CC:
SUBJECT: Sorry for the cockblock.
Aiden,

Thanks for getting back to me so soon, and I again apologize for pulling you away from more pressing matters. I cannot tell you how much this Lance guy makes my skin crawl, the muscles in the back of my neck scream for me to get out of this fucking desert and beside Harper. I worry now that she is alone as Kincaid is back here with me, almost to the point where I want to hire some form of protection for her. Tell me, Chief, you busy for the next few weeks? Or are you and Rachel still wrapped up tight as a pretzel?

This is hard for me to admit, especially to you, but I broke down and called a family friend, Senator Green. I know I swore I would finish my time here and do the right thing by Uncle Sam, but when they wanted to send me across the country to Twenty-Nine Palms, I couldn't do it. I can't be so close to her, and yet so far. Now before you threaten me, I asked for a change of duty station, not an early out of my contract. So in a few weeks, I'll be on my way to Norfolk, Virginia, where I will once again have a cakewalk of nine to five and holidays off. The best part, and the one, which is making this all worthwhile, Norfolk is a short distance from Chesapeake and my Harper.

Let me know if you're up to the challenge of watching over my girl. See you as soon as I get back to the States. The first round is on me.

Logan

Clicking on the second email, disappointment flooding me as it is from my realtor and not Harper.

TO: Logan .Forbes.LT@ OPS
FROM: Cutter, Violet @yournewhome
CC:
SUBJECT: Good news, I have a number of properties to show you.

Lieutenant Forbes,

As a proud supporter of our armed forces, I would like to thank you for your service and for choosing Your New Home Realty in assisting you with finding your new home. Given your healthy price range and all cash ability, finding you the perfect home will be effortless. In speaking with your attorney, Josh Houston, I have selected a wide range of options for you: from the southern charm, plantation home, to the more New York City Fifth Avenue style, with clean lines and polished surfaces. Attached you will find several homes in the area, with a number of useful photos and videos of the properties currently available.

I look forward to conversing with you and answering any questions you may have. Please do not hesitate to contact me in regards to the homes I have sent you.

Violet Cutter

I had sworn Josh to secrecy, if my mother found out I was buying a home in Virginia, she would be on the family jet to purchase one right beside me. She and I shared the belief Harper was my one, that mythical connection you read about in the books my aunt was famous for. Harper took my breath away, in how she carried herself and her generosity with others. But it was her blue eyes, like two tractor beams, digging into my soul and haunting me.

Instead of looking through the photos my realtor sent me, feeling wrong in choosing a home without Harper's input. I wanted her for all the new milestones of my life, everything I had yet to experience as a civilian. Clicking on the Skype icon, hovering over the connect button as the butterflies danced in my stomach. I'd never been apprehensive when it came to women. If I wanted a particular girl, I went after her, but Harper was different. She didn't bend to my way of thinking, available for my pleasure when I demanded. No, Harper challenged me, made me evaluate the person I am and made me remember what is was like to give a shit again.

"Attention all staff, Lieutenant Forbes you are needed in the trauma staging area, I repeat. Attention all staff, Lieutenant Forbes you are needed in the trauma staging area."

My heart dropped as the adrenaline rose in my bloodstream. Slamming the lid closed on my laptop, I took off at a run toward the trauma tent. Memories of the last time I had been paged like this flooding my mind, those of a much younger man with new skills I couldn't wait to use. A coveted title, and an ego to match, I assumed I was the greatest doctor on the planet. I know better now, all the skill in the world can't cheat death when he has come to collect.

The scene is organized chaos when I step inside the room, a pair of marines stand off in the corner, their sweat covered, horror filled faces look back at me. One of my corpsman stands over the patient, his arms locked as he performs chest compressions on the patient.

"Report," I command, unable to see around one of the staff nurses who is hanging an IV bag overhead.

"Sir, twenty-two-year-old male. Stabbed multiple times in the chest and back. No pulse or respiration since his arrival."

Moving to the end of the bed, my mind flashes to when Viper had been stabbed by a local during a rescue mission last year. Terror filled my chest as I took in the ashen face of the man lying on the bed. His bare chest, EKG leads scattered around, as my eyes move to the monitor out of habit. Ramsey has no heartbeat, nothing keeping his brain alive sans the chest compressions.

"How long has he been down?"

Rounding the table to examine him, I borrow the stethoscope dangling from the nurse's neck.

"Fifteen minutes."

One of the marines answers and I dart my eyes in his direction then back to Ramsey's lifeless body. I can't take the sadness in his eyes, the expectation the marine has for me to make him come back to life.

After forty minutes of throwing everything I had at him, "Time of death nine-seventeen." Tossing my gloves on the floor, needing to escape the somber mood in the room. I needed to be angry, hold onto the fire to keep from letting my inner emotions show. But as I hit the bright sunlight, I come face to face with the Captain, his arms crossed and a face which matches my insides, sad and falling apart. Several inches separate us, but no words are needed to convey what has happened.

"Beckman."

"Sir?"

"Let the staff know we are in River City."

Beckman, his assistant, scurries off to make the announcement and shut off our communication. Nothing would go in or out until Ramsey's family had been notified.

"Forbes, come with me."

Captain turns in the direction Beckman ran off to, not allowing me anytime to refuse. I'd pissed him off enough when he learned I called Senator Green behind his back, so I wordlessly followed his lead, staying a few paces behind him. Word of Ramsey's death will spread quickly through camp, questions as to why the woman who stabbed him was allowed to get so close will create more paperwork and training, a knee-jerk reaction from the powers that be. Before his body is released to the family, I'll have to sit down and sign his death certificate, something I can't handle doing today.

"Close the door, Forbes."

Captain sits hard in his chair, tossing his cover on the credenza behind him, the weight of the situation taking its toll on his face. With his head in his hands, something not normally shown by a man in his position, he looks in my direction as he slides a folded sheet of paper across the desk toward me.

"This was in my email this morning."

I stare at the sheet of paper, my heart in my throat as to what the transcribed ink will tell me. Will it separate me further from Harper, sending me into some remote jungle time has forgotten? Swallowing down the dread lodged in my throat, lifting the paper from his desk, one final breath taken in and held before my fate is sealed.

"I sent word to his LPO for him to come see me when his watch was over."

Captain looks out his window, the glass dirty from the constant wind which coats everything with the tiny particles it picks up as it passes by.

"I wanted to tell him myself, be the first to congratulate him on getting into the program."

In all the years since I had received the same news, the wording hadn't changed. I recall the relief I felt as I read the words over and over, unable to believe I was going to do something good for a change. Ramsey had worked so hard, conditioning every day, getting his mind in the right place.

"His brother is in prison, the same one his father died in. I'll have to call the Red Cross, see if they have any can give him a proper burial."

Ramsey told me of his family, the way his brother picked on him when he wouldn't follow him into a life of crime. Their father had been in and out of prison most of their lives, finding it impossible to do any legal work to support his family. He died in a riot, a few days before Ramsey graduated high school. His mother passed not long after, giving into the demons she found at the bottom of her bottle of cheap booze. Ramsey had been accepted to BUD/S, and I know my team would agree, he would have excelled and made a hell of a SEAL. In my eyes, he already was.

"Don't call the Red Cross. I'll handle getting him back to Arlington and a hero's burial."

Chapter Eighteen

HARPER

I had a meeting with the contractor to do the final walk through at Horizons. It never ceased to amaze me what waving money in people's faces managed to accomplish. When Meredith had the contracts signed, she had Josh put in a clause which stipulated for every day the crew went beyond the completion date, there would be a thousand dollar fine. If they finished early, and with quality work, they would receive a thousand dollar bonus per day.

Horizons was ready, all we needed was to move the clothing from the storage unit and onto the empty racks. Meredith had been in hyper drive planning a ceremony for the grand opening.

Everyone who was anyone wanted to be a part of this event, have their name grace the lips of one of the countries more generous families. The Mayor went as far as refilling the flower boxes, using a more reliable and hearty flower than what Mona had deemed appropriate. He even used his own money, something I believe he did to impress Meredith, rather than make the street beautiful.

My focus was slightly different. Although I wanted the event to go well, I hadn't heard anything from Logan in a week. I'd sent him three emails, all going unanswered, the only thing keeping me sane in all of this was how Ross hadn't contacted Amanda either. In the past when this happened, it was due to an emergency where they had to cut communications. We had been encouraged to continue emailing, as they would be welcomed when the ban was lifted.

It had rained last night, leaving my usual parking spot looking more like a lake and less like a free space. Having worn open toed shoes, I opted to park in front of my shop. Glancing at the exterior of the building as I shut off the engine, I spotted a young woman dressed in a conservative patchwork skirt, with a coordinating pale blue sweater. Her long, dark hair lay straight as a board against her back. Traces of sunlight, peeking through the leaves sparkled off the metal hair clip that held part of her hair back. She didn't flinch or move as I shut my car door, her focus remaining on the wedding dress in my display window.

"Good morning," speaking loud enough from the street so I didn't startle her, which worked as she looked over her shoulder, muttering a polite reply.

"Are you getting married?" Stepping onto the curb, the sounds of the waking city beginning all around.

"Yes," she admits, but doesn't turn from the window. "Well, maybe," she shrugs. "It's complicated."

"Men always are." A humorless laugh leaves my chest, my thoughts on Logan and not the young lady standing before me. The conflicted look on her face tells me she was warring with herself, much like the battle raging in me. Layers of doubt held together by the ghosts of my past, blocking out the rational side, the one who knew to expect the unexpected.

"How about you come in and let's see if we can uncomplicate it?"

I tried to coax a smile out of her by sharing one of mine as I slid my key into the deadbolt. She nodded and followed behind me, however, the smile never caught. Opening the door wide for her, I was surprised by the smell of coffee brewing. Amanda wouldn't be in for several hours, and Stacy wouldn't be out this early unless there was a sale on expensive shoes. Placing my purse on the counter, I noticed the hum of Sarah's sewing machine.

"Sarah?"

The humming stopped replaced by the sound of wheels on the floor. Sarah poked her head out, glasses on her face and a pencil clenched between her teeth. Her raised brow gave warning of her mood. Much like the past few days, she was full of new pregnancy hormones and not the brand which made you glow and happy.

"Why are you here so early?"

Removing the pencil from her mouth and the glasses from her face, the brows becoming more severe.

"Two words, boss lady: Khaki Ball."

Those two words sent military wives scurrying to find the perfect dress. For some, a push into a new diet and the gym membership they haven't used since Valentine's Day. For us, more specifically Sarah, it meant letting out seams and shortening hemlines, late nights and early mornings all to make our customers happy.

"How could I forget?"

"Could be all the knives you're juggling." Sarah tossed in sarcasm, sliding the pencil atop her ear as she eyed the young lady behind me.

"Who's this?" Tipping her chin in my direction, curiosity getting the best of her.

"I'm sorry," spinning around to find the young lady looking fondly at the wedding dress, her arms crossed in front of her, tears welling up in her tired eyes. "I didn't catch your name."

Startled, she uses the back of her hand to dry her eyes, shaking her head quickly as if to clear her head.

"Avery." Her name comes out as if it's her salvation, something to grab onto and hold until she can compose herself. "Avery Whitfield." Standing up straight, a firm resolve appears on her face. This girl is a fighter, one I'd want in my corner.

"Pleasure to meet you, Avery. My name is—"

"Harper Kincaid. I know, everyone in this town knows who you are." Her honesty catches me, and for a moment I am taken aback. My silence is taken in the wrong context by the look on her face. I know I need to right the situation, as there is no need for her to leave this shop due to embarrassment, or with a bad taste in her mouth.

"Well, hopefully you won't believe everything you've heard."

Sending her a wink and what I hope is a friendly smile. Internally, I hope what she has heard is in the positive and she hasn't come to right a wrong.

"Would you care for a cup of coffee? Sarah makes the best in the world."

"No, thank you. I don't drink coffee."

"How about some tea? I think we have a few good flavors back there."

"No, thank you, I'm fine."

Avery was beautiful in that girl-next-door kind of way: polite and gentle. What she wasn't was anything close to fine.

"You're sure?" Giving one last offer before I get to the root of the problem of why my wedding dress brought on a set of tears. Hell, if anyone was allowed to cry over that thing, it was me and the outrageous amount I paid for it.

"Yes, completely sure."

"Well, I'm going to have a cup as my morning started hours ago." Turning away from her, I shot a look at Sarah whose face had changed from the angry mother to be, to the much softer and compassionate one she wore most of the time. As I pass her, she rises from the chair and tosses her glasses on the desk, her work temporarily forgotten.

"I've got her," she whispers, and I know she will make Avery feel safe enough to open up and tell us what is going on. I listen carefully as Sarah walks over and introduces herself, complimenting her choice of clothing and inquires if she lives close. I take my time as I stir my cream and sugar, giving her all the time in the world to work her magic. When I hear the pair laughing, I know it is safe to return to the conversation.

"Avery, you mentioned something about a wedding and the dress in my window."

Sarah looks at me over her shoulder, sends me a knowing wink as the edges of her lips curl up in a smile. "I saw the flier about Horizons opening in a few days, and I had hoped there would be a dress I could wear to my wedding. But when I saw the one you have on display—" Her eyes drift to the bright white of the satin fabric. Full sleeves of sequined lace, with a four-foot cathedral train. I had the same look the first time I laid eyes on the finished product.

"It's beautiful, isn't it?" Sarah moves closer to the window, twisting the knob to open the case.

"Please don't," Avery cautions, her voice wavering with the emotions filling the room. "I can't bear to touch it when it is impossible to purchase it." Her bottom lip trembles as she releases the latter two words. I've seen the same look on hundreds of faces, all trying to make their lives better by finding a job, most coming from some form of addiction. This time is different, the tears aren't from struggle, but of facing an unknown future.

"On the sidewalk, you mentioned something about your situation being complicated. Why don't you tell us why you're about to twist your fingers off, and then we'll decide if you can afford the dress."

Avery separates her hands, her cheeks pinking up from getting caught. Rocking back on her heels, she places her hands on her side.

"You asked me if I was getting married, and I'm supposed to."

She ducks her head briefly and looks back to the dress. Golden hues of the early morning sun cascade across her face, giving depth to the sadness of her topaz eyes.

"Cole and I met when he pulled over to help me one night when my car broke down. He was all comfort and casual as he stepped out of his truck with a natural swagger that had my mouth dry as the desert and my heart hammering like a war drum in my chest. It was an instant attraction for me as he is a handsome man."

For the first time since she arrived, a smile emerged. Fondness streaks across her soft lips, leaving behind the memories she holds behind the smile.

"When he got to my driver's side window, he pulled his identification from his back pocket and told me to keep my window up and my doors locked. He told me where he worked and how he lived just off the next exit. He offered to take a look at the problem if I didn't have a tow truck on the way. I popped the hood as he walked around the front of my car, his ball cap shielding his eyes from my view. I was only able to catch the way the edges of his eyes wrinkled as he tugged on the release latch before he disappeared from view behind the hood of my car. He fixed my car in a matter of minutes and waited until I was on the road, before he drove off down the highway. I wanted to kick myself when I realized I didn't get his number."

The once shy smile has taken residence on her face, perfect teeth joining the celebration of what is destined to be an epic love story.

"A few days later, I got a call from my roommate who had too much to drink and needed a ride home. When I pulled up to the bar, she was leaning against the chest of a tall man, his friend approaching my car before I could put the vehicle in park.

The second he poked his head into my car, I was instantly mortified. I hadn't changed out of my pajamas before getting behind the wheel. Cole didn't seem to mind as the smile on his face grew tenfold and he called me beautiful."

Avery's words like a whisper at midnight, soft and reverent. Golden rays from the window glided along the caramel strands of her hair, giving her an angelic glow. I had to agree with Cole, the girl before me, bathed in the early morning sunshine, was indeed beautiful.

"After he and his friend helped get the passed out roommate of mine into the car, he asked me for my phone and put his number into my contacts list, under the cute guy who likes me."

Contagious smiles shine all around, as like minds rejoice in the pet name.

"He asked me to text him when I got home. When I did, he called me back, and we talked until the sun came up the next morning. Two days later, I showed up at his apartment with a plate of his favorite cookies as a thank you for fixing my car. He asked me to dinner the following weekend, and we've been together ever since."

I've always prided myself on my ability to read people, able to decipher the stories hidden behind the illusion of happiness they work so hard to create. Avery has the fairy tale beginning of a great romance, but her eyes tell me of the shadows of sadness, which darken the edges of her world, threatening to smother the life out of her dreams and the handsome man who stars in them.

"I met his grandmother, who raised him since the death of his mother. She's in a senior living facility as she has the beginning signs of Alzheimer's. Last month she had a bad episode and didn't recognize him at first. I tried to remain supportive and do anything to help him in dealing with her disease. After he got her settled and she seemed to know who he was again, he asked me to come to his apartment and stay with him for a while. I held his head in my lap, brushing my fingers through the hair at the top of his head, allowing him to get lost in his memories of the happy times he spent with her. At one point, Cole jumped from the couch and ran down the hall to his room. I assumed he was getting sick in the bathroom, but didn't want to barge in, so I stayed on the couch and waited, listening for any sounds of distress. Less than a minute later, he came back down the hall, a determined look on his face. He dropped to one knee in front of me and asked me to marry him. Seeing his mother die and now his grandmother losing her memories, he realized life is too short and he needed to live in the moment. Cole is in the Navy, at least for a few more months. His contract is ending, and he wants to attend college now that he has the money saved and the scholarship from his job. We had discussed him taking online courses so he can be available for his grandmother while I keep my job in retail."

Avery takes a look around the shop, a familiarity rising in the softness of her gaze. Reaching over she picks up the sleeve of a silk blouse, rubbing the fabric between her index and thumb, appreciating the quality of the fibers and the hard work of a skilled weaver.

"Neither one of us wanted a big wedding, but being married in the church was at the top of our must list. I suggested just friends and immediate family, a small ceremony with cake and punch afterward, and he wholeheartedly agreed. We booked the church, bought the flowers and the cake. He would wear his uniform, and I would find a dress."

Avery paused, taking a deep breath and then walked slowly to the counter where Sarah had draped the gown. Rainbows of iridescent colors shimmered from the sequins like a mirrored globe above a dance floor, sharing their brilliance with the rest of the world. Avery tentatively reaches out caressing the edge of the sleeve with the same care a mother gives the cheek of her newborn baby. Just like the silk of the blouse, she appreciates the feel of the satin and lace, the two fabrics complementing one another, creating a sea of wonder making the wearer the center of attention.

"I've been at my job since I was granted my first work permit when I was fifteen. Working my way up from housekeeping to cashier, then to customer service and, ultimately, department supervisor for women's apparel. I worked hard to prove to my bosses I had what it takes to attract the attention of their customers and help to turn a profit. I loved my job and everyone I worked with, considered all of them my family."

Avery picks the dress up by the top of the bodice, the look of longing covers her face and coaxes new tears to threaten to fall from her eyes. I send a side glance at Sarah, who face reads the same as mine. We choose to remain silent as Avery has time to confess her fears, telling the story that has been locked up inside, too consumed with the issues in Cole's world to voice the ones in hers.

"We got the word via a text message in the middle of the night, store closing in thirty days. No big meeting with our supervisor's, just five words typed out on a screen, sent to thousands of faceless people. Real families with mortgages and light bills, college tuitions and groceries to buy. What I assumed would be the worst, losing my job and only source of income, was only the beginning of a horrible nightmare. After I had helped them liquidate the inventory in the store, I began sending my resume to every store in the area. But with no way to call and confirm my previous employment, I had no proof of my worth. I haven't had a second interview in nearly two weeks. Now, I'm faced with paying my rent for the month or paying for my wedding. The worst part is, I can't bring myself to tell Cole I haven't found a dress yet."

Tears fall freely down her face, her hands still clutching the dress as her body jerks with her sobs. I'm starting to wonder if this dress is a beacon of bad luck as everyone who has touched it is rendered to a sobbing mess.

Sarah has reached her limit allowing the poor girl to cry alone as she pulls the dress from her fingers and wraps her in a motherly embrace, allowing all of the anguish the truth has released to hang in the air around us.

The store Avery had worked at was a member of a large chain. One I assumed was anchored in a long history of tradition and recognition. Their branding had been some of the industries best. Somehow they had been unable to evolve into the cyber age, trailing behind some of the smaller box stores who hired fresh-faced kids to make them marketable and rise with the times. I will admit to taking advantage of the rock bottom prices they advertised for display racks and hangers, wanting to save as much money as I could in hopes of spreading my grant money as far as it could go.

"You know something, Avery?"

Lifting the edges of the lace sleeve, trying to focus on defeating the tension around me, instead of the flood of memories trying desperately to clog my throat with too much emotion, forcing me to join the crying-fest before me.

"Last night when I was closing up, I noticed this dress had been in the display window for longer than it was supposed to be and I needed to add it to the next shipment for Horizons."

Grasping a hanger from under the counter, I carefully slide the edge into the neck of the dress, taking extra time to avoid damaging the dress. Moving my focus from the delicate material, unable to hide the hint of joy in my eye as I center in on her cautious face.

"Then you come in and remind me, not only of this oversight but of a position I have yet to fill at Horizons."

The first time I'd helped someone with an article of clothing, making them stand a little taller and prouder, it had been like a shot of heroine for me, trapping me in this addicting state of paying-it-forward. Offering to employ Avery as manager of the Center had the possibility of changing her life, not only monetarily, but by giving her a taste of the satisfaction of helping others.

"I need someone who can organize the floor, give instructions to the other workers as well as the few volunteers we have signed up.

Someone who can come over here a couple of times a week to pick up new merchandise and put it into the hands of those in need."

Sarah's arms remained snuggly around Avery's shoulders, a watery smile on each of their faces.

"The clothes aren't new, but if you're interested in the job, we would love to have you on our team."

The lack of a wedding dress was forgotten for the moment, tears of sorrow morphing into tears of joy. Avery cleared the space between us, skirting around the corner and tackling me full on with her appreciation.

"You won't regret this, I swear it." She promised, rocking the pair of us back and forth. Our bodies feeling lighter from the beams of hope I had started.

"I have no doubt you will do an excellent job." Untangling her arms from around me, I wiped away a single tear, which had managed to slip out in the excitement. "How about you take care of this dress for me and give it to someone who has a need for it?"

Sarah grabbed Avery, shoving her into the dressing room to check for sizing and proper hemlines. I messaged Meredith with the news we had a full staff including a manager with a lifetime of experience. Avery left the shop no longer feeling like the weight of the world was sitting on her shoulders, with a new dress wrapped carefully in a garment bag trailing behind her and an appointment to be back at this shop by seven-thirty tomorrow morning.

Today was destined to be busy as it was the last Friday before the annual Dine In event on base. A night where young couples with small children could enjoy a meal while their children were cared for, all free of charge. It marked six weeks until the coveted Khaki Ball, where the higher-ranking active duty wives dressed to the nines and got, what Sarah describes as, white-girl wasted. I took her word for it, as I've never had a reason to attend.

Normally, Sarah was polite and complimentary, ready to help anyone who walked through the door. However, with her new pregnancy and the hormones I could feel from across the room, she had apparently used all of her charms on Avery. Gone was Comforting and

Understanding Sarah, in her place was Raging Bitch Sarah, who would tell you in no uncertain terms the absolute truth, not giving two shits if you're feelings were left bleeding and battered on the floor.

Three young ladies had ventured in, shopping for the miracle dress and had each found a possibility. Girl number one, who I've labeled as 'Oh my, God girl', because in the six and a half minutes she has been looking in the mirror, she had said it fifteen times. She was a size two, with legs to die for and definitely the self-imposed ringleader of the group, speaking for *all* the girls.

Girl number two, 'Cell girl', as she'd had her damn phone glued to her ear since she walked in and hadn't said a word. I'll give her a pass though, if I had a friend like 'Oh my, God girl', I'd zone out on my cell too.

Girl number three, I assume is the new girl in the group, she was by far the prettiest in the bunch, but I've labeled her Gullible as her friends were trying to convince her the hot pink mini-dress they found was perfect for her. First, the dress was a double zero and wasn't going to fit the majority of the population on the planet, much less this chick.

Enter pregnant Sarah, walking out of her sewing room. "Oh, no! Girl, that dress is all wrong for you."

"Excuse me?" 'Oh my God girl' responded.

"Oh, don't play stupid! You and I both know that dress will barely cover her ass and she'll be the girl everyone whispers about."

"Don't listen to her, Lisa. She probably wants the dress for herself."

"No, Lisa, listen to me. I don't give two shits if you buy the dress or not, but your so-called 'friend' over here, wants you to wear it so she can talk shit about you behind your back." Sarah took the dress from Lisa and tossed it to 'Oh my God girl'.

"Here, if you like it so much, you wear it."

She went to the back of the store and brought out a gorgeous *Chanel* wrap-dress. "Try this on and see if I'm right."

Pissed off, 'Oh my God girl' tossed the pink dress on the floor at Sarah's feet.

"Oh, hell no! You better pick it up and hang it back on the rack."

The look Sarah gave her could have ended World War III. 'Oh my God girl' quickly picked up the dress and hung it back on the hanger. Lisa emerged from the dressing room and holy shit, she looked like a dream. The dress fit her like it was made for her and the smile on her face was priceless.

Once the girls were out the door with dresses in hand, I let loose the laugh I had held in. With the triplets safely in their car, I locked up the shop and shut off the lights.

* * *

Early the next morning, hours before the sun made a decision to rise or hide behind the clouds, my store was full of reporters, friends, and board members. Meredith came in late last night, she and Weston looking incredible as ever. The Forbes' possessed the ability to take any question head on and look fresh as the driven snow, no matter how much dirt the local paper wanted to toss their way. Mona stood among the press, her judgy eyes shooting daggers at Meredith. It was comical, watching the envy swallow Mona up, her flower boxes would never bring her a spread in People magazine. Even her attempts at photo bombing backfired, when a wayward cup of coffee went flying in her direction, its owner remaining a mystery.

Josh brought his wife and children. They arrived just as we were loading into the back of the limo, a jab at Mona I suspected, as they were brought in last minute. Amanda flanked my right side, nearly out of breath as she ended a call on her cell phone.

Kissing my cheek, "That's from Ross. He told me to tell you how proud he is and wishes he could have been here for you."

My breath caught in my chest, "When did you talk with Ross?"

Amanda was in the process of refreshing her lipstick, the applicator gliding over her bottom lip, leaving a polished shine in its wake.

"Last night, and again this morning."

Rubbing her lips together, spreading the gloss to her upper lip, she sends me a toothy smile and tosses the wand back into her purse.

Clearing my throat, a distraction to mask my disappointment. I had checked my email practically every minute in the last twenty-four hours, praying to hear even a short hello from Logan, but had come up empty every time. I'd rationalized the lack of correspondence to be from a communication freeze, something I'd experienced on a number of occasions. But with Ross's well wishes, my heart broke a little.

"Weston, love, didn't you say Logan sent you something last night?"

Meredith and Weston had climbed into the limo, giving a few last quotes to reporters who had traveled across the country to cover this event. Weston had removed a small tablet from his jacket as soon as the car began to move. Without looking up from his screen, dark glasses poised on the end of his nose.

"Yes, I did. He returned an email I'd sent him regarding Senator Green's phone call last week."

My belly filled with dread and with trembling fingers, I swiped the screen of my phone, my heart crumbling as I stared at an empty mailbox.

Chapter Nineteen

LOGAN

Red and white stripes, in perfect alignment drape over the coffin of Kevin Ramsey as it rolls down the conveyor belt of the airplane. White stars on a deep blue background come to rest directly in front of me. The American flag, a symbol of pride and honor, led the way to our fallen teammates final resting place.

The seven of us stand at attention, deep blue, crisp uniforms flanking each side of the mahogany coffin. Fellow passengers were asked to remain seated as I exited the plane in reverent silence. I take notice of the tear-stained faces pressed against the glass from the waiting area above, grief for a faceless man they will never know.

Reaper and Viper are the first to grasp the silver handle. White-gloved hands moving in unison to bring the coffin off the conveyer belt, and closer to the waiting hearse. Havoc and Ghost are next, as award metals move in the wind, the roar of the plane's engines drowning out the clang. Chief stands opposite me, his solemn face matching mine, as the silver handle comes into view. I watch as my own gloved hand reaches out to join the others, Ramsey's coffin now in our reverent hands. Diesel stands at the top of the coffin, his cover obscuring his face.

"Forward face."

I can barely hear Viper call out the command, but we've been a team so long it is more of a formality than a necessity. Using the ball of my right foot and the heel of my left, I drop my left hand and pivot to the left.

My heart is heavy as I place the edge of the coffin onto the guide at the opening of the hearse, the metal catching and allowing us to glide Ramsey into the back. From the corner of my eye, I notice the driver standing at attention, his arm raised to the edge of his brow in a salute, eyes fixed in the distance showing his respect.

We climbed into the waiting limo, an arrangement I asked my father to help me schedule. When the Red Cross returned the call confirming Ramsey's brother would not be allowed out of prison, nor had the funds to arrange a proper burial, I had less than two hours to pack my gear and get myself, and Ramsey's remains, on a cargo flight out, breaking my cell phone in my rush to get ready.

Kincaid helped me pack, offering to tell Harper I was on my way. Just as I was about to climb into the truck, I caught his attention and told him not to say anything to Harper, I wanted to surprise her. Viper had been available to come to Arlington, making the final arrangements for the honor guard and Chaplain. We all agreed, Ramsey deserved a funeral with honor and respect.

Being back in the States, something I had wanted with everything in me for months, seemed lackluster without Harper beside me. I'd nearly caved and called her several times, but I reminded myself I wanted to see the look on her face as I walked into her store.

Looking into the face happy face of Viper, the beautiful Kennedy at his side, I knew it would all be worth it. While I didn't have the closeness they shared with Harper, I was damned determined to get there.

"Hey, man."

Viper untangles himself from Kennedy's arms and moves in my direction. With an outstretched hand and determined look on his face, he leaves no room for doubt to fill the small space between us, that he has something he wants to discuss.

"I heard some bullshit story about you taking off with a Hummer belonging to Aarash."

"Something like that."

In all the hurried planning of this trip, I'd nearly forgot to speak with Zach about what we uncovered in Aarash's fortress.

"I'm glad you brought it up, though. We found something much more interesting, something you need to know about."

Zach's face contorted in worry as I told him about the files Aarash had in his possession. The amount of detailed information he had on each of us.

"You know, I've wracked my brain trying to figure out how he knew about my brother."

"I wish I could tell you how he got it. All I can say for certain is he won't be able to do anything with the information or causing any more problems for anyone."

"Oh, trust me, I'm thankful as fuck. But—" Zach tips his head to the side as his mouth contorts into a frown. "I still would have loved to wrap my hands around his neck until the truth came tumbling out as to who fed him the intel."

"Has to be someone on the inside."

We snap our head simultaneously in Ryan's direction. His eyes flashing between Zach and myself as he rocks back and forth on his heels.

"It's the only thing that makes any sense. He has the funds to pay someone in the right position for the type of information he had on this team."

Neither of us wants to imagine someone in Washington selling us out to a murderous prick like Aarash, but we've all seen how corrupt men can become when money is dangled before them. Those black-souled bastards crave power more than doing what is right.

After the last shovel of dirt had been tossed into the grave, we make our way to the parking lot where Diesel's family waited patiently. Two tall men stood on either side of him, muscular and built, much like Diesel, each with their own defining characteristics.

"Hey, Doc. I want you to meet my brothers."

"We're not in the desert anymore, Chase. Logan will be all right." His mega-watt smile comes out as his hands find his hips. Switching his feet back and forth, bouncing on the balls of his feet.

"Logan, this is my oldest brother Dylan." The largest of the three leans over, extending his hand in my direction. Dylan is my height, but if I had to guess, about thirty pounds lighter than me. It's clear he spends a fair amount of time in the gym, but is nowhere close to my muscle mass.

"Pleasure to meet you, man."

"This is my middle brother, Austin."

I'd heard about this one, some goddamn computer genius who has broken through every firewall ever put before him. Where Dylan has an edge of ruggedness, the same hard edges Chase has, Austin uses his brain over his brawn. Not that he is soft, the opposite is true, his build is solid, yet less so than his brothers.

"Logan Forbes graduated in the top three percent from BUD/S training. One of twelve physicians allowed to engage in combat operations outside of search and rescue."

His knowledge of my history didn't surprise me; hell the man was a master of the internet.

"Nice to meet you, Austin. Should I be worried you know my credit score too?" I joked, everyone joining in as the lightness of the moment helped to quiet the flurry of emotions around us.

"What this I hear about you going to Twenty-Nine Palms?" Ghost nudges me from my left, "Haven't you had enough sand and shit?"

Glancing back to Austin, his arm now around a beautiful girl I suspect is his wife, Lainie. "You got this one?" I tease, cocking an inquisitive eyebrow in his direction.

"I'm thinking the same thing he is." Nodding his head in Ryan's direction.

Taking a step back, needing room to collect my thoughts and the ability not to sound like a douche. "Remember when we were on the hill, listening to those Boots talk about warm pussy?"

My eyes flash to Lainie, unaccustomed to having female ears

around when I spoke with my team. "Sorry." I back peddle, but she rolls her eyes and snuggles into Austin's side.

"When you brought the mail over, Zach got a letter from Kennedy and I got one from Harper Kincaid, introducing herself. I assumed it was a mistake, but it turned out to be the best thing to ever happen to me."

Ryan nodded his head as Zach placed a kiss to the forehead of the girl standing beside him. How incredible was it to think all this happiness originated from a single mailbag.

"Harper and I have been exchanging emails and almost daily Skype sessions, building a friendship that has become a monogamous relationship. When I found out I was headed to Twenty-Nine Palms, I couldn't do it. I couldn't be so close and yet so far from the girl who has my shit wrapped around her little finger. So, I swallowed my fucking pride and made a phone call, cashing in a favor from a family friend. I'll still have to serve my remaining time, but it will be in Norfolk, Virginia, and not the fucking desert of California."

"Wait a fucking minute." Aiden interrupts, his hand gripping my right shoulder hard enough to make me wince if I'd chosen to let him see me, which I didn't. "Mr. Honor and Commitment did something selfish for once?" Exchanging a look with him, considering my answer carefully before letting it run free, once it's out there I will be unable to take it back.

"I love her."

Letting my admission hang in the air, the sound of my honesty settling well within my soul. Falling for Harper was effortless, her generosity and ability to love those around her called to me, pulling me into a place I have no desire ever to leave.

"Holy shit!" Aiden shouts, thrusting his head back in laughter. "Harper Kincaid is a goddamn miracle worker."

After a round of congratulations from my team, we make a firm plan to go forward with our mercenary for hire business. With the exception of Havoc, we all lived fairly close to one another. Alex made it clear he would not be leaving Florida anytime soon, his mother's plans to marry him off getting closer to reality. Aiden wanted to go and enjoy a beer, but I had a four-hour drive ahead of me.

"Sorry, man, I've waited months to meet her. With some careful planning, and my father's help, I will get to see her beautiful face in less than twenty-four hours." My dad was keeping me informed as to how Harper was doing.

"Any more trouble out of that guy you had me follow?"

"I haven't spoken to Harper in a few days. With Ramsey's death we went into River City. By the time it was lifted, I was boarding a plane home."

"You let me know if he starts any shit. I can be there in a few hours."

After giving Aiden and my team my word I would be in touch, Dylan and Austin started sharing the files on the latest requests for our teams help. The amount of money being offered for our services is absolutely ridiculous. Zach explained there was a need for men willing to ignore the rules of polite society. As SEALs, we didn't have any.

* * *

My need to see Harper clouded my better judgment to follow the speed limit between Arlington and Norfolk. Pulling into town much later than I had planned, her shop was closed for the day and the apartment above dark as a tomb. I stood on the sidewalk, taking in the stores around her, smiling as I saw the candy shop across the street and the salon where Amanda and Stacy worked. Ross had boasted about how the sidewalks rolled up as the sun dipped behind the horizon. The smallness of this section of the city, refusing to change with the new age.

Continuing down the street, the center of the city was illuminated by replica turn-of-the-century street lamps, their warm light chasing the dark shadows from delicate flowers, which surround a statue in the center of the square. A pair of stray cats riffled through a nearly full trash can, looking for what I would imagine were scraps of food. A subtle reminder I needed to find some food for myself, as the last time I ate was an MRE on the cargo plane.

My father selected a hotel far enough away from Chesapeake I wouldn't accidentally run into Harper, yet close enough I wouldn't have to fight the traffic Norfolk is famous for. Once inside my room, I changed out of my uniform and ordered room service. The polite lady behind the desk had handed me the package my father said he would send. Inside I found a new cell phone and bank cards, as well as some cash. It had been so long since I've needed these things, but I intended to take care of my girl. There was a note tucked around the cash, and I recognize my father's script.

I want to go on the record as saying I advised you to call her when you arrive. -Dad

After inhaling the first rare steak I've enjoyed in months, I climbed into a shower with endless hot water, letting the force of it redden my skin. I watched the water swirling around the drain in the bottom of the tub, taking with it the final remnants of the desert. I didn't bother to put any clothes on, as there was zero chance of a corpsman dragging me out of this bed for an emergency. Sliding between the crisp sheets, the soft give of the mattress extracting a sigh from my lips. With my hands behind my head, the firm pillows coaxing the sleep to take over sending me into dreams filled with Harper joining me in my bed, her hands appreciating every inch of me.

An alarm on my phone brings me out of the dream, just as I'm about to taste the juncture of Harper's thighs I've envisioned for months, creating the fantasy inside my head I used to release the tension in my brief shower back in Afghanistan. Today, I will get to see her, touch the skin of her face I've craved to all this time. Today, I would see for myself if her lips taste as sweet as I imagine they do.

When I thought of how I wanted Harper to see me for the first time, I recalled the first letter I received from her and the paragraph where she dispelled any officer and a gentleman notion I may have accused her of. Today, I will give her a reality, a new chapter in her world she can share with our grandchildren, a moment so incredible Hollywood will have a bidding war to own the rights.

As I finish shaving, the last one I will do for a while, as Harper prefers my 'sexy stubble'. I have to maintain regulations while I wear this uniform, but once I hang it in our closet, I'll make sure my girl has all the stubble she wants. My phone chimes with a message and I see Josh has sent me something. Opening the attachment, I see a picture of my girl standing beside my mother, her smile front and center as she shakes the hand of who I recognize as the Governor of Virginia and old admirer of my mother, Frank Borland. With the way, he appreciates Harper's chest, his taste in a younger woman hasn't changed, despite his run in with a jealous husband a few years ago. Motherfucker is barking up the wrong tree with my girlfriend.

Just as I was about to get into my rental car, my phone alerted me of another message, this time from my father. Harper is sitting in the back of a car, Amanda on one side and my mother on the other. Her face is breaking around the edges, sadness filling those beautiful eyes I loved to get lost in. Her hands are clenched in her lap; a black cell phone lay abandoned against the light fabric of her dress.

She knows communication was restored a few days ago and how I've been in contact with you by email. I stand by what I said earlier, this is going to come back to haunt you. -Dad

Tossing my phone to the passenger seat, I backed out of the spot and headed toward my future. A few blocks from the address I was given for Horizons, I had to park my car as the line to get to the event was endless. Finding a spot at the side of a convenience store, I locked the car and take off at a run, ignoring the thought of how much dirt was collecting on my white shoes. I could toss these and have plenty of time to order new ones, the next time I would need them would be the last day I wore a uniform.

Stepping around a number of people, calling 'excuse me' over my shoulder as I bumped into far more than I cared for. I could see in the distance the platform Josh told me to look for. Keeping as much of me hidden in the crowd as I could, not wanting Harper to see me before it was time. I notice to my left are a couple of tall guys and I slip as close as possible without being creepy. Two older ladies stand to my right, ignoring everyone around them as they watch my mother and Harper take their seats on the platform.

"She looks just like her mother."

"She may look like her, but she has the heart of her father."

Ross had given me the email address to reach Bruce Kincaid, but I preferred to sit down with him face to face. Once I introduced my lips to Harper's, I would plan a meeting between the families. Let Bruce see the kind of man his daughter had chosen.

Josh scanned the crowd as he took his place behind the podium, which I will admit was quite impressive. With all of these people here on such a beautiful morning, it was clear Harper had touched more lives than I ever imagined.

"Ladies and gentlemen, on behalf of the Reece International and the Forbes family, I would like to welcome you to the dedication of the new Horizons Center. Some years ago, a young woman we all know and love, took an idea she read about in a magazine, and brought it to life. Taking those principles and put them into a charity that has helped thousands. But she didn't stop there, not only did she help the citizens of this community, she dedicated herself to reaching across the oceans and into the deserts and jungles of other countries, sending a number of our single military men and women care packages during the holidays. Many would have stopped there, satisfied with the accomplishment of bringing a smile to the face of so many, but not Harper Kincaid. She continued to go above and beyond, adopting one of those recipients and sending additional care packages during the year. Building friendships and ironically bringing two people together, who might never have met if it wasn't for the giving spirit of one woman. Recently, the board of directors of Reece International learned of this courageous young lady and her mission to clothe her community, unanimously voting to pledge their support for a minimum of five years."

Just as Josh turns his body to look behind him, clapping along with the crowd as Harper's tight smile curls at the edges, he catches my eye but doesn't stop his progression. My focus flashes back to my girl, and the smile she is struggling to hold on to. I've seen this face on her once before when she discovered Goodman in my room, naked and lying through her teeth. I didn't like it then, and I fucking hate it now.

"I've had the pleasure of working for Reece International for a number of years, traveling alongside the wonderful woman who is going to say a few words before we proceed to the ribbon cutting and let you all have a look at what we've done to the inside of the building behind me."

My mother tugs at the edge of her skirt, the kind smile I've known my entire life gracing her face. Her left hand is clenched around her note cards, a waste of good paper since she always memorizes what she is going to say. I never thought I would ever meet a woman with the same values as my mother, someone with the same passion she does for those around her, until I met Harper.

The original plan was to wait until Harper took her place behind the podium, thanking everyone for coming and cut the yellow ribbon. But seeing how unhappy she is, how hard she is working to maintain what little smile she managed to paint on those lips, my feet decide the original plan sucks, and the rest of my body agrees. When I chose to be in her life, to stand by her side and protect her, I also accepted the challenge of making her happy. Clearly, my heart was in the right place, with good and honorable intentions. My delivery and inability to take the advice of a man, who had been married to the love of his life longer than I've been alive, was where I failed.

Working my way to the front of the crowd, I toss more of those apologies out to the strangers around me as I zigzag my way forward. I'm halfway to my target as my mother turns on her social graces. She may have been born and raised in Manhattan, but she can charm the pants off anyone. This crowd is no different as a collective cheer breaks out as she mentions the home team's football mascot.

Josh finds my attention once again, a deep wrinkle of confusion forming between his eyebrows. I motion to the side of the platform where the metal stairs leading up to the platform are. But there are three people in wheelchairs blocking my path, a little boy with a chocolate candy bar standing behind the one closest to me and I decide against taking a chance the chocolate won't end up all over my white uniform.

My only option is the jump up on stage directly in front of the podium, interrupting my mother's speech and possibly pissing her off. My need to change the fake smile on Harper's face to a real one, over-rules my avoidance of upsetting my mother. And as I increase my steps, gaining the needed momentum to propel my frame onto the wood of the platform and get as little dirt as possible on my uniform, my mother shifts her eyes and catches me.

Landing with a thud, the metal supports bouncing enough to sway the flag in the background. Dusting off my hands as I reach my full height, and then right my cover back in place. I stand quite a bit taller than my mother, even with the height of her heeled shoes. It's been awhile since we have seen one another in person, and by the smile on her face, I won't be begging for forgiveness in interrupting her speech.

Wrapping my arms around my mother, kissing her cheek and breathing in the scent of her perfume. I lean over and begin speaking into the microphone.

"Ladies and gentleman, you will have to pardon my interruption. My name is Logan Forbes," a loud gasp sounds from behind me, I don't have to turn around to know it came from Harper.

"And I have traveled a long way to be here today to celebrate this momentous occasion and honor one of the most generous women I know."

Smiling down at my mother, a quick kiss on her forehead, "My mother set the bar high for the woman I trusted with my heart. Her constant reminder of how to treat others, especially the less fortunate, as you want to be treated is something I have carried with me."

Unable to continue being this close to Harper and not touch her, I pulled away from my mother, and made my way toward the woman who had changed my life in a few short months. Seeing her beautiful face on my computer screen failed to show me the depth of her beauty. Her peaches and cream skin lacked even a single freckle, a product of avoiding the rays of the sun. Those almond shaped eyes, full of wonderment and disbelief shining brightly in my favorite kaleidoscope of blue hews. Her kissable pink lips, glistening from her lips gloss, one of the few vanities she allowed herself to have, and chocolate brown hair, streaks of healthy shine cascading down nearly every strand, giving her an angelic glow. She is breathtaking and so much more than I deserve, yet I cannot help but to fall further in love with her.

"Logan?"

My heart flips as my name leaves her lips, goosebumps take up residence on the flesh of my arms. From the first moment I heard her voice, I found myself anxious to hear it again, to memorize how her laughter sounds as it echoes in the room. I longed to taste her breath as she whispers her affection across my lips, bathing in the intimate way she calls me as she gives into my need to love her.

"Hey, beautiful."

My words are lacking, hollow even to my ears. She is so much more than beautiful, more incredible than any sonnet ever written. She is perfect, so motherfucking perfect.

"How?" She starts and I shake my head, reaching over to help her up from her chair. Calmness floods my body when my fingers touch the silkiness of her hands. I lack the control to maintain a proper distance between us, shielding the hundreds of spectators from being able to feel the love I have for her.

"I've waited so long," my eyes shifting between hers, feasting on the essence of her: the way her hair dances in the breeze. Most of all, I delight in the sliver of a smile growing ever so slowly as she realizes I've covertly decreased the distance between us. My hands travel up her arms, framing her delicate face as I clear the final inch, covering her lips with mine. I've kissed my fair share of women, some I liked enough to kiss a second time, while others I turned away and moved on to the next. Had I kissed this gorgeous creature first, I know beyond a reasonable doubt, I would never have stopped.

She is hesitant at first, her hands trembling against the skin of my arms, feeding the cockiness I've perfected over the years, using it to my advantage on numerous occasions. I don't give her an opportunity to second-guess this, my possessive inner core roaring to the forefront, claiming this beautiful creature as mine. Rubbing my thumbs over her cheekbones and pressing the tips of my fingers into the soft flesh behind her ears, I adjust the angle, deepening the kiss.

I nearly rejoice the moment she lets go of her hesitation, moaning into my mouth and parting her lips. Her nails dig into my skin, and I relish in the pain, which travels straight to my fucking cock. Her eagerness is catching up to mine as her fingers move up my arms landing at the skin on the back of my neck. Tucking a few fingers under my collar, she presses into the muscles there, silently telling me she wants this as badly as I do.

The majority of me is lost in this kiss, drowning in the love I have for her, with no desire to stop until she has forgotten her name. The SEAL in me is keenly aware of the crowd behind me, of my parents huddled together ecstatic with joy as they see how happy I am. When Harper lets her chest relax into mine, I know she has surrendered to the moment, ignoring the catcalls resonating around us. As badly as I want to stay in this moment, I love her enough to push my need for her aside and let her enjoy the reason everyone is gathered here.

Detaching my lips from hers, taking into account my level of control is a thread higher than hers; I take a half a step back, keeping her face in my hands, locking eyes with hers. Our breathing is labored, and her eyes are speckled with confusion. I have so many things to clear up, to remind her I the same man who swore to make her happy.

"Totally worth flying coach."

Harper blinks several times, her pupils dilate but as reality begins to set in she shifts focus from my face to the smiling faces around us.

"I'm sorry, what?" Her voice is shaky but sexy as fuck, and I wonder if she sounds like this when she first wakes up.

Unable to resist, I lean over and place a peck to her lips. "I said, kissing you was worth a cramped seat in coach."

"You didn't call. You always call or email."

"I know, I'm sorry." Looking over my shoulder, suspecting the novelty of the moment is wearing thin with my mother. "I'll explain everything later, when there aren't as many people around." Taking her hand in mine, such a tiny gesture but it's rocking my world. Josh pulls a chair from around the side of the platform, sitting it beside Harper's. Laying my right arm along the back of her chair, my fingers caressing the sliver of skin at her neck. The left is sandwiched between both of hers, our fingers interlaced. As I glance down at her, I'm elated to see the smile I've kept in my memory, the one I've claimed was made for me.

Harper leans into me as my mother continues her speech, sharing the story of how she initially came to Chesapeake to see for herself the woman who had captured my attention. As she prepared for the interrogation as she called it, gaining a round of laughter from the crowd, she found Harper to be much like herself: selfless and humble. I watched as heads nodded in agreement, blue haired ladies whispering to one another as they point to Harper. Out of habit, I surf the crowd, counting the number of men versus women, looking for anything or anyone unusual. A man sitting in the second row halts my perusal, deep-set eyes shooting daggers at me, the same eyes Ross and Harper shared.

Bruce Kincaid, possibly the biggest hurdle I had to face in dating his daughter. Ross had warned me his distrust of any man who came snooping around his only daughter, Lance Ranoka sitting at the top of the list. Mentally, I was ready for anything he could throw my way and physically I would show him how I had her happiness at the top of my priority list. While I knew it wouldn't be an easy task, I'd had years of training under my belt. If all else fails, I have a reference from someone he does respect, Ross.

The energy around us buzzed as the next speaker stood and took his turn behind the microphone. Josh gave the mayor all of three minutes to remind the citizens how he had watched Harper grow and create such a successful business, giving her the tutelage she used to make her shop so successful. I knew Harper was up next, Josh had emailed me the itinerary along with a few details involving the people

I would encounter today. Nothing pushes a man off-kilter more than someone knowing who they are and something about them when they have never been introduced.

"Our final speaker needs no introduction. She is the local girl who has shown more kindness to others in the past year than most people do in a lifetime."

Chapter Twenty

HARPER

Glancing out over the crowd, I see the smiling faces of my friends and neighbors looking back at me. Having Logan emerge, dressed in his whites and carrying the smile I'd pretended was reserved for me was enough to make the nervous butterflies fluttering around in my stomach vanish into thin air. Looking into his eyes, face to face and not through the filter of a computer screen, they captivated and enchanted me. His irises are so blue they are nearly white and are making my body take notice, any inhibitions take a back seat to what I wanted from him. Logan took charge, kissing me as if his life depended on it, showing me how it felt to be kissed by a man who not only knew how, but wanted to.

Sitting beside him, absorbing his warmth and the way his masculine scent surrounded me, blanketing me in a calmness that was foreign, yet comfortable. Relishing the way his fingers left a fire in their wake, as his gently glided them up and down the edge of my neck and arm, heating me to a point I wanted to straddle him, not caring if everyone watched.

"Hey, Y'all." Grasping the podium tightly, not because I was nervous or afraid to be standing here, but to keep me rooted long enough to say what I needed to say.

"I had a speech ready several days ago," picking up my notecards, I grip them between my fingers and with a firm tug ripped them in half, tossing the torn ends behind me. "But you guys don't need to be reminded of who is responsible for all of this or why we're here. I will say thank you to Dr. and Mrs. Forbes for venturing down south, even if it was to size me up." Craning my head over my right shoulder, sending a wink in Meredith's direction.

"And to Josh, for giving me fair warning what the Forbes family was capable of, especially Logan." I hear a unified rumble of snickers from some of the people before me. My eyes scan the crowd, landing first on my father who is trying to look intimidating in Logan's eyes, yet failing miserably, but I will give him credit.

Valerie Forbes sat in the third row, fanning her hand over her face and winking at me when she caught my eye. Somehow the reminder of how incredible Logan looked sitting in his chair didn't strike me as creepy, even with the close relationship they had.

"Thank you again, to Reece International for their generosity. Now let's go cut a ribbon and eat some cake."

Mrs. Dorchester, who owned the cake shop at the end of the block, had told anyone who would listen how the sweet and beautiful Meredith Forbes had phoned her personally, boasting about how she had heard from her New York society people that *Donna's Donuts and More* was the best bakery they had ever sampled. I don't know who she was trying to impress as most folks around here had never heard of Meredith to begin with, much less what high society was.

Strong arms surround me as the crowd applauds in appreciation of free cake. Connie Dorchester would have gotten more points had she skipped the society bit and gone straight to free sugar.

"Come on, I've arranged for seven minutes where we won't be missed." Logan doesn't wait for me to agree as he scoops me up bridal style and tears off down the steps, into the back seat of a waiting car.

Not a second separates the time between the sound of the door closing and Logan pressing his body to mine, lips firm and demanding taking control, cutting off the giggles which bubbled out of my chest without my permission. His hands trap my face, holding it firmly so he can explore my mouth with his tongue, rubbing his thigh against mine in tune with the talents of his tongue.

"My God, Harper, I can't wait to tear you up in the bedroom, and then cook you up something mouthwatering the next morning."

With his lips buried in my neck, his hot breath cascades over my skin. His voice is deep and drenched with wanton need. Parts of me want to hear more, getting lost in his description of how he would 'tear me up', leaving me a sweating and satisfied mess, only to pamper me in the morning with his refined culinary skills. But the rational and inquisitive parts, want answers as to why he chose to call everyone else but me and let them know he was safe. The logical thinkers, solidly getting me through unscathed when my past relationships fell apart, they remind me Logan is still a relative stranger to me. A man who has lacked female attention for who knows how long, telling me I should know better than to believe any sweet words which fall from his lips.

A knock on the window negates my need to refuse him, or any further exploration of my lack of defenses when it comes to Logan.

"Goddamn it."

He swears as he places his forehead against mine. His breathing comes out in labored pants, the hard muscles of his chest and arms slightly relaxing as he lets out a strangled breath. Pulling back as the knock sounds again, a deep growl escapes from his throat.

"Okay, let's give my mother her time to do what she does, eat some dry cake and shake some hands. However, the second the last smile fades, I'm whisking you off to a nice dinner including copious amounts of good wine to help relax the anger I know you're harboring against me right now."

His statement is bold and sobering, and as he leans away from me, I catch a glimpse of the position I allowed myself to be placed in. I was blinded by the carnal need of a handsome man, one who clearly took what he wanted, accustomed to following the rules he set for himself. Righting my skirt, which had risen to the top of my thigh, the lace edge of my panties on display all to see. Daring a glance into his face, his eyes are indeed on the area I had covered; a raised brow and cheeky smile tell me all I need to know.

Josh stands with his back to the opened car door, hands on hips bunching his jacket in the back. Logan offers his hand to assist me out of the car, his elongated fingers wrapping around my much smaller ones. I expect him to separate our hands when my feet touch the pavement, instead, he intertwines our fingers and pulls me close to him.

"Harper, Meredith wants Sarah and Avery to stand with you as the two of you cut the ribbon."

Tossing a look over his shoulder, noticing our clasped hands he looks back at Logan, a knowing look shared between them.

"You, my friend, are in a fair amount of hot water with your mother."

Logan pulls my hand to his lips, gently placing a kiss on my skin, "Completely worth it."

My heart skips a beat as I take him in. Tan skin a by-product of the time he has spent in the sun. His cover rides against his eyebrows, calling attention to the blue orbs I can't help but get lost in. Dark hair, freshly cut by the looks of it, a deep contrast between his skin and the white of his uniform. Sharp chin freshly shaved, something I'm not certain if I will have to get used to. With his unannounced arrival, for an uncertain duration, I'm not sure about anything right now.

Weston waves us over, Meredith is like a different person with the cameras on. Several big time news agencies patiently wait for their turn to ask questions. Sarah and Avery are posed at the edge of a red carpet, all smiles and wide eyes at the sight of Logan and I approaching, our hands clasped and bodies close enough to dispel any question of what is going on between us.

Avery begins to vibrate in her heels, the dark curls falling over her shoulders bounce from the force of it all. Meredith ends the interview, turning to face us, an approving smile crosses her lips, with her arms folded against her chest in an attempt to be intimidating. While she has never struck me as a person to fear, Logan has increased the speed and length of his steps, causing me to nearly trip as I try to keep up.

"Logan Marshall Forbes!"

Meredith's raised voice calls across the pavement, her smile falling into a severe frown. Her flawless forehead bows slightly but not a single wrinkle dares to show its face.

"Slow your steps, you're gonna cause her to trip and fall."

Logan immediately stops, looks from me to Meredith, "I could pick her up and carry her if you're really concerned." Weston hides a laugh behind a cough and a well-placed fist, while Meredith shoots him the same shameful look she shared with Logan. Not wanting to call any more attention to the situation than there already is, I step around Logan, ignoring his attempt to pull me back, and drag him with half-hearted effort to where the rest of them are standing. Flashes from the cameras startle me, nearly making me miss the edge of the carpet. Logan steps in behind me, lifting me at the waist without breaking his stride or alerting any attention to my near fumble.

"Hello, Logan." Meredith welcomes him with open arms. He bends down to embrace her as I step around the unit to stand beside a still excited Avery. Not having his hand in mine feels cold, despite the warmth of the bright sun shining down on us. I can still smell his cologne, masculine and fresh, the exact way I want a man to smell.

"I'm going out on a limb and assume this is *the* Logan Forbes."

Sarah had taken it upon herself to share the Lifetime Movie worthy story of how we met. Avery had practically sighed every third word as Sarah told her version of the events; minus the details I kept to myself.

"Yes, but don't ask me why he's here and not in Afghanistan. I had no idea he was considering a visit."

I ponder my own words, his appearance today was unexpected, and could explain his lack of contact with me in the past few days. Would his departure be just as quick, and secret?

"It's obvious why he's here." Bumping her shoulder against mine. "The question is," Avery looks around and then leans in close to my ear. "Why did you let him out of the back seat of that truck?"

A hand on my shoulder pulls me away from the conversation I have no real desire to participate in. "Harper, we need to get this moving." Josh leans into the space between myself and Avery, his interruption welcomed and I say an internal 'thank you' for the save.

I followed Josh's instructions as to where he wanted me to stand, turned and twisted to make certain we created a perfect picture. With Meredith on my right and Sarah and Avery on my left, I smile until my face hurt and held the over-sized scissors hovering over a bright yellow ribbon until I was instructed to cut. When the applause began to die down, and the questions directed at Meredith started again, I chanced a glance at the people gathered. Many friends and fellow business owners came out in support. Some of them genuine, while others like Mona and the Mayors, were parts played in a game of keeping face.

Logan stood beside Weston, their heads leaning in one another's direction, no doubt discussing his plans for his visit, perhaps a stop in New York to catch up with the rest of his family there. I tried not to think of how short my time with him could possibly be.

"That fucking idiot!"

Snapping my head in Sarah's direction, shocked at her crude choice in words. Her eyes were narrowed into slits and locked on something deep in the crowd, anger visible in the crevices of her furrowed brow. Following her line of sight, I search for half a second when I see what has her so pissed off.

Lance stands in the center of the sidewalk, arms crossed and a smug look on his face. A combination of anger and fear seethe through my body, and it takes everything I am not to run across the parking lot and ask him what his issue is.

Movement to my right brings me back to Logan, who must have been watching the pair of us and is already halfway to where Lance is standing. I'm about to take a step, and somehow stop any unnecessary confrontation from taking place. Logan is bigger, taller and, no doubt, smarter than Lance and while I have no loyalty or affection for him, I don't want him to get hurt.

"Don't even think about it."

Sarah grips my arm, keeping me from moving forward. I watch with my heart in my throat as Logan approaches Lance, the crowd parting like the Red Sea to let him through. His white uniform, high-lighted by the sun, causing him to almost glow. The pair stand parallel to me and I can see each of their profiles clearly. Logan looks down on the much shorter Lance, who doesn't change his stance or look the slightest bit intimidated. Logan stands with feet apart, his hands at his side, and appears to be speaking quite calmly. With the exception of the movement of his cover, I don't suspect his words are heated.

Several seconds tick by and as I'm ready to let out the breath I've been holding, Logan raises his right hand, tapping his index and middle finger in the center of Lance's chest. I pull in a quick breath as Lance attempts to knock his fingers away, but the size difference makes it impossible. Suddenly, Lance tries to grip Logan's fingers, but faster than I can blink, Logan has his hand bent backward, causing Lance to cringe in pain. Logan lets him go with a shove, and then lowers his head to the same level. As Lance rights himself, clutching his injured hand against his chest, Logan steps back and begins to walk away. He makes it three steps when Lance says something I can't hear. Logan stops, turns slightly and responds in a crystal clear voice.

"Try it and see what I do, motherfucker."

Chapter Twenty-One

LOGAN

"I've reasoned with your mother about how you won't be on the plane back to New York with us later."

"Good to know, considering I haven't asked for permission to do anything from my mother in over ten years."

I highly doubt I will ever grow tired of looking at Harper. Taking in her graciousness as my father prattles on in my ear.

"Hey, I'm trying to help you here. The least you can do is show some gratitude."

Looking away from Harper, I shoot my dad a go to hell look. The smirk on his face lets me know this conversation is light.

"She understands, but insists you join us for dinner."

I'm about to contest him, let him know I have plans of my own when he raises his hand to stop me. "She assumed you would want to have some private time with Harper, but she won't budge. She has also invited Bruce to join us."

I've planned to have a conversation with Bruce, approach him like a man to prove I'm a good match for his only daughter. That conversation wasn't in the plans for tonight, maybe breakfast tomorrow. Tonight was slotted for me to come clean with my girl, letting her know I was here for good. Glancing back at Harper, I notice she and

Sarah have found something or someone upsetting. The look of anger on her face has my need to protect her working overtime, so I follow their line of sight until I see him. Not bothering to excuse myself from my father, the conversation I need to have is far more pressing than dinner plans. Aiden had shown me a grainy photo of him, taken with a cellphone from quite a distance, so I immediately recognized the source of their anger. I wouldn't do anything drastic to him here, nothing that would cause the gossipers to speak ill of Harper. I would, however, give him a clear warning to keep his distance from the woman I loved.

"Lance Ranoka!" I called out his name from a few feet away. Dressed in light jeans and a long sleeved t-shirt, a little warm considering the temperature outside, but nothing too alarming. His dark eyes flashed to mine, running up and down my stature in an attempt to jog his memory if he knew me.

"Maybe."

"Did that sound like a question? I didn't mean for it too, as I know who you are. What I can't figure out is," stopping less than eight inches from him, my first attempt at establishing dominance. He doesn't flinch or waver his eyes from mine, so I plant my feet and square my shoulders. I've worked out hardcore to be as broad as I am, using sheer size to intimidate on several occasions. "Why the fuck you think you have any business being here?"

His smile elongates and lips part showing a full set of white teeth, complete with a gap big enough to drive a Mack truck through the front. "You have me at a disadvantage, my friend. You know my name, but I'm afraid I don't recognize you."

"Your friend? Sorry, that is something we will never be. However, I'm going to give you a piece of advice, call it friendly if it makes you feel better."

Reducing the distance between us to less than a few inches, I use my index and middle finger to tap the area in the center of his chest. It's annoying as fuck but more than an enough to drive my point home.

"Stay."

"Far."

"Away."

"From Harper Kincaid!"

Enunciating each word with a jab of my fingers, and increasing the force with each word. Her last name leaves my mouth through clenched teeth, and he finally grows a set of fucking balls by reaching up and grabbing my hand.

"Or what?" He returns, spit flying out of his mouth and landing on his shirt. "You going to go all GI Joe on me, threaten me while your boyfriend holds me down?"

Flicking my wrist, I twist his fingers and arm contorting it backward, effectively hunching him over and yelping in pain.

"GI Joe is a fucking pussy." Twisting his wrist a little more and I can feel him start to shake from the pain. "Consider this your last warning. If I ever hear about you going near her, you'll become acquainted with the business end of my .45."

Releasing his hand, I shove him back slightly, just enough to send home my point. I don't want to go much further with this asshole, but I won't back down either. Taking two steps back, I tip my head at the older gentleman who is wearing a veterans hat standing just far enough to the side not to hear the words we've exchanged. With fluid precision, I turn on my heel and ball of my foot, ready to return to the conversation with my father. I catch Harper's' eyes, her intent gaze locked with mine. I'll need to add this to the list of shit I need to discuss with her. We'll have no secrets between us that aren't necessary for her safety.

"You can't keep me off a public street, or prevent me from talking to her when you're not around."

I stop dead in my tracks, taking a moment to swallow down the rage I feel brewing inside. Everything in me, all of my training and experience, labels Lance as an enemy who needs to be annihilated. I remind myself this isn't a mission, I can't take care of the problem without suffering consequences. I've made my point, and now it's time to let him fuck up. Lance doesn't strike me as the type to fade into the shadows, so it's only a matter of time.

"Try it and see what I do, motherfucker."

Not bothering to wait for a rebuttal, I continue my forward momentum to rejoin my father. Needing the distance to tamp down my anger, and gain the control I know is in there somewhere.

"Logan?"

My father eyes me cautiously, he had never been comfortable with the changes I'd had to undergo to become a SEAL. He worried I had sacrificed too much of the caring side of me to become a lethal weapon. He is now joined by Harper's father, the two of them sharing the same concerned look.

"Care to explain yourself?"

Harper's father is the same height as my own, his dark hair matching the shade I love so much on his daughter. While I owe the man a certain level of respect, I won't let him steamroll me about anything.

"Which part?"

"Don't assume I will bend to you as easily as that piece of scum. My son has shared the nature of your character, I expected a visit to my front door would have presented itself before the display the entire town witnessed."

"With all due respect, Sir, I won't apologize to anyone for the message I sent to the city and most importantly to Harper. I want every man to know she is with me, while every girl wants to be her. Should I have come to you first? Maybe, but things happened fast and honoring a fallen SEAL took precedence over pleasantries."

Bruce's rigid face softens, "My condolences on your friend," his voice cracks and I wonder where the emotion is coming from. "When do you have to head back to your base? I'd like to have a few words with you before you go."

"Let me speak with Harper, explain why I'm here and how long I'm staying."

Chances are I should have taken my father's advice and told Harper I was on my way, but I'm smart enough to know she will be even more upset than she is now if I speak with her family before her. I also need to contact my team, have Ryan get me a tracking device for Harper.

Lance had been right when he said I couldn't be with her every minute of the day. In a few weeks I would have to go back to work, and she had her own responsibilities.

"Logan Marshall."

I caught the smell of her perfume a tenth of a second before I heard her call my name. "When did you get into town and why didn't you tell your favorite aunt?" Dressed in yellow from head to toe, wearing a wide brim hat and her everyday pearls dangling past her waist. Aunt Valerie always commanded a crowd, either from her striking beauty or the bottom line of her checkbook.

Opening my arms wide, I move my head to the side to avoid that hat of hers, which needed its own zip code. "No one told me you would be here, otherwise I would have been looking for you." Aunt Valerie and I had a unique relationship. Where most women her age, my own mother included, tended to stick with activities which kept their feet on the ground, Aunt Valerie had gone skydiving with me on several occasions. She climbed Mt. Fuji a few years back, and even drank most of my team under the table in Japan.

"And miss an opportunity to witness the next great love story?"

Piercing blue eyes, sparkling with mischief looked back at me. *Rolling Stone Magazine* interviewed her not long after she hit the best-selling list, even though her publicist warned the young reporter CJ Reece lacked a filter. The scared fucker dropped his ink pen several times as she told him about the extensive research she did for each of her books. The interview was cut short when she asked the guy if he wanted to see the callous she had on her knees after researching for a new erotica novel centering on blowjobs and penal jewelry.

"Uh-uh, good try, Aunt Val, but my personal life with Harper is private. Not for you to write about."

"Who said I was talking about the two of you?"

Her pursed lips are covered by an impeccably manicured nail, a single eyebrow raised in challenge as she drifted her eyes toward Bruce Kincaid. I returned with a raised brow of my own, adding a tip of my head in question.

"What? He's single, I'm single. And you," pointing the manicured finger into my chest. "Haven't decorated that beautiful girl with anything other than a mediocre kiss and a show of force to a Neanderthal."

"Shows you how perceptive you are." I teased, puffing out my chest like a goddamn rooster. "I've been sending her charms for her bracelet."

Aunt Valerie waves her hand in defiance. "What, are we in middle school? Harper is a beautiful, successful, and by all accounts, single woman. You better up your game before someone serious comes along." I fucking hated how right she was. Harper wasn't the type to run around town bragging about the boyfriend no one could see. Actions always spoke louder than words, and I was about to scream Harper Kincaid was my girl.

"Now, be a love and introduce me to your future father-in-law."

Bruce Kincaid stood dead in his shoes as Aunt Valerie laid on the charm. Had we been in a more private venue, I would bet the pair would have arranged themselves in a compromising position. When he offered to show her the tent where the cake and punch were located, I took it as an opportunity to go find Harper.

The cleanup crew has started their duties, breaking down the platform where the speeches were held, and winding up the fallen ribbon from the cutting ceremony. Josh and my parents spoke with the roaming reporters, giving insight into the next project on their lists. Harper stood to the side, Avery handing her a tiny white envelope, a shy, but enthusiastic smile on her face. Harper tucked the envelope into the pocket of her dress, as she enveloped the excited girl into a hug.

Drawing closer, I was able to catch the end of their conversation. "I wouldn't dream of missing it."

"What aren't we missing?" I interrupt, not giving two shits if I'm not invited. I'm about to do everything in my power to erase any doubt in Harper's eyes about us. I'll make sure everyone who sees us together walks away with envy and a dream of having a love like ours.

"Oh, Avery is getting married in a few weeks. Nothing too big, but she invited me." Avery is much like Harper in the modest way she dressed and carried herself. If I had to guess, Avery would be going to her marriage bed a virgin.

"Congratulations. When is the big day?" Slipping my arms around Harper, not waiting for her to melt into my embrace.

"Three weeks from tomorrow."

Pulling out my phone, keeping Harper caged in my arms,I bring up my calendar app. I can feel her quick intake of breath as she sees my screensaver, a photo I snapped on Skype and then downloaded to my computer. I had told her a funny story involving Ross and a pile of camel shit. Snuggling in closer, I let my chin rest in the space between her neck and shoulder. I begin typing in the words, *wedding date with my incredibly, beautiful girlfriend, who I hope wears a dress that takes my breath away.* "Okay got it."

Just as I'm about to put my phone away, it rings with a number I don't recognize, I press the ignore icon and place it back in my pocket. Avery has her eyes locked on my uniform, something I've grown used to in the years of wearing it. This time it's different, she isn't sizing me up for any fantasy or revenge sex.

"Can I ask you about your medals?" Her voice is reverent and soft, much like Harper's. She points to the spot on her own shirt as to which medal she is curious about.

"Of course," placing a kiss on Harper's cheek, standing to my full height. "Anyone in particular?" It's a redundant question, most people who recognize my Trident shield instantly know what I am. The intimidation is instant based on stories of missions and Hollywood's wild imaginations.

"The one that looks like a pitchfork."

"Ah," framing the metal with my thumb and index finger. "This is my Trident shield, it lets the world know I'm a trained SEAL." Avery takes a step back, as a flash of fear crosses her face.

Harper reaches out grabbing her retreating form. "Easy, Avery. Logan is a doctor, you have nothing to fear from him."

"I-I'm sorry. Cole wanted to become a SEAL, but he couldn't pass the mental portion of the exam." Avery's voice trembles and I have a suspicion this Cole has shared with her more than he should.

"And Cole is?" Prompting an answer from her, a diversion attempt to chase away the fear. A huge smile grows fast across her face, her features relaxing and it is my hope my name has the same effect on Harper.

"Cole is my fiancé. He's in the Navy, a Corpsman." The pride in her voice mirrors my own for being a member of the military. Avery has effectively secured a place in my world as the loved one of a shipmate.

"Is he stationed locally?"

"Yes, at Norfolk."

Knowing this is my perfect opportunity to surprise Harper, including her in the secret no one except my father knows.

"What's his last name? I'll keep a lookout for him when I report for duty."

It takes her a minute, longer than it does for Avery to answer. Harper looks up at me through confused eyes and attempts to take a step away from me. I've waited far too long to hold her, to be with her the way I want. Turning Harper to face me, "I was sick of being away from you, so I called in a favor." The need to touch her is too much, my hands crave the softness of her skin, the curve of her jaw and the way her hair feels like silk between my fingertips. Without much thought, I run my thumbs over the apple of her cheeks as my fingers disappear into her hair, engulfed by the luxurious feeling of the strands between my digits.

"I'm here," I whisper loud enough for only Harper to hear, placing a kiss on the corner of her mouth.

"In Virginia." Applying a kiss to the opposite side.

"To be with you." Rubbing my nose against the side of her cheek, losing myself in the essence of her.

"Forever." Unable to resist any further, I cover her lips with mine, losing myself in the softness of her mouth, the sweet taste of her tongue and how she exhales as she lets her body lean into mine. I should worry about the people around us, the judgmental eyes trained on the way I'm kissing her without abandon. But I want them pointing fingers, spreading rumors of what they have witnessed. Dispelling any questions as to what my purpose here is and how much I crave this perfect girl in my arms.

Chapter Twenty-Two

HARPER

When Meredith mentioned having dinner together as a family, I assumed she meant at a nice restaurant in town. I knew it would be a place with a name I couldn't pronounce, a menu I couldn't afford, and food I would need a magnifying glass to see on my plate. What I never, in my wildest dreams, imagined was the reality of sitting on the family jet to have dinner in New York City, at their home. But here I was, sitting beside Logan, his arm around me as I stared out the window, amazed at the bank of clouds creating a blanket, blocking my view of the ground below.

After the cake had been cut and the press got into their cars and left, Logan excused himself long enough to change out of his uniform and into a pair of dark slacks, expensive dress shoes, and a button-down gray shirt. The color contrast did incredible things to the irises of his eyes, highlighting the lighter speckles swirling in the blue. He had overwhelmed me with the news of his transfer, leaving me breathless with his confession of how he used his connections to maneuver his way to a position closer to me.

Logan had wanted me to ride over to his hotel room with him, but I needed a moment to compose myself, to wrap my mind around everything I'd learned today. Secluding myself in one of the available rooms at Horizon, I closed my eyes and tried to recall the time Ross had wanted to transfer to the UK and how he sat on pins and needles waiting for a call from his detailer to determine his fate. In the end, my brother didn't receive the assignment he wanted, instead he was sent on a three-month mission he refuses to talk about. According to Logan, he made a single phone call, and in a matter of minutes, he was handed the assignment he hand picked for himself. How big of a reach did the Forbes family have? Furthermore, what did Logan have to offer in exchange for the favor? Questioning the validity of why Logan was here cheapened the end result. I would remain cautiously optimistic until I was shown concrete evidence to the contrary.

My father sat a few seats over, Valerie all smiles at his side. Part of me was concerned with the quickness of their friendship. After her visit to my store, I wanted to know as much about her as I could. She was a free spirit, adventurous and outgoing. She was also filthy rich with four of her books having been made into movies. How fast would she tire of him? He was far from a wealthy man, with simple beliefs and community ties.

"Doctor Forbes, can I offer you a beverage?"

As we were greeted when we first arrived, the redheaded stewardess showed a bit too much enthusiasm when she noticed Logan. I tried to brush it off as loyalty, but during the time it took to reach a cruising altitude the top two buttons of her blouse had come undone.

"Melanie, I think we need a bottle of champagne."

Picking up my hand and bringing it to his lips, his eyes locked with mine. "We have so much to celebrate." Logan may be a trained SEAL with honed skills to fight an enemy, but he was clueless when it came to the woman who was currently panting in his face, arching her back in hopes of him catching an eyeful of her tits. I didn't trust this girl not to do something crazy.

"None for me, Logan. I want to remember everything about tonight." I wouldn't put it past her to dump something into my drink, something disgusting and unhealthy.

"Logan, I have an excellent bottle of champagne waiting at home. Pierre has it chilling for us."

Ten seconds ago I wanted to shoot daggers at Meredith, demanding to know why a local restaurant wasn't good enough for this dinner. Somehow I knew she saw what I did, and now I wanted to kiss her. As Logan turns to answer his mother, the end of his nose brushes against the top of Melanie's right shoulder, causing him to flinch back into the leather seat and grab my hand tighter. His face contorts in disgust, as if he has just gotten a whiff of something putrid and it takes everything in me not to burst out laughing at the embarrassed flirt.

"My apologies, Logan."

"Doctor Forbes, Melanie." Meredith words were coated with venom and rang with authority. I find it impossible not to shiver from the intensity of them.

"Yes, Mrs. Forbes." Melanie backs away in fear, disappearing behind the cabin door.

Logan relaxes back into the seat, his grip tightening as he whispers his own apologies into my ear. The flutter of his breath does insanely wonderful things to my body.

"You know, I should be angry at you for not telling me about moving to Virginia."

"But by the smile on your face and the way you kissed me back there, you're far from angry."

His deep voice reverberates against my heated skin, and I want nothing more than to lean back and allow him to devour me right here in my seat. But I need answers, reasons as to why he made me worry about him, knowing my brother would be in contact with Amanda and she would tell me.

"I was at first, but not anymore, not about that."

Logan adjusted in his seat, turning his body in my direction, his eyes locking with mine. "What are you angry about?"

Letting out a deep breath, attempting to categorize the many questions floating around in my head. "Angry isn't exactly the correct word. Confused is more like it."

Logan leaned over, placing a kiss on my forehead as his left hand caressed my cheek. "What can I clear up for you?" Pulling away from him, knowing I needed to have real answers for what was going to happen in the next few days. I had a business to run, a full schedule I needed to handle. How in the world would Logan fit into all of this?

"Well, what are your plans? I know you said you were here permanently, but how? Do you have somewhere to live? What about a car and your furniture?"

"Slow down, babe." Logan soothed, stroking my face as he kept his voice calm and low. "My immediate plan is to enjoy your company during dinner, and then have a much needed conversation with your father."

My heart sank as he mentioned my dad. It was no secret, no matter how hard he tried, my dad never cared for Lance. I had been vague when discussing Logan, more for my protection than his. I was still in disbelief this incredible man wanted to have a romantic relationship with me. Not to mention having to deal with letting go of the final thread of my past, something I didn't feel would ever happen.

"After dinner, we will climb back on this jet, minus one stewardess if I know my mother at all, where I will escort you back to your front door, and I will return to my cold, lonely hotel room. Tomorrow morning I have to hit the gym," patting his abs and puffing out his cheeks. "Where I will have to run twenty miles and lift ten tons of weights to get back into shape so I can keep my insanely beautiful girlfriend interested in me. After which I hope to take said girlfriend to a proper lunch." I start to interrupt, make it clear how turbulent this time of year can be for me, and my shop.

"Don't," he warns gently, gripping my index finger I've raised in rebuttal between his callused fingers. "I know you'll be at work and if you're too busy, then I'll occupy myself until you're finished."

"It's Saturday, so we are open until two."

"So, I'll hit the gym, call my realtor and make an appointment to see the property she has for me around say, four?"

"Is this a question?"

"I was verifying with you if four was a doable time for you?"

"Why?"

"Because I want your input."

"Again, why?"

A chill starting at the tip of my spine travels all the way to the bottom of my feet as Logan's face changes into an almost animalistic expression. His intense blue eyes, drifting to a dangerous level of black, frightening me and intriguing me at the same time.

"Listen to me, Harper." His voice has always affected me in ways I refuse to admit, but the depth of it at this moment is sending me to an arena I've read about, but didn't believe existed. "This isn't a temporary situation for me. Being with you isn't something I'm testing out to see if it fits. When I said forever earlier, I meant it, literally." My breath leaves me as the implication of what he said registers in my brain. Forever means dates, exchanging I love you's, and someday taking his last name. Rings and a church, kids and soccer, and trips to Disney.

"I want you with me when I see these properties and celebrate with me tomorrow night when I can take you to dinner." Leaning his mouth into my left ear, nipping my earlobe with the tip of his teeth.

"Alone."

The soft ding of the captain's announcement saves me from the internal panic of where my thoughts were heading. Being alone with Logan, no computer screen or chaperone involved is something I hadn't considered, at least not outside of my dreams. Logan Forbes started out as a name on a piece of paper, another friend I assumed I would add to my Christmas card list. Now, all six plus feet of him sat beside me, giving me tiny glimpses of what was going on in his head. Had I fallen into Alice's rabbit hole? Filled with strange characters and roles which modern society denounced as ridiculous. This incredible slice of man should be taking a tour of open vaginas instead of asking me to choose a home with him.

"Excuse the interruption, Dr. and Mrs. Forbes, we will be landing in twenty minutes. Mr. Berkley is waiting with the cars."

In the handful of times I've taken an airplane somewhere, I've never enjoyed the seemingly endless wait for the aircraft to open the doors and let passengers get off. Being pushed and shoved as the luggage is tossed down a metal escalator, only to be outdone by the two-mile walk you have to travel to find a rental car kiosk. Had I taken a ride on a private jet first, where the wait time is less than five minutes and the walk to your vehicle is seventeen-steps, I might have lost my mind.

The Forbes family didn't mess around when it came to getting a job done. Four full-sized SUV's lined up with men dressed in dark suits standing beside them, doors open and ready for us to climb in. Logan had intertwined our fingers before the door to the cabin opened, pulling me in the direction of the furthest Escalade after we descended the stairs.

"I'm sorry about this. I wanted to have time alone with you tonight, but you already know how demanding my mother can be."

"It's fine." And it was, granting me more time to get used to in the flesh Logan, instead of the Skype version.

"And I have to warn you about Pierre, my parent's housekeeper and chef. He can be inquisitive, to say the least. The man can gossip better than any of your Chatty Cathy's, but he does make a mean Beef Wellington."

In my mind, I pictured a tall, slender man with dark hair and a pencil thin mustache, dressed in a starched suit with tails and shoe covers. His nose pointed to the ceiling as he ignored anyone whom he didn't deem important. I nearly swallowed my tongue when a short, bald man dressed in a Chicago Cubs T-shirt, painter's pants, with bright pink nail polish on his fingers and toes.

"Corporal Captain," Pierre shouted in perfect English, as he raced down the steps toward Logan. Meredith clucked her tongue, shaking her head at the calamity going on outside of her upscale Manhattan home.

"How many times do I have to tell you its Lieutenant?"

"As many as it takes you to remember I don't care. What did you bring me?" Pierre stood in the middle of the sidewalk, his hand outstretched and his pink toenails wiggling against his flip-flops. He reminded me of a Chihuahua who had eaten too much sugar.

"Pierre," Weston warned as he assisted Meredith out of the SUV. His sunglasses gave him the appearance of a much tougher guy, one you see on one of those crime shows.

"I believe my wife requested champagne, not pool hall discussions in the middle of the street."

"Yes, sir, she did indeed." Pierre shifted his eyes to me, a smile attempting to escape as his eyes widened. Leaning closer to Logan, "Damn, man. Where did you find her?"

"One-eight-hundred-babe. You old bastard, put your tongue back in your mouth."

Nothing could have prepared me for the grandeur of the Forbes home. Deep mahogany furniture created a backdrop to the European feel of the space. Twelve-foot ceilings painted in Rembrandt settings, solid marble floor tiles laid in perfect alignment, making it hard to detect a seam. A giant crystal chandelier hung over a solid wood table in the center of the room and a large painting of Meredith and Weston hung on the wall to the left of the entry.

"Pierre, how close are we to serving? It's been a long day, and Harper and Logan are flying back to Virginia tonight." Meredith slipped out of her heels, leaving them haphazardly under the entry table, crossing the room and disappearing into the hallway. "And don't think I didn't notice you texting your friend Gregory on the elevator ride up."

Logan drops his face to the floor, his shoulder sagging as he lets go of my hand. "Pierre, you fucking traitor." Rolling up his sleeves, the silver of his watch reflecting the light from the chandelier. He stands in the center of the room, his back facing me, shaking his head as his hands finds his hips. I feel like an outsider, like I needed to turn around and leave the way I came.

Pierre returned with a tray full of glasses filled with champagne, his flip-flops and baseball shirt replaced with a jacket and dress shoes. Logan gave him a hard look, then took the tray from his hands and placed it on the wood table.

"You better not have used the good shit." Logan tossed, an edge of frustration coating his tone. Pierre remained rooted where he stood, his head held high, although he avoided eye contact with either of us. I've never trusted anyone who couldn't look me in the eye, and something told me the goosebumps on my arm were from more than the change in temperature in the room.

Meredith returns wearing a satin pantsuit and flats just as an odd tone sounded overhead. Logan and Meredith looked at one another, both wearing matching looks of disgust, as Pierre moved around me to the door.

"Be nice," Meredith demands, pointing a finger in Logan's face. Her once graceful demeanor has been replaced with the ferociousness of a provoked bear. Logan stands with his arms slightly outstretched, elevated above his waistline with his palms facing forward. His head is tipped to the side, raising his shoulders in a shrug, as if he were asking her, really?

"Meredith, darling."

My eyes grow huge, I could swear the nasal voice behind me was Miss Mona with a bad head cold. Both Meredith and Logan don fake smiles, as the clicking of heels against the tile grew closer.

"I hear you have wonderful news to share with me."

Refusing to turn around, too frightened to see if my suspicion was correct, Pierre hurried past me and into the hall to the left. Like a light switch, Meredith moved with the grace I was familiar with, grabbing Logan's outstretched arm and spinning him effortlessly as the pair glided past me to greet the owner of the voice.

"Jillian, you've arrived just in time as we were about to toast Logan's return to the States."

"Oh, I do love a reason for a glass of bubbly."

Fur and pearls filled my peripheral vision, the smell of Chanel swarming my nose and making my eyes tear up. Usually, I loved the scent, but when the wearer appeared to bathe in it, the fragrance became offensive.

"Penelope and Kiki will be so disappointed they missed this."

The owner of the fur and pearls doesn't waste a second as she stops at the table, snatching a glass from the tray like a free gift at a trade show. Holding the glass in mid-air, her eyes land on mine. Platinum blonde hair tossed up in one of the most elaborate up-do's I've ever seen, thick eyelashes, looking more like black chicken feathers, frame the surgically enhanced eyelids coated in sparkly eye shadow. Her cheeks are so severely hollow it looks as if she was sucking in her cheeks as she gives a man a blowjob. But it's her lips that make me look at her like a bad traffic accident; so full of silicone they look like duckbills.

"Oh," she looks at me, scanning from my head to the shoes on my feet. "I wasn't aware you were hiring more staff."

"I'm not." Meredith spoke with a edge to her voice, her rebuttal sitting on her lips, but Jillian was too quick.

"You should have said something. I could have given my agency a call, had them send someone—" Her judgy eyes scan mine once again, the chicken feathers rising with the motion of her brow.

"Less ordinary over."

I learned a long time ago how to deal with people like Jillian, you toss their venom back in their face and make them enjoy the taste. Stepping forward, my hand outstretched, and turning up the twang in my normal southern drawl.

"I am so sorry. My momma would tan my britches right good if she found out I'd forgotten to pack my manners. I'm Harper, from Virginia. Miss Meredith invited me to the big city to welcome her baby boy back home from the service." Not waiting for her to offer her hand, I took the glass of champagne from her fingers and slid my hand in its place, shaking so hard I wouldn't be surprised if I loosened a few fillings.

"It's a pleasure to meet ya."

Her eyes grew wide as the earrings dangling from her ears slapped against her neck from the force of my handshake.

"You know, my aunt Tilly has a housecoat just like yours. Bought it on sale at the five and dime by her house. My uncle Cecil offered to shoot her a raccoon to make her matching slippers, but she was too a feared one of them animal folks would throw paint on her like the lady on the television. I bet you wear yours around the house too, keepin' the chill off your old bones and all."

Jillian pulls her hand from mine with such force I had to take a step forward. "Meredith, I'm sorry, but I have an appointment," flexing her fingers, she wore a look on her face as if she had swallowed a fly. "Somewhere else. I will call you when—" She didn't finish her sentence, instead took one final look at me and pushed past in determined strides, not stopping until she reached the door.

When the wooden door slammed hard enough to rattle the crystals above, Meredith and Logan once again exchanged a look.

"She stays, Logan. I don't care how much you have to beg, she is staying."

Chapter Twenty-Three

LOGAN

"I'm sorry, Violet, I have to take this."

Excusing myself from my realtor's office where I'd been waiting for Harper for nearly an hour, hoping this call was her letting me know she was on her way. She had been too busy to stop and visit with me when I swung by her shop earlier. I wanted to stay and help, but knew my presence would be more of a hinder than help.

Glancing at my screen, my heart plummets as the digits were not that of my Harper. This particular number had called me a number of times, but I had chosen to ignore it until now.

"Hello?"

"May I speak with Lieutenant Forbes, please?"

"This is Lieutenant Forbes."

"Lieutenant, this is HM1 Gleason, one of the corpsmen at the branch clinic in Norfolk. How are you today, sir?"

Leaning my back against the brick of the building, my fingers find purchase in the thick hair at the top of my head. I suspect my old CO would have called my new command, telling my new Captain how I went behind his back and got my way. What I didn't suspect was a call this early into my leave.

"I'm all right, Gleason. But I have a feeling you're about to fuck that up."

"Sorry, sir. I've been instructed by Captain Vale to have you report to his office no later than thirteen hundred Monday afternoon."

"Let me guess, Gleason. You're short staffed and need my skills?"

"Well—"

"It was rhetorical, Gleason. I'll be in his office first thing Monday morning."

Not bothering to bid him farewell, I take my chances on the rumor mill spreading the word I was a cranky bastard. Every command had one, usually they are composed of people with too goddamn much time on their hands.

Shoving my phone in my pocket, I glance over in time to see my Harper pulling into the spot three over from mine. I wasn't a fan of the condition her truck was in, and while it ran decently, I would have preferred she be in something with a few more safety features.

Harper hadn't noticed me standing against the wall. Having pulled her sun visor down to check her face and hair, my inner caveman fist pumping at how she cared enough to want to impress me. Which was a wasted effort, I already believed she was the most beautiful woman I knew.

Last night as we sat down to dinner, my father explained the strange woman who had bounced in and looked at Harper as if she was the hired help. Jillian Stratton-VonLeure was a card-carrying member of the third wives club. She and her friends made marrying well an art form.

Her first husband, Wesley Stratton, was a fifth generation hotelier with more money than brains and an eye for a short skirt and even shorter attention span. He met and married her in less than a week during a meeting to purchase a hotel in Las Vegas, after a nasty divorce from his second wife, which left him a large settlement. Jillian worked as a cocktail waitress and managed to spill a drink in Wesley's lap. What started out as lust at first sight, turned into a drunken wedding with no prenup, which lasted five years and produced two daughters, their paternity questioned on numerous occasions.

Three months later, while shopping at an expensive store in London, Jillian met husband number two. Philipp VonLeure, an Indy car driver whose father was French and his mother of royal blood to the kingdom of Dubai. Philip's first wife, from an arranged marriage, failed to produce an heir, therefore nullifying its validity. Wife number two, a cousin to wife number one, had disappeared three days after the papers were signed, never to be heard from again.

Phillip also fell for the smoke screen Jillian had crafted in hopes of finding a new husband. While the royal family objected to the union, Phillip was killed in a fiery crash three months after the wedding, leaving Jillian to inherit all of his sizable assets. Now she is on a mission to marry off her two daughters, Penelope and Kiki, to the most eligible and lucrative bachelors she could find. I currently held the number one spot on the list.

Jillian traded in her moral compass to Satan himself to ensure she and her daughters would continue to live in the lifestyle they had become accustomed to. And where she may be ruthless, she isn't easily deterred. She wouldn't stop the pursuit of me until I had taken a bride or she found someone to surpass the allure of me.

Harper fell asleep on the flight back to Virginia. I couldn't help myself as I watched the rise and fall of her chest. The way her hair cascaded along her shoulder blade, curling around the swell of her breast, directing my attention, and my cock, to a place I was planning to visit soon.

"Hey. Sorry, I'm late."

Pushing a cluster of hair back behind her ear, giving me a glimpse at the silver crescent shaped scar on the edge of her chin. I'd ask her another time how she got it.

"You're right on time."

Harper's car door creaks as she opens it, the smell of her perfume hitting me as I reach in to take her hand. I love the way her skin feels against mine, soft and warm, the way a woman should.

"Your truck is way past its prime."

A look of pain flashes along her features, eyes slanted in an angry grimace and I could feel the hurt flowing off of her. With Jillian getting her riled up last night and the gentle way she allowed me to explain to her how I arrived in Virginia, I didn't want to risk crossing the line any further and creating a backlash.

"You, however, are scrumptious."

Burying my face in the crook of her neck, I nip not so gently at the sweet skin there. I know I've distracted her as she shivers in my arms, a throaty moan escaping her lips.

"Logan."

She warns half-heartedly, a sigh of pleasure leaving her lips. Her nails gently scraping the skin at the back of my neck, sending jolts of pleasure to my cock. I want nothing more than to shove her back into the cab of her truck, spread her open and devour her. Instead, I use the head on my shoulders and push her way from my raging hard-on.

"Come on, before I do something that will get me arrested."

As we walk hand-in-hand into the office, she leans into me, her head resting against my shoulder just as she did last night on the plane. I want this—her—to be right where she is, clinging to me as much as I am to her.

"I told the realtor we had time for two maybe three houses today."

"You know, you could have done this by yourself, chosen an apartment without my input."

Pulling her to a stop, lines forming on her forehead in confusion, the afternoon sun streaking her hair with highlights.

"Need I remind you of the conversation we had last night?"

Pulling her closer, my eyes flash to the pink of her lips, recalling how incredible they tasted, how supple they felt.

"We're not looking for an apartment. If I wanted to live like a frat boy, I would go back to college, or stay in the military. We are looking for a home. One with a spectacular backyard to have our friends over, plenty of bedrooms for us to christen, and one you and I can someday make our own."

Harper smiled but it didn't quite reach her eyes. She was holding back, too afraid to let out whatever it was inside her head keeping her guarded.

* * *

"Now, as I explained in the car, this particular home is five bedrooms and four bathrooms, with a mother-in-law suite on the first floor."

Violet Cutter, the realtor I had chosen, already had dollar signs dancing in her eyes. My mother proposed I let Josh handle this, but I wanted Harper with me when I made the final decision.

"The three-car garage was recently updated with additional storage for a motorcycle, and the schools are triple A rated."

Harper stood looking at the kitchen with its dark, dated cabinets and appliances which looked to have been installed by a fourth grader from that triple A school down the street.

"It's a gated community, with twenty-four-hour circulating security."

Violet may have started planning how she would spend the nearly seventy thousand dollars she stood to make in commission from this house. However, she was about to learn what is was to negotiate with a Forbes. Pulling out my phone, I opened the app Austin, Chase's brother, sent me. It was a copy of one we used all the time in combat. Entering the address of the house, I waited less than a minute for the intel to flash across the screen.

"Gates keep honest people in. With seventeen break-ins this year and two home invasions, it kept the criminals in as well."

Harper spun around, her lips ready to argue what I already knew was on her mind. I held my hand out to her, needing her to understand I had every intention of protecting her every single day of her life. Violet ducked her head, her years of being a seasoned professional teaching her she had met her match.

The next house sat not far from the water in yet another gated community. Violet showed us the game room and hidden area where our children could play, but just like the first, the number of reported crimes was high. This one had a governing board of directors to decide what could and couldn't be allowed inside the metal barriers.

Violet had one last house, the most expensive of the three and not in a gated community. Harper held my hand tightly as we maneuvered along the streets of Chesapeake. As we turned onto the main road, traffic was at a standstill, and I could see red lights flashing in the distance.

"Here, turn right," Harper spoke from my left, squeezing our clasped hands. "I know a side street where we can avoid the accident."

She and Violet exchanged ideas on direction and agreed we could get to the next house by taking her detour.

"I had a friend in high school who lived over here." A pleasant memory dances in her head as the emotions create a smile on her lips. "Her neighbor had horses, and they would come to her fence and let us pet them."

The two-lane, tree-lined road she told me to take was something out of a Southern magazine, with the Spanish moss draping the maple trees, the thick, green foliage snuggled up to the trunks of the tree. Thick, black asphalt splits the trees and allows us to get closer to our destination.

"Logan?"

Pulling my eyes from the road, the sound of my name crosses my ears as if a wish on the wings of angels. Harper has her index finger tapping on the side window, her eyes full of excitement.

"It's an open house, not far from where my friend lived." She doesn't have to ask me, I can see it in her eyes. Turning my signal on, I see Violet take a deep breath and look at her watch, but I could give two shits if this is an inconvenience to her.

The road is twisting like a snake back into the thick woods, the further we get into the dark green thicket, the more excited Harper becomes.

"There was so much empty land around her house, you couldn't see her neighbor unless you walked a half mile."

Sure enough, thirty-feet later the forest opened up, and the most beautiful home came into view.

Red and white balloons danced in the wind above an open house sign. The large black arrow pointed to the house that had stolen Harper's breath away. The same maple trees that guided us here continued up the drive, stopping just shy of the double garage. Sandstone covered the exterior, with two chimneys pointing to the heavens from the back side of the house. Clearing the trees, a circular drive showcased the grandeur of the front entry and the edge of what looked to be a pond or lake at the side of the property.

"I have no information on this house."

Violet remarks from the back seat, her frustrated tone giving me far too much permission to make this deal one the owners couldn't refuse. I had no problem leaving her with a more modest realtor fee, more work with fewer zeros.

Three other cars were parked in the drive, two with the same credentials as mine. I'd returned my rental ten seconds after the truck delivered one of mine from New York. Josh had taken care of the paperwork, making sure the fluids and tires had been checked. Harper hadn't bothered to show her opinion, it was evident having money and material things meant nothing to her.

"This was all forest the last time I was out here."

"You want to go inside or stay out here walking down memory lane?"

Not waiting for Violet, I took Harper's hand once again, following the sign on the door, which read come on in. We entered into a foyer which would make my mother green with envy, spying dual staircases running along the sides of the room. Wrought iron banisters filled with ornate flourishes gave dimension to the railing, giving the room a modern feel. What I assumed were the owners of the cars outside, stood with noses buried in cell phones, missing the beauty of the home surrounding them.

A slender woman stood off to the side, her hands clasped together in front of her, the lack of attention from the meanderers creating a wrinkle between her eyes. She swayed back and forth a few times before she noticed we are here. Violet is still trying to find the information on this house on her cell phone. The woman's eyes light up as she sees we are looking at the house and not our Facebook pages.

"Welcome to our open house."

Crossing the room, a colorful flier in her outstretched hand.

"If you have any questions, please don't hesitate to ask." I appreciate her smile and lack of excessive sales pitch. It shows she is confident in the house itself and not all the fluff it comes with.

As reluctant as Harper was to come along today, her mood changed as she ignores everyone and takes off to explore the rest of the house.

"Almost four-thousand square feet."

"The sprinkler system is on a well."

"Appliances new and still under warrantee ."

Harper rattles off the points on the flier, her eyes filled with excitement. I assume this is what impressed looks like on her. I like it, I like it a lot, and I will find a way to see it plenty more in the future.

"Oh my, God, Logan!" Her eyes grow huge as she spins around in the middle of what I assume is the dining room by the massive table and chairs in the center of the room. "It has a whole house generator." Her voice jumps a few octaves as her impression of this home increases.

"Which is good, why?" I tease, knowing full well why this is a huge selling point,

"Hurricanes, nasty things. They can leave you without power for days."

Harper moves across the room without waiting for any input from me. I let her go, keeping her swaying ass in my line of sight. I don't give a shit which house she chooses, as long as she sleeps in the bed beside me every night.

The dining room leads to the kitchen, it's décor more breathtaking than the entry. Harper is running her hands up and down the granite surface like she was stroking the face of a newborn baby. Off to the left is a set of French doors giving me a view which makes me stop in my tracks.

A wooden deck, large enough to throw one hell of a party, with a built in grill and what looks like an outdoor kitchen. A crystal clear pool sparkles just past the deck furniture and the body of the lake I first saw out front, which stretches along the entire length of the house.

Out of the corner of my eye, I catch movement at the edge of the deck and see a tall man with a glass of what I assume is beer resting along the wooden rail. I suspect this is the owner, and by the way his hair is cut short and the way he wears his clothes, this man is an officer.

"Excuse me, sir." He doesn't turn at first, and I wonder if he heard me. "Are you the owner?" He is my height, with significantly less muscle mass, yet he has spent some time in the gym. Glancing over his shoulder, patches of gray dust the area above his ears, placing him somewhere in his middle ages.

"I am."

"May I ask you a few questions?"

Picking his glass up and bringing it to his lips, I allow him to have a moment before I continue. I recognize the look he has, I've had it myself for the past few months, looking off into the distance for the one who holds my heart.

"Sure."

"Logan Forbes." Holding out my hand, inviting him to shake and become acquainted before we go any further.

"Forbes?" He questions suspiciously, a firm grip to his handshake and direct eye contact maintained even though he is sizing me up.

"You wouldn't be a Lieutenant by chance?"

"Depends."

"Good answer, Lieutenant. I'm Captain Vale, your new commanding officer."

"Pleased to meet you, sir. A little unorthodox, but still a pleasure."

Vale gives me the once over, the wrinkles around his eyes tracking the movements as he forms his opinion. I can still see Harper in the kitchen, opening drawers and getting more excited with each discovery.

"Your wife?"

"Not yet, but I'm working on it."

I turn to lean my back against the railing, mimicking Vale's stance. I don't have to ponder what his impression of me is, suspecting how much my old command filled him in, like a jaded lover meeting the new girlfriend in a public bathroom. Ready and willing to spill all the dirty secrets.

"Your reputation precedes you, Lieutenant. Although, I'm not sure I believe everything I've heard."

"Smart man, sir. I've found the legend is always better than the man."

"So you didn't buy your way into my clinic?"

"Buy it? No. Trade a favor? Yes."

"And does this favor have a price tag?"

"Sir, my father is a doctor in New York, he travels the world over trying to help the less fortunate. A few years ago, a friend of his came to him with a medical issue. He helped with treatment, and the friend wanted to repay him. I called in the favor."

"What about how you blew up a mountain?"

"Oh, that one is true. Killed one of the most ruthless men of all time in the process." I admitted, although I wasn't about to drop the name, let him search around and come to his own conclusion. "So why are you selling if you're still stationed here?"

Vale took another swig of his beer, his face contorting as he tossed the remainder of the cup into the grass at the edge of the deck.

"My wife and I built this house so we could retire. She was a consultant for the government on environmental issues and fell in love with this stretch of land. We purchased thirty acres of forest and had this house built. I had two years left on my contract, and we spent that time building what we considered our dream home."

He paused when the combination of a giggle-scream came from Harper when she found the hot water spigot above the cooktop.

"Two months ago, she got a call from an organization in Hawaii, wanting her to come out there and work with them. At first, she refused, swearing up and down this is where she wanted to be. They called back a week later, offering to have the both of us come and enjoy the island on their dime as they showed her what they needed her for. Three days later, she comes charging into our hotel room with the biggest smile on her face, her feet barely touching the floor as she starts begging me to consider moving to Hawaii. I was hesitant at first, reminding her of the beautiful house we had *finally* moved into. But she turned it around on me, reminding me of all the places I've dragged her off to over the years. How many projects she has left in the middle of to join me. She had supported me all those years, and now it was time for me to do the same for her."

"So you came home and stuck a for sale sign in the front yard?"

Shaking his head back and forth, the ire of a humorous laugh escaping his chest. "Not exactly."

Crossing my arms over my chest, slightly intrigued as to where this was headed. Did his wife decide to follow her dreams, leaving him in this massive house alone? I remained quiet as he crossed the deck to the bar area, pulling back on one of the beer taps.

"We came home and called a realtor, I went to my office and started the process for change of charge. Gail accepted the position and flew back out the following weekend leaving me to sell the house. What we assumed would be a quick sale has become a game of show and tell. Most of the people who look at the house find something wrong with it, mostly the lack of iron gates and a rent-a-cop to greet them when they come home."

Holding up his fresh beer, "Can I offer you one, Lieutenant?"

"No thank you, sir."

Harper sticks her head out the door, I want to pull her in beside me, but the look on her face is making me hopeful. She glances from Vale to me and then motions she is going upstairs. I nod my head in agreement as I wait for Vale to finish filling his cup.

"We've reduced the price twice, and my retirement day is fast approaching."

Taking a long sip from his cup, I can understand the frustration he is sharing. More than likely he and his wife have invested their savings into this home, expecting to take it easy for the rest of their lives.

"When do you retire?"

"Three weeks, the Thursday before Khaki ball."

He announces proudly, not bothering to cover up the smugness of getting to miss the annual event. It was one thing I hadn't missed while across the pond. Most commands forced you to attend, at least this year I would have Harper wrapped around my arm as I suffered through it.

"And what is the asking price?"

Once he told me the price he needed to sell it for, I climbed the backset of stairs, after Vale showed me the door, which concealed them. As I reached the top, I looked both ways in search of Harper, listening carefully for the sounds of her giggle as she unraveled more things she loved about the house. I found her sitting on the edge of the whirlpool tub in the master bathroom, looking longingly out the windows, which matched the view of the deck below.

"Too bad we don't have time for a bath before dinner." Leaning against the doorframe, careful not to startle her. With a smile permanently etched on her face, she looked over her shoulder at me.

"See the fence at the top of the hill?"

Moving closer, my eyes searching for the object she wanted me to see.

"The white one?"

"Yes. It reminds me of the same fence my friend and I used to sit on and talk about—well, everything."

Harper loved this house, that much was evident by the way she lit up when she walked in. Having her this motivated would make my plans for us so much easier. Besides, I loved the feel of it. Everything about it screamed home to me. Especially the beautiful lady lost in her memories.

"Tell me," I begin, tugging at a strand of hair laying perfectly against the back of her shirt. "If I were to buy this house, would you consider visiting me?" I wouldn't scare her with what I wanted or how I had fantasized about having sex with her twelve times since I walked up here.

"Of course I'd come visit you, but only if you let me cook in your kitchen."

Lowering my face within centimeters of hers, my eyes flashing between hers and our breaths mixing together. "How about spending a night or a weekend?"

"Not immediately, but yes."

Turning my head to the side and kissing her lips softly,I sent a silent prayer to whatever God was listening. I could work with what she was willing to give me, showing her how devoted and loving I could be. Pulling back from the kiss, not ready to break the momentum burning inside of her. I chuckle to myself as I look into her glassy eyes, drunk from the emotions I put into kissing her.

Pulling out my phone, I place the necessary call. "Josh, it's Logan." Harper blinks several times; trying to remove the haze I've created to distract her.

"I need you to finalize some paperwork for me. All cash, full asking price on the house I've just looked at. I'll text you the details."

Chapter Twenty-Four

HARPER

I felt an immense amount of guilt for letting my emotions come out and ultimately influencing Logan's decision to purchase a home. He hardly looked around while we were there, never bothered to lose himself in how the place felt or what he would need to change. I nearly swallowed my tongue when he told Josh to offer full asking price. I had the flier in my hand, the bright red numbers at the bottom of the page a few thousand dollars from half a million.

"I do have some bad news for you."

My heartbeat quickened in excitement as Logan returned to the table, needing to take a call he said was urgent. I began praying it was an issue with the house, a bidding war or the owner having second thoughts. Tucking my emotions away this time, no need to have them dancing in his face, giving him some signal to buy something else outrageous.

"That was my Captain."

"Oh?"

"He had one of the corpsmen call me earlier, telling me he wanted to see me Monday."

"Why, is there something wrong?" Ross had been called back from leave a few years ago. He couldn't tell us what happened, even when he came back a few months later.

"No, nothing is wrong." Logan reached across the table, taking the glass out of my hand and wrapping both of his around mine. I'd begun to crave his touch, welcoming his eyes on me. I wanted more, would give anything to be able to break the chains keeping me from letting him in.

"He wanted to have a formal sit down, which would have meant shaving the scruff you love so much. I assumed when he and I met at the house, there would be no need for me to come in. Unfortunately, he wanted me to understand our meeting today and his accepting of my offer had nothing to do with the order he gave for Monday."

My heart sank a little, my hopes of him getting out of the deal fading like light from a setting sun. "Wait, you bought the house from your new boss?" My brain was finally connecting the dots allowing the words, and emotions, to spill from my lips.

"Yes, he was the man I was speaking with out on the deck."

Oh that deck, even with the brief amount of time I spent there, I had envisioned friends and family enjoying the pool, Ross burning hamburgers on the grill while Amanda sunned herself as she watched the kids. Cool evening parties enjoyed with a fire roaring in the fire pit as beer from the keg flowed freely. Easter egg hunts, Fourth of July picnics, birthday parties, all celebrated and enjoyed on that deck.

"I introduced myself, he recognized my name, and then told me everything I needed to know about the house." His deep, blue eyes didn't betray him, confessing he was telling me the God's honest truth. He may not have searched every nook and cranny, but he took a tour of the house through the eyes of someone who loved it. "He's eager to join his wife and I know what it's like to miss the woman in your life, which is why I stipulated a ten-day close."

"You know, Doctor Forbes," swallowing back the pocket of doubt which had been living in my gut for years, inching closer to the day when I could set it free. "Just when I think I have you figured out, you change the rules on me."

As Logan drove me home, I let my mind wander over the past few months. This was what it was like to be on the receiving end of generosity. All those letters and packages I'd shared over the years, gave me as much joy as the ones who opened the lid. I never imagined what it was like to arrive at the end of the journey and find the beautiful gift of all-consuming love waiting for you. Somewhere along the line, I'd convinced myself I could never have a life like this, one filled with so much joy you practically drowned in it. Now that I found it, had it firmly in my grasp, I would treasure every minute and celebrate every day I was allowed to remain.

* * *

"Harper, I'm going to pick up something to eat and will be back in ten minutes."

Avery was a puddle of anticipation, with her wedding eight days away and her family arriving tomorrow night, she was burning the candle at both ends. She had requested to take a few weeks off for her honeymoon; she and Cole had reservations at a hotel on the beach somewhere, with no plans of ever seeing the ocean.

"Take your time. Sarah will be back soon and then I'll take a break."

"You want me to bring you something back?"

"No, I have something already, but thanks."

"Okay, but if you change your mind, I have my cell on me."

Avery slung her bag over her shoulder, turning swiftly and heading out the door, the bell clanging against the glass from her overzealousness. I stifled a laugh as I watched her nearly plow down a number of people on the sidewalk. This afternoon posed to be a busy one as the annual Khaki ball was a week away. Sarah had been flooded with wives and girlfriends needing her expertise, her reputation for her sewing skills a local legend.

With Logan still on leave, I had breathed a little easier when Ross told me he shouldn't be required to attend. He hadn't mentioned it, which I was glad as it was the same night as Avery's wedding and I had accepted her invitation weeks ago before I knew Logan was moving here. He had been so busy between opening the gym, *The Fitness Factory*, and moving into his new house, we haven't had much time to talk.

I'd recently contacted a friend of mine who worked as a buyer for one of the chain stores here in Virginia. She had one of her staff put back a sample dress from last season for me, marking it down to a price which made me feel as if I was stealing it from her. Sarah nearly fell out of her chair when I brought it to her, as it needed four inches taken off the hem. She made me swear to leave it to her in my will after I died.

"Excuse me?"

I'd managed to get lost in the daydream of new dress ownership and failed to hear the sound of a customer coming in. Looking in the direction of the voice, I found an Amazon beauty standing just inside the door. Long, blonde hair so thick I bet she broke a comb or two brushing it. Toned and clear skin that reflected a rigid diet or expensive salon visits. Dressed head to toe in cream, highlighting the tan of her skin which was most definitely achieved from a spray and not a weekend at the beach. She was a walking advertisement for Prada, and I bet everything was the current season.

"I'm sorry, how can I help you?"

With a gradual removal of her sunglasses, revealing a set of violet eyes, she took in her surroundings as if she had landed in Harlem, instead of downtown Chesapeake.

"Is this the establishment associated with Reece International?" Blondie didn't look like a reporter, though we'd had several of those lurking around after Meredith went back to New York.

"I'm sorry, I didn't catch your name."

Crossing the room, my outstretched hand in her direction. The light from the sun bouncing off a windshield, blinds me and causes me to retreat slightly. The door opens again, shifting the light and allowing me to open my eyes once again.

"Oh, good, Harper, you're here. Where's Logan?"

Lisa stands beside the glamazon, their attire complimenting each other. Clearly they are friends, shopping at the same expensive boutiques and hovering in the same circles.

"Hi, Lisa. How are you?"

Lacing my tone with a little bite, making sure she didn't think anything changed with the addition of her new friend here.

"I'm sorry, Harper. I'm dead on my feet as I've just finished back to back shoots."

Stepping away from her friend, she wraps her arms around me, hugging me close and then placing a side kiss to my cheek.

"Penelope called as I was getting off my plane in New York and told me she heard Logan was here."

So the glamazon was Penelope, Jillian's top contender for Logan's bed. "Neither one of us has seen him in a long time, so here we are." Raising her hands like Vanna White showing a new puzzle, Penelope waving as if on a Macy's parade float.

"I'm sorry, Lisa. Logan isn't here, he's either at his new gym or his house."

"Gym?"

"House?" The pair spoke over each other.

"Logan is using a public gym and has a house—here?" Penelope looked as if she was about to become ill, her nose turned up in disgust as she looked to Lisa.

"No," shaking my head, feeling the burn of disappointment settle in. "He co-owns a gym with my brother, and yes, he recently purchased a new home. Not far from here, actually."

"Logan Forbes owns a gym, you're sure?"

"Why are you so surprised, Lisa?"

Penelope stepped around Lisa the sound of her shoes clacking on the tile floor, rattling my nerves and making me clench my fists.

"Harper, correct?" She questioned, a seed of curiosity floating in her smile.

"Penelope—"

"I know who you are. I had the pleasure of meeting your mother in New York recently." I interrupted, hoping to save her the need to use any of her treacheries on me, keeping it for the next unsuspecting girl who stood in her way.

"Then you'll understand why we are so surprised. Logan is a trained physician, with a name notorious enough to open any door he knocked on. Why would he willingly leave all that behind to open a gym and buy a house so far from the life he has always known?"

Penelope posed an interesting question, one I considered several times as I tried to rationalize all of this inside my head.

"Tell you what, as soon as my assistant returns, I'll take you to the gym myself."

Twenty minutes and an uncomfortable car ride later, we pulled up to the front of Fitness Factory, the block letters against a camouflage background, the two T's exchange for trident spears. The glass front door was propped open, and three muscle-bound men carted large boxes inside. Lisa sprang from her seat, the rusted and aging door moaning in protest. Ross had begged me to replace this truck, pointing out its numerous mechanical issues and various safety concerns. But I couldn't let it go, not willing to let the last gift Alex had given me.

Penelope didn't wait for an invitation, as she too scooted across the passenger seat and out the door, not bothering to close it behind her. The men carrying boxes stopped dead in their tracks as the two beautiful women approached. Who could blame them? It wasn't every day a pair of runway models showed up in this town.

In a much more casual, and relaxed fashion, I found my way to the front door. Passing the same men, whose smiles and tips of their hats had been used up on the two ladies before me. The sound of blowing fans and angry rock music greeted me as I stepped over the threshold.

In the time since I'd last been here, Logan had managed to transform the space from looking like a tampon commercial, all soft and in different shades of beige. To one hosting cage fights and products related to hard-core men, with black ceiling tiles and gray walls, the carpet ripped up, and the underlying concrete polished to a bright shine.

Scanning the room, over the rows of treadmills and past the army of elliptical machines, some wood like structures sat against the far wall. Logan was balanced on what appeared to be a straight bar suspended on a pair of wooden pegs. His back was glistening with sweat as he heaved the bar up the wooden structure, using his upper body to move the bar to the next peg, climbing the structure. With each heave of his arms, his lower body would swing slightly and his tucked in heels almost reaching the edge of his shorts covered ass, building momentum to move the bar higher.

The muscles in his back corded in response to the weight of his body, flexing and relaxing in time with his movements. When he reached the highest peg, he lifted his feet and draped them over the bar, allowing his body to relax as he hung upside down. His chest heaved with each intake of breath, but his eyes remained closed, stretching his arms several times over his dangling head and then returning them to his side. I wasn't certain who was breathing harder from his workout, him or the three of us? Lisa and Penelope stood slack jawed just a few steps ahead of me as we all watched Logan open his eyes.

"Hey!"

He shouted over the thumping base of the music coming from the speakers above our heads. Removing a black object from his pocket, he presses a button, and the music abruptly stops, leaving my ears ringing and my body still panting with unbridled desire.

"Now this is what a guy wants to see. Three incredibly beautiful women watching him sweat out his frustrations."

If watching him climb the ladder made me want to do dirty things with him, it was nothing compared to what I felt when he came back down.

"Lisa, how the fuck are you, sis?"

She squealed as he lifted her off the ground, his laughter bringing me out of the sex driven haze his pecks had lead me to.

"Pep, always happy to see you. Does your mother know you left Manhattan?"

"Who do you think told me you were slumming it down South?"

Where Jillian seemed to be deceptive and calculating, hiding behind her clever choice of words and social standing. Her daughter appeared to be the polar opposite, brutally honest with no hidden agenda. Still, there was something there, some deep-lying secret, poisonous enough to do real damage.

"It appears some things never change do they, Pep?" A moment of silent slips between the pair, Logan's eyes drift between the two, waiting for something, but I'm not sure what it is.

"And some things, thank God, do change." Penelope fires back. A sliver of disbelief flashes across Logan's face and then it's gone. I would ask them about it later, but I fear it's like Ross and his missions, unable to tell the real story of what happened.

"Well, at least Jillian pointed you in the direction of my Harper."

Logan stepped around the two, his bare chest disorienting me and confusing me further. His warm arms and musky man smell solidified the spell he was placing me under, making me forget temporarily what I'd heard.

"Hey, baby, I missed you."

Without care of who stood in the room, he lowered his mouth to mine, his tongue crossing the boundary of my lips, meshing the two of us together. His exploration of my mouth as if we were in a dark room and the promise of much more to come, bloomed in the distance. A loud crash from behind us pulls Logan's attention to the men carrying in the boxes.

"Hold that thought, I'll be right back. Pep and Lisa showing up reminded me of something." The huskiness of his voice rekindling the fire in my belly, pushing me closer to the edge of giving into him.

Logan walked over to the men, his chest still bare and his calf muscles having their own audition for my needy eyes. He helped right the tipped over box, assuring them nothing inside was break-able. Winding around the large desk in the front, he reached behind it and grabbed what looked to be his shirt, sliding it over his head and covering those delicious muscles I wanted to run my hands all over.

"Ladies, I'm glad you're here." Logan stood before us, hands on his hips and his feet apart, the gym logo splash across his massive chest.

"I have an event I have to attend next weekend, and I need you to go with me. It's formal—"

"Khaki ball." I interrupted, knowing full well where this conversation was leading.

"Yes, I found out today. My new Captain has selected and directed everyone who is eligible to attend."

"I'm sorry, Logan, it's the same day as Avery and Cole's wedding. I've already RSVP'd I would be there." My heart sunk a little as I watch his face fall, but the loyalty I have to my friend overrode my need to comfort him and give him a false hope I would go.

"Damn it, I'd rather go to the wedding with you." Rubbing his chin, the scruff filling in nicely, giving him that bad boy persona I loved so much.

"I'm sure one of these lovely ladies would be happy to be your arm candy for the night."

Penelope's phone rang from her purse, "Care to guess who this is?" Logan and Lisa snickered as Penelope examined the phone in her hand. I hated being on the outside, not familiar with inner workings of this relationship to understand the offhanded jokes. I considered leaving the two of them with Logan and heading back to my store where I knew I was wanted.

"Hello, Mother." Penelope rolled her eyes, the condescending tone in her voice almost at a disrespectful level. "Of course I've located Logan. Who do you think you're talking to?"

I turned away from the trio, not interested in conversations I couldn't understand. Penelope made it seem like a joke, how her mother encouraged her to pursue Logan. Was there perhaps someone who Penelope favored, a forbidden love out of her social status or economic reach? Or maybe it was all a show for Logan, giving her an inlet to make him laugh, sharing stories of her mother's desperation over a bottle of wine and ending with breakfast in bed and a baby on the way. Whatever the reason, or whomever he chose, one thing was certain; Lieutenant Logan Forbes was going to be the envy of every man in attendance.

Chapter Twenty-Five

LOGAN

"Ross, I need you to calm down and trust me, okay?"

Harper's brother had called me the day I bought the house when he received news his time and service had been miscalculated, and his contract was up. He was given the option of signing a new contract, receiving a sizable bonus, or parting ways with United States military. He chose option B.

"But dude, I don't want this to be as fucked up as when you went home. Pissing off all the girls in your world and making my father doubt you."

Sitting down to breakfast with Bruce has been one of the easier things I've had to endure. In the end, we both agreed we had a common thread, both of us love Harper and wanted what's best for her. We disagreed slightly on whether or not that was me. Not surprisingly, he wanted to see how I treated her. He would make up his mind when, as he called it, I was squeezed. In other words, when I was put in the position where my looks, money and family name would do nothing to help me. *"Character is who we are in the dark,"* he told me, *"let's see who you are on the inside."*

"Listen, I've got it. You make sure your ass is on that plane, and I'll take care of the rest."

Ross and I devised a plan where we would use the ruse of my house warming party as a way to surprise his wife and sister. I had invited everyone we knew, every member of my team and even some of the guys I would be working with. I wanted to introduce my old life to my new one, meshing the two together into one cohesive unit.

Harper was a seasoned military family member, she would understand my need to disappear from time to time to help my brothers and the new missions we accepted. Ross included.

"Dude, I fucking owe you one."

"Yes, you do, and I know just how you can pay me back."

"Name it, man."

"Go to this fucking Khaki Ball for me."

I half teased, knowing full well we couldn't pull that bullshit off. It was my fault, I've been too wrapped up with all the shit in my world, thinking I was practically bulletproof and wouldn't have to follow the rules once I got back to the states. But the cocksucker of a new Captain I had, needed to have his rank stroked and put out the official order, all senior active duty would be in attendance. Which meant I had no choice in the matter.

"I thought you jumped at the chance to go with my sister."

"I would love to go with your sister, but she's already RSVP'd to a wedding."

"Still not seeing an issue, go to the fucking wedding."

"Can't, ball and wedding are on the same damn day."

"Logan, for a smart man you are pretty stupid right now."

"Fuck you, I'm trying to be helpful, and you're making fun of me."

I was half tempted to leave his ass at the airport, or let the word slip out he was packing it in and coming home. But I wanted to see Harper's face and let her thank me personally for the joy of her brother being home.

"Listen, man, I got a plan."

"Yeah, motherfucker. So did General Custer, and we all know how that shit turned out."

Early the next morning, using the advice Ross had given me last night, I phoned Harper's shop and asked to speak with Sarah. She nervously gave me the information I needed and made me promise I wasn't going to hurt anyone. I needed her on my side, so I told her as much of the story as I could and still keep my word to Ross. I reminded her of the party and how much I wanted her and Mitch to attend. She assured me they would both be there, as they wanted to see what was going to happen.

Ross's plane was due to land in fifteen minutes. I had turned down a home cooked meal from Harper in order to be standing here helping her brother. She was under the impression I was meeting up with an old friend who would only be in town one night. I didn't want to lie to her, but I knew she would forgive me when she saw her brother's face.

I had to laugh as I watched Ross walk down the jet way, his sea bag thrown over his shoulder and a day's worth of good scruff on his face. He looks like some hippy on the pilgrimage across the country, instead of the trained killer he was.

"Never thought I would ever say this to you," extending out his hand to shake mine. "But you're a fucking sight for sore eyes."

After assuring him a multitude of times that his wife and sister were clueless to his arrival, and a firm and definite no to his begging of letting him drive my car, we hit the road. Where Harper was not impressed with the sports car I had shipped down, Ross was about to lick my leather seats.

"Dude, come on, it's your payment for letting you date my sister."

"Um, that would go to your father and not to you. And the answer would still be no."

Our first stop was the gym, where he stood like a kid in the candy store, touching and testing out every piece of machinery we had. Finally, he noticed the salmon ladder in the back of the room, and jumped over the ellipticals as if they were sawhorses.

"Come on, man. I'll race you."

The look on Harper's face hadn't escaped me as she watched me tackle this particular piece of torture the other day. First time I used one of these bastards, I thought I would throw up. But after a few attempts, I found I enjoyed how it made my upper chest look and the amount of strength it gave me. I'm not ashamed to admit, my dick got a little hard what I saw the lust in her eyes.

"You're on fucker, but I've been making it my bitch since I had it installed."

Competing with Ross was like having the brother my parents failed to give me. He knew which buttons to push and how hard to push them. But he would be there if I needed him, and I would return the favor. When I stomped his ass at climbing the ladder, I offered to make him feel better by buying him a beer. As we wandered down the twisty road leading to my new house, he mentioned how he dated a girl who lived back here. I told him of his sister's excitement and her story of a girlfriend with a horse. He and I laughed as he admitted the girl was one in the same, the pair keeping the relationship a secret from Harper.

"Logan, man, if my sister doesn't want to shack up with you out here, I sure as fuck do." Ross accepted the beer I handed him, giving him permission to drink as much as he wants.

"Sorry, man, she's a fuck ton prettier than you."

Shortly after I moved in, I found the fire pit was remote-controlled. I called around and found a company who came out and made my house Bluetooth compatible. Now instead of keeping up with remotes, I tell a computer to turn things off and on.

"Don't tell her I said this, but she's fucking smarter than me too."

"Trust me, Ross, she already knows."

"You get everything set up like I told you?"

"Yes I did, I made a phone call and with a little persuasion, managed to get what I needed."

We talked and drank until the wee hours of the morning, stopping long enough for me to call Harper and tell her good night. She questioned if I was having fun with my friend and I said it was boring as fuck. She giggled and said I must be having a little fun as my words were slurred. She made me promise to be careful and that she would see me tomorrow night at my party.

* * *

The caterers arrived mid morning, setting up three full bars and several food stations. Harper called and asked if I needed any help, but I told her I was headed to the gym in just a few minutes. Ross came downstairs looking like death warmed over. Being in the desert for so long, he wasn't used to drinking as much as he had.

"Hey, Doc, any magic cure for a fucking hangover?"

He grumbled as he took a seat at the bar, accepting the fresh cup of coffee I poured for him.

"Yeah, avoid getting drunk." I teased, receiving his middle finger back as a thank you. He closed his eyes as he savored the hot liquid, leaning back and staring out into the open field.

"Promise me something, Logan."

"Sure."

"My wife never hears about how drunk I was."

"Sure, bro, what happens here stays here."

The plan was for Ross to stay upstairs until a particular song came on over the speakers. I planned the party early enough so the kids can enjoy their dad and he and Amanda could go home and enjoy each other once they were asleep.

With the relatively short notice, none of my team had been able to get away to come. However, this morning I had received an invitation to Zack and Kennedy's wedding, and everyone confirmed by text they would be there. I needed Harper to meet them, show her the caliber of men I would be surrounding myself with. There was time for all that, I still have a few months left in my contract with the military, but as soon as it was over, I was joining my team.

"Logan you ordered plenty of food, right?"

My mother was the first to arrive, pulling into my driveway shortly after I got off the phone with Harper. She had her design friend in tow. Jacques had been a big help when picking out fabrics for the house, but I drew the line at touching anything associated with this party.

"You can always send the extras to the homeless shelter." My mother fails to remember how I have attended more than my fair share of her parties where there's more food than people invited.

"Yes, ma'am," kissing her cheek, showing her the respect she was unquestionably due. "After all, I learned from the best."

"Would you listen to that, my little boy is developing a southern accent."

"Give it a rest, Mom. The military taught me 'ma'am', not the state of Virginia."

Her attention was soon captured by the staff, who was setting up the bars to close together in her opinion. While she was correcting them, I made my way back upstairs to get ready. Harper called me as soon as she left her house, making sure I didn't need her to stop anywhere and grab anything. I wanted to get this party over as quick as possible, getting these people out of my house and a few hours alone with my girl.

By the time I made it back downstairs, my party was in full swing. I hadn't realized how many people my mother had invited until it became difficult to walk around, even with the massive size of my house. Not surprising, the guys I invited from my new unit had all congregated on my deck, taking full advantage of the stocked bar out there.

"Hey, handsome."

Harper's soft voice called to me, as I was about to step onto the deck. Her radiant smile and mischief-laden eyes made my heart skip a beat, and I wasted no time separating the distance between us.

"I'm so glad you're here, beautiful," Pulling her in as close as I could, not wanting a fraction of a centimeter to separate us. She was my world, and I wanted to celebrate everything about her, show her all the many ways I wanted to love her. "I have a surprise for you."

With a tremendous amount of self-control, I pulled away from Harper, the smile at the corner for lips dropping slightly in confusion. Knowing the sooner I got Ross and his family united, the quicker I could get Harper upstairs and in my bed.

"Alexia, play song three."

A heavy beat filled the air as I turned Harper around to face the stairs. Planting my face into the area between her neck and shoulder, losing myself in the smell of her perfume. I wanted to worship her neck; kiss, lick, and bite every square fucking inch of it. I wanted to bathe in the moans, which I knew I could elicit from her.

"Logan?"

My name came out in a wanton whisper, her ass grinding into my pelvis, kneading the rock hard erection I had waiting for her. One of her hands grips they hair at the nape of my neck, pulling just enough to coax a sliver of pain, which travels directly to my now aching cock. Sliding my hands around her waist, my thumbs brush the edge of her firm breasts. Just as I'm about to capture her earlobe between my teeth and her soft mound in my hand, I hear the words that act like a bucket of ice water being doused over the top of my head.

"I'm home, bitches!"

Ross practically dances down the stairs. Amanda's scream is enough to shatter all the glass in my house, but as he picks her up and twirls her around, the smile on Harper's face makes it all better. "Did you do this?" She spins in my arms, taking my face between her palms.

"Yes, this was my friend I told you about. I didn't want to lie to you, Harper, but Ross is my friend, and he wanted to surprise you and Amanda. But I will tell you, he's home for good."

Ross had such a charisma about him, meaning even people who had never met him were laughing and joining in on his antics. I introduced Harper to everyone I recognized, and she returns the favor for the ones she found familiar. I wasn't ready to unleash the men I would work with on her just yet, saving that for a time when I knew more of what to expect from them.

I've never seen Harper as happy as she was, surrounded by her family. Playing with her nephews and cuddling with the baby, which admittedly, created a few ideas in my head. This was how life was meant to be, surrounded by those you loved and planning for the future.

Harper was safe within these four walls, surrounded by those who cared the most about her, but I knew of the evil that lurks in the shadows outside. Those who took great pleasure in the pain of those they inflicted it upon. I would destroy those people, do anything to hear the laughter that made my heart sore, to keep the girl who owned my heart right where she belonged.

As I bid goodnight to the last guest to leave, I found Harper asleep on one of the deck chairs. My original plans of loving her until she forgot her name were temporarily placed on hold. As I carried her upstairs, being careful not to wake her, I pondered what it would be like when the girl was much smaller and a product of the love I wanted to share with her mother. I wanted a family with Harper, with as many children as she would bless me with.

With the surprise of bringing her brother back to her complete, I couldn't wait to see her face when I showed her what I had in store for her next.

Chapter Twenty-Six

HARPER

What is it about weddings that put everyone in a good mood? Is it the anticipation of two souls joining together? Or perhaps it's the nostalgia of those who remember when it was their special day? For me, it's about finding the one special person who brings out the best in you. The one who will let you laugh at yourself, and holds you when you cry.

When I woke up this morning, nestled deep in Logan's bed, I knew today was going to be spectacular. Last night, as I watched my brother jog down the steps, something told me Logan was my one. All his recent endeavors had a common goal, keeping me happy. Helping my brother surprise Amanda, solidified what a great man he is. He could've woken me, testing the waters to see if I was willing to sleep with him. Instead, he ignored his own desires and tucked me into bed, holding me all night.

As midday approached, I dragged my feet, not wanting to leave his house and pop the bubble he'd created. I wanted to thank him, let him know his generosity and selflessness had not gone unnoticed. But I had made a promise, and by extension, so had he.

Avery and Cole had chosen St. Luke's Catholic Church as the place to start their new beginning. While the church wasn't the newest or the grandest inside, it was perfect for them. She wanted the ceremony to be simple yet elegant. With the church's high ceilings, marble tile and stained glass windows, I think she chose well.

The ushers were dressed in Navy dress uniforms, each so young, I found myself questioning if they had started to shave yet. With the low number of invites, Avery and Cole chose not to have the tradi-tional bride and groom division of the room, allowing everyone to choose their seat. The handsome usher who showed me to my pew called me ma'am and wished me a good day. I winked at him and told him I planned to.

As the light filtering through the stained glass windows grew dim with the setting sun, the ornate lights and glowing candles increased the romantic setting of the church. Surveying the room and admiring the way couples sat together, my heart sank, I knew Logan was about to sit down to the dinner portion of his ball. How I wish I could've joined him, sat beside him and held his hand.

But I reminded myself, this is the beginning, and another wedding will surely come our way. I tried not to think about who he chose to go with him tonight. Which leggy blonde would raise the eyebrows of the men he would be working with? Penelope would have an opportu-nity to remind him of the life he had in New York and Lisa was comfortable for him, someone he knew like the back of his hand. Tonight was for sharing in Avery's happiness, I would deal with the aftermath tomorrow.

Cole and his groomsmen came out from the side door, each dressed handsomely in their Navy uniforms. The priest, whom I was not familiar with, took his place at the end of the aisle. As the music began, one by one Avery's attendants came down the aisle, each wearing a pale yellow dress and carrying bouquets of white daisies.

Finally, the priest motioned with his hands for everyone to stand, and a murmur floated across the guest's eager to catch a glimpse of the bride. Turning to look at the back of the room, the doors to the foyer now closed. Anticipation built in my chest as the organist began the wedding march. With a nod from the priest, the two ushers opened the doors revealing an angelic looking bride. Even on my best day, and with all the magic in the world, I couldn't have looked as beautiful as Avery did.

Marrying Lance would have been one of the worst things I could have ever done. He allowed me to remain stagnant, never growing, never failing, and never living. I shivered to think of what would have happened to me had I continued in the relationship. Maybe someday, he too will find happiness, preferably not at the end of a line of cocaine .

As Avery passed me, her bright eyes and white smile reflecting every ounce of happiness she had in her tiny body, she blew me a watery kiss. Had I not met Logan, I would be green with envy right now, saddened by the lack of a true companion. But all I could feel was immense joy. She glided as if on a cloud, her dress flowing behind her just as I had pictured when I purchased originally it. There was no sadness for me, the right girl was wearing that dress.

Avery took her place beside Cole, handing her bouquet to her maid of honor. I wasn't sure if I could decide whose smile is bigger, his or hers?

"You may all be seated."

The priest took the couple's hands, guiding them to the steps on the altar. After instructing them to face one another, he opened his massive bible and began to read.

"Dearly beloved—"

I nearly screamed as a hand touched my right shoulder. Looking up into the owner's eyes, I came face-to-face with suit-clad Logan.

"Hey, beautiful. Anyone sitting here?" He whispered as he moved around the end of the pew, forcing me to scoot to the left.

"What are you doing here?"

"I'm attending the wedding of a friend." His blue eyes danced, as he pulled me into his side. Crossing his right leg over his left, his ankle resting on the opposite knee.

"Seriously, Logan, are you crashing this wedding?"

I hissed, looking around as if the wedding police would come marching up the aisle to arrest him.

"No, Harper, I'm an invited guest."

"Who?"

The priest had begun the exchange of vows, and the woman seated three pews ahead of us looked over her shoulder and scowled. Logan pulled me closer, leaning down into my neck, his lips brushing against the shell of my ear.

"I have to give credit to your brother. When I mentioned we each had plans tonight, he suggested I contact Cole and see if I could persuade him to invite me. It just so happens, my father needs some supplies in Thailand. Cole has volunteered to take the needed supplies to him and Avery will tag along with him."

"What about your ball?"

"Well, my Captain said we had to attend, but he never stipulated how long."

"My God, Logan, you're going to get in trouble."

"For what? Following orders? He said to attend, he never said stay."

"What about Penelope and Lisa? Where did you leave them?"

"They left me, jumped back on a plane headed for the south of France. They have a house there."

Looking at him through confused eyes, I had the feeling he wasn't telling me the whole truth about his relationship with the two of them.

"Lisa and Penelope have been in a relationship for the past three years. Jillian likes to pretend her daughter is straight, hoping she'll grow out of this phase of liking girls. She tolerates her relationship with Lisa, because of who her parents are."

Never in a million years would I have suspected Lisa and Penelope were lesbians, as they showed no connection when they were around me.

"Then why didn't you tell me? I could have waited for you or gone to the ball with you."

"Because I wanted to see the surprise on your face." His voice dropping low, the base of it wrapping around my soul and stealing my breath. "Seeing those eyes sparkle and the way your face flushes, makes me forget who I am."

I turned back to the front just in time to watch the priest pronounce them husband and wife and for Cole to kiss his bride. I wouldn't question how Logan was here, but enjoy him, all of him.

The reception was held in the church rectory. Logan held my hand as we walked along the broken sidewalk leading to the party. Several of Cole's friends stood meandering around outside the doors smoking cigarettes and telling jokes. Logan had changed out of his uniform and passed by them with a simple nod. How many of them would call him 'Sir' when he returned to work? Regretting any words spoken with the help of alcohol and a lose mind.

The rectory was as old as the church, its character bleeding through the cracks in the paint. A small kitchen sat opposite the entry, a bar to the right, and several tables had been decorated with Avery's colors.

Strands of Christmas lights flickered from the ceiling, draped between flowing sheets of sheer organza and tulle. The simplicity of the room made me smile, until I noticed a team of men finishing a parquet dance floor. I knew this had to be a mistake, as Avery had commented on having a friend download music to play during dinner, as there was no money for a formal DJ.

"There has to be a mistake," I mumbled, trying to locate the person in charge.

Logan pulled at my arm, once again leaning over to whisper in my ear. "Harper, I couldn't sit back and let them have their first dance and not have it done correctly."

There were no words for the way I felt about this man. His endless generosity, never ending compassion, and it appears he is a romantic at heart.

"You did this?" I questioned, the emotion of the moment threatening to strangle me.

Shrugging his shoulders, "Well, I didn't know what else to get them for a wedding gift."

Wrapping myself around him as tightly as I could, I rested my cheek against his, the prickly stubble from his morning shave lightly scratching my skin.

"Do you know how wonderful you are?" Closing my eyes, I wanted to commit everything about this moment to memory.

"Care to dance with me?"

Not allowing me to answer and taking our still clasped hands, he leads me onto the dance floor. Raising our joined hands above my head, spinning me twice as the music began to play, a soft melody filling the small amount of space around us. The last time I danced with a guy, was with my brother at Ashton and Stacy's wedding. Ross was more of a prom sway kind of dancer, where Logan knew a variety of steps, moving me around the floor with ease. With his hand on the small of my back and his eyes fixed on mine, I could feel the shift in the air around us. I could almost taste the sweetness of something wonderful.

Logan spun us to the center of the dance floor, tiny squares of light danced off his features. "Harper," gently gliding his hands to either side of my face, his eyes bore into mine. "You have to know, every-thing I've done; moving here, Horizons, this wedding..." Shaking his head, a glimmer of a smile dancing on the edge of his lips. "It was all for you. All because I love you."

A smile I had no control over broke out on my face, as incredible jolts of pleasure grew in waves over my body.

"I love you, too."

The air around us shifted, growing thick with the desperation we shared for one another. Logan's hand caressed the skin on my face as his eyes held mine in a measured gaze. He dropped his hand and reached into his jacket pocket, his footsteps never faltering as he dangled a silver chain from his index finger.

"I picked this up the other day as I was shopping, it reminded me of the way you make me feel when we're this close."

The delicate chain held a tiny heart, the left side of it dusted in what I assumed were diamonds. "I wanted you to hear the words before I gave this to you, having something to remind you of how deep my feelings are for you."

All those years I unintentionally helped single souls find their other halves, giving a gift there isn't a big enough thank you on the planet to express, until now. Now it was my turn, as I too had found my match.

"Put it on me?"

Logan stopped our progression, ignoring the couples who danced around us. Unclasping the closure, he walked behind me, grazing his warm fingers along the tender skin of my neck. Welcomed chills floated across my skin as the cold of the metal came in contact with my heated flesh. Once the latch was secured, he placed his hands on my shoulders, pressing his pelvis against my back, his lips ghosting along the side of my neck.

"Let's get out of here," he whispered in that husky voice I loved so much, pressing his taught body to mine.

"My house is four blocks away."

* * *

Clothes landed haphazardly as we tripped through the back door. Logan wrapping his body around mine and devouring my neck, as I silenced the alarm and reset it. Once secured, Logan leaned back long enough to unzip my dress.

"You have no idea how bad I wanted to rip this dress off you."

His fingers felt hot against my skin as the satin of the dress fell from my hips and gathered around my feet on the floor. Sarah had taken one look at the dress and claimed something that sexy deserved to be on the floor of an expensive hotel.

Wet lips, followed by nips of perfect teeth found the flesh of my collarbone, eliciting a hiss from me. Mouths colliding, tongues battling for dominance, as Logan's strong hands took hold of my bra cover breast, kneading and creating a fire deep in my core. Reaching for him, I discovered somewhere along the way his jacket and tie had been removed.

Knowing he wouldn't give a shit about his shirt, I grasped the seam and tore with all my might, the buttons rick-a-shay off the walls surrounding my stairs. My actions spur Logan on as he picks me up, my legs wrapping around his waist, while his hands grasp my ass at an almost painful level.

"Which way?" He pants into my ear, his lips continuing their assault on my neck and shoulder.

"Left, end of the hall."

Until this point, my father and brother had been the only men ever to come up here. Until now I had preferred it that way. I'd always left the lamp on my bedside table on, not wanting to trip as I clambered into my room at night. The warm glow of the light showed the hunger in Logan's eyes, his usual light blue eyes now dark with primal need. Laying me down gently in the middle of my bed and climbing his way to join me, he continues to shed his clothing.

"I'd hoped to love you for the first time in my bed. The one I bought for the two of us."

Sliding his hands behind my back, his fingers finding the clasp of my bra and in a single attempt, the offending garment is flung over his shoulder as his lips find my nipple.

"We can stop and do this another time."

Arching my back as his teeth scrape the sensitive bud, the action traveling to the junction between my thighs.

"Next time."

Breaking away long enough to answer me, his hands taking over for his mouth. Lowering his mouth to my lips, his knee between my thighs, giving me enough of a solid surface to create some needed friction for my aching core.

"It's been a while for me."

"Me too, almost a year."

"I'm clean, and I take birth control because of my periods."

Logan accepted my admission with a nod of his head, lowering his face to trail kisses from my shoulder to the top of my lace panties. Hooking his thumbs on each side, he slowly drags the fabric down my legs, his eyes never wavering from mine.

I rise up on my elbows, not wanting to miss a second of being with him. My legs fall open automatically revealing his steely erection, long enough to reach the center of his ripped abs. I recalled watching him at the gym as he used the bar to climb the wooden planks, a surge of heat erupts inside, and I want him to touch me, to help turn this inferno to smoldering ash.

Using his index finger he blazes a trail along my lower lips, dipping inside as he reaches the bottom, and then circling my clit. Lifting his finger to his lips, he slides the digit into his mouth, closing his lips around and moaning while he hollows his cheeks as he sucks. With a pop, he removes the finger and his eyes open slowly, a mischievous grin growing on his face.

"I've always preferred to sample from the source."

Without warning, he dives into my pussy, his tongue lapping at my clit. I cry out in ecstasy, my head falling back against the pillow as I give myself over to him.

Feeling the pressure build in my belly, the painful tingles starting as I feel my orgasm just out of reach. Logan suctions his lips around my clit and begins to hum as he shakes his head violently. It's the final shove I need to fall over the edge, shouting his name as white spots cloud my vision and my limbs feel as if they weigh a thousand pounds.

My breathing is as rapid as it would be if I had run a marathon, and I hear the faint sound of foil ripping. I can feel Logan kissing me from the middle of my thigh and progressing higher, laying his body between my legs as he continues to worship my skin with his mouth.

"I love you, Harper."

Feeling the head of his cock just outside my entrance, I raise my hips hoping to push him in further.

"I'll go slow, so I don't hurt you."

He whispers with truth wrapped around each word. Excruciatingly slow, he begins to push into me, spreading me and leaving the most delicious burn behind. Logan Forbes is blessed with so many things; a kind heart, abundant muscles, and thankfully, a big fat cock.

"I love you, too."

I confess, taking hold of the back of his neck, driving my tongue between his parted lips. When he is balls deep inside, he shifts his hips, giving me the friction I need to bring on another orgasm. He pumps in and out several times, each stroke hitting a new angle, bringing me closer to the finish. My world shifts on its axis as Logan brings my hips off the mattress, the angle causing my world to shatter and his name to echo off the walls.

"That's two," he says, looking down at me from his extended arms, the muscles straining with the position. "Let's see how many more I can find?"

Chapter Twenty-Seven

LOGAN

The soft hum of the ceiling fan above, provides enough of a breeze to create a chill in the room and the right amount of white noise to soothe me. It felt good against my overheated skin, my body wrapped around a sleeping Harper.

She'd drifted off a few moments after I took her for the third time, riding me as I had fantasized about at least a hundred times.

I wanted her again, craved the way she screamed my name and told me where she wanted me. How she pushed me back against the mattress as she took what she wanted from me, the necklace I had given her dangling between her luscious breasts. I hadn't told her everything about the heart she wore, omitting the slight alteration I had Ghost make in the design.

Lance had been dead on when he boasted how I couldn't watch her every moment of the day. The bastard was far too cocky for my liking, not knowing when to back off when threatened by a valid opponent. Until I could find the source of my unease where Lance was concerned, I would continue to have her monitored, and Lance investigated. Harper was too important to me to risk even a second of her safety. I wanted to keep her close, but most of all, I wanted to hear her say she loved me again.

Her body bathed in moonlight, the silvery rays casting a magical glow around her. Having turned off the lights after round two, she wanted to feel more of me, said the lights took away some of the sensation, and I for one, could deny her nothing.

Running my index finger over her bare hip, goosebumps pebble up in my wake. She shifts her hips, the curve of her ass brushes my rock hard erection, a delicate moan escaping her lips as she reaches her arm around my neck, pulling my lips down to meet hers.

Lifting her leg slightly, I slide the head of my cock between her wet folds, she is so ready for me. Even half asleep her body craves mines as much as I do hers.

"Logan," she breathes against my lips, the sweet taste of her washing over me.

"Yes, baby?" Reaching between her thighs, finding her warm and slick, pressing on her swollen clit, her ass rocks back against my pelvis.

"Harder." She demands, tugging hard at my hair between her fingers.

Pistoning in and out of her, I release her clit and travel my wet fingers up her body, finding her nipple and pinching it hard enough to make her pussy clamp around my cock. Harper shakes as she rides out her orgasm, but I'm far from done with her as I spin us around, putting her on her hands and knees. Grasping her hips, I continue the speed she insisted on, laying my chest to her back, my fingers back on her clit. It's never been like this for me. I've never been so desperate for the girl in my hands, never needed to connect to another human being, the way I need her.

Harper knocks the breath out of me when she reaches between her legs and takes hold of my balls, massaging them as her fingers hit my swelling cock diving in and out of her. Her movements are tender, but enough to force my orgasm to bypass my brain and hit with the same force as a wrecking ball.

"Goddamn."

I curse, slamming into her several more times as I continue to come. As gently as possible, I lower us both to the mattress, covering us with the sheet. "I love you," I mumble into the back of her neck, smiling when she mumbles it back.

* * *

Years of waking before the sun has created a habit I've found impossible to break. My eyes open as the first rays of the sun began to announce the new day. Harper is sleeping soundly, her head pressed against my chest, leg draped over mine and my arms wrapped around her. Running my free hand through my hair, I stifle a yawn begging to come out. I glance to my right, unsure where Harper keeps her alarm clock, only to find a chair with an afghan draped neatly over the arm.

Turning to my left, where I recall the lamp had been, I crane my neck to see the time. But as my eyes scan beyond the lamp and the bottle of lotion, the air leaves my lungs as I take in the photo sitting in an antique frame.

Two fresh face kids smile back at me; the beautiful girl on the right, a much younger version of the one who lies across my chest. But it's the boy in the photo, the one who has a big smile on his face, wrapped around the girl I professed my love to. His eyes have haunted me, made me seek out the SEALs to help me to forget my promise to a dying man.

"Tell her I always loved her."

His desperate plea echoes in my head. How he took my hand, shoving in it the one thing of hers he kept close, wrapping my fingers around the tiny treasure.

Ross had told me about his best friend growing up, how he had waited for years before pursuing Harper. The news of his death coming to her on Valentine's Day, making her justifiably jaded against the theme of the holiday. Harper said his name was Alex, such a common name yet I never made the connection. The statue in the town square, the charity Harper created using the money from his death benefits. Alexander Gray sacrificed himself so that many could live. He also gave me the one thing I've regretted all these years; the knowledge that I would never locate the nameless girl he left behind.

As quietly as I can, I slide out from under Harper, being careful not to wake her. Collecting my clothes, I make my way out the door. Recalling the code from the night before, I punch in the numbers and reset the alarm as I escape into the morning air.

How was I going to fix this? I knew how to disarm a man, stop a bleeding wound with ordinary objects, and silently rappel out of any aircraft shown to me. But how was I going to defend myself against the ghost of her first love? The man she has spent every waking moment remembering and immortalizing to the world. I could eliminate any real threat that came my way, but this was different. How do you fight a man who is already dead?

After arriving back home, I rush upstairs taking the steps two at a time, needing to get back to Harper before she woke. I'd placed the chest in the back of my closet the minute the delivery company arrived with it. Over the past few weeks, I'd allowed the contents to fade from my mind, concentrating more on the beautiful woman who had taken possession of my entire world.

Dropping to my knees, the malaise of the moment making me weak and weary. I don't want to open the lid, like somehow seeing it would make this nightmare a reality. But I had to know, Harper had to know, and I had made a promise to a dying man. I watched as if it was someone else's hands, shaking like a leaf in an earthquake, pulling at the latch, the metal clanking against itself, shattering the silence in the room. Tipping my head back, the panic rising in my chest as I draw in a deep breath, preparing myself for the inevitable.

"Quit being a pussy, man."

Reaching deep inside, my adrenalin pushing aside the panic as I hear the words echo off the walls. Lifting the lid, the sparsely used hinges protesting my use of excessive force. Dirt and sand escape and fall to the carpet from the inner edge of the locker, and I want to laugh at how I still can't escape the tiny particles. Reaching in, I pull out the stacks of awards I tossed in here over the years, laying them beside me.

Old magazines and newspaper clippings my parents sent me, documenting the good things I had missed while I was away. Finally, an old college sweatshirt is all that remains between me and the talisman, which has haunted me. Lifting the soft fabric, the small treasure still wrapped in paper towels and plastic. With the most amount of courage I've ever had to muster, I snatch the plastic from the cold confines of my past, shoving it into my pocket.

The drive back to Harper's goes by in a flash, the sun skirting the horizon on what could be the beginning of the end for this relationship. Parking in the same spot I had last night, recalling how she had commanded my lips as I tried to shift my car into park. Feeling the bag in my pocket, I considered for a tenth of a second tossing the whole thing in the dumpster behind me, taking away the shit storm I was certain I was about to create. But I couldn't do it, Diesel's words echoing inside my head.

"No regrets."

Silence greeted me as I re-entered the shop. Disabling the alarm, I took the stairs one at a time, each one feeling as if I had shoes full of cement, growing heavier with each step. As I stood on the top, I could hear the sound of water running. Stepping into her bedroom, the sheets already pulled back into place, her dress from the previous night neatly lying on the chair in the corner.

Stepping around the bed, my undershirt from last night peeks out from the edge of the bed. I wonder if Harper saw it, choosing to leave it instead of covering her naked body in it. I would have taken her again if I had seen her wearing my clothes, unable to resist the monster inside who would have forced his way out.

Lifting the dress from the chair, I bring the silk fabric to my nose, memorizing the essence of her as I slump into the firmness of the cushion. How beautiful she looked when I walked into the church, the fabric accentuating the curves and dips, which drove me crazy. I owed Ross a huge debt of gratitude, and yet felt like a complete idiot when he suggested I make an appearance at the ball and then get the fuck out. Finding Cole took less than five minutes after I brandished my rank and reminded them of my arrival. He agreed to meet me after his shift, and after my offer of an elaborate honeymoon and reception, I had an invite to the wedding.

"Hey, where did you go?"

Harper stood across the room, hair still wet from her shower, pulled up in one of those clips women use. She had dressed in a pair of yoga pants and simple t-shirt, the casual look taking nothing from the sexiness of her. Taking her in, I contemplated telling her a lie, offering to make her breakfast and then messing up this perfectly made bed as I reacquainted myself with her inner thighs.

"Harper, I need to tell you something." My upbringing instilled value and morals, being a SEAL chiseled honor and respect into my moral fiber. In truth, I had no other option but to tell her everything. She deserved everything, and so did Alex.

I watched as her face shifted from inquisitive to fearful, her pupils dilated slightly but returned as she blinked. Her fingertips held the heart I had given her last night, her thumb rubbing the tip of the heart.

"First, I want you to know I don't regret what happened last night. I can see worry in your eyes, and there's no reason for it."

Her chest heaves as she lets out a sigh of relief. Guilt filled my belly, as I knew the news I had to deliver would be worse than what she had feared.

"I meant what I said when I told you how much I love you. Please —" my voice faltering as the weight of it all constricted my throat as if I've swallowed a mouth full of cotton. "Remember that, no matter what, okay?"

Harper moves to the edge of the bed, collapsing onto the mattress, her frightened eyes trained on me. "Remember when we first started exchanging emails and you told me of the young man you loved? How he died a hero, and the whole town mourned with you?" Harper nodded her head, the fear in her eyes begging me to stop, make the tears collecting there go away.

"What I didn't tell you was why I chose to become a SEAL, to run away from the skills I had spent years learning, ignoring the needs of the Navy for my own personal agenda." Putting her dress back on the arm of the chair, resting my forearms on my thighs. "I came into the Navy for all the wrong reasons. I wanted to be a doctor so fucking badly I was willing to do anything to get into medical school. When they sent me to Afghanistan, I thought it would last a month, and then I would be right back in my cushy apartment and fucking any girl I wanted. When the weeks turned into months, and the enemy started fighting back, I knew I would be there for a while."

Recalling how fucking cocky I was, arrogant as a result of the importance they placed on my skills as a surgeon. "When the insurgents started fighting back, killing as many of our men as we were theirs, my conceit grew ten-fold. They needed me, couldn't win the fucking game without these fucking hands." Raising my spread fingers in the air, shaking them with the anger growing inside. I wanted to kick the shit out of the young man I once was.

"When the wounded started pouring in, the need to fix them and return them to the front line was emphasized to me on many occasions. Liberty chits were dangled in front of my eyes, my time away from all the bloodshed just a few skillful surgeries away. But when the men came in beyond repair, torn apart by the bullets some cocksucker back in the states sold these bastards, I knew I was fighting a losing battle."

The leather of my dress shoes glistens from sun's rays coming through the window. Giving me pause to collect the right words, discarding the ones, which would do neither one of us any good. "I used to brag about how clean I kept my boots. Even poked fun at the other doctors who walked out of post-op with dried blood covering their shoes." Swallowing thickly, I recalled the night that changed everything.

"It was hot a fuck when the call for incoming wounded sounded over the PA system. I'd just finished stitching up several guys who had arrived a few hours before, and my body was feeling the effects of lack of sleep and the heat surrounding me. Something held me up as I stood at the edge of the helipad, the blades of the helicopter sending dirt and sand spinning in the air around me. The first guy I saw on the stretcher had a few cuts and a gunshot wound on his shoulder. His injuries were superficial, so I moved on to the next one. The darkness of the helicopter cabin kept me from seeing more than his boots, so I jumped in to get a better vantage point. From the second I laid eyes on him, I knew his time was limited. He had lost so much blood his uniform was discolored to a dark crimson, his name tags unreadable. He had taken several shots to the chest, his lungs full of holes and he struggled for every breath. The corpsman behind me pulled his stretcher from the cabin, but as we ran toward the OR, the man grabbed my arm and called me sir."

Reaching into my pocket, just as I had watched Alex do all those years ago, my fingers grip the plastic bag as my voice cracked with emotion.

"He took something out of his pocket and made me swear to tell the girl who this belonged to he would always love her."

Carefully, pulling the plastic from my pocket, taking my time as I opened the bag and grasped the paper towel, just as I'd noticed when Alex pulled it from his pocket, the fucking dust and sand fell from the cracks and crevices.

"I never thought I would meet the girl he spoke of, the one he thought of as he took his last breath."

I hadn't laid eyes on the cluster of hair wrapped in a satin ribbon since I placed it in the bag all those years ago. Running my fingertip along the dark strands, the frayed edges of the fabric showing the decay the elements had started.

"But when I woke up this morning and saw the face of the man on your nightstand, I knew I had to give this to you."

Harper sat with her legs tucked under, both hands covering her mouth as the tears began to journey down her face. She shook her head, I assume trying to make this all go away.

"Alex loved you, Harper." Laying the hair and ribbon on the bed beside her, I retreat to the corner where I waited for the fallout.

Chapter Twenty-Eight

HARPER

My heart was pounding inside my chest with such force, I worried it would break through my ribs and land on the floor. The last time I saw the lock of my hair was in a tiny motel room, hours before I said goodbye to Alex. I remember jumping off the bed and grabbing the scissors I used to cut his hair, snipping off the long lock before I could chicken out.

"I thought he would think me silly or old fashioned for making it."

My voice sounded scratchy, foreign to my own ears. My eyes never wavering from the pink ribbon encircling the brown hair like the red stripes on a candy cane.

"If he did, he never said anything, just put it in his pants pocket before wrapping me in his arms again."

Tentatively, I reached out testing the waters on the last gift I'd ever given him, half expecting it to leap off the bed and slap my hand away.

"I shopped with a friend of mine, behind my parents back, for the nightgown I wore. Alex had been so patient waiting for me to be ready to be with him. I didn't want him going off without something to remind him where he belonged. I was a virgin, he most definitely was not, but he took his time and made it easy on me."

Sand fell away from the strands as I finally picked it up from the bedspread, wrapping my fingers around the fabric, closing my eyes as I traveled back to the moment when he kissed my forehead and pushed past my barrier. The way his body felt against mine, the tenderness in his touch and the way he spoke my name.

"When the Chaplain came to the door, I wondered what happened to this. I always suspected he lost it somewhere along the way."

I couldn't admit, even to myself how I questioned if he tossed it out the window the second the bus rounded the first corner.

"For years I had to bite my tongue with every flower delivery that came into the shop on the day I marked as a bullshit holiday, jealous of—"

I couldn't continue, not with the truth out here like an infected wound. I had allowed my need for love to start erasing the oath I swore to Alex, to wait for him and be here when he returned.

"I'm sorry, Logan."

I managed to get out before the bile in my stomach began to rise, storming down the steps and into the street. I had to put as much distance between myself, and the man who had helped me forget as I could. Tears streamed down my face as my feet continued to hit the pavement. With the earliness of the day, the streets were thankfully empty, making my escape so much easier.

With my lungs burning and the muscles in my legs resembling Jell-O, I slowed to a crawl in the middle of Front Street. When we buried Alex's body, the funeral procession came down this way. I stood beside his mom as we walked behind the horse-drawn carriage she had insisted on using. The American flag covering his coffin as two black steeds led the way to his final resting place. Years later any sound resembling a gunshot would send me into a panic attack, the memory of the twenty-one gun salute flashing before my eyes.

I've come to visit Alex's grave at least a hundred times since that day. My way of letting him and myself know I would never forget him. But time had been a thief, stealing away the love and devotion I once felt for Alex, replacing him with a new man, one with a new uniform and a kind heart. The Grays were not showy people, and therefore the gravestone was nothing grand. An American flag etched above his name and the dates of his birth and death below. I'd traced the letters and numbers a thousand times with my fingers, hoping he would tell me to stop, anything to hear his voice one last time.

"Thought I'd find you here." My father had been beside me as the men in uniforms had expressed their condolences, handing me a number to call about claiming his body and the forms I would need to file for his life insurance. I had refused at first, convinced they had made a mistake. "Logan told me what happened."

When I felt my father's arms wrap around me, I allowed myself to collapse into his embrace. Sobs broke free, much as they did the first time we sat like this. He didn't shush me or say anything, letting me rid myself of all the pain I'd swallowed over the years.

"I let him down, Daddy."

"Who?"

"Alex. I swore I would wait for him and I didn't."

My admission made me cry harder, turning and burying my face into his chest. He held me tightly as the guilt took over, stabbing me with it vicious claws and stealing my breath away.

"You know, time has a way of making us forget."

Clinging to his chest, nodding my head in agreement. Time was a selfish bastard, skipping through life stealing the gift it had given us and continuing on, only to suggest we had plenty of opportunities to live it all again.

"It allows us to keep the good memories while forgetting the bad ones. As I recall, Alex Gray was not always the man you make him out to be."

Pulling away from his chest, anger bubbles inside me. How dare he disrespect a dead man?

"Hold on, Harper, hear me out." Moving away from his embrace, using the hem of my T-shirt to wipe my eyes. "You have forgotten all the times you came storming downstairs after Alex had chased off another young man you found a fancy in." Opening my mouth to argue, my father held up his hand to continue.

"Wait, I wasn't finished." He paused, as I closed my mouth and leaned against the hard surface of the gravestone. "Alex was an honorable man, but he was also a mischievous boy. One who, on several occasions, made you cry. He chased many a cat up a tree, set fire to the Duncan's trashcan, and spray painted another girl's name on the side of a school bus."

Claudia Shipley, how could I forget? She moved into town on a Saturday, and the two of them were an item by Monday afternoon. I had walked in on them having sex in the library after school one day.

"And remember the time he told you he was going to Parker Lawson's to help work on his truck? But you found out he went to a strip club instead." I had been so mad at him that night. My mother sent me out for eggs, and as I drove past the club, I noticed his truck in the parking lot. He came clean the next morning, but it caused us to take a break for a few weeks. Or the time he went to the lake without you, and the rumor got back to you how he kissed Becky Mooney after they had both been drinking."

He called me the second he woke up in the bed of his truck, Becky passed out beside him. He swore nothing happened, but I questioned it every time I saw her out in town.

"Harper, the last thing Alex would want is for you to spend the rest of your life waiting for him. He died so someone else could live. And, if I'm being honest, I think he picked Logan to bring you the lock of hair as a sign he is who you're supposed to be with."

As much as I wanted to argue, my father was right. Alex did try and make me happy, he failed many times, but he wouldn't want me to sit here and waste away either.

"Now, I think you should take a few minutes, get your thoughts together and then head over to Logan's and let him know this wasn't his fault."

As my father stood, getting ready to leave, a question hit me. "Hey, Dad, what were you doing out and about this early in the morning?" My father loved to enjoy his morning coffee and newspaper. Allowing the sun to come up and get a good distance in the sky.

"Well, if you must know, I was escorting Valerie Forbes home." The glint in his eye made me gasp with joy.

"Daddy!" I exclaimed, jumping from the ground to stand with my fits on my hips.

"What? She is a beautiful woman who is single and enjoys my company." I didn't want to know what level of enjoyment he was referencing. Parents aren't supposed to enjoy such things as kissing and sex.

"Life is too short, Harper. Take happiness wherever you can find it."

After my father left, I sat back down leaning against Alex's headstone, the sun high in the sky as I leaned my head back and soaked in the warm rays.

"I think my dad is right. I believe you did have something to do with Logan and I meeting." Crossing my legs in front of me, taking my father's advice of getting my thoughts together.

"Logan is a great man, one you would have been friends with had you returned. I was angry with you, so pissed off you chose to sacrifice yourself and rip us apart. And, while I'm being honest with you, I know about the girl in boot camp. The one you met in the bar off base. She filed for benefits for her son the same day I filed my claim for your death benefits. I never told anyone about them, and I will take that secret to the grave. But it's time I let you go and get to living the life I still have left to live."

Listening to the sounds around me, the birds in the trees, the grass as the wind tickled its blades, Mother Nature playing her symphony of life going on. By keeping Alex's memory alive, I kept alive the lie and deceit he had shown, but also how he did one final act to make things right with me. Opening my eyes, the clouds drift aimlessly in the sky.

"Goodbye Alex,"

I whispered to the Heavens. Feeling as if a layer of weight had been lifted off my chest, I place my fingers to my lips, kiss the skin, and then send if off to join those clouds. Pain in my back alerted me to how long I had been sitting here. Logan would be worried and thinking the absolute worst was happening. A rustling to my right made me turn my head, the sun was high in the sky and blinded me with its intense rays. Before I could open my eyes again, I felt something hard against my forehead and a cloth covers my mouth. I tried to scream, but the smell from the fabric made me choke. I struggled as hard as I could until everything faded to black.

Chapter Twenty-Nine

LOGAN

Watching Harper tear down the steps ripped my heart out of my chest. I expected to feel free after delivering the news I swore I would, but instead I felt defeated like I had stolen the life out of the girl I loved.

I felt out of place sitting in her room, surrounded by the memory of the love we made and the haunting photo on the bedside table. I needed to leave, to give Harper all the space she needed to sort through all of this.

Securing the door, I half listened as Bruce assured me everything would work itself out. Patting my back in comfort while his eyes showed me pity. I fucking loathed pity, a bullshit emotion you saved for the losing team. I left my car parked behind Harper's shop, we had left her car at the church last night and I didn't want her to be stranded. The gym wasn't too far away, and the run would give me a reprieve from the bone crushing pain in my chest.

A few years ago, I met this drill instructor on leave in Thailand, he was beating the hell out of a speed bag, and I asked him what the trick was. It took him an hour to teach me how to steady my breathing while letting my mind go blank as my hands found a rhythm with the bag. My walk over here turned into a run, which in hindsight was a huge mistake, my dress shoes were not designed for the exertion, giving me two new blisters on the bottom of my foot. I changed into some workout gear I kept here, and for the last hour, have made the speed bag my bitch. I wanted to call Harper's shop as the third hour passed without a word from her. Instead, I moved to the salmon ladder, further punishing my upper body.

On the third trip up, my phone began to ring. I let go of the bar and fell to my feet, stumbling over the mat to get to my phone.

"Harper?"

"No, man, Ryan Biggs."

"Oh hey, listen this isn't a good time—" Ghost would never call me to shoot the shit, but in my current mood, I wanted to leave the line open in case Harper needed to talk.

"Too fucking bad, I have shit you need to hear."

My back shot straight as I heard the urgency in his voice.

"Okay, what's up?"

"Plenty." He shot back, an edge to his voice I associated with nervousness. It was never a good thing when a SEAL became alarmed.

"You remember when we were monitoring Aarash outside his compound? The time we found all the shit he had on us?"

"Yes, the last mission."

"Exactly. Anyway, part of this new job is listening to radio chatter and following the leads. Last week, I saw the notes of one of the other team members and found where he had been listening to the same intel we were acting on. Remember the name of the guy who pissed off Aarash, Ecnal?"

"Yes, the guy who sent him the Hummer." The hairs on the back of my neck stand up, my knuckles clenched at my side.

"Ever since that night, I've been searching for anything on this guy. A few days ago, I spoke with Aiden who told me about the mother-fucker sniffing around your girl and how he had some pretty big balls to stand up to a guy like you. This morning, I sat in on a transmission. Nothing at of the ordinary at first, but just as it died down, I heard Ecnal's name mentioned, followed by an order."

"What kind of order?"

The sinking feeling in my stomach shoved bile into my throat. Only two kinds of orders came from the kind of radio chatter the Secret Service would want to know about, neither one of them involved a pizza or chicken wings.

"They've activated a sleeper cell." Ryan was far too calm for this to be the only ounce of news he had for me.

"And?"

"And I had to find out where this cell was located. While I waited for the coordinates, I wrote down Ecnal's name ready to plug in the numbers and get a team over there. But as I waited, I kept looking at the letters on the pad of paper, and something hit me."

"Ghost, quit fucking with me."

"Invert the letters, Doc. Ecnal is Lance spelled backwards, the same name as the motherfucker messing with Harper. I confirmed the coordinates with the address of the storage unit Chief found him going into."

"Motherfucker!" I roared, my training in dealing with terrorists kicking in. "Keep me posted with any further chatter, I'm calling in the team."

Ending the call, I began to formulate a plan in my head. I needed to get to the storage unit see for myself how far they had acted. But as my hand landed on the metal of the front door, my cell vibrated and Harper's name scrolled on the face of my phone.

"Harper?" I answered in a rush, both grateful and terrified of what she needed to say. "I'm so sorry about Alex."

"Oh, isn't that sweet, Lieutenant." The voice on the other end was not my Harper's, but the sinister son of a bitch I needed to annihilate. "I almost believe your sincerity."

"Lance," I growl, careful not to show my hand before I had the information I needed. "What are you doing with Harper's phone?"

"I told you, Doc. You can't watch her every minute of the day. She's safe, for now." Switching the phone to the speaker, I open my message app and typing a message to Diesel.

GHOST IS ROAMING THE HALLS AGAIN.

He would know to contact Ryan and the severity by all caps I used. Diesel had been with us a few times when we neutralized an active sleeper.

"Let me talk to her so I know she isn't hurt."

"You think I would hurt her?"

"Yes, I do. Now put her on the phone."

Several tense seconds clicked by followed by the sound of Harper telling Lance he was hurting her.

"Logan?" Harper's strained voice came through the speakers. My blood boiled at the thought of him hurting her.

"Yeah, baby, it's me. Listen to me, I know Lance is listening too. I'm coming to get you, but don't believe anything that pathetic motherfucker tells you. I love you, and when this is over, it's just you and me."

Hoping my true meaning was reaching behind the fear she felt and made it to her heart.

"And Lance, I'm coming after you. And when I find you, I'm going to show you what happens when you fuck with what is mine."

I-95 IS A PARKING LOT

Diesel's reply message meant I had roughly an hour and a half before the team would arrive. Chief was up the road in North Carolina and would be the first one here. Reaper lived between Viper and me, but had a bad habit of going balls to the wall when he drove. Havoc was way down in Florida, it would take him the better part of a day to get here, but I would hook him up by satellite if I needed his expertise.

I'd used one of the storage lockers built into the back of my gym to hold my equipment and a Jeep I'd had outfitted to match the ones we used on missions. According to the rest of my team, we each had a similar setup, complete with enough explosives and ammunition to do some significant damage. I donned my gear, adequately housing all my favorite guns and knives in various holsters and pockets on my camos.

Taking the side streets and alleyways in an attempt to hide from the prying eyes of any other members of Ecnal we had yet to learn about. Pulling up along the side of the storage facility, the iron gates separating me from my target.

Checking the app Ghost had given me to track Harper's location. The red dot on the map flashed a few hundred feet from me, confirming he had her in the storage unit. A white van sped down the road to my left, stopping at the gate. The man inside enters a code, and the gate moves to the left to allow him through. Taking out my binoculars, I observe as two men get out of the van, take a look around, and then hurry inside one of the storage units.

Less than a minute later, a black full-sized truck pulls up beside me. The passenger side window rolls down, and I see Reaper nod his head in my direction. Now that I have a second set of eyes and another trained gun, I jump from my Jeep as Reaper does the same.

"Sleeper cell, huh?" Reaper raises his boot to the hitch on the back of my Jeep. "Ghost says this one is personal."

"You could say that," My game face is firmly in place, still mentally trying to wrap my head around it all. "Half of my fucking heart is across the street with a fucking mad man."

"Do we have visual confirmation or one of Ghost toys?"

Opening the gate of my Jeep, I pull out the zippered duffel I kept some of my gear in. "Now that you're here, going in for a visual."

Reaper wasn't the biggest fan of Ghost gadgets. He trusted his eyes, ears and what he knew. This time I agreed with him, we needed to see Harper and make sure this wasn't Ecnal setting us up. "Trouble is, the bastard knows us both. There's a chance they've figured out the necklace she has on is a tracking device and have it instead of her."

"Too bad those bastards have never seen you use that beautiful face for evil instead of good."

Reaper tipped his head toward the road. A bright red VW Beetle is sitting at the gas station next door to the storage unit. Two young ladies are attempting to pump gas, but by the looks of it, were having trouble getting the pump to work.

"Oh, fuck me!" Slamming my gear bag back into the Jeep. "Reaper, if this gets back to Harper, you had better defend my fucking ass."

"Nah, man." He stops me with firm grip on my shoulder. "I'm going to help her kick it."

Crossing the street, twisting my ball cap backward and sliding on my shades, a move I'd been told made a woman stop and take note. As the girl closest to me looked over her shoulder, the bottle of water in her hand crashes to the ground, I knew this would work.

"Whoa there, darlin'."

Picking up the bottle from the ground, flipping it in the air before returning it to her hand. "Careful, now." Sealing the con with a wink and a smile.

"Gas pump kicking your pretty ass?" Turning my charm on the second girl, who looked more cautions than the first. I knew her type, had been the wingman on a number of occasions while I captured the attention of the third-wheel friend. She eyed me suspiciously, her mistrust coloring her face. Adding a flex of the muscles in my arm, a bitch move on my part, but the distraction worked as she let me slide around and fix the pump for her.

"Y'all headed for the beach or something?"

"Or something."

"Yes." They answered at the same time.

"Shush, Kristen, he could be a serial killer. Don't tell him where we are going."

"She's right," flexing my arms one more time as I finished filling the car, giving them a view of my ass as bait for what I needed next.

"You don't know me. How about we fix that?" Looking over my shoulder, I catch the pair with their wide eyes fixed on me.

"My name is Dustin, I live just up the road. I've been waiting for my sister to come out of the storage place over there, but she is taking too long, and I'm going to be late for work. Do y'all mind helping me get through the gate so I can get my car?"

"Why can't you just walk up and let yourself in?"

"Well, I would, but if you look over your shoulder there, it says *no foot traffic admitted*." Both turn to look at the sign on the gate. "Hell, I'll even pay for your gas. Everything I just put into your tank."

The pair shared a look, but decide to toss caution to the wind and get me past the gates. Looking in Reaper's direction, I signal for him to get me the code to open the gate. Before the first girl has her seatbelt on, Keys was rattling off the code in my ear.

As she pulled up to the keypad, I pretended to tie my shoe to hide my face. Not coming back up until she had driven around the corner and stopped the car.

"Thank you, ladies." Tossing some money in the front seat as I climbed out of the back. "Y'all wear sunscreen, wouldn't want you to look like a lobster."

I listened as the gate opened again, letting the car of girls back out into the street. I noticed the van I had watched enter earlier, parked in the middle of the drive, the two men nowhere to be seen.

"You should be ashamed of yourself," Reaper chastised me through my earpiece. "Making those poor girls think they were something special."

"Fuck off, dude." Locating the security box on the side of the office and sliding in a USB, which would freeze the monitors and make anyone watching blind to our movements. "Get your ass over here so we can LoJack this van."

"Keys, you got eyes still?" Diesel's brother, Austin, had proven himself to my men when he assisted Viper, tracking down a man who was terrorizing Kennedy, his then girlfriend.

"Yes, Doc. You RSVP to Viper's wedding yet?" Reaper pulled up as I scanned the corner for the two men from the van.

I had wanted to share the invitation with Harper, excited to see her name printed on the envelope as well. But the shit storm that is my life happened before I had a chance. "Reaper, toss me a Nanny." Ignoring the question Keys asked, more than slightly worried I wouldn't get the opportunity to dance with her again. Reaper pulls my Jeep into the space between the office and where the units start, tossing me a tracking beacon as he jumps from the driver's seat.

"Doc?" Ghost calls into my earpiece as I switch on the tracker and secure it under the wheel well of the van. If these bastards decide to go anywhere, we will have their location and can follow them.

"Go ahead."

"A rendezvous point has been assigned. A cargo ship is currently scheduled to leave the Port in two hours."

"Find me the ship, Keys. I want to know everything about it."

After tagging the van and having a good look around, I found no evidence Harper was here. Her red dot on my app flashed, but I had no visual confirmation. All we could do now was wait and see if Ecnal showed up. Taking out my phone, making a call I didn't want to make. I'd hoped we would be able to swoop in, take out Ecnal and call it a day, but that wasn't the case.

"Blaze, get your ass to the storage facility off Main. It's about Harper."

Chapter Thirty

HARPER

"I'm coming for you."

Logan's promise had been on repeat in my head since Lance ended the call, and pocketed my phone. Gone was the gentleman who let me hide behind my grief, a cruel and calculated demon in his place. After kidnapping me with his chloroform cocktail, the effects lasting less than twenty minutes but left me with a killer headache. He tossed me in the back of his delivery van, ignored speed limits and the fact I was unrestrained, rolling around in the back.

Lance made several phone calls, speaking in a language I assumed was Arabic. Whoever he spoke to last made him angry as he slammed his hand on the steering wheel several times. I remained quiet, something Ross had taught me if I ever found myself in a situation such as this one. When he finally stopped, and the back door opened, the smell of the ocean and something rancid hit me full force.

"Enjoy the ride, Harper?"

I wouldn't feed into his madness. Instead, I remained quiet and still, celebrating internally as the smile on his face faded and disappeared into a flat line. Frustrated with my lack of participation in his game, Lance grasps my ankles, pulling me from the van and shoving me toward a metal container waiting to be loaded on a ship.

"Hurry up, Harper. I have much to show you."

Shoving me through the open door of the metal container, the hinge creaking, and then shutting with a thud behind us. I expect the interior to be dirty and stacked with boxes. Instead, there was electricity, or at least a generator, as several television screens lined one of the walls. It was cool inside, not hot like a metal box should be in the afternoon sun.

"Welcome to my office, temporarily at least."

He walked over to one of the rolling chairs, sitting down in a huff motioning for me to sit beside him. I hesitate, considering for a minute bolting for the door. The idea of escape fades as I see the gun he has tucked in the waistband of his jeans. Switching gears, I take a seat and attempt to formulate a new plan.

"I bet you're wondering why I brought you here? Gone to all this trouble to get you alone?"

Twisting his chair back and forth, his dark eyes fell on me, his relaxed stance worrying me.

"I suppose you've earned the right to know who I am, considering how close you came to marrying me. Who knows, perhaps I can convince you to wear my ring again." The sting of a tear prickled behind my eyes, and I take a deep breath to contain them. When I woke up from the chloroform, I found I had lost my necklace in the struggle.

"My name is not Lance Ranoka, it's Ecnal Konar. My family owns thousands of acres of land in Afghanistan, Iraq, and Pakistan where we harvest poppy plants to make heroine. We sell our drugs to the world or trade for things we need, such as guns or young women to entertain us."

The night I found him snorting coke while two girls sucked his dick made perfect sense.

"I came to the States originally to help my older brother, Aaron. But that changed when the US military started targeting our poppy fields, destroying the way we live and trying to enforce a new way of life for my people. I've spent the last two years collecting information and making new alliances." Something told me I didn't want to hear him go into any detail regarding the kind of alliances he spoke of.

"What does kidnapping me have to do with all of this?"

"That's all you get, beautiful Harper. I have something to show you and an appointment to keep." Lance or Ecnal, whomever he is, turned from me to the monitors on the wall. Picking up what I assumed was a remote, he pressed several buttons until all the screens came to life. The first screen showed what looked to be the outside of a security gate, the metal fence at the bottom and a pole with a keypad to the side. The second screen looked to be the inside of a room, although the walls resembled the ones in this metal container. Two men sat in the center of the room facing each other, a small table separating them. Looking closer at the top of the table, I noticed two cell phones and something much smaller, the pendant Logan had given me last night.

"Your little boyfriend and his team has created too many problems for us lately. Cheating us out of a lucrative deal with a Russian business partner."

I remember the news report announcing the death of Pavel Kumarin, a Russian mobster, who died in an explosion. I also recall the name, Aarash Konar being reported as dead as well. This had to be one of Ecnal's brothers.

"His actions took away a lot of money, and I plan to collect payment, from all of them."

Pointing at the second screen, "I noticed you recognized the locket on the table. Did you know he planted a tracking device behind the fake diamond chips?" This didn't surprise me, Logan was a trained SEAL, and he had confessed he loved me. As far as the term fake, I highly doubt it. It was just another jab in an attempt to get a reaction from me.

"Want to know why those men are sitting on the floor waiting?" Keeping my focus on the two men, I avoid answering his question. "Look at the walls, Harper. What do you see?"

Straining my eyes, trying to see what he was trying to point out, but the picture is too dark to make out what was against the wall.

Leaning over and resting his chin on my shoulder, he whispers in a chilling voice.

"It's enough explosives to blow up a city block. I arranged for some information to be leaked earlier today. And by my calculations, your boyfriend and his gang of misfits should be congregating outside my storage unit right about now. You and I are going to watch as they storm the unit, looking to rescue you, and blow themselves up instead."

Chapter Thirty-One

LOGAN

Having Harper trapped in the same room as a mad man is stretching the limits of what I can stand.

"Fuck this! Everything tells me she is in there, inside a metal building, with no air-conditioning. I'm going in."

Grabbing a couple of grenades and some flash bombs, I check the chamber of my gun, as I got ready to move.

"Doc," Reaper cautioned but didn't try to stop me. The sweat beading at the base of my neck, rolled down my skin and collected somewhere near my belt.

"Let's wait for Blaze to get here." Ignoring his rationale, the girl I loved with every fiber of my being needed me to get her out of there.

"And then what? We wait a little longer for Diesel and Ghost to show? No thank you, I'm done waiting." My frustration is greater than my clear thinking. My need to keep Harper safe outweighing the rational part of me that agrees with Reaper.

Keeping my back to the metal exterior of the building, I edge my way over to the unit, which the white van is parked in front of. Glancing over my shoulder, I notice Reaper has my six. Even when he doesn't agree with me, he is still willing to follow me into a possible ambush.

Earlier when we put the tracking unit under the van, I noticed a grassy area with several tall bushes. It was close enough to see the door, yet far enough away not to be noticed if they opened the door to leave. I give Reaper the signal to go around the opposite side of the building and wait for me in those bushes. He silently takes off around the corner, as I continue my forward progression to the door on the end of the aisle. As the door grew closer, I began to question the validity of the intel Ghost had been given. Sleeper cells tend to blend into their surroundings, keeping to themselves and not seeking attention from those around them. Lance Ranoka drove an expensive car, attended public functions where he openly confronted people. He had been arrested for possession with intent to distribute. Not to mention how he stalked Harper, allowing her neighbors to ask questions about him, know who he was and where he lived. All of the above are out of character for a sleeper cell.

"See anything?"

Reaper had his rifle pointed at the closed door, his belly against the ground the way he preferred it.

"Not a fucking thing." He mumbled back, checking the sites for placement. We sat in silence for several minutes, neither one of us wanting to admit this felt all wrong.

"Blaze should have been here by now." My thoughts somehow make their way past my tongue and out in the open before I can stop them.

"Maybe he got caught in traffic." Reaper had complained about the traffic around Norfolk since he came down here for some training a few years ago. Reaper preferred the quiet of the mountains, where he could do as he pleased and not be bothered by rules and regulations.

"Cover me," I ordered as I stood from our hiding spot, pulling one of the grenades from my pocket and stepping close to the white door, which mocked me. Over to my right was an empty lot. I could create a diversion, which would make them come out to investigate, giving Reaper a clear shot to take them out. As I hooked my index finger through the pin, something hard hit me from my left, throwing me to the ground and knocking the wind out of me.

Lying on the pavement, trying like hell to regain my breath a cell phone is shoved in my face. In the center of the screen is a flashing red dot on what looks like a map of the Port of Norfolk.

"Stand down, motherfucker, she ain't in there." Blaze stood over me, a determined scowl on his face.

"What the fuck man?" I coughed out, as my muscles relaxed and air filled my lungs. I attempted to get up, but Blaze had his boot in the center of my chest.

"Ghost called me thirty seconds after you did. When he mentioned Lance called you from Harper's phone, I knew he was up to something more than pissing you off." Blaze removed his boot from my chest, extended out his hand and helped me stand.

"I've had every phone Harper has ever owned equipped with a tracking chip. One I created myself and undetectable, even by the hardcore hackers."

"So if Harper isn't in there, who is?"

"A couple of members of a well know terrorist organization, waiting for the go ahead to blow up this entire fucking block." My heart skips a beat as what Blaze is telling me finally sets in. I had been seconds away from killing us all.

"I called in an ATF friend of mine who is on his way with a team of experts to safely defuse the situation. Meanwhile, we have got to get the fuck out of here before Ecnal catches on to what we know."

We pass Blaze's friends as we hauled ass to the Port. I know this is difficult for him as not only is his baby sister involved, but he lives for blowing shit up. Creating big fires out of tiny little things earned him his nickname.

Security at the Port is a huge joke, the guard waving us by without looking up. "There, by the crane." Blaze pointed at a group of containers stacked four high. One on the lower level caught my attention, the markings on the side not making sense. The arm of the crane was in the process of moving the container to the waiting ship. The one scheduled to leave in an hour if this intel was correct.

Reaper pulled his truck around the back, giving us the advantage in case Ecnal had cameras trained in our direction. While we suspected he had guns and ammunition inside, we also had Keys confirming there were two humans in the container.

"Blaze, you'll position yourself beside the crane, ready to take out the operator if he's on Ecnal's payroll. Reaper, I want you as hidden as possible, but with a clear shot to take him out if he gets past me." On the ride over, we all agreed this was personal, a vendetta he needed me to pay. He had planned on using my emotions against me, and it would have worked if Blaze hadn't been in the position of Harper's protector since her birth.

Maneuvering around the containers, I could hear the sound of a man laughing. As I grew closer to the container, I knew it was Ecnal inside. "Did you see that, Harper? Your boyfriend charged in there like the idiot I knew he was and now he's in a million teeny-tiny pieces." As his laughter faded, I could hear the sobs of Harper loud and clear. His delight in her misery carried the stamp of a sick individual, and it was time he was taken out.

Not giving a shit if he heard me, I pulled the metal doors open, rust falling around me acting as a lubricant to quiet my invasion. Ecnal stood over a crying Harper, his hands in the air in triumph as he watched the fire trucks extinguish the flames on his monitor. Too bad for him it was all bullshit. Keys had located his feed and interrupted it, giving him a slice of action from a movie that didn't make it past the cutting room floor. Aiming my gun at his pathetic head, I waited until he turned around before I put my finger on the trigger. His face fell as realized his plan had backfired, all his efforts and secrecy for nothing.

"You touched something of mine. Worse than that, you made her think I was dead and made her cry."

Ecnal looked from the barrel of my gun to the action on the monitor, his eyes and gaping mouth not believing what he was seeing.

"I told you earlier I was going to find you and let you see what happens when you fuck with what is mine."

Ecnal reached for his gun, but he was too late. I'd left the doors wide open giving Reaper a clean shot. Ecnal cried out in pain as he dropped his gun to the floor. Reaper knew I needed to handle things, his shot taking off his hand, but leaving his life for me to take.

"Harper, come here, baby."

Holding my arm out for her, I needed to feel her and know she was okay. Harper jumped from the chair, knocking it over in the process, rounding my body and tucking herself safely behind me.

"Did he hurt you?" I questioned loud enough for Ecnal, and my men outside, to hear, giving Blaze the go-ahead to create a diversion.

"No, just scared me." I could feel her body shaking as she pressed against me.

"Close enough, motherfucker. Say hello to Aarash when you make it to hell." Shielding Harper's eyes, I unloaded my magazine into Ecnal's chest. His body jerked and spun several times as my bullets hit their target. As the last shell casing landed on the metal floor, Ecnal lay dead against the far wall.

"Harper?" Turning my eyes from Ecnal's dead ones to the beautiful face of the woman I would do anything for. Holstering my empty gun, I frame her face with my hands. "I'm sorry, I didn't think to have him run through the proper channels. Are you okay?"

Her face is covered in dirt and dust, the side effects from the distraction created by her brother outside. My adrenalin ran so hot I missed the firestorm, which shook this container to its metal fillings. Blaze created a blast so severe it buckled the walls, causing the monitors to crash to the floor, scattering glass and plastic at our feet.

"I'm okay. A little shaken, but I'll live." Licking her lips, her eyes drift closed as she collects her thoughts. "None of this is your fault. Ecnal, Alex, they were grown men who made choices."

"I know, but if I would have gotten to Alex sooner, you would be happily married with a ton of kids."

"Maybe," she shrugs. "But I wouldn't have met you, or had the time I needed to become the woman I am today." Pulling my face down to her level, "A wise man once told me how time has a way of making us forget the bad in the people we love. I made Alex into a superhero, with standards even *he* couldn't meet if he were still alive. He's always going to have a place in my heart, be a part of who I am. But—"

Searching her face, I knew I was about to go mad as she considered her final thought. I could feel my heart hammering like a war drum, every beat on the edge of a sword. Harper had become my world, the reason I woke up and tried as hard as I did. Without her, my life was destined to be lonely.

"You're my future."

Lips crashed in a hurried craze, bodies pulled together so tightly the lines of where one began, and the other ended blurred until we were one. Tongues caressed each other in a desperate game of cat and mouse, chasing after the other, and then starting again.

"Come on," I panted, not ready to stop loving her, but the creaking of the weakened metal told me we needed to get the fuck out of here. "Let's get you home."

Exiting the container, ash floated in the air around us. Reaper stood just outside the door acting as sentry to anyone who dared ruin our moment. Blaze stood off to the side, his arms crossed over his chest, the look of a happy man on his face. The crane, which had been transferring containers to the waiting ship, was now on its side, the operator nowhere to be seen. Black smoke billowed from what was left of the top row of containers. The bottom of the stack, vibrating as smoke and dust swirled through the cracks, announcing the collapse of the structure.

"I leave you alone for a minute and this is what you get yourself into." Chief stood off to the side, his hands on his hips, a triumphant look on his face.

"Took you long enough."

"Someone has to be on cleanup."

Closing the distance between us, his hand outstretched in Harper's direction. I felt her get close to me as he approached. "Harper Kincaid, I'd recognize your beautiful face anywhere. A pleasure to meet you, I'm Aiden Sawyer, or as these losers know me, Chief."

"Please to meet you, Aiden. Or do you prefer Chief?"

"I'd prefer dinner with you, but I'm fairly sure this motherfucker will slit my throat if I tried." Harper's eyes grew large as she received her first dose of an unfiltered Aiden.

"Ignore him, Harper. He's been trying to compensate for a small penis for years." Pulling her close, I place a kiss on the top of her head.

"Ghost filled me in on what happened." Motioning to the smoldering debris behind us, tiny flakes of ash falling into his dark hair. "Aarash and Aaron had a little brother, huh? Never saw that one coming." He laughed humorlessly, his eyes trained on the scene behind us.

"He said he had associates, relationships he has been forming since he quit helping Aaron." Harper pulled back, her arms remaining wrapped around my waist. Her worried eyes drifting back and forth between mine.

"Don't worry, Harper. Mad men are schoolyard bullies who finally got chest hair and a deep voice. They still find pleasure in torturing the weak. We know how to handle bullies, hell, its what we live for."

As we drove back to pick up my Jeep, I couldn't keep my mind focused on the conversation going on around me. According to Harper, Ecnal had been sent to the States to help his brother Aaron, but with what? As far as we knew, Aaron was the more refined brother. His interests leaned toward having a perfect manicure and away from growing dope. Had Ecnal been the mastermind behind the family, or was he trying to fit into his big brother's shoes?

"What do you think, Logan?"

Shaking my head from my mental ramblings, I turn to see Harper sitting beside me looking at me through questioning eyes.

"I'm sorry, baby, I was daydreaming. What did you ask me?" Harper had a smile that could light up a city block, one she bestowed on me at regular intervals.

"Ross and I were discussing how now Aarash and Ecnal are dead and can't hurt anyone anymore, the government could lower the terror threat to a lower level. Would you agree?"

Harper lived in a world where she had no real understanding of the threats surrounding her. As the man who loved her and knew the warning signs, it was my job to protect her, keeping her ignorant of the evil all around her. Reaper hadn't been mentioned in this conversation, and as I glanced in the rear-view mirror, I caught his eye, sharing a knowing look with him.

"I think this has just begun."

Epilogue

"Hey, man. When are you going to put a ring on that girl's finger?" Zach touched the tip of his bottle to mine, his face covered in post-nuptial bliss.

"Not today, but hopefully soon."

Harper had been leery of attending Zach and Kennedy's wedding with me, worried another bomb would fall from the sky like the last time.

"Listen," he leaned in, attempting to speak in hushed tones over the music in the room. "She has accepted what we do, knows how this lifestyle works and has a good head on her shoulders. I wouldn't wait too long, man."

I heard stories of how Zach had to keep things from Kennedy, how he disappeared for hours and even days with no real justification. At first, it put a wedge between them, but once he was certain about her, they talked and here we are at their wedding.

"Harper isn't going anywhere. And I want to be done with the Navy before I jump into a marriage."

Ross confided in me how Harper swore she would never marry a man in the military given the way Alex had died. It was important to me she keep the promises she made to herself, even if it meant I wouldn't be in Zach's position for a while.

"You got what, four months?"

"One hundred and twelve days."

"But who's counting?" We said in unison, chuckling and tapping our bottles together again.

The music changed, and the DJ made some comment as to the elderly lady in front being a hot momma with her dancing skills. A new song started, and the tiny women got back into her groove.

"Honey, come dance with me."

Kennedy Forrester-Michaels, the beautiful new bride and keeper of Zach's balls, called from the edge of the dance floor. Her white dress glittering from the candlelight around us, the back tied up in one of those bustles and the hem nearly black from being dragged along the dance floor. Given the smile on her face, she didn't give two shits about the dress, except how quickly Zach would be able to get her out of it.

"Duty calls." Handing me his beer, he joins his bride without another word.

Tipping my bottle back and draining the remaining beer as I scanned the room for Harper. We had spent the last four days here in Atlanta, taking in the sites and enjoying one another's company. Kennedy and Harper became best friends in the time it took us to get drinks the first night we arrived. They both enjoyed charity work, Kennedy with her horses and Harper with her clothes. They had made plans for Kennedy to come to Virginia and spend some time in the city.

"Logan, have you spoken with Matthew?"

Aiden took the spot Zach vacated. He had come down the same time as we did, enjoying the area and a few of the female flavors. Aiden had a thing for Southern women, the way they could insult the fuck out of you and make you ask for more. I had to agree with him, Harper had a hell of a twang when she was tired.

"I haven't seen him tonight. Did he come to the wedding?"

"He showed up close to the end, stood in the back as Zach carried Kennedy back down the aisle." Kennedy and Zach both came from influential families. As a man who was also raised in a privileged home, I understand the need to break society's rules every once in awhile. Zach didn't wait until the kiss was over before he scooped Kennedy up and carried her at a jog down the aisle, leaving a lot of stuffed shirts wagging their tongues at him.

"He's been sitting at the bar since the reception started, tossing back Wild Turkey."

When you depend on another person the way we have all these years, you learn when they are doing good and when they are trying to numb something. Matthew Parrish was a silent but deadly individual, who only drank the hard shit when he wanted to either start a fight or pass out. By the way Aiden described it, Matthew was self-medicating whatever is bothering him.

"You're the doctor, Logan. He'll listen to you long before he will any of us." Aiden was right, it was my duty to check on him, to see if I could help him figure shit out or get him the help he needed.

"You guys see Matthew?" Ryan made his way out of the crowd, motioning over his shoulder at the bar behind him.

"We were just talking about him." I went to leave when Ryan grabbed my arm, his eyes full of worry.

"You should know, he came without Rayne and his face is covered in two days growth."

Crossing the packed room, Zach and Kennedy must have invited the entire city of Atlanta to this thing, you couldn't take two steps without bumping into someone. Harper caught my eye as she danced with a girl I didn't know on the dance floor. I waved to her and pointed to the bar, letting her know where to find me.

Matthew Parrish was not an easy man to hide. Although, if he didn't want to be seen by his target, he had the skills to make it happen. He occupied the last seat on the far end, shoulders hunched over and his hands wrapped around a highball glass.

"Motherfucker, don't you know Zach is rolling in fucking money. You ain't got to drink the cheap shit."

Matthew's attention never left his glass as he greeted me in the most broken voice I'd ever heard.

"Logan."

Taking the seat beside him, ordering a new beer for myself, I kept my focus forward so as not to crowd him. "Want to tell me what's so bad it warrants a nasty hangover tomorrow?"

Matthew huffed as he raised his glass to his lips, draining the amber liquid as the ice cubes clinked in the glass. "I fucked up, Logan." Turning his head in my direction, turmoil rolling off him as sadness clouded his eyes.

"Must be bad if Wild Turkey is involved."

Matthew motioned for the bartender to refill his glass, the young man behind the bar flashing me a look. I motioned for him to go ahead and fill the glass. His speech was still understandable, and he looked too tired to start a fight.

"Worst thing I've ever done in my life."

"This I have to hear if it beats Kosovo."

Three years ago we tracked a group of arms dealers to an abandoned warehouse on the outskirts of Kosovo. It was the middle of the night when we found them and had to clear a barb-wired fence to get into the warehouse. The night was so dark we couldn't see a fucking thing. Matthew found a hole in the fence we could crawl under, but there was this stench all around. One by one, we got down in the sludge like stuff. I assumed it was old wastewater from the factory, but it turns out it was what was left of the victims these guys had killed. They had tried to melt their flesh by wrapping them in plastic sheets and tossing the corpses into a sauna. After we had bathed in bleach, we all agreed this was the worst condition we had ever faced.

"You remember Tombstone and the time he spent in the hospital in Germany?"

"Yeah, his wife couldn't be contacted. When he got home, she had taken off with the kids."

Matthew nodded his head. "I found her and the new fuck buddy in an abandoned hotel in Arizona. She was prostituting herself while he took all the money they had and injected it into his fucking veins. Those kids saw it all and were practically starved to death."

"Okay, but it doesn't explain why you're drinking the way you are. You've seen worse than that. So what gives and what's with the beard?" After Matthew got out of the military, he found a girl who shifted his world. Her name was Rayne, and she pulled him out of the shell his ex-fiancé put him in. For the longest time, he hid the scar on his face behind his beard. Rayne changed all that, made him comfortable in his own skin.

"Tombstone's little girl was afraid of me, screamed like hell when I picked her up. She saw this fucking scare on my face and it terrified her—a little girl." He shook his head, defeat written all over his face.

"When I got back to Charleston, I couldn't get the little girl's face out of my head, and it got me to thinking. How in the hell would I feel if it was mine and Rayne's baby? I couldn't stand hurting an innocent child, especially one I helped bring into this world. So I broke things off with Rayne."

"You did what?" I shouted, a bit too loud as the entire bar area looked in our direction. Matthew held up his hand to stop me, letting me know he wasn't finished.

"After I said some horrible things to her, Tombstone called me up to thank me and let me know his daughter, Macy, had drawn me a picture to say she was sorry for how she acted. He said his ex-wife told the kids if they said anything to the authorities, she would send in a big man to take them to the desert and eat them. She assumed I was the monster from her dreams."

"Oh fuck, man. What did you say to Rayne?"

"I lied and told her I didn't love her anymore." Matthew's voice cracked as he confessed what he had done. Taking the last of his drink into his mouth, he slammed the empty glass on the bar, the ice jumping around inside.

"She ignored my calls and then changed her number."

"Do you still see her in town?"

"Yes, she works the graveyard shift. So I follow her and make sure she gets to work and home safely."

"Then there's still hope, she hasn't gotten a new man and she's still employed. First things first, we get rid of this nasty shit." Taking the empty glass from him and sliding it down the bar out of his reach.

"Second, we pour you into bed and you get a good night's sleep."

"Then what?" He scoffs, leaning back against the chair.

"We get your girl back, that's what."

The End

THE OFFER

Join my mailing list and I will send you a FREE eBook.
https://www.instafreebie.com/free/62GAn

ABOUT THE AUTHOR

Cayce Poponea is the bestselling author of Absolute Power.

A true romantic at heart, she writes the type of fiction she loves to read. With strong female characters who are not easily swayed by the devilishly good looks and charisma of the male leads. All served with a twist you may never see coming. While Cayce believes falling in love is a hearts desire, she also feels men should capture our souls as well as turn our heads.

From the Mafia men who take charge, to the military men who are there to save the damsel in distress, her characters capture your heart and imagination. She encourages you to place your real life on hold and escape to a world where the laundry is all done, the bills are all paid and the men are a perfect as you allow them to be.

Cayce lives her own love story in Georgia with her husband of eighteen years and her three dogs. Leave your cares behind and settle in with the stories she creates just for you.

caycepoponea.com
caycepoponea@yahoo.com

ALSO BY CAYCE POPONEA

Signed, SEAled, Delivered

Book One

Lieutenant Zach Michaels is in the middle of the Korengal Valley. On the eve of a new mission, he receives a desperate letter from a young woman. After he discovers the letter belongs to another soldier, he takes on a new mission; making sure it finds it's intended recipient.

Kennedy Forrester has spent her life pleasing others, specifically, her social ladder climbing mother. When an internet search done in hopes of finding love, introduces her to the charm and charisma of Lieutenant Michaels, she is tossed into a world she never dreamed existed.

As the two continue to correspond from half a world away, will either of them figure out the common link they share? With their lives interconnected, and his SEAL days in the past, can they find a balance allowing a blossoming relationship to thrive? Or will a new mission, one involving Kennedy's safety, be too much for this new love to survive?

Code Of Silence Series

SHAMROCKS AND SECRETS

Book One

Event planning, dealing with demanding clients and defusing situations before they get out of hand are all in a days work for Christi O'Rourke. But when a mystery man seems to appear at every turn will she have the ability to handle him as well?

Power and wealth are staples in the world of Patrick Malloy. But when family obligations dictate his future, a future involving a certain spirited young woman, will Patrick have what it takes to win her heart or will his lifestyle place her in more danger than he ever dreamed of?

CLADDAGH AND CHAOS

Book Two

Shamrocks left us with Patrick posing an intriguing question. What exactly happened during those twenty-five years? We know that they got their happily ever after, but how did Patrick and Christi get there? Could love have a shelf life?

STOLEN SECRETS

Book Three

Arianna Covington's world is turned upside down after the tragic death of her fiancé. Her friends watch as she tries to put the pieces of her life back together, only to fall further into the depression and seclusion her loneliness creates. To them, a trip to New Orleans for Mardi Gras will somehow make the demons, which haunt her, vanish into the sweltering heat of the night.

What they don't know is, Arianna has been living a lie, a spider web of secrets she keeps in order to stay alive. Using the city's reputation for lost inhibitions and excessive celebration, she vanishes into the sea of spectators. She emerges with a new look and endless choices, leaving behind the secrets and lies she never wanted or earned. How can one night of burying your past, turn into a war with Dominick Santos? A man even the devil himself fear.

Secret Sins

Book Four

A powerful man living in the shadow of his father. An innocent girl crying desperately for help. A suspense-filled, romantic story of self-discovery.

Declan Malloy was born into a lineage of great and powerful men. Molded from birth to one day take over leadership of the Malloy Family. His position dictates he must protect those who have been given certain badges of honor. Keeping them safe has never been a question on his lips until a late night cry for help places him at a crossroads. One decision with two choices. The first, lined in shrouds of secrets, lies, and deceit. The other, a clear path to living life on the edge, continuing his fast-paced world of power, money, and an endless supply of women.

But when a secret is revealed after he announces his decision, will Declan hold on to his need to step out of his father's shadow? Or will his obsession to stand tall cloud his judgment and jeopardize his reputation, while costing him his heart.

SOUTHERN JUSTICE TRILOGY

ABSOLUTE POWER

Book One

Dylan Morgan has it all; a prestigious career as a Detective for the city of Charleston, devilish good looks and a selection of girls whenever he chooses. Southern born and raised, he lives by the pearls his Granddaddy imparted to him. But when he questions his worth to the citizens of Charleston, his fears are realized when someone close to him is in danger. Does he follow the letter of the law as his position dictates, or does he follow his conscience, which will cause him to straddle a fine line? Can Dylan overcome the demons he creates for himself? Or will he toss everything away in a moment of reckoning?

Claire Stuart has fought hard her whole life not to fall into the same trap as her mother. She refuses to allow men to use her and toss her away. Needing to escape the hardship her family creates, she seeks education over acceptance and uproots herself from the backwoods of Kentucky to the charm of Charleston. She knows all about Dylan Morgan and his choice to bed every woman he comes across, yet she finds herself unable to listen to the warnings her mind and friends give her. Can Claire ignore Dylan's past and allow herself to let someone in? Someone who could shatter her very soul

ABSOLUTE CORRUPTION

Book Two

"Hold a door open for your girl, not because it's expected of you, but because it gives you a moment to appreciate her as she walks ahead of you."

Austin Morgan left the safety of his home in Charleston, accepting a position in New York City to make a name for himself. He wanted to earn his reputation through hard work, inventive ideas, dedication, and not by the legacy or influence of his family's name. His dedication to work leaves little time for a social life or the promises forgotten, creating the perfect opportunity for deception to reach its greedy hand out and grab ahold of this Southern born gentlemen. What will happen when he has to make an unexpected trip home and rediscovers what is really important? Will his eyes finally be opened to the deceit and misplaced trust of those around him?

"Never let the fear of falling keep you from learning how to fly."

Lainie Perry has never backed down from a challenge her entire life. She has come to count on her wits and stamina in achieving her goals. She has left her fears and those who would prey upon them in the dust. What happens, though, when her latest adversary exists only in her mind? Can she win the battle when the imagined enemy is already dead? Or will she need to seek help for this struggle?

Can these two find the help they need in each other?

ABSOLUTE VALOR

Book Three

Chase Morgan said goodbye to the Marines, believing by removing his uniform, the hero persona would go with it. But when he meets the girl who shows him how the hero lives in the heart of the man and not in the clothes he wears. Will he be able to ignore the demons of his past, which plague him with reminders of cruel intentions? Or can he let true love move in and take residence in his heart.

Audrey Helms describes herself as a bad country song, complete with a boyfriend who treats her badly and more baggage than a Kardashian. Can this timid southern girl be the one to mend the bonds of brotherhood? Or will the sins of her past be too big to forgive? Will Audrey and Chase learn the meaning of true love, and how to live with no regrets and absolute valor?

CRAIN'S LANDING

When life threw her a curveball, Natalie Reid adjusted her stance and hit a home run. With her life packed neatly into the back of her SUV, she bids goodbye to her college life and steers toward adulthood. With the help of her father, she has been given the opportunity of a lifetime. Will she be able to win the hearts of the sleepy southern town. Or will it's hidden secrets be more than what she bargained for? How long will she be able to resist the persistent Grant Crain?

Grant Crain is well acquainted with the joys of living in the south. All his life he's known that when Ms. Connie makes her famous pecan pie, you better hurry and get a slice. That when the fireflies dance in the dusk, it seems to make the heat of the summer day a little more bearable. He had decided long ago this town would always be home to him. He never expected that a tiny, Yankee girl would turn his comfortable and carefree world upside down. Or that a ghost from his past will do more than come back to haunt him.

Made in the USA
Lexington, KY
27 July 2017